MINDING HORACE

D.S. Lewis

G

The Glanville Press

Minding Horace
ISBN 978-0-9955089-4-1

Cover art: Svetlana Aganina (2023)

Published by
The Glanville Press
Holywell House
Bradford Street
Shrewsbury
SY2 5DP

to Wendy

whose absence launched this voyage
and whose presence spurred its completion....

ONE

The old bastard hadn't made an appearance in almost twenty years, not since my eighteenth birthday, yet there he was, standing on my doorstep, about as welcome as the remnants of a worm in a half-eaten apple.

It's funny really, because I almost didn't answer the doorbell. In the light of how things turned out, I sometimes wonder at how different my life might have been, maybe his too, had I not opened the door. Often I didn't in those days, not unless I was expecting something. And this was a particularly spiteful morning, wet and flat and drab, the sort of day that never truly clears before sliding into another weary evening. April, *the cruellest month, mixing memory and desire, stirring dull roots with spring rain*; Eliot got that right. Late April, when Hart Crane—who had forsaken poetry for alcohol and then abandoned the bottle in favour of suicide—jumped overboard from a steamer in the Gulf of Mexico. Maybe he got that right too. But the doorbell was followed by a flurry of authoritative raps that had the promise of a delivery, and I was anticipating the arrival of some face cream I had ordered—on special offer, of course.

Besides, I'd left my desk and gone downstairs to check out the weather from a different perspective. I was tempted to go into town and buy something, anything, just a little anything to lift the mood. Shopping therapy. It works, but only if you can afford it. There is nothing therapeutic about spending money you don't have. Drowning in debt is worse than drowning; it's like slow drowning. From the kitchen, the street looked even less inviting. The only visible life was a fat man, swaddled against the day, trying to manage a dishevelled dog that squirmed like a ferret on a string, straining for shelter. Then the squalling rain began once more, sweeping down from an iron sky and smattering against the glass with the rhythm of an inconstant heartbeat. It was the sort of day where life clung on, where it endured but would never flourish. Who but a postman, a dog-walker or a desperado would venture out in such conditions?

There was an empty wine bottle on the cluttered table, but its neighbour still had some life. I rinsed out a tumbler, poured a small measure and then a dribble more. I took only a few sips before pushing the glass away. It was at that moment that I heard the bell and then the rapping on the door. I stepped over the junk mail, slid the bolts and opened my house, my life, to the tempest. He was there on the step, an elderly man in a dark overcoat and black trilby, leaning casually on his silver-handled cane. Under the hat's battered rim was a tanned and heavily lined face, lean and leathery flesh stretched taut over sharp cheekbones. Beneath unruly white eyebrows the pale blue eyes smiled as though there had been no chasm of intervening decades between us.

"Jesus Christ!"

"Not quite, Lizzy, but I'm flattered."

"Where the fuck did you spring from?"

"You wrote to me. Remember?"

"That was eighteen months ago, Horace."

"Really? Well it took an age for the letter to reach me. I've been on the move you see. May I come in? I'm finding your weather significantly more hostile than I remember. This tempest is particularly tiresome."

He stepped into the dark hallway; I added his coat and hat to the heap that was propagating on the hooks near the front door. I led him through to the kitchen. Bereft of his coat he looked more insubstantial, his shoulders a little stooped and his gait uncertain as he negotiated the unknown topography.

"You want tea?"

"Terrific. Earl Grey, please."

"You didn't write back." I filled the kettle. "So even when you finally got my letter you didn't write."

"I was going to, but I received it only recently. I was due to make a trip over anyway, so I thought I'd surprise you."

"You succeeded."

"I had to come for a college reunion. Class of '52 and all that. Probably the last, actually. We're dropping like flies."

"But not you." I handed him the steaming mug with its floating tea bag.

"Thanks. No, not me. Not yet. Not quite. Any chance of a sliver of lemon?"

"Yeah, there's a grocery shop on Mill Road."

"Oh Lizzy. Still angry? All these years of silence and yet the anger is still unquenched." The pale eyes were staring, imploring.

I felt an urge to cry. "I'll check the fridge. There might be a slice."

"Let me look at you." He took my arm gently and turned me to face him. "You look marvellous. As always."

"Liar. I'm fat and I'm getting old."

"You're neither. You're thirty-three. That's young."

"I'm thirty-seven."

"Well, that's close to thirty-three. Try being eighty-six. That's old, believe me. I'm so close to kicking the bucket that I hardly dare move my foot. I'm... well, I'm close."

"It's possible to be closer. But not to feel older than I already do. The last few years, they've been... hard, Uncle. Very hard."

"Yes, I gathered that from your letter. I'm so sorry. I wish I'd known sooner."

"Well try opening your mail from time to time. Anyway, there's nothing you could have done. I don't want to talk about it. It's pointless. Talking doesn't change anything." I pulled away and wiped my eyes.

"England has changed," he said. "Everyone here is angry it seems. So angry all the time. Scratching and biting like rats in a sack. It's different at home, we have more space, more sunshine, more guns."

"And guns don't make it more dangerous?"

Horace snorted. "Nah. Australia's not like America. But you do think twice about road rage or robbery when you know you could get shot. And you don't pull a knife on someone when they might pull a gun."

"Who'd have thought guns would have such a civilising influence."

"Oh, I almost forgot," he said brightly. "I brought you a present." He took a small hardback book from his jacket pocket and passed it across the table. Its ornate leather binding was scuffed and battered, the embossed gold lettering indistinct. "It's from my father's library. He translated it in fact, your great grandfather. It's a work of natural history by the great explorer, Georg Steller. The original was written in the eighteenth century, in Latin. Father translated it after the war and published it privately. It's a limited edition, very rare. You should give it a try, it's an interesting read."

"Thank you," I said instinctively, turning the little blue volume over in my hands.

"You should bear in mind, of course, that many of Steller's observations were made under extreme conditions, after he was shipwrecked. He was one of a group of survivors who found themselves marooned on Bering Island, in the strait between the Russian Far East and Alaska. I went there once, you know, many years ago. It's indescribably bleak: cold and barren, windswept, treeless, permanently shrouded in fog and rain. Frequent earthquakes, too. Tough environment."

I opened the front cover. The yellowing title page read "*De Bestiis Marinis* (*The Beasts of the Sea*) by Georg Wilhelm

Steller." Below was a reproduced line drawing of a strange sea creature with a small head and an enormous body and tail; a sort of cross between a whale and a dolphin. Near the foot of the page, in small print, it read: "Translated and arranged from the original text (published St Petersburg, 1751) by Professor Alexander Cunningham (Oxford, 1947)." Opposite, on the inside front cover were faint brown mould spots and a faded handwritten inscription, "*Acta deos nunquam mortalia fallunt.*" I looked up to see Horace watching me intently.

"It's from Ovid," he said. "The deeds of men never escape the gods."

"Does that apply to the deeds of women too?"

"Probably. But best check with the gods." He winked. "Just to be on the safe side."

We sipped our tea in silence. Then he said, "Is Will here?"

"William's got a place in London. We... we're sort of apart. Trial separation sort of thing. We needed space after... after everything that happened."

His face lit up. "Well now, Lizzy, that's actually a spot of luck."

"Luck? Oh yeah, I'm forever counting my blessings. I barely have time to get anything else done."

"No, really. I come armed not just with a gift, but also with a proposal."

"What sort of proposal?"

"The nice sort. It's like this..."

And that's when he laid it on me. He spoke as though it was the most natural proposition in the world. He had "long contemplated" taking a cruise and the time was now "propitious." He was in "sound health," but his advancing years meant that it was "desirable to have the assistance of an agreeable companion." He was looking for a "chaperone" to shield him against "the unwanted attentions of ladies of a certain age and disposition." The cruise company was insisting that he be accompanied on the voyage, and he would consider it "an honour, nay a privilege" if I would consent to be that companion. All expenses would be covered, "of course," and he would be happy to "compensate" me for my time, should I consent. The duration would be "approximately twenty-one days;" the weather "clement;" the itinerary "redolent with historical interest." "We leave from Southampton at the end of the month," he said. "Do come, it'll be a hoot."

My first reaction was one of incredulity. When he showed me the brochures it was like a surreal sales pitch and I was thinking, *You're fucking insane.* I mean, what sort of person rocks up at your door after decades of neglect and—ignoring the bitterness of unresolved issues between you—invites you on a fucking cruise? But the more he talked about it the more the absurdity melted away under the onslaught of his enthusiasm. There was something touchingly childlike in his desperation. The rain ran rivulets down the window behind him. On the table lay the open brochure for the *SS Evening Star*, a luxury cruise ship, and among the sun-drenched images of enjoyment was an itinerary of stops on a three-week voyage through the Mediterranean and the Indian Ocean. The ship looked fantastically sleek, its curved white prow rising from the carved blue water like a cruel beak. Above the hull towered a metropolis of terraced apartments, phalanxed by tiered balconies, overlooking decks studded with swimming pools and bars where happy bronzed bodies, trim and toned, lounged and played, casual in their ease.

Great Uncle Horace was silent, his patient eyes fixed upon me with dog-like expectation. I stared at the images strewn on the table, aware of the drumming rain, aware that I was prevaricating.

"You know Lizzy, I'd like the chance to know you again before it's too late."

"You never knew me the first time around."

"Well let's put that right. But we'll have to look lively about it. I'm running out of time."

I raised my eyes. "There are things I still want to talk about. Questions that only you can answer."

"Yes, that too. And what better opportunity for civilised discourse than whilst dipping through the tropics by the calm green shores? I shall be your captive and you can interrogate me at your leisure. You may have your answers and I can spend some quality time with my most beloved niece, whom I regard as great in every way."

"I'm your *only* great-niece."

"And all the more precious for that. It'll be terrific. We'll talk, have fun, see some sights and catch some rays as we glide through the wide blue water. You should see the Indian Ocean, Lizzy. It's magical. The birds, the fish, the azure sea and sky stretching all around you, stretching beyond vision, holding you forever in a cobalt spell, a sphere of beauty and light. I crossed that ocean a lifetime ago to make a fresh start in Australia, and I'd love to see it once again, and for you to see it too. What do you have to lose except a few weeks of grey rain? And it's not like we're travelling in the wilderness. The ship stops at major cities all along the way. If you don't like it you can simply get off and fly home. So, do we have a deal?" He extended his scarred old hand. "Shall we shake on it?"

"I've never been on a cruise."

"Well now's the time. There's really nothing to it. You just get on, have a good time, try not to fall overboard, and then get off at your final destination. For you that will be Cape Town, from whence you fly home, business class of course, and I'll stay put and sail back to Oz. What could be simpler? Do we have a deal?"

I shook my head with incredulity and gave an exhalation that in previous times might have morphed into a laugh. But I took his proffered paw. "Okay, Uncle, stop with the sales pitch. I give in. I'm convinced. Let's go cruising."

He grinned. "Excellent. Excellent." He raised my hand delicately to his lips and bestowed an ostentatious and whiskery kiss. I withdrew it quickly.

TWO

The morning after Horace's visit I woke with a slow, dull headache. I lay in bed listening to the rain. Sammy the Bad Cat hopped up and wanted to play but I wasn't in the mood. He got the message and soon stalked out but in doing so nudged open the door to an unacceptable angle. I wanted to get up and return it to its correct position but felt too tired and so I closed my eyes instead and tried to blank it out. I needed coffee but there was nobody to bring it. I took some painkillers and lay perfectly still, my eyes shuttered against the dull light. I reproached myself for having skipped dinner. It was good to try to lose a few pounds, but the good had been undone by the wine I had inadvertently consumed. I resolved not to drink again until the weekend. I made a plan: get up; shower and wash hair; make progress with the book, putting in a good shift, working unbroken until my first appointment of the afternoon. But first I had to pause, allow the pills to work their magic, give them time to soothe away the long, slow pain that arced from the shadows.

I thought of Horace and wondered if yesterday's visitation had been real. For a year the medication had suppressed all dreams, rendering sleep a monotone, fumbling void. But since stopping the pills the dreams were back, more vivid than ever, exotic and exhausting, too real, too tragic. I longed to turn them off; retreat to the woolly comfort of colourless nights, shapeless and familiar, empty of memory. Though even as I considered it, I knew Horace's visit had been real and that I really had agreed to go on a cruise with the old rascal. The thought made me smile and I felt the flicker of unrecognised muscles and an intensification of the pain behind my eyes. The whole idea was absurd, but then again, maybe it could be fun. At the very least it would be a change of scene, a bit of pampered luxury. And better weather.

Above all it would provide an opportunity to glean some information on a family about which I knew so little. Over time I had become more curious but they were few in number and had left impermanent tracks, as though they had passed through the world in water. My grandfather—Horace's twin brother Virgil—had committed suicide at an absurdly young age; my grandmother, Amelia, had barely made it into her middle years. I had never shared the Earth with either; I had barely seen a photograph. As for my father, he was unknown, even to my mother. She said it could have been either Steyn or Dieter, but as neither had hung around for my birth she considered it unimportant to be overly-precise in matters of identity. My mother had never been overly-precise about anything, including the responsibilities of parenthood. And though, unlike most of my family, she was still alive, she had escaped extinction only on a technicality. Dementia had robbed her of memory, and as memory confers identity, the loss was fundamental. Her lungs still breathed, her heart still throbbed, and her body continued its weary cycle of curated eating and excretion. So I performed visits of filial duty, but she was dead to me as a person, as a mother, for hers was a death of the mind.

And so it was that when I looked back across the generational wreckage, Horace was the only survivor, the last man standing, stooped and alone in the debris field. We had never been close. I remembered him from a few family occasions, times when my mother was still unbroken. But he had lived his life on the other side of the world. I still possess the battered, blue kangaroo that he sent over as a birth present, nine months after I was born. Thereafter he sent sporadic birthday or Christmas gifts which invariably arrived late: stuffed toys; a wooden boomerang, which would never return when thrown; a hat with corks dangling from the brim; a couple of T-shirts; and, in the wake of my thirteenth birthday, a satin ball gown which my mother had immediately confiscated on the grounds that it was "unsuitably adult." I used to send thank you letters and even received the occasional reply, his writing small and neat but hard to decipher. He wrote of exotic animals: koala bears and kangaroos, sharks and dingoes; of spending Christmas at the beach, and how uncomfortable Santa was, carrying his sack of presents through the summer heat. Sometimes as a child I would lie in bed in the dark and imagine him doing stuff in daylight on the other side of the world, but I was never quite sure what stuff. He was a colourful component of my life, but the colour was vague and indistinct, drained by inconceivable distance. Horace was exciting in theory but absent in practice, always very absent.

Now, this last living repository of the past was failing and our bizarre expedition, even in its absurdity, could be the last chance to gain some insight into the impulses, the decisions, that had created the circumstances of my life. So much had been broken and obscured, even before my birth, as though a curse had tumbled down the generations and was tumbling still, still wreaking its destruction, still shearing off phantom limbs from our overly-coppiced family stump.

By late morning I was at my desk in the back bedroom that I grandly thought of as my study. It was small enough to be snug and looked over the little garden. The master bedroom at the front, which was now the mistress bedroom, was for sleeping; it faced the sunrise and the street and had the double bed that Wat was born on. The middle bedroom, painted blue and white, was Wat's room. He no longer lived there, of course, but all his things were still there, as was his smell and his memory, for memory lingers in the scent of the past.

I was trying to write a book about the past. About a family, another family, not mine. This was a fictional one, a saga of three generations set in the late eighteenth century. I was going to have one of the characters shoot himself at a tender age, for this family was as robust as an oak and could afford the loss, but otherwise any similarity to my own lopped-off kin was purely coincidental. I had jotted notes, many notes, but progress was slow. Still, one has to persevere. I mean, what's the alternative to perseverance? Giving up.

I'd always intended to write a novel, or maybe a play. I did act for a while, actually. After university (Cambridge, English Lit.) I joined a women's theatre project that put on all-female productions of Shakespeare. Technically it was gender-blind casting, but as we were all women the technicality was purely technical. We weren't bad. I played Hamlet once, the highlight of my career, and got some pretty good reviews. But there were personality clashes and political differences and when I broke up with Heather, the director, I knew that I wanted out. I mean, the shards of broken love are too sharp to inhabit unless you want to bleed forever. I drifted into teaching, not because of any particular vocation or inclination, but simply because it was there; it's always there, always available for those with an education and a lack of any discernible skills. In the event I was good at it and loved that light bulb moment when a kid suddenly understands something and you know you have made some small but permanent change to their life, an enduring mark left like a sculptor's thumbprint in the clay. I qualified, got a job locally, married a nice guy, became a mother. It was a pretty effortless progression. I was happy, I think, but busy, busy as Hell. And though the vague desire to write never really left me, it just got eclipsed by all the other stuff. I never had time to write; I never made the time. I was too busy being happy.

But by the time that Horace washed up on my doorstep I wasn't teaching any more, other than some home tutoring via the agency. It was enough to cover the bills; at least, most of them. By then I had ceased to be a wife or mother. I had an ocean of time in which to write, but it was so slow, so hard to do, so easy to get distracted. The past pulls and snags. It's greedy too, it takes huge bites out of the present.

At lunch I mistakenly had a small glass of white wine with my sandwich, not really from desire but rather because I had forgotten my previous injunction not to drink for a few days. I rectified the error by sticking at one glass only. Then I idly browsed the book that Horace had given me. I looked again at the handwritten inscription and wondered who had written it and when. I often inscribe the books I give as gifts, and I write my name in a book when I buy it, but always in conjunction with the date. Signed but not dated is like being only half-dressed.

The little blue volume began with a preface by the translator. It was a curious read for it held the distant echo of the voice of my great-grandfather, long dead, describing the life and significance of a man even longer dead, a man who had been long extinct when great-grandfather was still alive. The preface consisted of a biographical sketch of Georg Steller who, it turned out, was a Bavarian naturalist and a member of Imperial Russia's Great Northern Expedition of 1741, led by Vitus Bering, the man who gave his name to the Bering Strait. Bering had been charged by the Tsar to map the Far East and find a north-east passage from Europe to the Pacific, thus resolving the question of whether there was a land bridge between Siberia and North America. The Great Northern Expedition was Bering's second, and final venture. It was successful in that they discovered Alaska, with Steller being the first European to set foot on its frozen soil—though Bering (who came over as a bit of a bastard) only allowed him ten hours ashore in which to make scientific observations of the pristine wilderness. But on their way back to Russia, four months later, in November, with a crew that was ravaged by scurvy, the ship was wrecked. The survivors were trapped on Bering Island, an uninhabited territory (56 miles long and fifteen wide), which is part of the Commander Island archipelago and lies to the east of the Kamchatka peninsula. Bering was already ill and soon died, but more than half of his crew survived because Steller convinced them to eat seaweed, which is rich in vitamin C. Great-grandfather had helpfully added a footnote at this point, informing the reader that whilst most animals produce their own vitamin C, humans do not, and without it one cannot produce collagen, and without that "the body must inevitably succumb to the inescapable depletions of scurvy." But because of Steller the stranded men did not succumb to inescapable depletion. Instead they survived on that godforsaken island for ten months, living in an abandoned fox den complex that they enlarged by excavation and covered in sailcloth "as an ingenious means of securing shelter from the harsh and unrelenting elements." And during that time they laboured to build a makeshift boat from the wreckage of their original ship, eventually using it to escape over the water to the Kamchatkan mainland.

Herr Steller, the gentleman naturalist, did not engage in the boat-building project. Instead, writing in Latin with quill and ink, he produced "one of the eighteenth century's great works of natural history," *De Bestiis Marinis*. It was published posthumously, for he died at the age of thirty-seven, without making it back to Europe. In fact he was under arrest at the time of his death for being too sympathetic to the native peoples of Siberia, a stance that led to accusations that he was fomenting rebellion against the Tsar. But his book, which later appeared in German and, finally, at the beginning of the twentieth century in English, contained a scientific observation—in fact, the only scientific observation—of what is known today as Steller's Sea Cow, a creature that sustained the castaways during their months of privation on that island but which is now, sadly, "lost to us forever."

The Preface ended with a plea for readers to be "cognizant of the conditions of extreme adversity pertaining to the creation of the work," citing weather, wildlife, the absence of "scholastic support" in the form of reference works or "collegiate fellows of education and substance." Furthermore, because of Steller's premature death, "the work had not been completed to a standard fit for publication." Thus, Steller had had no opportunity to check the material nor to give "sufficient time and care to consider its arrangement." Inevitably, therefore, mistakes and omissions had been included and these had been amplified in translation to a degree that Steller would have "reviled for their offence against his certainty in science and his unflinching search for truth." Only by going back to the original manuscript, written in eighteenth-century zoological Latin, and by "rationalising aspects of the presentation of the text," could justice be done to the work of "one of the Enlightenment's most eminent but neglected scientists." My great-grandfather had freely undertaken this task and asked only for "the indulgence of his readers" and their understanding that any mistakes which he might have inadvertently introduced "be laid forever at my door and not at the lodge of him who laboured with such diligence to bring light to a dark corner of human understanding and knowledge."

I put the book aside and searched online for information about Steller. I was surprised at the extraordinary range of his discoveries: Steller's eider (*Polysticta stelleri*), a small sea duck; Steller's jay (*Cyanocitta stelleri*), the only crested jay west of the Rocky Mountains; the sea otter (*Enhydra lutris*), which looked as cute as an aquatic teddy bear; Steller's sea eagle (*Haliaeetus pelagicus*), an imperious bird of prey; Steller's sea lion (*Eumetopias jubatus*), also known as the "northern sea lion"; Steller's sea cow (*Hydrodamalis gigas*), a huge marine mammal, now extinct; the spectacled cormorant

(*Phalacrocorax perspicillatus*), the largest breed of cormorant ever to have lived; the gumboot chiton (*Cryptochiton stelleri*), a weird giant mollusc with armoured plates and leathery skin; the hoary mugwort (*Artemisia stelleriana*), a plant from the sunflower family; Stellera, a pretty pink, mountain flower in the *Thymelaeaceae* family; and even a rare mineral, Stellerite, a crystal with light-bending properties that is found in the fractured cavities of volcanic rock. It was undeniably impressive. It made me pine for a world where there was so much still to discover.

Apparently, Steller even reported sighting a marine mammal known as Steller's sea ape (*Siren cynocephali)*, which he described as 5 feet long, with a dog-like head, drooping whiskers, a fat, fur-covered and limbless body, with two tail fins. This animal apparently cavorted around the ship for two hours—in full sight of the naturalist and the crew—performing juggling tricks, playful as a monkey, and only disappeared when Steller opened fire, determined to bag it as a specimen. Fortunately he missed or, at worst, only wounded the poor creature. It was depressing to learn that most of Steller's discoveries were now endangered and that two—the sea cow and the spectacled cormorant, the latter being a large and almost flightless bird that had existed for at least 120,000 years but which had the misfortune, unlike most types of cormorant, to taste good to humans—were now extinct. Three, probably, if one includes the mysterious sea apes, not seen much since his initial sighting and not at all since 1965.

I rested my heavy eyes, drifting and dreaming of a world where giant cormorants peered beakily over their spectacles at herds of lowing sea cows grazing on kelp fields, common as cattle, while Steller's sea apes frolicked offshore, joyfully alive, nimble as monkeys and playful as children.

My first appointment was at 4pm, with little Connor Hastings, a ten-year old who was being trained by his parents to get a scholarship to a public school. I was part of the training. Apparently they were unable to afford school fees but could pay the agency which, after taking its disgustingly large cut, provided the Hastings family with me. For the family, as for the agency, I was cheap. But I knew also that I had once been valued, just as I was once loved. At least young Connor was keen. He seemed to enjoy our grammar drills and lit crit sessions with unseen poetry and prose. He was an enthusiastic reader but I wished sometimes that I could have taken him to play in the local park. It's just across from the house and I often sit there and watch the children play.

At 5pm I had Ashraf, a lazy kid being crammed for A levels with a view to getting an Oxbridge place. He was nineteen and had already flunked once. He always turned up late and tried to sidetrack the lesson into other areas. We were supposed to be doing *Mansfield Park*, but he still hadn't read the bloody thing. So I put up minimal resistance and let him steer us into the shallows of contemporary music. I was tired and he did have a sort of self-serving conversational charm. He thought he was being clever, but not so clever that he could see the opportunity he was wasting. Or maybe his family was rich enough for education to be of no consequence. So be it. I let him go early.

When you're a whore you get paid for making yourself available. You get paid for your time, even if the john wants to talk not fuck. The money's the same either way.

THREE

Happiness, I have always believed, derives from order. Order is a form of individual precision that defines who we are; it is specific to each of us. Happiness relies on that specificity. Chaos can be stimulating, sometimes liberating, even exhilarating, but it's as unsustainable as permanent revolution. Whereas order is the creation of a harmonious framework within which happiness can flourish, assuming, of course, that it is not snuffed out by some extraneous act of God.

Over the ensuing days, in preparation for embarkation on Horace's ship of dreams, I began making lists, and these, in turn, spawned sub-lists, revisions and clarifications. The core lists were simple: Diet; Closing up the House; People to Inform; Work; Mother; and Packing. The little cork notice board in the kitchen was already bristling with several layers so I relied instead on notebooks and a sunflower meadow of Post-it notes that sprouted on the door of the cupboard near the cooker.

I began with Diet. This involved devising a menu plan for the ten remaining days prior to departure with a view to eating healthily and dropping a few kilos in preparation for emerging prematurely from winter hibernation and exposing my sleepy white skin to the sunshine and spa treatments of the voyage. It also involved identifying and acquiring essential foodstuffs that would be required on board. Fine dining was all very well, but having an essential supply of healthy and familiar snacks for comfort was an obvious requirement. The diet/food category also included using up stocks of fresh food and undertaking a deep clean of the kitchen, a task long overdue. This, of course, spilled over into the preparations for Closing up the House. Here I set up timers for the lights and devised a programme that most accurately replicated my own normal habits, whilst also throwing in the odd bedroom lamp coming on in the middle of the night to simulate that unpredictable 'awake and unable to get back to sleep' moment that could strike without warning.

I booked Sammy the Bad Cat into Moira's and gave my itinerary, contact details and a spare key to the neighbours. We, or rather I, had long shared a reciprocal arrangement with Petra and Gavin—keeping an eye on each other's house, picking up post, watering plants—although of late I had had little need to call upon it. But they had been supportive since the separation and Petra seemed genuinely pleased when I told her of my plan. She made coffee and scrutinised the itinerary, purring with vicarious pleasure. "The Med is always lovely at this time of year... Lisbon is beautiful, we were there last year on a city break." I smiled, determined not to be drawn into a competition for the veteran traveller award. "But if you go ashore in Rome beware of pickpockets, they're everywhere, like rats. Most are gypsies. They call it dipping."

"I'm sure they're not all Roma," I said, and then immediately regretted it.

She ignored the challenge. "They distract you. We had a woman come up to us with a piece of paper, asking for help. And while we were trying to make sense of it, of the words, Gavin caught her companion trying to dip a hand into his trousers. Not his pocket mind, actually into the waistband of his trousers would you believe."

"You sure she was after his cash?"

Petra frowned. "Yes, it's where he keeps his money belt."

I drank my coffee while Petra informed me of the wonder of Santorini's black lava beaches, where I had camped as a student, and the magic of the Red Sea and the quaint exoticism of Madagascar. I smiled but in my head I pictured the two pickpockets, perhaps a mother and teenage daughter, migrants living on the streets, living on their wits, avoiding rape and violence from criminals and authorities alike. It seemed an unimaginable life. Not rats but rather fragile birds gone astray, scavenging for food in a predatory world of concrete and traffic. What desperation had they fled for this existence to be deemed preferable? Were they still alive? Later, when I got home, I went online for information on how many migrants were actually trafficked women. The statistics were unclear but the anecdotal evidence made for grim reading.

By going to see Petra I had strayed across the border of Closing up the House and into the territory of People to Inform about my impending absence. This raised the issue not merely of whom but also of how. Moira was already done as I had called her to check that she could look after Sammy the Bad Cat. I told her all about the cruise. She listened with that quiet warmth that has always been such an evident aspect of her character. I had known her for most of my life. She was Mum's companion since I was a little girl. In that sense she was like a second mother to me, a calmer and more considered mother. She still visited Mum regularly, way more often than I did. Sometimes our paths would cross at the home and we would have a drink afterwards. I loved the way that Moira's hands always bore the traces of paint and how from this residue you could discern the pigments she had recently applied to the canvas. She was probably working on a painting when I phoned, but she still made time to talk for almost an hour. I could feel the warm smile in her voice when we discussed the voyage, and the sadness when we talked about Mum. On the eve of departure I dropped off Sammy. Moira's hands were smeared with orange and ochre.

When it came to telling William, I decided email would be best. After the separation we had tried to do phone contact but it became ever more difficult. Email was almost as immediate, but it deflected some of the tension and allowed us both to take a moment, or longer, to consider a response. It meant an end, almost, to the rows and recriminations, and that, however you measure it, represented a form of progress. I kept it brief, playing down the 'free holiday' angle and emphasising instead the 'dutiful niece co-opted into caring for eccentric elderly relative' approach. He shot back a pretty immediate response that was quite constructive. He said it was a good move as I "needed a break" and that I should try to enjoy the change of scene "by focussing on the present rather than dwelling on the past." Frankly, I could have done without the proto-Buddhist homily. Still, I knew that he meant well, in his way, and his injunction to enjoy myself seemed genuine and well-intentioned.

I called a couple of friends to let them know the news. The responses were not uniformly positive. Lucy's take on it was to emit a strange shriek and shout "It's totally bonkers!" into my ear. I tried to put forward a carefully reasoned case but she repeated the same response, this time with hysterical laughter. Twenty minutes later, by the end of the call, I hadn't made much progress. I said in parting, "Try to be happy for me, try to say something positive." There was a prolonged moment of silence, and then she said, "Good luck." A couple of days later I had regrouped sufficiently to try Aisha, perhaps my most empathetic friend. She listened quietly, only occasionally asking for detail or clarification. I made the case for the free holiday of a lifetime so powerfully that I enhanced my own level of certainty. I paused, awaiting her verdict. "Okay," she said. "I get it. I really do. It makes sense, sort of, if you take out all the weird bits." I took it as an endorsement; I figured it was the best I was going to get.

The Work category was necessarily messy because it overlapped with People to Inform. I put it off for as long as I could before I called the agency. They were pissed off, naturally. Anything that interfered with their bloodsucking always pissed them off. They liked a clean puncture and a stable line into the vein; no kinks, no clots. I had to play up the 'elderly relative in desperate straits' narrative hugely in order to clear the coming month of my commitments. They exacted a small "administrative charge," of course, as an unguarded vein was obviously irresistible, and eventually we reached a compromise whereby they rescheduled some sessions and I got to keep my students and promised to make up lost time as soon as I returned. I taught my last lesson on the afternoon prior to my departure.

The Work category also included my private work, my real work: the novel. I opted to take several files of notes for use at sea. But in case of disaster I also wanted to ensure that all of the material was backed up electronically and on hard copy at home. I was mindful of poor Coleridge who, when living in Malta, had sent back to England a year's worth of writing in the care of a friend, but the man had died of plague in Gibraltar and all of his effects were burned by quarantine officials. The backup manuscripts that Coleridge had laboriously copied out and sent home via a British frigate were thrown overboard in accordance with naval regulations when the ship was pursued by French privateers. He never quite got over the grief of his loss. My backing-up was more automated than his but no less laborious, for it involved copying files, printing, labelling, cataloguing, hiding memory sticks but keeping lists (in cryptic form) of where they had been secreted. I planned to take my laptop, naturally, and so that meant backing up its drives in their entirety and taking advantage of that opportunity to also streamline the structure of my directories. It took a little longer than I had anticipated but was a worthwhile labour.

There was also, of course, the matter of my Mother. I have a photograph of her in a blue enamel frame. It was taken in 1978 when she was twenty-one. It was the year that she got together with Steyn and Dieter and God knows who else; the year that she fell pregnant with me. (Though in Mum's case I'm not at all sure that she fell, more a case of dived, I think.) I don't know where the picture was taken—Germany, Scandinavia, Amsterdam? The buildings in the background suggest a northern European city and she was a woman who, in her youth, had liked to wander. It's a head and shoulders shot and she is looking directly into the camera. She has a dark shirt and a grey jacket of shaggy fur. Her hair is dirty blond and long, almost unkempt, with a centre parting. Her eyes are dark grey-blue and heavily made-up. There's a half-smile on her painted lips and she is staring intensely into the lens. She knows she is attractive but she also knows that she is so much more than that. It's a look of defiance. She is staring down the camera, staring down life, with a look of amused contempt.

I always liked that photograph and I kept it close to remind me of what she once was. After her admission to the care home it became ever harder to equate that proud young woman in the picture with the anonymous old lady in the bed. She was barely fifty when she had her stroke. The doctors suggested that a lifetime of drug use had been a contributory cause. Ten years later her dementia had left her incapable of living an independent existence. I tried to maintain a weekly visiting schedule, but it was difficult to find the time. On good days she knew me, or said my name at least, or that of someone else she had once known. But increasingly there was no real recognition and I have never had Moira's patience or shared history of intimacy.

But I made time to visit her on the eve of my departure. I had informed the care home that I would be travelling and left dates and emergency contact details. The manageress became the 114th person to congratulate me and tell me what a lovely time of the year it was to take a holiday in the Med. Mum was lying, as she always did, in her high, single bed with bars, in her small first floor room with its small north-facing window that looked out over the car park. The television was always on although I never saw any indication that she was following its cascade of images. I muted the moronic babble, as I always did when visiting. I mean, there is no shortage of moronic babble in the world, and it will always find its way into one's life without needing to be given an open conduit. There was an uneaten bowl of sickly dessert on the tray that bridged her bed. She stared incuriously, her grey eyes vacant, a line of drool creeping from the drooping left side of her shrunken mouth.

I affected an air of jollity and announced my presence. She did not react. I kissed the top of her head, where the shorn white hair accentuated the worn look of her ancient skull. *That skull had a tongue in it, and could sing once.* With a tissue I gently wiped the corner of her mouth. She pulled away.

"Mum, it's Lizbeth. How are you today?" I put my face in her eye line, close enough to smell her. I smiled but the eyes looked through me. "Your daughter. Lizbeth. Remember, Mum? Your daughter." The explanation was familiar but still sounded unnatural, particularly when delivered almost at shouting level. I tried to breathe away the panic that stuck in my throat. *Suck down the agony. DO NOT cry. Tears change nothing.*

"Lizbeth." The pronunciation was slurred but close enough to remind me of an earlier time of tenderness. "You just missed him."

"Who, Mum? Who did I just miss?"

"Your father. He was just here."

I smiled. I was never sure how to respond to these claims. When her illness first manifested itself the advice had been to challenge the delusions, demonstrate their falsehood by slaying them with truth. That stage was now long past but the impulse remained. "I don't think so, Mum. He hasn't been here for a long time." It was a sort of weasely compromise.

"Your father."

I felt like saying, 'Which one? I never met either of the bastards and you never knew them beyond a few nights of lust.' I felt like it but I didn't. Instead I settled for the trusty but feeble, "I don't think so, Mum. It was just a dream."

"He was standing where you are. He came in his balloon, floating, and then he stood where you are. Your grandfather was with him, too. He had a big net and was catching things. Fishes, I think. Big fishes."

When I got home I had a drink. It was not quite the weekend, but a trip around the ruins of my mother was always enough to warrant a moderate measure of anaesthetic. I checked the lists. The one great outstanding task, the one that overlapped with no other, was Packing. I had made a start but had then become discouraged. My two suitcases were splayed on the landing, half-full of carefully folded garments. Around them lay neat piles of clothes, queuing patiently for a berth in the diminishing transports. I felt like Noah, but unlike Noah I had no clear idea about what to take. I had never been on a cruise and knew nobody who had.

I spent an hour online trying to check the weather that we mariners were likely to encounter. I had a glass of wine. I tried to imagine myself in different areas of the ship: the pool, the spa, preparing to disembark to sun-drenched shores, casual wear, casual evening wear, formal dinner attire, night clothes, foul weather clothes, slobbing about in one's cabin clothes, lifeboat wear. There were infinite possibilities and yet here I was, constrained by geometry, the limits of space. In the end I began throwing stuff into the bags. Well, folding rather than throwing, until each was full to bursting. I zipped them up, with some difficulty, and then carefully checked my hand luggage. The last thing I picked up was Benny, Wat's little blue bear. He sleeps with me on the vacant pillow of my bed. I couldn't leave him alone in the empty house.

And thus it was, in the early morning of the next day, I stood nervously in the hall at the appointed time, waiting with my luggage for the car to pick me up. It was only a little late, the driver was quietly competent, and I arrived at the dock in Southampton in good time and decent shape.

FOUR

I had expected to saunter along a sunlit pier beneath the shadow of a great white Leviathan until ushered up a gangplank and welcomed on board by a handsome officer gilded with gold braid. In the event, as with so many events, the reality was disappointingly pedestrian. The surroundings were grey and congested with traffic. The sky was overcast, with dirty drizzle falling from dirty clouds.

The driver made a point of dropping me at a specific berth inside a vast terminal that reminded me of an airport. My luggage was carried by a porter, and a uniformed shepherdess escorted me through a busy passenger lounge to a more discrete area reserved for priority boarding. A smiley young blond woman with a crisp white blouse and the sort of neck scarf worn by airline cabin crew welcomed me by name. She checked my documents and labelled my luggage before it was whisked away. She asked me some questions, most of which seemed designed to ascertain if I had had any symptoms of illness in the preceding two weeks. Happy with my responses, she concluded the process by issuing me with my boarding pass.

I went through an airport-like security check and then entered an enclosed gangway of steel and glass that zigzagged upwards, snaking to its entry point in the ship's side. Beyond the glass, one was always aware of the vast white mass of the hull; below me were the small, round portholes of the crew's quarters, while ahead and above were the flat windows of the cabins without balconies, and above these—towering towards the sky, with tiers of balconies running like dark gills along the length of the crisp white vessel—were the quarters of those, like me, whose privilege accorded them a scrap of private outside space, with ocean views. Finally, I passed seamlessly from land and air to sea and steel and, after a woman at a desk took my boarding pass, I found myself in a cavernous space that looked like an amalgam of the lobbies of every posh hotel I had ever visited. It was bubbling with passengers whose excited conversation scrabbled above the soothing piped music. All around were beaming crew members in starched uniforms, eager to help, aching to anticipate a need so that it could be satiated. And all were smiling the white cult smiles of those who are certain of their role within the world.

Once again I was greeted by name and, after a further passport check, was issued with my ship card which, explained the polite Indian lady, must be safeguarded at all times as it gave me access to my stateroom as well as allowing me to make onboard purchases in what was, it seemed, a cashless society. I said that I wasn't planning to buy anything as I understood that it was an all-inclusive cruise. She smiled and said, "It is all inclusive, Ma'am, but there are always things that you might want to add in order to enhance your experience." She also told me that a credit card had already been logged with my account in the name of H.E. Cunningham and so I was "all set to go." She wished me an enjoyable voyage and I returned her smile as I thanked her. I was shown to my stateroom by a beaming young North African, dressed in a crisp white jacket and smelling of sandalwood. He insisted on carrying my scruffy shoulder bag and wanted to take my handbag too, relenting only when I had adamantly refused for the third time to surrender it. His dark eyes looked even sadder when I declined to use the ornate elevator. It was as though I had spurned his hospitality in some fundamental way. But then his frown passed like a cloud and his smiling white teeth shone once more as he walked me to my destination.

We took the opulent central stairs—each riser discretely lit at floor level with ambient blue light—to Deck Eight, officially called the Horizon Deck. I liked the name, it felt full of possibility, though as we made our way along the endless corridor it began to feel a little too like being trapped in a plush but inescapable hotel hallway. My escort opened the door to my room and bade me farewell with a final flash of white. I entered a cabin where even the air smelt freshly laundered. My accommodation was, according to the brochure, "a deluxe stateroom with veranda." It was, apparently, 273 square feet (with veranda), smaller than the penthouses and suites above, but larger than the staterooms (without verandas) that lay below.

Its layout was that of a standard hotel room: bathroom next to the outside door, opposite a wardrobe, shelf and drawer unit cunningly designed to maximise storage. The main part of the room had a queen-sized bed (complete with padded leather headboard), wall-mounted flat screen TV, small sofa, round glass table, and desk unit and chair. The far wall comprised a sliding glass door that led out to the veranda which was, in reality, a cute little balcony with a small table and two chairs. On the glass table was a basket of fruit, covered in cellophane, and on the desk unit were bottles of water and soft drinks. Accompanying notes informed me that my TV included blu-ray and a DVD-CD player; the desk area had a data port for hooking up a laptop, with complimentary wireless internet access; my wardrobe had a "secure safe unit;" and my one touch lighting system included a "Do Not Disturb" electronic doorbell, a necessity that I was amazed I had managed to live so long without.

The bathroom, like the bedroom, was immaculately clean and softly scented with the smell of a fruit that I could not recognise but which seemed both exotic and comfortably familiar. Opening the door caused the fan to start and the light to come on. The latter was clean but not brutal, as though somehow it had been diffused without losing its clarity. There was a deep basin with a brushed steel soap rack designed to vent excess water and prevent the development of a soggy underside. Above it was a large mirror with good light and opposite was a reasonably sized tub with a built in shower. A notice on the loo proclaimed that it was a part of the ship's "vacuum sewage system" and that no "non-lavatory waste" was to be disposed of via its pristine porcelain bowl. I used it and I tested its flush: there was a momentary silence after touching the sensor and then, a micro-second later, the toilet gave a terrifying roar as the water was slurped from its bowl with a degree of violence that seemed both alarming and wholly unnecessary. It was as though something inconsequential was being ripped from a small and orderly world of white ceramic and stainless steel and shredded to sub-molecular level within an unseen labyrinth of pressurised pipes.

My bags were already stacked on the luggage rack near the door and so I spent time unpacking, arranging hangers and filling drawers. I worried whether I had brought the right clothes, for even my two or three formal outfits looked overly casual in their new setting. I drank some of the complimentary bottle of wine. I unpacked my laptop and books, clearing the clutter of brochures and safety instructions from the desk to make room for them. I arranged the books in alphabetical order although, because they were so few, I permitted the miscegenatory lapse of mixing fiction, non-fiction and poetry.

I also put out the two photographs from my bedside table at home. One was the small snapshot taken in the garden of me sitting in a canvas chair with Wat in my arms. It was early summer and he was only a few weeks old. You can barely see his features. He is so swaddled, swamped in his babygrow with a knitted cap pulled low and just his little nose peeking out. It's not a great photograph but it captures that moment. I remember Will taking it. I'm wearing a loose denim shirt and stretchy black leggings. No makeup. My hair's a mess and I look tired, even with sunglasses. I was exhausted, totally exhausted but serene. No, much more than just serene, I was happy, so incredibly happy. It felt as though we had taken some momentous step into a new life, a more profound and meaningful existence. And I felt a Zen-like calm when I held this tiny creature close, his fragile arm extended like a wing as he slept, his impossibly tiny hand, new and unblemished, resting on my upper chest, his skin against my skin, as though his tiny fingers were reaching deep into my heart. The other picture was a little larger. It sits in a frame decorated with the hand-painted faces of animals. It is Wat's fourth birthday and he is standing next to a gnarled old tree peering with fascination at its partly stripped bark. He is so focused that he's unaware of the camera. He is wearing blue jeans and sandals and his green puffer jacket. Beneath it you can just see the top of his stripy T-shirt. His face is so delicate and there is a slight flush on his perfectly smooth cheeks. His light brown hair is a little dishevelled, pushed back carelessly and damp from the rain. That same arm is outstretched, but this time it touches the tree, his fingers following the tracery of pale silver lichen. His stare is intense and there is a half-smile on his soft lips. I often wonder what he was staring at. When I took the picture it had not seemed important; now I am haunted by not knowing, by the knowledge that I can never know. I wonder sometimes if he was staring not at the tree itself but at something beyond it, something forever out of shot.

With the room arranged and ordered I grazed on the fruit bowl, eating a mango that was chilled but juicy and then picking off plump indigo grapes in twos and threes. It occurred to me that I had no idea of Horace's cabin number. In fact I was unsure whether he was even on board. But as I lay on the bed drinking another glass of what was a reasonable bottle of chardonnay, the absence of certainty did not disturb. My room felt like a sanctuary, a luxurious cell, and though there were background sounds of boarding, occasional voices in the corridor, the thick carpets and steel walls muffled and protected, guarding against the sea, shielding away the sky and the world outside.

I flicked through some of the literature, trying to familiarise myself with the layout of the ship. I knew that I was on the port side and somewhere amidships, but much of what lay above and below was uncharted territory. The booklet contained a helpful diagram of the fourteen decks. One to four, those with the small portholes, were the crew's quarters and were "strictly off limits to passengers." Five was "Fifth Avenue," where we had boarded, the location of Reception and concierge services, the main dining room, the medical centre and a shopping plaza. Deck Six was "Monte Carlo," "a fusion of bistros and restaurants." At its rear was the Starlight Club ("a constellation of dancing and stage shows") with the Owls Night Club "situated conveniently close by." Towards the bow was the Celestial Lounge (a "choice of bars" located around an auditorium and stage), whilst amidships was the Klondike Casino; a large 4-D cinema ("Poseidon's Sensorium"); and the "Sea Garden," consisting of bars, plants and a "breathtaking aquarium" beneath a huge glass atrium. Deck Seven was the "Promenade," a residential deck of deluxe staterooms with "picture windows" but free of balconies so that its teak boards could be trodden, trundled or jogged upon by those wishing to maintain their fitness by making circuits of the entire ship. Towards the stern were more bars, lounges, the ship's library, the "Nautilus University," and a broadcasting studio, the purpose of which was undefined. Next was the "Horizon" deck, with ranks of deluxe staterooms (with verandas), an area that I was rapidly coming to think of as home. Above that was "Belleaire," an identical deck of staterooms with, presumably, purer air by virtue of their greater elevation. I felt a sense of curiosity and kinship towards these unknown neighbours and wondered if Horace might be amongst them. Deck Ten, the "Champs Elysees," was a mixture of staterooms and suites, and above it was "Serenity," comprising penthouses and penthouse suites, with private terraces. Deck Twelve, "Poseidon," was described as the "Lido Deck," a complex of cafes and bars surrounding the "luxurious Seahorse Pool Complex." Above this, beneath a giant retractable glass roof, was the "Apollo Sun Deck," studded with myriad sports facilities, including gyms, spas, wellness centres, paddle tennis courts, a golf driving range and ski centre. The mind boggled. And finally there was Deck Fourteen, the "Eye of Zeus," a half-deck occupying a portion of the stern, which served as an observation platform and helicopter pad.

The booklet showed interior shots of a host of locations—Captain Cook's Cove, the Darwin Room, Churchill's Grill, Neptune's Playground, Covent Garden, the Cakewalk, Star of India (international cuisine), the Magellan Bar and Grill—each inhabited by smiling staff and happy cruisers. There were people watching shows, dancing, sunning themselves, frolicking in water or being massaged, listening to a lecture, driving a golf ball, laughing and eating, always eating. And all around them hovered crew members in sharp white uniforms, their gaze slightly lowered but ever attentive, poised and waiting to be allowed to facilitate, and smiling, always smiling as though they too were having fun. It was repellent but it also exerted a gravitational pull that was hard to resist. It drew you in, making you want to join the legions of the blessed and experience "the holiday of a lifetime" in the land of lotus eaters. Passengers and crew alike, it seemed, were all players in this enchanted theatre of dreams.

Reading on, I was informed that the *Evening Star* had a gross tonnage of 69,340, which sounded impressive, although I had no idea what gross tonnage actually measured. (An asterisk led my eye to the bottom of the page where a small note helpfully explained that gross tonnage was "a non-linear measurement of internal volume" and was not to be confused with measurements of mass or weight such as deadweight tonnage or displacement. So that quickly clarified matters.) More comprehensibly, the ship's length was 877 feet, its beam was 111 feet, and its draught was 29 feet. It had a cruising speed of 20 knots (37 mph) and a maximum of 23 knots (43 mph). Its passenger capacity was 1,052 and its crew numbered 879. It was described as an ultra luxury vessel, "a floating palace where opulence prevails and desire is made real." It was owned by Blue Water Cruises and registered in Nassau, in the Bahamas. It had been built in 2012 at a cost of over 600 million dollars, and had completed its maiden voyage in 2015.

The brochure referred to the ship as "it" but the term "maiden voyage" echoed an earlier time when ships were routinely denoted as female. Was it sexist to personify them as female, I wondered. And why had that convention arisen? Because they were vessels, because they contained other things, other lives? That would explain why "she" was also used for cars, trains and countries. But why not buildings or cities? And why was "she" used for some institutions (the church) but not others (the government). Nature was traditionally a "she," as was the sea. Storms had always been female, until some recent administrative decree had alternated their gender, and yet not earthquakes, eruptions or tidal waves, none of which had ever been gendered. Some abstract ideas were female ("justice shall unleash her fury"), but others, including love and loss, were without gender. I tried to think of inanimate objects that were referred to as "he." God was a "he," always a "He," but then the Judeo-Christian God was male. Not male in the sense of having male sex organs, of course, but indisputably male in character. But why were there no others? Even fierce phallic things like cannons or swords or guns were not male. So it seemed that the choice was actually confined to "it" or "she" but how did an object find itself in one category or the other? Even if it was as simple as having been consigned there by male grammarians or theologians, it still would not explain the logic behind the taxonomy.

Perhaps the female category encompassed objects that were necessary but potentially lethal, like ships, cars and aircraft; phenomena that were capricious (and potentially lethal), like sea, storms and Justice; or that which could not be fully understood or controlled, such as Nature, Fate and Lady Luck. Things upon which men were dependent; that they knew intimately but could not alter or fully control; things that they held in affection and wanted to appease or coax; things that had the potential to kill them; that which they could never fully possess: these things it seemed were typically female. Did that constitute sexism or was female anthropomorphising a tribute to female strength and the uniqueness of our containing? Language had become a minefield, a war zone where the fighting was so intense that much of the landscape, much that was beautiful, had been reduced to ugly ruins.

"Evening Star" made me think of Venus, a classical goddess and a feminine planet associated with love not war. It made me think of Keats pouring out his passionate soul, his ardour, to a woman he would never possess and with whom he would never know the joy of physical love. I lay back on the soft clean pillows and closed my eyes and listened to the faint throb of the ship's engines, a sound not heard through the ears and brain but as a vibration felt in some deep and secret place, like the memory of a maternal heartbeat. I thought of "moving waters at their priest-like task/Of pure ablution round earth's human shores." This ship, my ship, I concluded, was female and I was safe and warm, cocooned content within her protective body.

FIVE

I was woken by the buzz of the phone on the bedside table. For a moment I thought I was at home. I had been dreaming that I was going upstairs, except it wasn't our house, my house, it was somewhere different and the stairs were different and went on forever. I knew that William and Wat were waiting for me at the top and I was late, and wanted so much to see them, but the stairs kept rising and the light was fading. For a moment I heard their voices but then they were drowned by a foghorn blaring out a warning to the unseen ships passing in the darkness below me.

I answered the phone and a soft, accented woman's voice confirmed that I was Mrs Tyler and then, after apologising for disturbing me, extended an invitation to take tea with Horace in his suite. I washed my face and made my way to Deck Eleven, Serenity Deck, using the main staircase. The ship's horn blasted several times. I could feel the shuddering vibration pass through me and I sensed that we were underway.

Outside Horace's door I was greeted by a stiff young steward with almond eyes and olive dark skin who seemed to appear from nowhere. Her hair was scraped back into a tight bun which emphasised her highlighted cheekbones and heavy eye makeup. Her smile revealed teeth as white as her jacket. Addressing me by name, she introduced herself as "Monique, Mr Cunningham's butler." Then she used a card to open the door and announce my arrival, before inviting me to enter with an exaggerated sweep of her starched arm. I passed a white and blue mosaic-tiled bathroom with a marble, double-width tub at its centre. The bathroom looked bigger than my entire cabin. The main room was even larger, large enough to require zoning. There was a dining zone with a huge glass table and eight chairs; a work zone with a grand, mahogany, leather-topped desk and bookshelves; and a sitting zone near the plate glass window, with several coffee tables and three geometrically arranged sofas. It was all cool creams and greys, with rich curtains, crystal light fittings, and a vibrant smattering of abstract art. Beyond the window lay a deep sweep of veranda.

There were several interior doors, one of which was ajar and gave the glimpse of a huge ebony bed and brocade sofa. Horace appeared from a doorway near the bathroom. He was studying a sheaf of papers but his battered old face glowed when he saw me and he opened his arms. We embraced and when he double kissed my cheeks I felt the scratch of his wiry old beard.

"What d'ya think, Lizzy?" He gestured with both arms spread. "Best suite on the boat."

"It's astonishing," I said. "Vulgar, but astonishing." It felt mean to be negative in the face of his childlike enthusiasm.

"I've got a bed the size of a football pitch, a whirlpool bath I can swim lengths in, and a terrace I could play tennis on."

"That sounds a little exhausting. Besides, wouldn't you keep losing your balls?" How often envy dons the guise of humour.

He looked at me for a moment and then guffawed with laughter. "And that would be a shame because I get Monique as part of the deal." He gestured to the silent presence standing near the door. Her porcelain mask of non-expression flickered with a discreet smile. "We'll take tea whenever you're ready, Moni," he said to her. She nodded and withdrew.

He led me to the sofa nearest the huge window and bade me sit. "You're just in time. We've cast off. We're on the move, Lizzy, sailing out into the wide blue yonder on a voyage of wonder and exploration."

"It's already mapped out, Uncle. I think you'll find it's been well explored and charted."

"Yeah, but not by us. Not yet. Anyway, the sea's a capricious mistress, Lizzy. Who knows what'll happen. And isn't she a beauty?" His arms gestured in all directions. "The ship, isn't she marvellous?"

"Is it a 'she' or an 'it', Uncle?"

"A 'she', of course. She's a ship. Ships are always female."

"And why is that? Just because it's traditional?"

"No, not because it's traditional. Never follow traditions just because they're traditions. But accept that traditions become traditions for a reason. So the question here is why is it traditional that ships are female? And the answer is because traditionally they needed paint and powder and regular exfoliation to keep them looking their best, just like women. Though these days it's more paint and cordite. But the point remains, ships are never male. Men don't wear makeup."

"Sometimes they do."

"Not where I come from."

Monique knocked and entered. Behind her followed a steward pushing a trolley. Monique spread a white cloth on the low table before us and laid out the elaborate elements of an afternoon tea that might have been taken by a landed family in the Edwardian era. She worked methodically, without glancing up, placing each item with the utmost precision. Horace told me that she was from Haiti and was highly qualified, having studied with the Guild of Professional English Butlers. I asked where she had lived whilst studying for her diploma. She glanced up at me with expressionless eyes. "In Port au Prince, Ma'am," she said softly.

Horace did not bat an eyelid. "Never been there but I've heard it's a fascinating city," he said. Then he went into a riff about French colonial architecture and the differences in the legacy of French and British imperial possessions in the Caribbean and beyond.

I watched the land slip away as the great ship slowly left the quayside, manoeuvring with an intricacy and precision that belied its enormous bulk. I thought of a sightless whale patiently bouncing its sonar against the rocks in a search for open water, blindly following an instinct for freedom.

We ate delicately cut sandwiches, pastries, and dainty scones served with jam and cream. Monique poured the tea and used silver tongs to add translucent slices of lemon. I noticed that the painted nail of the fourth finger on her left hand had broken, but otherwise she was immaculate. Not a hair out of place, nor a drip of tea on the pure white tablecloth. She stood silently at a studied distance, discreet but close enough to pounce should any need be anticipated. It was as though she wanted to apply the fix before we had felt the deficiency. If your plate became empty she offered you more; if you refused she offered alternatives until you acceded, worn down by her persistence; if you looked a moment too long at anything on the table she stepped forward and offered it. I found her presence uncomfortable and the conversation stilted. Horace, however, seemed unfazed, munching cheerfully, making small talk, asking how I had been, asking after my mother. When Monique had filled our cups for a third time he told her that she could go. She cleared the table and silently wheeled away the trolley.

Beyond the window the sky was a brooding grey. The little boats around us had dropped away and though there was still land visible, we were in more open water. The sea was as grey as the distant land and the hanging sky. I felt tired and sad. I wanted a drink. I regretted coming but I wasn't sure why.

Horace smiled. "And what about the old mal de mer, Lizzy. You don't get seasick do you?"

"I'm not sure. I've never really been to sea. Cross channel ferries are the closest I've ever got to a cruise. Though I always felt okay on those."

"Ah, but ferries are different beasts, very different. Still, you'll probably be fine." The qualifier was smuggled aboard like a stowaway. He patted my thigh. "I haven't been to sea in more than fifty years but it won't matter. The thing is, you either get it or you don't. Some people are simply programmed to feel nausea when there's a disconnect between the body being in motion—through some separate agency, can be boat, or ship or plane or whatever—and their natural yearning for balance. Got to not fight it, that's the secret. That and ginger. Root ginger, crystallised ginger, ginger tea, anything with ginger in it helps."

"I'm feeling fine."

"Really? I brought along some ginger just in case."

"I really don't want any. I'm full of scones."

"Ah yes, well that might not have been such a great idea. I meant to mention it. Brandy's good too."

"Well let's have a brandy. As a precaution."

"Are you beginning to feel it?"

"No, absolutely not."

"You know, Lizzy, it's like going into combat for the first time. You can't predict how you'll react. Nobody can, not the first time. Some men are heroes and others break down in a blubbering heap. Wailing and paralysed with fear. Can't tell which are which, not until it happens. And by then it's too late. Women and children are more at risk than men, especially women who have had a child."

I winced but stayed icy cool. "At risk of what? Combat or seasickness?" I tried to affect disengaged curiosity.

"Seasickness of course. Women and children don't belong in combat."

"That's a convention at odds with the modern world, Uncle."

"But not children under two. They're always completely immune. And do you know, old people get it least? So I'm covered both ways. And you'll be okay. You look fine, for now." There was that treacherous little qualifier again.

"I feel totally fine."

"That's good, because it's been shown scientifically that people are also susceptible to seasickness by suggestion. Even those not physically prone to it can succumb if they convince themselves they're going to get it."

"Maybe other people convince them."

"Don't worry, Lizzy, you'll be fine, but you won't know for sure until we reach open water. We're still in the lee of the shore. And the forecast is for heavy weather ahead. The Bay of Biscay can get awfully rough this time of year. It can test the stomach of a veteran mariner."

"Horace, why are we talking about fucking seasickness? I haven't seen you in twenty years and the last time I did you were a total arse."

"I'm just concerned, Lizzy. I don't want you to feel ill. It'll spoil our holiday. I remember years ago, one day when I was out fishing with a couple of fellas, in the days when I used to fish. One of them was prone to seasickness but he had really wanted to come out with us in the boat. He'd stocked up with a tin full of ginger and one of those fancy wristbands that compress the median nerve and are supposed to prevent nausea. But he'd made the fatal mistake of eating sausages for breakfast. We'd all had a big breakfast because we knew we'd be out in the bay for twelve hours or more and we were pushed for space in the boat, with all the fishing gear and whatnot. And though the sea was pretty calm, there was very little wind so the diesel fumes from the engine were hanging. Anyway, this fella began chucking up before we'd reached the first pitch but, to give him his due, he was experienced. I think he had a diploma in nautical vomiting. He was belching a bit and went green around the gills but you could still banter with him. It was just that every once in a while he'd stick his head over the gunwale and throw up. Then he'd continue the conversation just where he'd left off. And the weird thing was that though he was chucking up this greeny-yellow slime, with plenty of lumps in it, there was nothing that looked even remotely like the sausages he'd just eaten."

"This is a gripping narrative but..."

"Nah, hear me out, Lizzy. The wind got up and the sea became bit more choppy and he was spewing more regularly and definitely talking less. I was baiting up, and I was upwind of the bastard which was lucky as there was definitely some blowback. I had a ringside seat and I couldn't help but notice there was still not a hint of sausage in his spew. Just that weird slime, that was greener every time he chucked until it was almost luminescent."

"I'm glad to hear you kept such a sharp eye on him and can recall the details so precisely."

"I did keep an eye on him. See, the way he was going, I was worried he'd get dehydrated or choke on his spleen. Eventually he had nothing left to toss and was groaning a bit so I gave him a nip of brandy. He got it down and it seemed to settle him. He was a bit brighter and he gulped a full bottle of water. After that he was fine, well, for a minute or two anyway. But then he started groaning and shaking and finally he hit the mother lode. He didn't even make it over the gunwale. He let rip with a bright green spray, full of half-digested sausage. It was like all that sausage had sunk beneath the rest of his breakfast and so was last to abandon ship. And my God, even upwind the stink was abominable. The breeze took it aft to old Joey who was at the rudder. Hit him like a shit shower. And it sparked a chain reaction. You know what, until then old Joe had never been seasick in his whole life, but as soon as that tsunami of vomit hit him he was chucking too. And the sight of old Joe going at it with his head over the side set the other fella off again. When we finally got back to harbour, I swear that little boat was one-third full of vomit. In fact, on the way back I had to throw some gear overboard to stop us sinking because of the extra weight. Took two full days to clean her out. And you know something, I never felt sick for a moment. Not once that entire day. Just goes to show, you never know when you're going to blow, but once you start you never know when you'll stop."

"Uncle, just to be crystal clear. I've never been seasick; I don't feel seasick; I'm not going to be seasick. And you are not going to make me feel seasick. So can we talk about something else? Anything."

"What would you suggest?" Horace seemed momentarily crestfallen and his English accent was suddenly much more evident.

"How about the past."

"You mean that party? When I saw you last? It was just silliness. I don't even recall what we argued about."

"You were being beastly to Mum."

"I'm not sure that's an entirely accurate memory, Lizzy. You'd had a few glasses of bubbly and were a little tiddly as I recall."

"And you, as I recall, had had a few too many tumblers of brandy and were as drunk as a skunk when you arrived."

"I was jet lagged and I was going down with the 'flu. I had a temperature of God knows what."

"That's not how I remember it."

"We all have individual perspectives on the past, Lizzy. Put things down and just enjoy, that's my advice. Enjoy what exists in the moment, accept it for what it is. Otherwise this voyage is going to be a pain in the ass for us both."

There was a wounded pause and we looked out to sea. Rain pattered against the window. Horace got up and opened a cupboard that contained glasses and an array of bottles. He poured two generous measures and handed one to me, ruffling my hair affectionately. "Here, get that down you, my girl. Good French cognac. It'll settle you."

The fumes were delightful and I drank willingly. I felt the familiar warmth and sense of fusion, the softening of hard angles of irritation. "I don't want to argue with you, Uncle. I'm just not sure what we're doing, what this represents, this whole escapade."

"You over-analyse, Lizzy. Why can't it be simple. Two chums taking a little holiday together."

"Is that what we are? Chums?"

"Closer than chums, you dolt. We're family. And family's important, not just for humans but across a huge spectrum of species. Do you know, Lizzy, when I was in east Africa I saw wild elephants display a whole array of emotions: joy, grief, anger, love, compassion, self-awareness, altruism. Way more than I've seen in most people. Mothers show such love for their offspring, nuzzling, stroking, bathing them, gently guiding and protecting them. The bond between mother and daughter lasts more than half-a-century. And when members of families are reunited they run towards each other roaring and trumpeting with joy, and then rub against each other, flapping their ears, clicking tusks and entwining trunks. Touching is fundamental. And they go through an excited dance, spinning and leaning into each other, making contact, skin to skin. Sometimes they're so happy that they urinate or defecate, they just can't contain their joy. And they also exhibit grief. I saw a weeping mother carrying her dead calf on her back for hours, and when she finally chose a spot to put it down, family members all broke off branches and pulled up clumps of grass to cover the body. They understand death you see, Lizzy. They return to the bones of their dead, touching and smelling them, caressing them with their trunks as though trying to reconnect with a loved one. And when they stand there in silence, their eyes overflowing with tears, it's impossible not to believe that their gentle minds are full of memories. And what are memories but a reliving of the past?"

"That's fascinating, Uncle, but I still don't know why I'm here."

"Because I invited you."

"But why?" I could hear the insistence rising in pitch as it approached a whine.

"Because I wanted it. And you wanted it too. Isn't that enough?"

"But will you talk to me? I mean really talk."

"We're talking now."

"You know what I mean, Uncle. About family. My grandfather. About Virgil, your brother."

"We'll talk, Lizzy, past, present and future. It's one of the reasons I invited you. We can talk about the past, although you have to understand my memory's not what it once was. We'll talk, but we've got almost a month. No need to charge at it like a wounded bull." He patted my knee. "Come on, drink up. We've got to explore the ship. Let's take it deck by deck. And when we're done it'll be time for dinner."

SIX

I'm trying to be careful; trying to be precise and true. Looking back, it's easy to misremember. One cannot always recall exact emotions or motives, so it's tempting to make them up, smooth out and neaten the jumble of the past. Or, sometimes, you remember too well, and shudder, and then there is an overwhelming temptation to alter what you know. Either way, the result is a re-burnishing, a process of colourisation to restore what once was, or should have been. Fresh emotions and coherent motives are overlaid upon a sequence of fixed events, or things perhaps that were never completely fixed. It's not fiction exactly, but neither is it fact. I guess it's how humans deal with the past. It's how history is laid down.

When we set off on that expedition to explore the ship it felt like a voyage within a voyage. There was a sense of anticipation, heightened by the delay of necessary preparations. Horace fussed around, moving papers, choosing a jacket, tidying his books and generally indulging in the endeavours of someone planning a significant absence from base camp. I took the opportunity to check out his absurdly ornate bathroom, with its Carrara marble, classical columns and Italian mosaic walls. The grandeur demanded that one should not inhabit such space alone. There were deep twin basins, a double shower, and a twin-sized whirlpool tub next to a full-length plate window (with one-way glass) so that you could luxuriate in a warm and private ocean, while looking out at the real thing, grey and shuddering, 150 feet below. As I perched on the loo I noticed my reflection in three separate mirrors, the images bouncing back upon each other all the way to infinity. I wondered what spectacles of excess this room had witnessed as the rich frolicked, like steam-shrouded hippos at a waterhole. When I flushed I noticed the same phenomenon that I had observed earlier: that click and fractional pause before the awful roar, and then the hurling velocity of water.

With preparations complete, we paused so that Horace could conduct an elaborate pocket-checking routine for cards, wallet, pen, glasses and handkerchief. Monique appeared, a silent and submissive apparition, asking if she could assist in any way—perhaps a reservation for either of the dinner servings in the main dining room, or a priority booking at the table of our choice in one of the ship's speciality restaurants? With buccaneering confidence Horace declined and thus we set forth in a spirit of rugged self-sufficiency. I remember thinking that we looked like Don Quixote and Sancho Panza, the hidalgo leading the way with a sprightly gait born of self-belief, easy in his baggy flannel trousers and crumpled tweed jacket. He strode, stooped but jaunty, down the corridor, his thin cane with its ornate silver head silent on the carpet, clicking only when it struck the wall. I followed, half a step behind, moving to a different rhythm.

But—and this is important in the context of the way the evening ended—I wasn't counting doors or seeing abstract patterns in the paintwork. And there were no intrusive thoughts. I was feeling relatively relaxed. After our initial skirmish it seemed we had reached an accommodation that was more than a mere ceasefire. There had been terms, and within them lay the germ of a settlement that promised the possibility of historic grievances addressed. I was also warmed from the brandy, and that, too, was undoubtedly a factor in how things played out. But at the outset, I remember feeling an imprecise sense of optimism as though, in moving through our moving vessel, we were actually getting somewhere. The ship felt like a protective rather than a constraining element, a Noah's Ark of humanity carving its way through a vast sea that was alive with all manner of unseen, exotic life, though not, as it turned out, blessed by the presence of Steller's sea creatures, cows or apes.

Looking back on things, I think maybe we were too relaxed. It began well enough, with a climb up to the Eye of Zeus where we braved the wind and gazed out at a 360 degree panorama of the grey sea and its white, painted ship. After panting for a minute or two, leaning heavily on the rail, Horace recovered his breath and produced a pair of binoculars ("special forces issue," I was informed) from his capacious jacket pockets. Braced together we watched skuas and fulmars shadowing the ship, crying and circling, banking above us, hanging weightless on the wind. There was such easy joy and fluidity in their movement that I thought of Coleridge's albatross, a Christian soul appearing through the fog to cheer and guide the faltering mariners. Below us, on our ship, there were only a hardy few outside, but looking down through the glass to Apollo deck one could see the swarm moving with considered chaos, bereft of a single Christian soul. Brightly coloured bathing caps bobbed and splashed in the pool. In the bars and restaurants ragged groups or neat pairs were talking, reading newspapers or books, staring at screens, and all simultaneously engaged in that default cruise activity: eating and drinking.

And that's where we made our mistake. We came down from our lofty perch and, as we descended through the decks, we paused a little too frequently at a few too many watering holes. We spent a while on the Poseidon deck, checking out the bars around the pool complex. Later, we passed through the residential decks before arriving at the Promenade, where we circumnavigated the vessel and explored its lounges, library and bars. Horace declared sniffily that he had seen better libraries in public bus stations, but when challenged as to precisely which bus stations he claimed a memory lapse. Memory certainly did become an issue when we arrived at the bright lights of Monte Carlo where, within the huge atrium, we were borne along on the human tide that washed through the restaurants and bars. I remember that we paused for a while at a table in the Sea Garden, where we sat amid an artful combination of real and artificial plants and foliage. At its centre was a vast circular aquarium of curved glass. There were banks of brightly coloured coral alive with an array of grazing fish, from small orange specimens that reminded me of the goldfish I had kept as a kid through to silver and black striped beauties and clownfish with painted faces peering from thickets of gently swaying sea anemones. There were yellow and white butterfly fish; bright blue damselfish; lionfish with scarlet stripes and spines; black trigger fish with yellow noses and round white spots; drifting yellow sea horses with curled tails; starfish; crabs of varying size and colour; baby sharks, with gunmetal mottled skins, gliding with the precision of bullets; and rays, flying as effortlessly as eagles over reef and sand. In a separate but adjoining tank was a rock arch and an old anchor, picturesquely encrusted with barnacles. A large octopus was perched upon it, tentacles wrapped around the metal hook. It was absolutely still, but as we gazed its colour changed from rusty red to olive and then shivered to silver.

As for the other ports we called at during that first night, I remember Fizz, the Magellan cocktail lounge, Shooters, the Paper Moon and Club Kryptonite. I think that there were a few more, too, but as Horace always liked to say, the past can be a little hazy when viewed from the present, but from anywhere else you can't see it at all. Also, whilst in retrospect it might seem like a pub-crawl, the thing to remember is that when there is no cost it's all just too easy, way too easy to consume. When everything is free, everything loses its value. You can order at whim and leave it unfinished, even untouched. There is no requirement to finish anything, or even to start it. Consumption can be subsumed within the act of acquisition—the joy of ordering and seeing it brought to your table and presented with a bow.

We, however, were old fashioned; we consumed in the traditional way and in our wake we left a flotsam trail of bobbing bottles and empty brandy balloons. I tried to mitigate the inevitable: I ate those tasty little plates of crisps and canapés that accompanied our drinks; I even switched from brandy to gin at some hazy halfway point in an evening devoid of normal time, where our actions were governed not by the clocks of land but the soothing insistence of the sea. I was in favour of getting dinner in the main dining room but we had missed the first sitting and so went to have another drink and then missed the second. Horace did not seemed bothered. He said that the problem with the main dining room was that you were seated on communal tables and thus ran the risk of being trapped with "a heap of old bores." He said not to worry as we could swing by one of the speciality restaurants at any time. The problem was that "any time" proved a slippery schedule.

There came a moment when I knew that I was utterly hammered. Horace was flushed but still conversing in his clipped and regular tone, old school English enlivened by vivid flashes of Australian. He was talking about elephants again, citing a long litany of human cruelty. He told me about Topsy, a female Asian elephant who had responded to gratuitous human ill treatment by attacking and killing several of her tormentors. Condemned as a killer, it was decided that she should be hanged in January 1903, before a crowd of paying spectators (25 cents per head), in the Luna Park amusement complex that was being constructed on Coney Island. The American Society for the Prevention of Cruelty to Animals ruled this to be needlessly cruel and so an equitable solution was reached whereby Topsy would be put to death by being poisoned and electrocuted prior to strangulation with a pair of steam-powered nooses. The crowd was limited too, with only around 1,500 (plus press), but as the execution was filmed and released under the snappy title *Electrocuting an Elephant,* those unable to attend in person could still enjoy the event at cinemas. On the day itself Topsy refused point blank to go to the designated spot of execution, and so they brought death to her, feeding her carrots laced with potassium cyanide, and then wiring her up with a copper-lined sandal on her right front foot and rear left. The 6,600 volts killed her in ten seconds, before the poison could do its work, but they went ahead anyway and strangled her corpse for ten minutes.

So, there we were, talking. But it was not an elevated conversation. Rather one that left me distraught over the inhumanity of humanity. Elephants good, humans bad, was our mantra. And we were still walking too. Horace insisted that our swaying gait was the result of the ocean and the motion of the ship, but I knew we were succumbing, becoming more sedentary, dropping anchor for longer intervals at our chosen ports of call. And that was dangerous, because if you sat with an empty glass someone in a white tunic would come along and replace it with a full one. I knew that we should eat something, a proper meal, but I no longer felt hungry. I remember wondering if we looked anything like as drunk as I felt.

Horace was now telling me about "Mighty Mary," an elephant calf who had been captured in British India and sold to a circus in America. He was describing events that happened in 1916 but was doing so with an immediacy that made me think for a moment that he had actually been there, until I laboriously counted back the decades and calculated that he had not been born. As a 5-ton adult, Mary was caged and beaten, malnourished, bolstered with cheap whisky and made to perform under the Big Top at the Charlie Sparks travelling circus. And Horace was quivering with indignation as he related the indignities and privations that had been heaped on poor Mary, the largest of the circus's five elephants, as "she shambled through a repertoire of tricks—playing tunes on a horn, pitching a baseball, dancing and sitting up on her hind legs—for the amusement of the greasy crowd. And beneath the lights and paint her untreated skin sores chafed against the saddle and harness, and her jaw was swollen with a puss-filled abscess that had been left untreated for years."

"And do you know, Lizzy, on 12 September 1916, in Kingsport, Tennessee, Mighty Mary was leading the five-strong elephant contingent to a watering ditch and was being ridden by a drifter called Red Eldridge who had been hired the previous day by the circus, hired as an elephant-handler even though he had no expertise or experience. And there he was, riding Mary, when she paused in the street to pick up a watermelon rind. She was hungry, you see. In response, Eldridge hit her on the side of her face with an iron hook, close to the site of her abscess. Mad with pain and fury she reached back and grabbed him with her trunk, dashed him to the ground, and then calmly walked over and stepped on his head, crushing it like an over-ripe melon. A local blacksmith called Hench Cox rushed out and shot the elephant five times without much effect. That evening she even performed at the circus as scheduled, but a mob of townspeople was demanding that she had to be killed if the circus were to be permitted to continue. They did not have the electricity to kill her like Topsy, but they considered all manner of alternatives, such as crushing her between two trains or using engines travelling in different directions to rip her head from her body. Finally, circus owner Charlie Sparks agreed that Murderous Mary should be hanged as part of a grotesque public spectacle. The next day the circus travelled up the track to Erwin, Unicoi County. Mary was excused participation from the matinee performance, which was by all accounts well attended. Afterwards she headed the trunk-to-tail elephant parade for a last time, being led to a nearby rail yard where there was a derrick that was to be her gallows. It had been raining but a crowd of 3,000, including many children, turned out to watch her hang. The other elephants were led away, although they were reluctant to leave her. One of her back legs was shackled to a rail to prevent her following them and an iron chain was fastened around her neck. The crane hoisted her up but her leg was still tethered and so she was stretched taut, her sinews snapping, bones popping, screaming, until the chain broke and she fell to the ground, her hip bone shattering with the sound that observers later described as a rifle crack and ricochet. She lay crying in pain while they untied her leg, and found a heavier chain to attach to her neck. This one proved up to the job and so, to the cheers of the crowd, Mary was dragged into the air. She choked and writhed for ten minutes, her eyes running with tears, while her four companions trumpeted their grief. And even today, Mary's bones are there, in the mud of some unmarked grave beside the railway track.

"This magnificent creature, born on the other side of the world, was enslaved after watching her mother murdered, and then moulded by the whip and the repetition of command. But here's the thing, she was never completely broken. She would have retained memories of an untamed life and so, on an ordinary day, after a commonplace jab from that routine spike, she killed one of her tormentors. But only one. Note what she did not do. She didn't run amok, trampling anyone in her path. She didn't even run. She transgressed enough to get a cut-price crucifixion. And so, though she was born free in the heat of India and died in chains amid the laugher and rain of Hicksville, she transcended the misery of her life by leveraging human depravity. So it was suicide really, but then suicide comes in many different forms. And so does narrative. Other versions and reports of the story say that there was no abscess of the jaw; that Mary was a killer, with a dozen or two victims, who struck down Red (or Walter) Eldridge for no reason; that

Sparks and his wife, Addie, loved the elephant and raised her as a pet; that she was well treated and trained with kindness; that she killed Eldridge with a blow to the head from her powerful trunk, or used it to strangle him like a boa constrictor; that she had been bought and sold before, under different names, including Queen and Empress; that she gored Eldridge with her giant tusks; that after Eldridge's death she was arrested and chained up at the Kingston jail; that the townspeople tried her in an impromptu court and sentenced her to death; that her body was burned on a pyre of railroad timbers; that after her death Sparks had three of his men dig around in her face to retrieve her valuable tusks; that, as a female Asian elephant, she had no tusks; that the night after her execution the other elephants broke free causing panic; that they were seeking to return to her body to grieve; that Mary killed Eldridge during a circus performance and after stamping out his life hurled (or kicked) his mangled corpse into the shocked audience from whence Hench (or Henry) Cox rushed out to fire five (or more) shots which gravely wounded (or barely inconvenienced) the huge elephant. Even the famous photograph of Mary's hanging corpse is disputed, credited to Eddie LeSeurer or others; accused of being faked; undoubtedly retouched many times to enhance its subject and overcome the limits of the medium on what was, it is only fair to say, an overcast and intemperate day where there may or may not have been rain. It was said that the local railroad company was offered money by the Associated Press to exhume and re-hang Mary from the derrick so that better quality snaps could be taken, but the company refused (probably)."

It was getting late when we shambled into a seafood restaurant somewhere on the Monte Carlo deck. The maître d' looked at us sceptically but Horace's old school accent and his Diamond Plus status were magic keys that overcame all prejudice and unlocked the table of our choice. I ordered lobster but Horace said, a little too loudly, "No way." Then, with the waiter waiting, embarrassed and patient, Horace lectured me on the cruelty of how lobsters are cooked alive and on the sophistication of the lobster's nervous system. He told me how they react to damage, to pain, both physically and hormonally. They exhibit symptoms of distress, try desperately to escape the torture of the pot, and they release cortisol into the bloodstream, just as we do. But unlike us, their nervous system does not alleviate suffering by producing a state of shock, so they feel everything with the same level of acuteness, right up to the moment of death. I've never eaten lobster since.

Horace cancelled my order, substituting two seaweed salads served with rice vinegar, toasted sesame seeds and ginger. The waiter politely informed him that the salads were side dishes rather than mains, whereupon he upped the order to six, explaining that we'd have three each. I ordered a bottle of chardonnay, more from habit than from desire. When desire is sated, when it has rolled off and gone to sleep, habit remains, throbbing silently in the dark. It's predictable, you can rely on the steady pulse of habit.

The lobster thing had led to an increased awkwardness. So there I was, picking at one of the half dozen plates of seaweed salad. It wasn't bad actually, although in those days I was still a prisoner of the misplaced view that a meal was not truly complete unless it contained some part of a dead creature. Horace came shambling back from a visit to the Gents, swaying out of time with the ship and talking too loudly.

"God that's better. First proper opening of the bowels for days."

"Uncle!" I hissed.

"What?" He sat down heavily, almost knocking over his glass.

"Too loud. Too much information."

"Not where I'm from. My old mate Jimbo, he always said that a good shit was better than sex."

I was aware of heads turning at the neighbouring table. "He sounds a real charmer," I whispered. "Maybe you should have brought Jimbo on the voyage rather than me."

"That would have been difficult." Horace half-stifled a burp. "He's dead. Eaten by a croc, actually. The bastard was more than five metres long!"

"Jimbo?"

"Nah, the croc. It was a monster. Some of the locals killed it later, poor devil. And do you know, when they opened that bastard up they found Jimbo's orthopaedic plate with six stainless steel screws inside its gut. He'd had it fitted when he broke his arm, years before when he came off his dirt bike. And you know what else they found in there?"

"Surprise me, Uncle, but do it quietly."

"A walking stick and two pairs of glasses."

"More of Jimbo's possessions?"

"Nah, that's the thing. Jimbo's legs were fine. He didn't need a stick. So were his eyes. He didn't even wear sunglasses. What they found in there belonged to other poor buggers that the croc had already pouched. Impossible to know how many. Up there in the swamps, people can disappear without trace." He resumed work on his salad.

"I feel sorry for the croc," I said.

"Yeah, so did I. It was a real killer, but that's what crocs do. Top predators. It's in their nature. Jimbo was out hunting and so he got what he deserved. To tell the truth, he was a bit of a shit actually. Treated his woman abominably. Do you know what he did to her one time?" Horace took a large mouthful of seaweed, chewing it thoughtfully, with the deliberation of a manatee.

In truth, I was quite intrigued about what Jimbo had done. I was fascinated to know what constituted abominable treatment of women in Horace's world, but I was wary about straying too far into that territory, or even crossing the frontier actually: too much alcohol consumed, too public a venue. Instead, I tried to change the subject. I had no idea—I think that I had no idea—what it was destined to produce. "Can we talk a bit about the past?" I said.

"The past?" Horace snorted derisively. "Western culture is obsessed with the past. Know why? Because it has no future. It's finished, economically eclipsed, scientifically outstripped, culturally decadent. It's gone soft, rotten as a tooth, hollowed out by political correctness, social media, and a culture of weakness."

"I meant our family's past."

"We promote weakness and reward enfeeblement. People no longer have the balls to think for themselves, they're too busy searching for things to take offence at. You know Lizzy, when I was a kid people wanted to be heroes; now they just want to be victims. Right there, in that aspirational arc, hero to victim, that's a perfect reflection of a culture in decay. We live in a perpetual oppression-Olympics where everyone's competing for maximum victimhood. And you know why? Coz it gives them a voice, gives them status, gives them unearned privileges. They don't have to work for it, they don't have to strive or think. Christ, they don't even have to be oppressed, they just have to be able to claim victimhood. And that's piss easy because there are so many seams they can mine: ethnicity, gender, sexual identity, sexual preferences, disability. The list is bloody endless because new claims are being staked out every day. There's enough for everyone, as long as you're not white and male and old. And the more victimhood you lay claim to, the more privileges you get, and with the privileges comes the money." He rubbed his fingers together ostentatiously. "Blood money, the money that salves the sins of the past, real or manufactured."

"Are you setting yourself up as a victim, Uncle?"

"Nah, my lot are the oppressor. We're the bastards responsible for everything that has ever gone wrong with anybody's life. It's not their fault, it's ours. We owe them an eternity of apologies, lifetime privileges and an ocean of cash. And no matter how much we pay, how much regret we express for things we didn't do, it's never enough because new victims are coming forward every day and fresh crimes are being cobbled together and added to the charge sheet."

"Well, I'm not saying I'm oppressed and I don't use social media, but I can see that people like you, and me for that matter, have benefitted from privilege. History is full of wrongs, don't you think we should right some of them?"

"History is full of wrongs but you can't right them, you idiot, you can only learn from them. Rewriting the past doesn't undo what actually happened. And how dare you compare us. I'm much worse that you are. You're white but you're a woman, you get points for that. I'm old as well as white, and I've got a cock. I'm the fucking devil."

"Hey buddy, keep it down will you." The guy at the next table was middle-aged and pumped up.

Horace turned towards him. "Ah, one of our colonial cousins. You've got a few years on me matey, but you're still white and male. And you lose points for being a Yank. So you're a devil too, a cock-wagging, white devil like me."

"Buddy, I'm just trying to have a quiet dinner with my wife."

"I'm not your buddy, Buddy. But pull up a chair and join us, you might learn something. We can talk man to man, one devil to another. Let's measure diabolicals and see whose is bigger."

For a moment I thought the guy was going to come over and thump him. I heard myself apologising, hissing at Horace to keep his voice down. The man looked at me with something nearer to pity than hostility. "You should take your grandfather back to his cabin to sleep it off," he said.

"I'm not her grandfather," declared Horace loudly. "I'm her lover. And yes, I know she's only with me for my money, but I'm only with her for her body. It's a relationship based on honesty, and the sex is fan-fucking-tastic." He emphasised the final compound adjective, stretching it for maximum effect. "We'll be out of your hair—what's left of it—shortly, when we retire for our all-night fuck fest. We do it every night but I'm not bored with her yet. She's new, I just plucked her from the shop floor a few weeks ago. You could say it was an unexpected promotion. I'm still breaking her in. How long have you guys been married?"

"It's not true," I remember saying. And then to Horace, "Shut the fuck up or I'm leaving."

Just then a waiter appeared. "Please sir. You're disturbing our other diners."

"We were just discussing marriage," explained Horace. "Are you married?"

"No sir," he said. "But please don't talk to the other guests." He went over to apologise to the American couple.

"Wise man," said Horace as he shovelled in more seaweed.

"What the fuck, Uncle," I hissed. "You want to get us thrown out? Thrown off the cruise?"

"I was only having fun. He's just a heckler."

"No, Uncle. He's not a heckler, he's a guy having dinner with his wife."

"Yeah, well there's nothing else you'd want to do with her."

"And it wasn't fun. Not for him, not for me, not for anyone in here. And just because you found it funny doesn't make it alright. Can't you see how entitled you sound?"

"Lizzy, don't try to use that shit to flip what I was saying. I'm telling you it's lost. The scum has risen to the surface of the tank: looters, venal politicians, self-serving bastards, half-witted bureaucrats. It's inevitable. The West fought two civil wars in the last century, internecine fratricidal bloodletting. We killed the brightest and bravest and best. It's the flowering of a poisonous seed, one that begins with high culture, honour and chivalry and duty, but grows into frightened young men bleeding to death in some shitty pock-marked wilderness, raped women crying for lost children, dying behind the barbed wire of camps. It was a suicide. And now it's done—Europe, America, Australia—we're a busted flush, and the rest of the world is on the move, they're coming for us, coming to take what's left."

"I don't agree. There's plenty of evidence to..."

"It's over, I tell you. Look around you, the crisis is here, it's now. It's there, right there, and there," he said, jabbing the air wildly with his fork, shedding bits of seaweed. "It's everywhere, and the catastrophe is just around the corner. All we can do, all anyone can do, is have a glass of bubbly before succumbing to the great inevitable. Let's have a glass to toast the victors who have crossed continents and oceans to inherit our ruins."

"That's the last thing you need. You've had enough. And don't ever say what you just said about me and you, not even as a joke. It's humiliating. It's also fucking disgusting."

"Ah, yes, I know I'm old and withered, but I was once beautiful, desired by many."

"It's nothing to do with your being withered, Horace. We're fucking family."

"Ah yes, a family of fuckers. And the family that plays together stays together. After we've raised a glass to the victors we should have a toast to families. I know how fond you are of families."

He reached for the empty wine bottle but knocked it over. I tried to catch it but in doing so upset a glass, which broke against the side of one of the many plates of seaweed. The carafe of water went over too, emptying its contents into my lap. The noise was horrifying and our sad Filipino waiter swooped in to deal with the wreckage.

"Fuck," I said.

"Not yet, Honey," Horace laughed. "Fucky later, when we're back in the cabin. First we have drinky, then fucky, then sleepy."

"Shut the fuck up, Horace."

And then, suddenly, the other table was back in communication. "Will you stop cursing." It was Mrs American now, tanned, bejewelled, quivering with Evangelical outrage, baring her perfectly regular, manicured little teeth. And her husband was limbering up too, waiting to re-enter the ring as soon as he was tagged.

"We're leaving," I said.

"We haven't had the toast yet. You, sir," Horace beckoned to the waiter who was still clearing debris. "Mr Bachelor man, we need more wine for the toast."

"Sir, the restaurant is closing now."

"But there are people still eating. Besides, I haven't finished my seaweed." He reached with his fork into one of the bowls that the waiter was stacking.

"Okay, I'm leaving," I said. I could see the maître d' approaching.

"You see," said Horace, shouting over to the Americans and gesturing with an overloaded forkful of seaweed. "See how keen she is, like a dingo with a doughnut."

I stood up and bent to retrieve my bag. At that moment the ship pitched and I went over, scattering the bag's contents. I scrabbled on all fours, trying to retrieve them. The waiter bent down to help me. I heard Horace shout, "Get your paws off her. She's mine, all mine. I won't share her with anyone. Go and find one of your own." The seaweed fell from his waving fork and landed with a splat on the carpet. "Damn," he said. "I need more food, anything but lobsters. And where's that wine I ordered? Service here sucks." He looked down at me. "My God, Lizzy, your pants are all wet. Are you excited or did you just piss yourself?"

I should like to say that I got to my feet and swept out of the restaurant with the dignity of righteous outrage. I'd like to say it but it wouldn't be true. Slopping out of a crowded room, drunk on a bucking ship, whilst wearing wet trousers is never going to be a good look, never dignified. I'd like to say that I got back to the privacy of my room before beginning to cry, but the tears began sooner than that, though the real sobbing, the gulping that came later, was confined to my cabin.

The bed had been turned down and someone had taken Benny from the bedside table and put him on my pillow together with a little ship-shaped chocolate in a sheath of blue paper embossed with "*Evening Star.*" I curled up on the bed and hugged him, my wet face against his blue fur inhaling his scent. And then I sobbed.

SEVEN

With consciousness comes pain. In those first few seconds of self-awareness, before you even open your eyes, you feel its percussive presence, the shells bursting and sending shrapnel ricocheting around your skull. Unsticking your eyelids, opening a crack to the grey light, unleashes a fresh barrage of head artillery. And then, just as you remember the slough of your body, it chips in with a discord of imprecise throbbing, sweats and aches and feverish chills, and somewhere on the inside, somewhere that's hard to place but you know is important, there's a sour burn, the aftertaste of poison. And following in the shadow of the pain comes shame as you piece together recollections of the evening, fitting the fractured images together like shards of coloured glass. And each one cuts as you fumble it, so you wince and cringe while you assemble the ramshackle framework of horror and regret, that misshapen thing that appals and humiliates as it grows into a hazy and incomplete record of the night before.

I needed to pee; I needed pain killers to dull the machete blows of the maniac in my head. I didn't flush; my body was too delicate to risk in the vicinity of the awful snort and unnatural force that ripped water and waste from one world to the next. In the mirror my skin looked too white and my eyes too small and yellow. I picked off the flattened chocolate that had stuck to my cheek in sleep. I downed a glass of water, took two aspirin, peeled off my remaining clothes, and retreated bedways, cocooning myself beneath the covers, willing the dawn to disappear and the pain to disperse into the gentle darkness of night.

I had been dreaming of a lobster boiling and screaming in the pan, scuttling in blind circles, thrashing in its futile desperation to escape. I thought of Horace's pointless, senseless cruelty and behind my clenched eyes I drifted among images of horror: a dolphin helplessly trying to free her drowning calf from a gill net; a seal on a crimson ice floe unable to save her pup from the hunters' clubs. I thought of God, and wondered how I could have once had such faith in a being so cruel, so compassionless, or perhaps just merely uninterested. Once, I would have said that God was there, bleeding on the ice, drowning in the net, but now I think him absent, or careless in the face of cruelty, preferring to look away when the blood flows.

I hunched in my anonymous bed, afloat on some unknown fleck of ocean, beyond frontiers, and I wished I could feel the hug of strong arms around me. I wished William were with me, with his familiar smell and his clumsy bear embrace. That's what I called him sometimes, Clumsy Bear. He had wanted to be a father from the start. He told me the first time we met, sharing a playground supervision one lunchtime at a school where I had just been appointed and knew nobody. He had ambled alongside me while we chatted of the future, and had said that his greatest ambition was to be a Dad. And later he was, and then he wasn't. I thought of little Wat and then scrabbled for Benny, who had become lost in the tangled sheets of the night. I pressed my face into his fur and drifted back into the oblivion of sleep.

Three hours later I was swimming lazy, regular lengths in the pool. The pain was under control now, the shame too, and it felt good to move through the slick water. I felt relaxed and warm, though filled with loathing for Horace. And buoyed by my hatred, I swam like a sealion.

After dousing the pain, my initial inclination had been to abandon ship, just get off at the next port and leave him to find an alternative victim for his fucked up idea of fun. I contemplated this as I ate breakfast in the buffet, staying well clear of the location of the previous night's humiliation. The ship was quiet, the heaving sea apparently keeping many in their bunks. I ate and read, anonymous and alone, and I realised that it was unlikely that I would ever come across any of the handful of people who had witnessed last night's cabaret in the lobster restaurant. And even if I did, it was unlikely that we would acknowledge each other or the unpleasantness that linked us. The shame existed only in my mind and thus could be set aside as an act of will. It was Horace who should feel ashamed. He had behaved like a thoughtless, boorish bastard, whereas I was an innocent and injured party, slightly culpable only through accidental intoxication.

And thus it made no sense to run away. I was here, put in this place at this time and I should enjoy it, freed from the responsibility of chaperoning a fucking maniac. When I returned to my room to get my swimming stuff the phone was ringing. I let it go to voice mail. And after I had swum my twenty-eight lengths (in four groups of seven, each group comprising three lengths crawl, three breast stroke and end-stopped by one of backstroke), I sat in a hot tub and was sort of hit on by Brian, a retired bank manager from Devon. He had a fascinating absence of hair, head and body, though he was otherwise unremarkable. But he seemed kind and was mildly amusing in a lonely guy sort of way, and I was almost sorry when I had to leave for the appointment I had made at the salon. But the body massage and facial were more than worth it, clearing my pores of the last of the alcohol and blotting my mind of the memory.

Later, smelling of rose oil and buttermilk, I lunched lightly, chatting confidently in the main dining room to Egon and Art, a pair of gay guys from Bethnal Green who had recently got married; a charming Belgian couple whose names I can't remember but who spoke excellent English and were celebrating their fortieth wedding anniversary; and Pam and Stanley, a jolly and well-padded couple whose tireless, joyful eating induced in me a vicarious sense of satisfaction that was almost as good as the real thing. There was an easy familiarity and friendliness about it all and, after ordering another non-alcoholic cocktail and choosing a moderate dessert, I was aware of a sense of contentment, a growing feeling of belonging. In fact, I did not think at all about Horace until later in the afternoon as I was browsing the shopping mall on Fifth Avenue. I guess that in truth it was more grazing than browsing. And what began as mere window shopping, little more than light flirtation really, ended in a more prolonged and serious clinch that stopped only just short of full penetration.

Initially I had thought that it would feel odd, maybe wrong, to spend his money. But the problem was that there was no discernible point of transaction, just the flip of my cruise card; a tiny movement to initiate an unseen electronic pulse that legitimised the purchase by charging it to his account. And after this effortless moment came the curiously liberating act of walking away with an item where the only real decision had been whether or not to have it gift wrapped. The distinction between looking at stuff and acquiring it had been seamlessly fused, so much so that it seemed as though people were giving me stuff for free. And they were so helpful and nice, suggesting other things I might like to consider, bringing me alternative sizes and colours, eager to please, devoted in that moment—totally devoted—to making me look good, feel good, to increasing the sum of my happiness. I mean, entire religions have been founded on less devotion than that. So although it felt odd at first to be spending his money, I adjusted quickly. Besides, I was owed.

And this was a high-end shopping experience, strolling through the halls of a palace of glass and mirrors, a crystal plaza where clothes and shoes and accessories were displayed with the reverent care of art works in a gallery. They had prices to match, but these were so discreetly placed as to be almost irrelevant, as unobtrusive as the soft music and the perfume-freighted air, and it all became more normal as the afternoon wore on and I became attuned to the opulent splendour. But first one had to adjust. Initially the grandeur of the luxury was wildly unfamiliar and I wandered disorientated, almost overwhelmed, unable to gain any traction on the shiny surfaces. My deliverance came when I was snagged by a pair of shoes. And these were no ordinary shoes. These were ebony black, high heeled sandals, sculpted, with a thin toe-strap of sequined black rose clusters. The silver instep soared elegantly to delicate satin ankle straps. The flared heels were a perfect height—chic but not vertiginous—and made of smoked glass (probably Perspex, actually). They looked like something worn by Cinderella's trashy twin. They looked great. Even on my feet they looked great. They felt great, too, different from any shoe I had ever worn. With these as my foundation I felt elevated, a step or two closer to the heavens. So there was no real decision. I pouched them as instinctively as a crocodile, like the one who had inadvertently avenged the unspecified wrongs that Jimbo had done to his nameless woman. I thought about how long the taproots of vengeance can be, and how tangled, while I picked out a pair of deck shoes that were expensive but, as any fool knows, essential on a ship. When I offered my card as payment I sort of expected it to be declined, but it was done in an instant, as easy as blinking, and there I was, a moment later, walking free with two pairs of new shoes including my black-rose-smoked-glass beauties.

After that initial snog, there was definitely some heavy petting. I needed a dress to go with my new shoes. With a little searching, assisted by Eva, a soft-spoken Norwegian with eyes the colour of irises, I found a strapless little number that screamed—or, rather, huskily whispered—sophistication and elegance. I was torn between classic black—beautiful and versatile—and a colour somewhere between ivory and burnished silver, which shimmered like a breaking wave. As I twisted with indecision it was Eva who came to the rescue by suggesting that I take both. It was a simple solution, like slicing through the Gordian knot. They were doing a promotion too, so it was a good deal. Not exactly a saving in the strictest sense of the word, but certainly an economy. Eva also found me a clutch bag that went with both colours, so that was a definite saving as it meant that I only had to buy the one. And then, after a tiny electronic bleep and a warm farewell from my fairy of the fiord, they were mine. As the dresses were strapless, I obviously had to get a strapless bra to go with them. I got two, one to match each dress, and a couple of pairs of matching pants. I was fitted by Mahalia, a sweet girl from the Philippines, who recommended Spanx for an even, flattening, all-over-body effect. Anything smaller, she warned, could produce a "muffin top," a condition that she pronounced in such a cute way—"muphen tope"—as to render it almost benign. The Spanx were certainly big, stretching from mid-thigh almost to armpit, but once on, they held everything in its rightful place. My tummy disappeared, almost, artfully redistributed to other regions without being squished sideways into love handles. They also made my bum look pretty good, flat and toned; I wondered how many pairs you'd have to wear before your bum became invisible to the naked eye. I was sold on Spanx. Mahalia suggested that I take (note that pain-free verb of acquisition) a regular pair and a pair with a thong-finish for when VPL would be a problem. I took her advice. I mean, it would have been foolish not to. She was the expert whose mission was to use her hard-won expertise to make my day nicer, my life a little better.

Before I returned to my stateroom I stopped for a pedicure, which seemed only fair to my new shoes. When I got back the cleaning fairies had been and the food fairies had fluttered by to replenish my fruit basket. And so I lay on my freshly laundered bed, surrounded by my purchases, munching my way through a bunch of grapes. Later I checked my phone messages. All four were from Horace: one was a 'good morning, hope you're not too hung-over' call; the second was 'let's meet for lunch;' then there was a more business-like 'please can you call me so we can finalise arrangements for the day,' and finally, in the afternoon, a rather forlorn invitation for tea.

I read for a while and wrote my journal, recording a heavily curated version of the events of a night that was already sliding away from history, drifting into the haze of unsubstantiated hearsay. Soon it would be mere rumour. I browsed my email. There was nothing from William, but Moira had checked in to reassure that all was well with Mum. I sent her a brief note to say the weather was improving and that we had crossed the Bay of Biscay without my having succumbed to seasickness. I thought about checking the News, but the affairs of the land seemed of diminishing relevance as we slipped south around the western edge of Europe.

Instead, I read some more of the book that Horace had given me. After my great-grandfather's preface there came an introduction by Steller himself. Or, to be absolutely accurate, its words were Steller's but it had been embellished by my great-grandpa. He had taken material from elsewhere in the original text and transplanted it to create the introduction that he supposed Steller would have written had he not died before completing his book. I was not sure how I felt about this piece of surgery. The words were still authentically those of the original author, but the restructuring did raise the issue of when does editing—and for that matter translation—become rewriting? And yet these changes made the text more coherent and therefore more accessible.

Steller's book was a study of four particular creatures: sea cows; sea bears (a type of fur seal); sea lions; and sea otters, though as the introduction was at pains to point out, "one must not suppose that these places do not contain more great and magnificent animals that are still unknown, besides those which I shall describe. For if weather, time, and place had smiled upon my desire, I should have enriched our natural history with many such curiosities, as indeed I desired when I took the risk of this journey to regions so remote and unexplored." This was a general point from the original introduction. As was the consideration that, "So long as things elude us and fade unknown with our acquiescence, and in our silence are perceived as beyond belief—things which could be seen with little effort in the very land where we, with all our curiosity, inhabit—it is not strange that things which we are prevented from observing by the great sea that lies between, have remained to the present time unknown and unexplored." I glanced out at the great sea that lay beyond my window and contemplated the depths of all that lay unknown and unexplored.

And then there came specifics, material that had (as a footnote indicated) been moved from the sea cow section of the original to the newly-constructed introduction to give a flavour of the difficulties under which Steller had worked whilst marooned on Bering Island. "The weather...was almost constantly rainy and cold; my observations had to be made in the daytime; then there were the tides of the sea; and the droves of blue foxes (*isatides*) that would damage everything with their teeth and steal from my very hands; they ran off with my charts, book, and ink...and harried me when I was writing." When studying the sea cows, "the great size of the animal itself and the bulk of its parts were also a hindrance, for I had to be both observer and labourer, as all the others were busy with the construction of a ship to free us from the island. By paying men from my own pocket I could hire them for an hour or so in the evenings to lend some basic assistance, but in their ignorance and disdain for the work they would rip specimens to pieces, acting in accordance to their own inclinations... so that for all the pleasure I got from certain observations I had twice as much trouble and annoyance in consequence of those useful things which I had to leave alone. So I beg of my kind readers, when they have finished reading this feeble description, that they will judge it by my will and my zeal rather than by the circumstances." Even the specimens that Steller did prepare had to be abandoned when the new boat was completed as, "on account of the small size of our craft" there was insufficient space for them. But he did keep his notes, his scientific account of the "most minute circumstances" of all those months of "careful watching," that contained "nothing that is not most true," justifying his level of detail on the grounds that "an account can always be made shorter, but not longer or fuller, if it has been from the outset restricted within rather narrow limits." Or at least, this is what Steller had said in a passage lifted from the latter part of the book, dealing with sea bears. The end of the new introduction had a peroration taken from an earlier sea bear passage, in which he wrote defiantly that because of his many difficulties, "I have set out my porridge in carefully made earthen pots. If these offend anyone, he may perform a friendly service for me and others by pouring all into a vessel of gold or silver."

Porridge indeed. But it seemed that my great-grandfather had taken Steller at his word and had fashioned a golden vessel for the great man's hard-won observations. And though I had not yet tasted the porridge, there was something inspirational in Steller's story. Some of this lay in what did not happen. Shipwrecked, with their captain dead, the expedition could have quickly fallen apart. They could have given up and died. They could have descended into barbarity, a welter of murder and cannibalism, venting their hopelessness and desperation through bloodletting.

There were plenty of examples of such descent. When more than 150 passengers and crew from the French frigate *Medusa* spent thirteen days drifting on a hastily-built and overcrowded raft off Mauritania in 1816, only fifteen survived. The others were killed by the elements, committed suicide, or died in the series of wars that broke out over space, where the strong prevailed, throwing the sickly overboard or killing the weak so that their butchered flesh could provide sustenance. Even when resources were plentiful, the outcome could be dark. The mutineers from the *Bounty*, together with a group of native Tahitans, settled the Pacific island paradise of Pitcairn in 1790 but within a decade all but one of the men were dead from racial wars, alcoholism, suicide and murder. Maybe that is how unchecked human nature manifests itself. But not on Bering Island in 1741 where the men, even without their captain, hunted for food, collected seaweed to ward off scurvy, and laboured together to build the boat that would carry them home to the human world. And thus they survived, and Steller, a man of learning, survived with them not by sacrificing his refined and learned mind through a descent into savagery but by using his intellectual gifts, his scientific training, to make observations in the field despite all of the difficulties that he was forced to endure. And he did not just observe with a scientific eye, he wrote it down and managed to preserve his notes for posterity.

And suddenly I could see why my ancestor had felt it worthwhile to translate this man's work, and why it had been important to him to fashion the golden vessel that Steller himself had not lived long enough to make. I went out onto the balcony and sat watching the sea. I felt transported through other worlds and time, but also rested, calm and positive. I was forgiving enough even to answer the phone. I was braced for Horace but was flattered to receive a slightly gauche invitation to join Brian for aperitifs. I accepted. Of course I accepted. It was a great chance to wear the new frock.

Horace called me shortly afterwards and, from a position of strength, I extended magnanimity without warmth. I was super cool, even in my moment of triumph when I turned down his offer to meet up, informing him with carefully calibrated casualness that I had accepted a prior invitation. He affected insouciance, but when he asked where and with whom, I could sense the outline of his hidden hurt. We kept it vague and he wished me luck and agreed that maybe we would cross paths later in the evening. He asked if I was planning to go ashore at Lisbon, reminding me that he had priority disembarkation and a car and driver. I told him, with delicious ambiguity, "We haven't decided yet." What strength there is in such a little pronoun.

It turned out that Brian was a bit of a bore, whose principal love was buying and selling vintage cars. Nor were the others at the table much of the partying type. His mother must have been ninety but was sufficiently desiccated, under sympathetic lighting, to be able to pass for an undead eighty-five. Her neediness was mixed with a haughty snobbery and an antipathy towards anyone likely to outlive her. Thus, Miriam regarded me with suspicion from our first handshake. Also along for the occasion were two couples whom Brian and Miriam had met since coming on board: Doug and Eleanor, a former pharmacist and physiotherapist, who were now plump, Scottish pensioners; and Charlie and his wife Vicki ("with an i"), who ran a property empire in the West Midlands.

Brian sat next to me and maintained a steady patter of sweet banality. Though trying, this was preferable to the inanity of the forced conversation amongst the others, which Miriam steered with grim control. Occasionally I glanced at the clock, wondering how much more I had to endure before I could reasonably make my excuses and leave. Rescue came from an unexpected source. Horace entered the room dressed in whites with a navy blazer. His hair and beard were freshly washed and trimmed and he appeared perfectly sober. With a flourish of his cane he made straight for our table and then, just as he was about to pass it, did a slightly over-elaborate double take and stopped to say a cheery hello and to express his pleasure at having run into me. Introductions were made and hands shaken and he naturally accepted the invitation to join us, insinuating himself into the heart of the group with an open smile. He ordered a round of drinks and then, like a seasoned predator, went straight for his targeted member of the herd.

"And how are you finding the cruise so far?" he asked Miriam. The tone was solicitous and the cut glass accent had been polished to gleam, the Australian boor entirely superseded by an English gentleman.

"The sea air is bracing enough. Beneficial for the lungs of course. But it's hard to sleep with the perpetual motion of the ship. It is unnatural."

"But think about how soothing the motion of a cradle is to a baby," said Horace sympathetically.

"A baby has not yet become attuned to a stationary bed. It has been in motion for nine months, living *in utero*. Whereas I, by contrast, boarded this vessel only in Southampton."

"A loss from which that fine city must surely now be grieving." Horace beamed. "But, you know, all humans once slept in the tree tops in nests that swayed with the wind." His hand, raised head high, moved delicately from the wrist as though touched by a zephyr of air.

"I believe you must be thinking of birds."

"No, our ancestors lived in trees," said Horace firmly. "Our closest relatives—chimps and bonobos—still do. In fact," he moved his face closer to hers, "Once when I was lost in a forest in Kenya, I slept in a chimp's bed in a treetop. The air was clean and I was rocked to sleep on currents of gentle breeze. It was the best night's rest I ever had."

"The chimpanzee was not, I take it, present."

"No, the nest was abandoned but in excellent condition. Its erstwhile owner had built it well, weaving twigs and branches together securely and lining it thickly with leaves."

"And you could fit within this structure?" Miriam did not attempt to hide her scepticism.

"Indeed, the centre was depressed and there was a wide rim around the outside that proved perfect for resting one's head and legs upon. It was superbly comfortable. I was tired, exhausted from walking, but after a night in that nest I woke with the dawn feeling utterly refreshed. Not an ache or a pain anywhere in my entire body. I felt as though I had slept in the bed of my ancestors."

"*Your* ancestors perhaps, but I, for one, would not care to sleep in a chimpanzee bed. And I could not imagine climbing a tree each night in order to reach my bed."

"I could not imagine your doing that either, madam. But for me, I can say only that it was truly exhilarating."

"Truly terrifying, I should say."

"Not at all. In fact I found it so satisfying that when I eventually returned home, my odyssey at an end, I built a bed based on its precise design."

"You sleep in a tree within your house?" Miriam's tone had moved to incredulity.

"Not a tree. I replicated the nest's gentle motion by constructing a wooden frame and suspending a mattress within it. The frame has no solid centre and thus there is a natural declivity. The structure hangs from ceiling hooks and so it sways gently."

Vicki (with an i) jumped in. "I mean, correct me if I'm wrong, but you know that horrible feeling of jolting just when you're about to fall asleep. Isn't that a leftover from back in the day when we slept in the trees. Our ancestors, I mean, and they were terrified of falling out of their nests? I get that a lot and it's awful. It's always just when I'm getting off and it makes me jump awake so much it causes my back to spasm. Wouldn't your swaying bed make that even worse?"

"And if you fell out it could be dangerous. You could break something," said Doug.

"The bed is not mounted at great height," explained Horace patiently. "It hangs close to the floor but clear of the ground."

"Well, I wouldn't sleep in it," said Miriam.

"Be assured, there is no possibility of that," replied Horace lightly.

"I wouldn't sleep in any bed that was designed like a monkey nest," said Miriam. "Even if it was in my house. After all, we are clearly not chimpanzees are we? We are a different species, with a different shape."

"Indeed, some more so than others," said Horace.

I smiled. You couldn't help but smile when Horace was on form. There was the merest flicker of an eyebrow as he looked over and caught my eye, but then he sat back in his chair, poised but casual, head slightly cocked, attentive as a well-mannered host but slightly detached, like a scientist observing a chemical reaction that he had set in motion.

Eleanor was speaking. "We are certainly different. Great apes can stand on two legs, but it's not comfortable for them. They're naturally bow-legged and they can't run upright. Our bipedal ability is considerably more evolved."

"No disrespect to chimps," said Vicki (with an i), "but their posture isn't great, is it? I mean, it's not just that they're bandy legged. They don't sit up straight or walk tall. I wouldn't be surprised if all those saggy beds they build are the cause of their problems. Comfy isn't always best. In fact it's often bad for you."

"They're not like that because of their beds," said Eleanor. "We've just evolved differently. Our legs are straighter and longer, they're better positioned beneath our core centre of gravity. That's not to mention our more stable feet and our more dexterous hands. I have a professional interest in posture and how muscles evolved."

Horace returned to centre stage, gently agitating the test tube. "It is indeed the chimp who makes the bed, rather than the reverse. And if you view progress as being a mere journey towards bipedalism—which, I should add, is a highly contentious thesis—then chimps have not completed that journey. But then nor have humans. That's why we have so many back problems."

"I agree with that. My chiropractor is a second home for me." Vicki (with an i) was gazing at Horace, slightly star-struck, wanting to be liked.

"Absolutely. And just ask an ostrich or an emu if they get those kind of back problems. You won't see those at your chiropractor's surgery. So by that index they're more highly evolved than we are." Horace was having fun.

"I'd never thought of that," said Vicki (with an i). She leaned towards him, "Can I ask, without meaning to pry. Is your bed for one person or do you share?"

"Depends if I get lucky," said Horace. "It is most comfortable for one, but two can be accommodated, even three at a push." He winked ostentatiously. "But really it's for sleeping. I do my love-making elsewhere, the sofa, floor, pool, terrace. Wherever takes my fancy. When the blood is up there's no time to lose."

Vicki (with an i) giggled, but elsewhere there was an awkward silence. "Your bed sounds fascinating," she said. "A bit like a hammock, wouldn't you say?"

"Not really," said Horace. "Not remotely like a hammock."

"But hammocks can be very comfy though." She blundered on. "Futons are good too, especially for the back. I slept for two years in a hammock."

"Slept for two years? My goodness," said Horace, "You must have been very tired when you turned in."

"A clear conscience," said Charlie. "In my experience that's the bedrock of a good night's sleep."

"Spoken like a true insomniac," quipped Horace. Vicki (with an i) giggled again.

Miriam looked disapproving. "Sleep is not a laughing matter. Nor is it a luxury. It's as essential as food or water."

"Absolutely," agreed Horace, "But it's possible to sleep too much. In fact, some people are never fully awake. Most actually. But on that note, you must please excuse me. I have some pressing matters to attend to. It's been an absolute pleasure." He rose to leave, glancing over to me as he did so. And then, after a round of polite goodbyes, he walked briskly towards the exit without a backward glance.

I caught up with him at the top of the stairs on the next deck. He smiled when he saw me, and held out his hands. "I'm sorry, Lizzy. Forgive me for last night, I behaved like a cad."

"Yes. Yes, you did."

"A few too many sherbets. I was absorbed in your company and I lost track of the empties. The booze reacted a bit with the medication I'm on. Do you forgive me?"

"I'm trying to decide." Though in truth, I had already reached my decision.

"Tell you what, let me make it up to you. I know you probably want to get back to your friends, but I have a terrific dinner due to be served on my veranda in ten minutes. We could sit and watch the lights of Lisbon, and we could talk. Talk about the past if you like. Thing is, Lizzy, it's a meal for two, so if you don't accept I'll have to invite Brian."

I laughed and stepped towards him, accepting his proffered hands with their gnarled rough skin. "Okay, Uncle, it's a deal."

"Wonderful." He took my arm as we headed off towards his suite. "You look great, by the way. I love the dress."

"Good. You bought it."

"I did? Good. I have excellent taste, it seems."

EIGHT

I have come to believe that the past is a tangled labyrinth of other worlds. Some are public spaces but others are private arbours, walled gardens and mausoleums, open to the sky but protected by sentinels of the heart. We enter the public places as travellers, but for those reverent private worlds we need to be invited. That evening, as the light faded and the coast of Portugal hovered on the horizon, a smudge of grey flecked with passing dots of orange light, my Great Uncle Horace, for the first time, invited me across his threshold.

The veranda was resplendent, burnished by lamps. The table was laid for two, a starched white cloth set with china and glass, an ornate ice bucket and an elegant ceramic vase of pale pink roses. Horace poured champagne which seemed to dance on the tongue as we stood together at the rail, looking out to sea. We toasted our new beginning. I asked him if he minded about my shopping spree. He laughed and said, "Of course not. That was part of the deal. Besides, Lizzy, I have more money than I need, more than I can reasonably spend." I felt close to him, closer than I could remember ever having felt.

We were sipping our second glass when Monique arrived with the food. She gave me a fierce look, but said nothing, serving in silence. Horace and I talked about Lisbon, a city I had almost been to as a student when I inter-railed around Europe one summer. Almost but not quite. He listened politely, and asked about the other places I had visited. We discussed the ranking of European railways, the relative merits of steam engines and the advantages of a public transport system that was not required to turn a profit. Monique cleared plates and we nibbled on cheese and fresh dates, salted crackers and thick dessert wine. Horace thanked her and said that she could go. The door to the corridor clicked shut behind her and we sat for a moment, silent in our pool of yellow light.

"You said that last night's alcohol was exacerbated by medication. What medicine are you taking?"

"Lots, Lizzy. I'm old, and the years come not unattended. There's a litany of things wrong with me that's as long as your arm, both arms in fact. They come not as single spies, but in battalions. Though I'm still here. For now at least."

"Why do you have such difficulty talking about personal stuff, Uncle, acknowledging your past?"

"Actually, I'm not sure that I do. But I come from a generation where the personal was personal, not something to be blabbed about to all and sundry, tweeted and bleated and paraded in front of the world and his wife. As for the past, I just prefer to live in the present. At my age it makes sense. It's a survival mechanism. When you get to be as old as me the past is like an immense ocean. It surrounds me with its vastness, and I'm a tiny island becoming more eroded by the day. Time will come, one day soon, when I'll feel the cold ellipse close over me. I'll be submerged; as insubstantial as a memory."

"I hope not. As family goes, you're almost all I've got. And you promised to talk to me, talk properly."

"I can... I do... I will." He twisted his left cuff link and then refilled our glasses. I waited him out. He coughed and squeezed the bridge of his nose, massaging the deep horizontal crease at its top. "It's just that I'm not sure what you want exactly."

"Start from the beginning. Imagine describing yourself to someone you have never met before."

"Okay, I get it." He cleared his throat and pitched his voice up an octave. "My name is Horace Cunningham. I live in Queensland, I have land there, just over a thousand square kilometres, in fact."

"Relax, Uncle. It doesn't have to sound like Edward VIII's abdication speech. Just speak normally."

"Yes, yes of course." He cleared his throat once more and, after a couple of deep breaths, began anew with a self-conscious casualness. "It's not really a farm, as such, more a sort of nature reserve. I have an estate manager, Pete Boyden, who helps keep the place ticking over. I have two dogs, one's a German shepherd, Miro, which is a kind of spear in the Nyungar language of the aboriginals. And then there's Jiemba, that means 'laughing star' in the Wiradjuri language. She's lovely, a crossbreed I found abandoned as a pup. I have a parrot, too, called Megan. She has a big vocabulary, but seems particularly drawn to obscenities. I love those guys, that place, it's the best home I ever had. It's the sunshine state. We've installed solar panels, loads of them, and wind turbines too. We're not just energy independent, we sell it back to the state grid and use the revenue for conservation work. We even had... we have plans to use excess solar power and waste water to create an onsite hydrogen plant. Oh Lizzy, this feels silly."

"I'm listening, Uncle. You're doing fine. Tell me about your parents, my great grandparents."

"My mother was Rosa Lucciano, the daughter of a well-to-do farmer in Le Marche, it's in the calf of the Italian boot, in the east. It stretches from the Adriatic to the Apennines, beautiful country with rolling hills and lakes, but not rich. The family farm was inland from Ancona. I was born there in 1934. I arrived seven minutes after Virgil, my brother, your grandfather. Our father was Alexander Cunningham, who met my mother when he was out there on a hiking trip. He was a bit older than her, an Oxford classicist, hence our names. I think it was a sort of joke by a man not renowned for his sense of humour. We were brought up in Oxford, went to prep school in Dorset at six and later to Shrewsbury. We boarded, of course. It was normal in those days. It was a tough time, with the outbreak of war. I remember my mother crying on the station platform. She was dark haired and very beautiful and her face was soiled by tears and she was reaching up at the window when the train pulled away. She was trying to say something but it was lost in the noise and the smoke. But I can still see her lips moving and those yearning fingers. My father took us to our prep school. I think he forbade her from coming. I suppose he thought it would be easier for her and for us. He was very much old school, it didn't do to show your emotions in public. He said goodbye with a firm handshake.

"In his uniform he looked very grand. He was in Intelligence and had been serving in North Africa. He never talked about what he did, even after the war, but as children we were enormously proud of him. I later revised that opinion. I came to hate him for a while. Now, when I look back, I just feel despair at the choices he made. The thing is, I believe he thought he was doing right. Maybe he knew what was coming. When the Germans overran the Low Countries and France in the summer of 1940 the British government panicked. They rounded up foreign enemy nationals, about 30,000 Germans and Austrians, most of whom, ironically, had fled to Britain to avoid Nazi persecution. Italy had joined the war on the German side, and so about 4,000 Italians were also interned, including Rosa Cunningham née Lucciano. She was considered low risk. Like many, she was confined in a requisitioned boarding house on the Isle of Man. Our father lied to us, told us that she had gone back to Italy to see her family and that she could not come home because of the war. We used to write to her. My father would stamp the letters and take them for posting, but she never replied. After his death I found our letters among his papers. They were unopened. Unopened, Lizzy. I still find that incredible, unforgiveable. He wasn't even curious enough to open them."

"Maybe he was respecting your privacy. Maybe he couldn't bring himself to read them because he found it too hard, too upsetting."

"You didn't know him. Why didn't he just send them to her? They would have been a comfort. But he didn't, and he didn't read them or even destroy them. Ever the classicist, he just preserved them and in the process killed the content." Horace replenished our glasses. "In the school holidays we were mostly looked after by Mrs Warner, our Irish housekeeper. She was a keen Christian, but not one who was overly familiar with the notion that love lay at the heart of the Gospels. We never saw Mother again. She died in February 1942, shortly before our eighth birthday. There was no funeral to speak of. Father told us when we were at home that summer. I remember his hand on my shoulder. He told us not to cry. He blamed the war and he blamed Hitler for starting the war. So Hitler was responsible for the death of Mother, and my father was doing all that he could, fighting hard in the desert, to make Hitler pay for it.

"Years later I visited the house where she died that winter. It's a family home now, she would have liked that. I found her ashes too, amongst my father's stuff. Still in the original wartime carton. Just fine grey powder really, could have been anything. I took them home to Le Marche and scattered them on what used to be the family farm, the fields that she would have played in as a girl. And after Father died, I didn't just find our letters to her, I found a stack of letters that she had written to us from her detention. Sad imploring letters, sometimes with passages excised by the censor, begging for news, for contact. He thought it best not to let us have them. Too upsetting I suppose. Or maybe as a serving officer he didn't want to acknowledge having a wife who was interned as a threat to national security. I don't know his thinking, but I hated him for it, for that misguided cruelty. Sometimes I hate him still for that."

He was silent for a moment before saying softly, "I have a picture." He fumbled for his battered cloth wallet and extracted a creased black and white photograph. He passed it to me. The image shows a woman sitting outside on an ornate cane bench. She is half-turned towards the camera, leaning forward slightly with crossed legs, her hands clasped with interlaced fingers around her left knee. Her black hair is centre parted and has deep waves and curls. She is looking at someone off camera, looking and smiling.

"She's beautiful," I said.

"Yes, yes she was. Everyone said so. I don't remember as much as I would like, but I remember that smile. She always smelt lovely too, I wish I knew the name of her scent, and she had a wonderful voice. She used to sing to us at bedtime. We missed her terribly. But you know how it is, you just have to get on with things. We were at school most of the time and it didn't do to show your feelings in that environment. But as long as you conformed, school was alright. I was pretty good with most subjects and was above average at games. Virgil was better, mostly. He was in the Firsts for rugby and cricket and won our year's Athletics Cup for three years running. He was a bit like that; he won things without really trying. Sometimes I envied him for it.

"I went up to Cambridge in the autumn of 1952, the same time as Britain conducted its first nuclear weapons test. The site they chose was the Montebello island archipelago, off the coast of Western Australia. Montebello means beautiful mountain in Italian. That first test, and there were two others later, was an underwater explosion that blasted a huge crater in the seabed. Nobody bothered to measure the long-term contamination, but fallout certainly reached as far as Queensland. The area is a designated park now, but the official advice is not to spend more than an hour there and not to take home any rocks as souvenirs.

"Anyway, I went to Trinity Hall, just as you did later. I was proud of you for that. There weren't many women at Cambridge in my day. I graduated in Natural Sciences and stayed on for a doctorate but gave it up in 1956, after Virgil's death. He'd followed in Father's footsteps but had dropped out in his second year. We weren't that close at the end. Our lives had taken different courses and nobody realised quite how much he was struggling. His suicide was the most awful shock. There was no note, no explanation. He left a pregnant fiancée, Amelia."

"My grandmother."

"Yeah, Amelia Heyward, it's where you get your family name. Anyway, Father never really recovered from Virgil's death. My way of dealing with it was to get away. I travelled the length of Europe, taking jobs when I needed to. Just kept moving. Father died the following year. I was in Greece and it took them three weeks to contact me, so he was already buried when I got back. I had no desire to stay. There was nothing to stay for. So I sold up, made sure that Amelia was provided for, and then went on my way. I travelled widely in North America, even crossed the Bering Straits into Siberia before I was arrested and deported by Soviet border guards. They weren't at all bad actually, once they had satisfied themselves that I wasn't a spy. After I got kicked out I made my way through India and Afghanistan and eventually to Egypt. Then I spent a year travelling down the length of Africa until I ran out of land and arrived in Cape Town.

"So you really did sleep in a chimpanzee bed in the tree tops."

"Of course. Did you think I was lying? I'm hurt, Lizzy."

"It just sounded improbable."

"Well sometimes improbability is an indicator of truth. If you want a lie to be believed, make it sound plausible, make it mundanely probable. Having said that, improbability can also be an indicator of falsehood. I was in a bar a while back and a fellow there told me that he had discovered the secret of cold fusion. All he needed was distilled water, sunlight and electricity. When I asked him how it was done he wouldn't say. In my experience, that's usually a tell-tale sign."

"What happened after Cape Town?"

"At Cape Town I rested up a while. I was anaemic and I had lost a lot of weight. When I started coughing up blood they found that I had copped a dose of Bilharzia. You get it from water-borne parasitic worms. They're incubated by snails and then the tiny bastards burrow through your skin and surf your bloodstream until they pitch camp in whichever of your internal organs takes their fancy. Took a while to clear it and even longer to fully recover. My immune system is still compromised. So I dropped anchor amongst the Boers for a bit, just while I recovered. I mean, you couldn't stay there permanently, not if you had a shred of decency. Apartheid was utterly obnoxious and it was impossible to avoid, impossible not to see, even when you looked the other way.

"When I was strong enough I moved on. Australia was one of the few places I hadn't been to. So was South America. I actually flipped a coin on the quayside, heads for Perth, tails for Rio."

"Really?"

"Really. And on the counsel of that coin I took a boat across the Indian Ocean and tossed up in Oz. I liked it from the start: good climate, great country, honest people. You can be accepted for what you are rather than for what you might have been or where you came from or went to school. It took a while to settle. I needed to make a living and so I tried a few things. I worked on a sheep station in Western Australia. You know, we have 74 million sheep in Oz and 23 million people, that's a ratio of three to one in favour of the sheep. I worked on a place at the edge of the Great Victoria Desert, couple of hundred miles north of Kalgoorlie, 500 miles north-east of Perth. It was 50,000 acres, the size of a small country. You needed a light aircraft to get around.

"In the end I opted for opal mining. It's not an easy game. You live in the outback in remote camps with temperatures around 40 degrees C. If you hang a water bag up to shower you'd better get under it quick, otherwise it'll boil and take your skin off. But most of the time you don't have that sort of water to spare. And you have to watch out for snakes and spiders that will kill you soon as look at you. And then there's the human vermin. Ratters who sneak into another man's shaft out of hours and try to steal his opals, or claim jumpers who'll try to steal your title through fraud or on some legal technicality. It's better now than the old days but it's still a pretty lawless and extreme place to be.

"Thing is though, you can do well: a good opal is worth more than a diamond. But you have to know what you're doing, and where to look for them, and you have to be lucky. You stake a claim and then you look for opal-bearing dirt. You have to find that before you can begin mining and even if you do, what you find in it is pretty much down to luck. You know, some folks say that you can divine the presence of opals, just like you can search for water with those rods that cross when you're above an underground stream. Others search with various scientific rigs, some look for types of vegetation. I've known fellows swear by magnets, animal tracks, even prayer. The truth is, there's no reliable method. And you can burn through tens of thousands of dollars just test drilling. The old timers say that the most accurate method is to throw your hat in the air and start digging wherever it lands. There's something in that. It's like Life: hard work is not enough, you also have to be lucky.

"Some guys take exhausted old workings and dig out everything in between them, making open cut mines. That way if there's any opals that have been missed they'll find them. It's called noodling, and it's expensive. You need the machinery to shift a hell of a lot of dirt, and these days you have to fill in the excavations when you're finished. The two traditional methods for the small scale prospector are trench searching or drilling. I preferred drilling. It's more like traditional mining for coal or tin, just not as deep. You sink a shaft, which means hiring a drilling rig, which is not cheap, and then you dig a drive, which is basically a tunnel. If you're lucky, you find opals in clusters or nests, and if you're not, then you die from noxious air or collapses. When the drive is a long one you cut larger chambers. We call them ballrooms..."

"Ballrooms?"

"Yeah, but they're not as grand as the name suggests. Though some people live down there to avoid the heat up on top. Either that or you tunnel into a hillside and make a dugout to live in. The longer a drive is, the more prone it is to collapse, even though you leave pillars of untouched dirt for pit props. It's hard, filthy work, and dangerous. I had a mate, Brett. We dug together in three states over the years, New South Wales, South Australia, and Queensland. The best opal miner I ever knew. One time he was working at a face at the end of a long drive when it collapsed. Took all night to dig him out. When I found his body he had a big, pinfire opal in his pocket. The black tone was beautiful and it had stars of electric blue and green, and deep inside it there was an amazing red flash that came out like a rolling flame when you angled it away from you. It was a beauty, the best we ever found, but I never cut it up or sold it. Wouldn't have been right. Cost the poor bugger his life. He must have found it just before the cave in, maybe he was coming back to show me or he was looking for more. I was on the surface and I felt the collapse, but when I looked down the shaft it was a real turkey's nest, it was impossible to reach him.

"And speaking of opals, I want you to have this, as a peace offering, an apology for last night."

He reached into his jacket pocket and handed me a small cotton pouch. Inside was a polished stone. It was irregularly shaped, somewhere between a disc and a rectangle with smooth edges and rounded corners, maybe two centimetres long and just over one wide, perhaps half a centimetre thick. The light danced on it, picking out liquid patches of iridescent colour.

"It's a polished up black boulder opal, a Queensland speciality. It's actually a mixture of opal and ironstone, which means it's very stable, won't craze or crack. It's strong, Lizzy, like you."

I turned it over in my fingers, feeling its coolness and weight. The base colour was a deep indigo and this was overlaid by clouds of green and yellow, changing to pink and white towards the edge of the narrowest side. It was breathtakingly beautiful, as if you were looking down from some great altitude, gazing at the surface of an exotic planet where clouds of vapour, glowing green and gold, swirled and skittered over the surface of an ocean so pure and deep and blue that you wanted to weep for its sheer loveliness.

"It's beautiful. How old is it?" I asked, without lifting my eyes.

"Hard to say. Truth is, no one knows how they're formed. It adds to their mystery. But there's a consensus that it takes five or six million years to make one centimetre of opal. So they're old, you can bet on that. When you dig for them it's not unusual to find dinosaur bones, and fossils of lung fish 400 million years old. In that era, Australia was part of Gondwana, the ancient southern super-continent, and it had a huge inland sea. My guess is that silica-laden sediment was deposited around its shoreline and, over time, it got washed by rain into fissures in the rock. Alternatively, the aborigines believe that opals were made by the creator's footprint, when it touched the Earth at the base of a rainbow. I like that version too. The ancient Greeks thought they were the tears of joy that Zeus wept after overthrowing the Titans. They're all theories. Take your pick."

"It's breathtaking," I said, turning it over in my fingers. "But I couldn't accept it, Uncle. You've already been more than generous."

"Yeah, not bad for a bit of silica that's got trapped in a rock. That's a nice one, actually, it's about ten carats, worth about three grand on the open market. But it's more precious than that. It was one of the first boulder opals I ever found, and it's always been a favourite. I've had it a long time, but now I want you to take it. It would make me happy, Lizzy. Maybe get it made into a piece of jewellery, you know, something nice that you'd want to wear. And when you do, remember me."

"Thank you, Uncle, I will. I'll treasure it."

"Good, you do that." He shivered and then gave a huge, slow yawn. "Night's getting cold. I'm going to have to take my leave. This old man needs his bed. But just to finish the story, I did well, you know, some good investments and we found some nice nests. The dirt of old Australia was good to me. Twelve years ago I sold up and suddenly I found I was decently placed. So I bought a pristine piece of Queensland. It's remote, gloriously beautiful and utterly untamed. Mind you, it's land that's always trying to kill you. It's not really mine, I've just been living there and looking after it. It's a sort of unofficial nature reserve. It's good to give back to the country that made me rich. And that brings us bang up to date." He laughed with a dry cackle of relief. "There, it wasn't so hard to do, was it? As long as I didn't bore you to death."

"Nobody could ever accuse you of being boring. Thank you, Uncle. It's been fascinating. You've travelled so much." I hugged him goodnight and kissed his cheek.

He escorted me to the door, moving stiffly with his cane. "You know, Lizzy, a lot of the time when I was travelling, I was just a kid running away, fleeing the past. But as anyone who has ever fled from the past finds out, it pursues you and it can outrun you. And wherever you hide, it always finds you. And you know why?"

"Tell me."

"Because the past is shackled to your damned ankle. I'm old, Lizzy, but one thing I've come to understand is that you have to lay down hatred or it will etch you with a mark that you'll carry forever. Forgiving can't change anything that happened, but it can help you remember differently, remember with less pain. And that enables Life to go on. In the end it's not about trying to forget something, it's about accepting it."

NINE

It was my first, and thus far still my only, visit to Lisbon. Less than a day's stopover, long enough for our fellow mariners to enjoy a controlled taste of foreignness without being away too long from the security of the mother ship. Even then, I was surprised by how many chose to stay on board; and those who were brave enough to risk the swarthy, alien streets did so via the fleet of air conditioned tour buses that lined the quayside, offering not just comfort but safety in numbers. Horace and I, however, were independent travellers, exploring at will, supported only by a guidebook and the private car and driver that were at his disposal.

We began by checking out the Museu Nacional de Arte Antiga, where Horace made straight for *The Temptation of St Anthony*, a triptych by Hieronymus Bosch. I had never seen anything like it: a meditation on mental and spiritual suffering pursued through fire, air, earth and water. It was astonishing and horrifying in equal measure, surreally alive with demons, hybrid creatures, armoured dogs, a ship-shaped bird, flying fish and boats with wings. But there was also a treacherous and provocative beauty within the monstrous, and a profound statement in the core narrative of temptation and seduction by demons resulting, eventually, in salvation via the simple virtues of life as a hermit. It was one hell of a way to kick off the morning. Afterwards we were driven to the Mosteiro dos Jerónimos, a stunning gothic pile of cloisters and cathedral, built to commemorate the voyage of Vasco da Gama, and funded by the spice trade that had been unlocked through that expedition. Then we went on to the Moorish castle of São Jorge, with its picture book crenellations, standing tall on a hill that had been fortified since the Iron Age. Afterwards we wandered through the narrow streets of the Alfama, a labyrinth of houses and hidden squares where from time to time you got unexpected glimpses of the Tagus River and the Cathedral.

All day we bumbled along harmoniously, sometimes arm in arm, discussing art, architecture and history, subjects upon which Horace was surprisingly well informed. The sun was shining. It was warm but not uncomfortably hot. We walked easy in each other's company, pausing to look, to consider, sometimes sitting in the shade while Horace recovered his breath. It was one of those occasions where you realise, when looking back, that you were happy. Not leaping about, screaming, joyous happy, but warm and contented, happily engaged in the process of sharing. I've never had much luck with families, neither the one that I was given nor the one I tried so hard to create. But on that sunny Lisbon day I felt what many must simply take as normal: a closeness, an instinctive connection. Horace felt something too, I think. He quoted a Spanish proverb: "An ounce of blood is worth more than a pound of friendship." I like that. Though later I thought of something George Eliot wrote, about human souls joined for life "in silent unspeakable memories." That, too, seems an accurate summation of families.

The night before, with my sea-and-clouds opal glowing on my bedside table, I'd had a nightcap or two. I checked my email but skipped the News, for Britain seemed a distant memory, lost in the foam of our wake. I was aware of the great ship slowing and delicately turning, treading water as it changed its inclination and pirouetted into its berth. I went out onto my balcony and looked down at the harbour lights and the city beyond. Before bed I wrote my diary. I saw on the flyleaf the quote by St Paul that I had inscribed and underlined: "I die daily."

I slept in the company of difficult dreams. I woke early with a sad song playing in my head. I can't write music, I'm illiterate, so I transcribed it as a poem. I used to be able to hum the tune but I've forgotten it now. I still have the words though.

> The festivals are finished
> in the season of St Paul,
> but though she knows he won't be coming
> she's still setting out her stall,
> and she longs so much to see him
> she still wants to have it all:
> the patter of his footsteps
> still echo in the hall,
> the chatter of his laughter
> the bouncing of the ball,
> but there's really just an absence
> beneath the shrouded pall
> of another season's grieving
> in the silence, the empty
> winter silence, of St Paul.

I lay in bed and read some more Steller, marvelling at his description of the sea otter, whose beauty, he maintained, was "incomparable, without a peer; exceeding all other inhabitants of the boundless ocean." He described how, "On warm days they seek out shady recesses and frolic there like monkeys, for they surpass all other amphibia in their playfulness and frolicsome nature, as well as their fleetness of foot.

"On the land they rest like dogs, their bodies curled up. When emerging from the sea, like dogs they shake the water from their pelts before lying down to sleep; and with their paws wash their faces, as cats do, smoothing their bodies and straightening their fur, turning their heads from one side to the other as they inspect themselves, seemingly deriving great pleasure from their personal appearance. I have also seen males play with their genitalia like monkeys. When they are engaged in sleeking their fur they are so intent that they can be easily killed." There was a coldness to that final sentence that sat ill with the gentleness that had preceded it. Similarly, "They never exhibit conflict for they always live on the best of terms with one another. They play together, and, like humans, embrace with their arms and kiss each other. If they escape the club, they gesticulate in a comical manner, as though mocking the hunter. With one paw raised over their eyes, as if shielding from the sun, they lie upon their backs and continually rub their pudenda. Then they take to the water, still staring at the men and urinating as they do so.

"They suckle their young for almost an entire year. They maintain their conjugal affection most constantly, living together both on sea and on land in a state of contented monogamy... In sea or on land they carry their cubs in their mouths; but when they sleep at sea they fold their young in their arms just as mothers do with their babes. They throw the youngsters into the water to teach them to swim, and when tired they bring them to shore and kiss them just as humans do. At sea they toss their young and with their paws catch them like a ball, and with them engage in all the delightful and gentle games that a loving mother can play with her children. When the mother sleeps on shore the cubs keep watch, clinging to her dugs or arms. They embrace their young with an affection that is scarcely credible. When hunters press upon them, whether by land or by sea, they hold their young with their mouths and never let go of them except when compelled by extreme necessity or death itself. And so they are killed often when they might otherwise have saved themselves by abandoning their babies."

The poignancy of those last sentences made me want to weep. In fact, the reference to their killing made me uncomfortable as it was ever present, mingled with the description of their lives. For as Steller noted, "because of their beauty they are very valuable," their fur "much more constant than the sables, and sable skins never shine with so deep a natural blackness as the otters." In a pre-Darwinian insight, not fully explored, he noted that the more beautiful the hide of an individual otter the more difficult it was to capture because the desirable ones had learned to be "so careful about their own safety that they come out on dry land alone to sleep" and only after carefully checking that "no man is in the neighbourhood." He noted, too, how the price of skins had increased recently because of demand from China where it had become fashionable to use them for fur borders on the robes of "both sexes." Plus ça change.

Despite his obvious affection for the creatures, he described with a curious detachment the detailed hunting methods used to trap them and noted casually, "We killed them on Bering Island with spears and nets, and—when they were lying asleep or in the act of copulating—with clubs." For not only was their fur of value. "The flesh of the adult otter is much more tender and savoury than that of the seal. The flesh of the female is best, for it is fatter and more tender... The flesh of the young otter is most delicious; it cannot easily be distinguished from the flesh of an unweaned lamb, whether roasted or boiled, and the gravy from its preparing, in either way, is most delicious. Otter flesh was our principal food on Bering Island; it was also our universal medicine. By its use we were saved from scurvy, and no one got sick of it, although we ate it every day half raw and without bread. The liver, heart, and kidneys tasted exactly like those of calf..."

The flesh I could just about deal with, but half-raw internal organs before breakfast was too hard core. I put aside the book and went for a morning swim. I found Horace already in the pool, red eyed and beaming like a whiskery old sea lion. His body was tanned but surprisingly thin, as though the muscle mass had dropped away and left the flesh hanging empty on its bones. His skin was scarred, especially his arms and shoulders. Ancient scars from decades of tunnelling, I supposed, but there was also a more recent one, still pink and fresh, running down his left side and snaking back beneath his rib cage. When we sat together in the hot tub I saw that he had some sort of abstract tattoo high on his left bicep, the ink a faded blue.

"Light breakfast and then an excursion into Lisbon, I think. Haven't seen the old place in years. Care to join, Lizzy?" He stood up and the waistband of his swimming trunks slipped enough to expose a birthmark on his hip. It was small and leaf-shaped, the skin slightly darker than that which surrounded it. I knew it well. I have the exact same mark.

"Love to," I said.

As we wandered through the Alfama with the sun on our backs, I decided to try a test bore into the warm seam of our togetherness. I asked, as innocuously as I could, "Were you never married, Uncle?"

He laughed, which was promising. "No, but enjoyed some berths along the way, even dropped anchor a few times but never a permanent mooring."

"Don't you get lonely out there in the jungle, with just your dogs and your parrot?" I teased. "Nobody to share your chimpanzee bed with."

"Lonely? No." The tone was more curt. "Do you?"

"Yes, yes I do."

"Then you should sort that out, my girl. Everyone should have someone to reach for in the night. It's hardwired into the species. And as it happens, I have Maya, she's a native Australian from the Kimberly area in Western Australia. Her name means home or house in the Kiwari language."

This unexpected information took me aback. "You never mentioned her. What's she like?"

"About your age but taller. Very beautiful. She's an artist, and a damned good one, too. But she's also very practical, grounded. She understands, understands the country, and what I've been creating there. She has an extended family. We're a sort of community really, living in harmony with the land, with Nature. You know what, Lizzy, it's not quite Eden, but it's the closest I ever got."

We walked in silence for a while. Then I said, "Tell me about Amelia. Mum never really knew her. She doesn't... didn't remember much about her, and what memories she had are gone now."

"Poor Amelia. She was a lovely girl."

"How did she and Virgil meet?"

"I introduced them. I met her at Cambridge. She was very bright. She was one of those people who understands things very quickly, instinctively. Ferociously bright. Her people came from Hove, her father had a grocery shop in the High Street. She went to the grammar school and got a scholarship to Girton to study English. We met at a party in May Week. She had big eyes that were a beautiful blue, such a dark blue that in some lights they appeared black. Dark blond hair, quite short, sort of messy, but in a good way, with a fringe. She was stunning, so much so that it took me an hour to go over and speak to her. She was standing off to the side and I'd seen a few boys go up to her and talk but they didn't get anywhere. She had a natural aloofness which I later discovered was a sort of shyness that she had learnt to manage. After watching those other chaps get dispatched, I tried to think of some opening gambit that might impress. In the end I plumped for a few lines from *The Wasteland*. These days I think it vastly overrated, but back then it was all the rage. I only knew a few lines actually, the beginning of the chessgame, "The Chair she sat in, like a burnished throne/ Glowed on the marble..." I know even less of it now, but she,

Amelia, she laughed and then rattled off another dozen lines before, and mark this, quoting the barge scene speech by Enobarbus in *Antony and Cleopatra* that Eliot had based it on. I felt totally outclassed but at least it got us chatting, and the chat became talk, and we talked together for the rest of the evening. You know how sometimes when you meet someone there's that instant connection? It's like you have known them forever. Or known them in some former life. Maybe been joined together in some earlier creature, and though the atoms later separated, they retain a memory, an instinctive longing to return to where they belong. That's how it was with Amelia: an instinctive longing to be where we belonged."

"That sounds amazing."

"She was amazing. Wonderful to talk to. She was cleverer than me, better read, too, but she wore it lightly. She didn't suffer fools, but she was tremendously kind. Her only shortcoming, if it can be called that, was an unworldliness. She'd spent her life in Hove, working hard in school and helping out in the shop. She had a naivety about the nature of the world, the manner of human beings and the depths to which they'll stoop. She was too trusting, especially with those who got beyond her outer shell. You see, she had no nose for deceit, for lies. She was too good for all that, but it meant that she walked in the world unarmed."

"You sound as though you were smitten."

"Well, I was terribly keen on her. She was special, very special. I never met anyone like Amelia."

"I wish that I could have known her. She sounds as though she would have been a cool grandma."

"She would, Lizzy. You would have liked her, and she you. And you know, I love that some part of her lives on in you. You have her DNA. I sometimes see flashes of her in you."

"But she ended up with Virgil."

He laughed bitterly. "Yes, she ended up with Virgil. Introducing her to my brother was a huge mistake. I lived to regret it. He did too, or he would have done if he'd lived longer. But you know, there was an awful inevitability to it. I understand why she fell for him. Amelia hadn't been inoculated by life, she had no resistance to Virgil and his kind."

"That must have been hard."

"Yes. Yes it was. Very hard." He stopped walking and mopped his brow with his handkerchief. "It was hard but it wasn't as if I had no experience. I was used to Virgil taking things. It was his way. If he liked something, or sometimes even if he didn't much like it but just wanted it, he'd take it. That's how he was, a creature of habit, the Golden Boy who inhabited a world that he believed had been created entirely for his pleasure and amusement. We were all extras, drafted in to play minor roles in The Great Virgil Story, a Technicolor spectacular with no intermission."

"That doesn't sound very fraternal. You really disliked him that much?"

"I loved him," said Horace fiercely. "He was my brother. I loved him but I knew him, knew him better than anyone else did, including Amelia. He broke that girl, that special, lovely girl. After his death she was inconsolable, unreachable. She went back to Hove and had her baby, Amber, your mother. But she never got over it. She died of pneumonia in 1962, a month shy of her 25th birthday." He shook his head as though trying to dislodge intruding images. "It's the waste that gets me. The sheer, utter waste."

"So why did he do it, Uncle?" I asked quietly. "Why did he kill himself?"

"Why does anything happen, Lizzy? Sometimes there are no reasons, or none that make sense at least. Shit just happens. The natural world is full of it, compassionless random stuff that just occurs. And of course, it can have consequences, sometimes significant consequences, but that doesn't mean it must have rational causes. Sometimes it just happens. There's no regulatory framework, no external control or moral guidance from above. Good things come to bad people, the undeserving; and sometimes, too often if you're unlucky, bad things happen to good people, people who deserve better, people like Amelia. We all just blunder through, looking over our shoulders from time to time, playing the percentages, keeping our fingers crossed and casting the odd supplicatory glance up to the empty sky."

"Okay, maybe. Maybe that's true. But it doesn't explain what we're talking about. Suicide is a conscious act. It doesn't just happen, it requires agency and choice. I don't understand why Virgil threw it all away."

"Oh Lizzy, leave it be won't you. Why are you so interested in this?"

"He was my grandfather. I have a right to know."

"A *right*? Do you know how entitled that makes you sound? Like a spoilt child."

"It's part of my history."

"It's not yours. History doesn't belong to anyone. Leastways, no one except the winners."

"Okay, then it's part of my narrative."

"Narrative doesn't belong to anyone either. You can live it, or read it, you can even make it up, but it still doesn't belong to you. It's not a possession. You can't own it. That would be like trying to own an ocean."

"I don't understand why you're so reluctant to share it."

"It's personal. He was my brother. I loved him."

"It's personal to me too. He was my grandfather. I could have loved him. He might have loved me."

"You didn't know him."

"That's right, I didn't. And I want to know why that was denied to me. I need a reason."

"You think there are always reasons?"

"Yes."

"Oh Lizzy. If I were to give you one, a reason, would you then be content?"

"Maybe."

"Alright. He was depressed. He shot himself. He chose not to live anymore. People do it all the time."

"Not enough. I need more."

"Dear God, is there no end to your insatiable curiosity?"

"If it had an end would it be insatiable?"

"Christ, I'm going for a drink."

"I'll join you."

"Actually, Lizzy, I'd prefer it if you didn't."

I tracked him as he made his way down towards the seafront. He was walking stiffly with his cane and I thought for a moment that he was dabbing his eyes, but I think he was just mopping his brow. I trailed him to a bar and even before he had been served I approached his table, guidebook in hand, and asked, "Com licença, senhor, is this seat free?" He looked up from beneath the brim of his Panama hat and smiled sadly, "Talvez, it depends on what you want to talk about."

We drank sangria and ate a plate of vegetarian petiscos, with chickpeas and local cheeses served with coriander and olive oil. We chatted about the present and the future, discussing which onboard activities we should check out. I mentioned some of the lectures that I had earmarked as possibilities; he suggested we see some shows, starting with that evening's cabaret which he said would be a "hoot." With regard to the past, we congregated only in the safety of public spaces: the history of Lisbon, the politics of Queensland, and the imperative of marine conservation.

Only at the end, while we waited for our driver to reappear and whisk us back to the towering white sanctuary of our ship, only then did I extol the virtues—without being overly oblique—of shining a light on the past, even if doing so disturbed dark places and the things that lived in them, cold and frigid creatures, fashioned by depth and pressure.

"Oh, Lizzy, whatever am I to do with you?" he said with exaggerated exasperation.

"How about just telling me everything you know?"

"Everything I know?" He paused, his eyes distant and troubled. The car pulled up alongside us. "Not everything can be known. Some things don't want to be known. They need to rest in the dark forever."

"Uncle, that sounds like something from Lord of the fucking Rings."

"Possibly, but no less true for that." He nodded to the car. "The driver's waiting."

In the evening, we put to sea once more, leaving the lights of Lisbon and sliding away to the darkness of open water. Horace and I grabbed a quick bite to eat at the buffet before going to the cabaret. We were late arriving in the theatre as Horace got distracted by the casino that we passed en route. I have never been a gambler—the unpredictability of life itself always seemed risk enough—and so had never set foot in a casino before then. There was a plush quietness to it that I had not expected. It felt cushioned, a space soft with muffled sound and subdued lighting, where people gathered in pools of yellow light around green baize tables, or roulette wheels that span with a mesmerising motion and around whose perimeters clattered a hard bouncing ball, small as a satellite, until it came to rest, trapped in a tiny numbered notch, red or black. The atmosphere of the place, or at least that area where there were no gaming machines, struck me as a cross between an exclusive library and a traditional gentlemen's club. Sustained concentration prickled just below the surface as players counted cards, calculated odds, and desperately willed the clacking track of the ivorine ball as it rattled within the blur of the wheel.

Red or black, win or lose, life turning on the flip of a card or the call of a colour. I wondered how much money had been lost or won here, in the shadow of that turning wheel. I thought of St Catherine, starved and tortured in her prison, her wounds so grievous that spectators wept in pity, and yet she would not recant her faith. So they broke her on a spiked wheel but even then, when they struck off her head, it was not blood but a fragrant milk-like substance that flowed from the severed veins of her incorruptible body. They founded a Cambridge College in her honour in the fifteenth century, but these days she is believed to be entirely mythical. But the wheel was genuine, a spiked wheel of death, the dark twin of that most quintessential symbol of human progress.

By the time we got to the Celestial Lounge the show was already underway. Monique had reserved seats but getting to them proved tricky. Horace seemed in no great hurry, talking loudly as we squeezed along a row, oblivious to the evident irritation around us. The auditorium was in darkness and there was a dance troupe in action. Their black-clad bodies were invisible, reduced to outlines and highlights, strips of light that changed colour in unison. The effect was quite dramatic and had a balletic beauty. Horace, however, did not approve. Even as we were still blundering to our seats, he paused to bellow in my direction, "I can't see a bloody thing." The dancers were followed by Selene, a tall, black soprano in a full length dress of shimmering gold who did a mishmash of operatic lollipops and numbers from hit musicals, ending with a version of Mamma Mia that reached screeching heights unknown to the original. Then there was a stand-up comedian called Deaf Com, whose best line was, "I was watching a programme about how ships are made. It was riveting." Amid the polite laughter that followed Horace told me that he had to "nip out to the Gents." Once again he disrupted the row, slowly squeezing past.

Deaf Com gestured towards him, "Don't tell me you're leaving sir. The joke wasn't that bad was it?"

"Not at all old boy," Horace shouted back cheerfully. "Just going for a slash. I'll be back in a mo."

Deaf Com yawned and tapped his foot. "No worries," he said. "Take your time Pop, looks like you need it."

"No need to wait," said Horace. "I'll be back in time for the comedian."

True to his word, he was back in good time. Moulin Rouge, the next dance set, involved women in red and black striped tutus and fishnet stockings cavorting with men in black tunics and shiny red waistcoats. The stage was festooned with drapery and washed with light that slid from lurid prostitute red through to vomit-inducing Barbie pink. Horace caused a degree of mayhem by clambering initially along the wrong row, then looking around in confusion before retracing his steps. He arrived, panting, in time for a lame cover of the title song from *Cabaret*. Horace missed most of it as he was bending over rubbing his trouser leg with his handkerchief.

"Slight accident," he explained. "The ship rocked and it affected my aim."

"Perhaps you should sit down to pee," I whispered.

He looked up with appalled disdain. "Never. Not while I have breath in my body."

By the time Horace had finished mopping up, *Cabaret* had morphed into a lumpen, booming version of *Voulez vous coucher avec moi ce soir*, which massacred the suggestive playfulness of the original. It also featured a large, heart-shaped frame of pink feathers that descended on a line and upon which a woman writhed. Her toned body had the strength and grace of a gymnast, but one whose hunt for medals had been replaced by the desire to cash in on the years of training and abstinence, before Time galloped her into middle age. When she hung, lithe and graceful from the heart, she still looked every inch the gymnast; when she sat within it she looked like a coquettish harlequin, and when she finished her act with her impossibly long legs spread wider than any natural anatomy would permit, she looked like a porn star. The audience applauded wildly and Horace rose from his seat in a one-man standing ovation, his hands clapping above his head. This meant adopting a slightly crouched stance so that he could hold his cane between his knees. In his enthusiasm the cane escaped and fell beneath the seats in front of us. I was still trying to retrieve it on my hands and knees, down there with the unmistakeable whiff of urine, when the next act came on.

And so it went: a trite but pretty boy band; a troupe of clunky flamenco dancers; and then a dull group of statue people, the sort who infest parks and the environs of public buildings in tourist season. Their principal skill was to be able to stand motionless. Then lights would go out, the music would change, and, when the lights came up again, lo and behold the statue people were in a different part of the stage, having adopted new personae and new positions. It was uncanny, almost as though they were moving around when the lights were out. And then, just as it seemed that we had hit the rock bottom of banality, one of them—the smallest one, naturally—began twitching when the others weren't looking. With every little movement, the audience roared in complicit laughter. I glanced at my watch and wondered how much more of this I would have to endure. It was so bad that I was actually pleased to see Selene return, alone in a spotlight, now in a delicate white gown that gave her an angelic aspect as she trundled through some classics of yester-year. It ended with a full throated medley of interlaced ABBA songs and a thunderous wave of applause, which she rode with evident pleasure. She bowed, blew kisses in all directions and then said, "See you after the interval." It felt like a threat.

We filed out into the adjacent Neptune bar. I proposed that we find somewhere quieter but Horace reacted as though I had made an improper suggestion. He wouldn't hear of it in case we were late for the second half. He was particularly taken with Selene, noting her "rich, sensitive voice" and "commanding stage presence... clearly classically trained."

He was firmly of the opinion that her presence on the ship, whilst being a stroke of good fortune for us, was indicative of the impoverished state of the arts in Britain. "I think I'll send a bottle of fizz backstage for her, or maybe we should take it round personally and express our appreciation." I played the exhaustion card, saying I was tired from Lisbon, developing a headache, in need of an early night. He was understanding and bade me goodnight, saying that he was heading back to his seat to be in good time for the resumption. I reminded him of his seat row and number and then unleashed him back into the auditorium.

I was glad to return to the sanity of my room. I had a couple of glasses of white wine and read some more Steller. It was the section on the Sea Bear, a creature known to us today as the northern fur seal. Steller made them sound almost human, describing how "the male places his lips to those of the female as if in the manner of a kiss." He also noted that "the parents love their young exceedingly. The females, after parturition, rest in crowds upon the shore with their pups and spend much time in sleeping. The pups, however, directly in the first days play together like children... The fathers display particular affection for brave offspring, making vigorous demonstrations of love for the youngster who displays courage. Thus he rejoices that he has a son worthy of himself, while being less fond of the lazy and ease-loving pups." This sentence was faintly underlined as though it had been marked by pencil but subsequently erased.

Steller's eye ran to all aspects of parental relations, describing how "they cohabit as in the manner of humankind, the female below and the male above, and especially near evening time do they desire to indulge their passion. An hour before their lovemaking, the male and female take to the sea and swim around quietly together. Then they return and the female lies flat upon her back while the male emerges from the waves upon her. He seizes her in his arms and indulges his passion with the greatest urgency. During their union he presses upon her and by his weight buries her in the sand so that only her head is visible, and he himself digs into the sand with his front feet, his whole belly pressed down upon her. For this they choose a sandy spot upon the very shore, where the waves come gently even to the place. And so absorbed are they, and so forgetful in their passion, that I could stand beside them for more than a quarter of an hour without being observed. And even then I should not have been noticed had I not struck the male a heavy blow, whereupon with a great uproar he attacked me so wrathfully that I managed to get away only with difficulty."

I paused and considered the passage. Was this Steller the scientist or Steller the Peeping Tom, observing a pair of sentient mammals, a loving couple, having sex? And why stand so close? And why in God's name was it necessary to reach out and hit the poor creature in the throes of his passion? Where was the science in that? I mean, everyone has probably had the unfortunate experience of interrupted sex, but who has ever been doing it when a lurking stranger decides that his perving is not complete without reaching over and hitting the bloke mid-thrust? I had a vision of a man leaping off me mid-act, with his trousers down, roaring as he gave chase to an intruder who had crept up and whacked him on the arse for no reason. No wonder the poor sea bear was wrathful, and it made me almost sorry that Herr Steller had escaped retribution. It put into perspective his descriptions about how the sea bears "rage with exceeding fierceness at all who pass by." It made you wonder what exactly he had been up to when trying to pass them.

This was confirmed in a later passage where he wrote, "When we were forced into conflict with them because of the necessity of continuing our journey, we threw great stones at them. They in turn would rage at our missiles, just as a dog would do, and stand in defiance, filling the air with terrible roaring. We attempted to knock out their eyes and break their teeth with stones, but even wounded and blind they would not give way." The coupling on the wave-lapped sand had now, it seemed, given way to all out war, and he noted ruefully that "there is no doubt that many of us would have been killed by them if their legs were as good on land as they are in water. And, indeed, we learned it was not wise to fight them in a large and open space, for there one could escape only with difficulty. Instead, steep places were always our refuge, because the beasts could not climb. Even thus secure, however, sometimes they laid siege to me for more than six hours, and at length compelled me, at very great peril of my life, to ascend a precipice, and in such way effect my escape from the infuriated beasts."

And then, of course, there was the hunting. "Those that we first blinded on land with stones were afterwards dispatched with clubs without ceremony. But the beasts are so tenacious of life that two or three men beating their heads with clubs could scarcely kill them with 200 blows, and thus would have to rest two or three times and refresh themselves frequently. When the cranium is broken into little pieces and most of the brains have gushed out, and all the teeth have been broken, still the creature attacks, fighting on with his flippers. I have purposely broken the skull and put out the eyes of one and then left him, and afterwards for more than two weeks he still stood alive and unmoved, like a statue, in the same place."

This was becoming unreadable. The native hunters were altogether more refined, using an iron harpoon on a cord to spear the sea bear and then moving on to "crush his front flippers and head with axes and clubs." They were selective, too: "By preference, in spring they kill the pregnant females and young males."

I put the book aside. It was impossible to get beyond those words. *In spring they kill the pregnant females and young males.*

TEN

It's hard not to feel a tad smug when you wake up after a night out with not even the trace of a hangover. Abstinence might feel bad at the time, but the next morning... damn, it feels good. That morsel of smugness is a by-product of exactly how good it feels. You're congratulating yourself on exercising control, commendable foresight, and you're enjoying the rewards and wondering why it is that so many people struggle to exercise similar levels of restraint. And credit where it's due, I had shown restraint. The sangria hardly counted as proper alcohol and so, effectively, the small glass of wine that I had (well, two glasses, if one is being perfectly accurate) before that wretched cabaret and the nightcap back in my room—two nightcaps, I guess, which, given the darkness of my reading matter, had been pretty restrained—were the only drinks I succumbed to during the entire day.

I leapt up, took a few brisk turns around the promenade deck to savour the sea air, and then had a light and healthy breakfast. Afterwards I swam, luxuriated in the pine and menthol vapours of the steam room, and then had a body massage. This one included aromatherapy and hot pebbles, which were placed with great care and ceremony on the naked skin. Sometimes they were left to sit there, sometimes they were rubbed or pulled, kneading and scraping the flesh to a degree that stopped just short of inducing pain. It didn't seem very dignified but it felt pretty good, better than anticipated, actually, and my cooling eye mask meant that I did not have to confront the indignity of lying stretched and naked in a small cell, at the mercy of an unknown assailant armed with stones. It did, however, make me think again about the poor sea bears.

After that I had a well deserved coffee, sharing a table with fat Pam and Stanley, who it turned out were from Sussex. They were pleasant enough but, like so many seasoned cruisers, their greatest pleasure (after eating and drinking) was to reminisce about past voyages and in doing so impart endless advice to a novice about the do's and don'ts of cruising. But I was feeling rested and pampered and so could endure a bit of patronising. I guess they meant well, apart from the constant name-dropping, one-upmanship and sheen of smug entitlement. So I guess that they meant well in a sort of well-concealed way.

Having made my escape, I headed to the ship's "university," a purpose-built room off the library, where I took in a lecture on the Romanovs. It was surprisingly well attended. The woman giving it was a suave, blonde academic, a few years older than me, with a commanding and elegant presence, and an enviably deep voice. In charting the lives and deaths of Russia's doomed imperial family, she avoided the usual clichés of butchered innocence and bestial Red murderers. The core of her talk was the interface between the public and the personal lives of the Romanovs, twin existences of carefully crafted artifice. She illustrated the lecture with a series of photographs from the vast archive of a family that had, at the time, been the most photographed in all of human history. As well as being the objects of photography, they were also keen practitioners, constantly snapping each other as they engaged in the humdrum activities of everyday imperial life. There was a terrible poignancy in the monochrome images: people who had been dead for a century staring back at us with frozen faces and living eyes, oblivious to the oncoming train. And there was genuine tragedy in those four daughters in white dresses—beautiful girls vibrant with life, desperate to assert their individuality, impatient to begin living—caught forever on the cusp of becoming women, their images floating free of the wreckage of bullet-riddled corpses strewn in a small, smoke-filled cellar. And then there was Alexei, the prince who never grew up, the little boychild ripped from the world in an instant of careless slaughter. I struggled not to cry; not for them exactly, but for the monumental cruelty of life and the arbitrary nature of unwarranted death.

After the applause I wanted to thank the lecturer but she was surrounded by a knot of amateur history buffs, including a loud and eccentric Russian lady, all of whom seemed to know far more about the subject than me. So I left without catching her eye.

I looped back via my room in order to check for messages from Horace but there were none. I thought about calling, but I assumed that he was sleeping off a late night and so left him to it. How easy it is to be considerate when your act of courtesy coincides with your preferred choice of action. I had lunch. Having narrowly dodged Brian the Bore in the dining room, scampering a few paces behind his dreadful mother, I opted instead for the buffet, where I maintained my regime of abstinence by restricting myself to a single glass of white wine. Then, after the tiniest bit of shopping (a scarf, lipstick and some mascara) I took myself off to Poseidon's Sensorium, to watch a movie. I had never seen a 4-D film, and was curious to experience it. The movie itself was utter crap, a nonsensical journey-to-the-centre-of-the-Earth type narrative, where zombie aliens had to be overcome in the cause of planetary survival. Together with its faux environmentalist credentials, it trumpeted its diversity with a multi-ethnic cast that included several forceful women in bandanas and stripped-down battle dress, their scalpel-sculpted faces artfully smudged with oil and ochre, flexing gym-toned biceps and growling orders with the same obnoxious imperative as men. It was the repurposing of something that had not been fit for purpose the first time around and, as such, it was merely a vessel for the special effects. But oh what special effects! My seat moved and vibrated with the shudder of earthquakes and gunfire; I was assailed by heat, lightning, drifts of fog, spray, wind and air; teased by a succession of ever-changing scents: salt, fragrant flowers, fire, rotting flesh and melting rock; whilst being pummelled by a sound track so loud that you experienced it viscerally through your internal organs rather than via the ears. I stuck it out to the end but could not say that it was enjoyable. It felt too much like a calculated assault on the senses. And more to the point, the tsunami of sensation was hugely distracting and, therefore, detracted from the film. Given the quality of the film in this particular instance, that distraction was no bad thing. But in a wider sense I was struck by how futile it was to invest so heavily in ancillary technology that—when you see past the bells and whistles of the "extreme sensory experience"—serves not to enhance but only to undermine and diminish the core of the work: character, exposition, and the compelling clasp of narrative.

I called in at Fizz to compose myself after the cinematic assault course. Then, bolstered by a couple of glasses of Prosecco, I felt sufficiently recovered to trot over to Horace's suite to check on him. He was in the sitting room and opened the door remotely, calling out a cheerful greeting without looking up.

"Forgive my not getting up. Be with you in a mo."

He was dressed smartly with a dapper blue jacket and indigo cravat and was perching on the sofa tinkering with an array of metal parts laid out in a highly ordered pattern on the coffee table. One glance was sufficient to determine that they were the pieces of a dismantled handgun.

"Horace, is that a fucking gun?"

"No. It's a Webley Mark IV, 38 calibre, top break, double action service revolver. Army issue. Officers only."

"What are you doing with it?"

"Cleaning it, of course. The Webley is a very robust weapon but, like all firearms, it benefits from being cleaned from time to time. Particularly in this environment. The sea air, you know, salt and water are a corrosive combination. Very hard on moving parts."

"I meant *why* do you have it?" I was trying to stay calm, glacially cool.

"It's my sidearm."

"Your sidearm? Horace, you're not in the fucking army."

"All gentleman should have one."

"Oh, that's a good idea. Let's have loads more guns in the world. That'll help with law and order, harmony, social cohesion. How the hell did you get it on board?"

"Like this, in pieces. Actually, dismantling it was probably an unnecessary precaution. Still, better safe than sorry. In the event though, they were actually pretty lax about checking the luggage of Diamond Plus passengers. Seemed to be considered a bit of an impertinence."

"Okay, next question. *Why* did you bring it on board?"

"I like to keep it close. It's been through some tight scrapes with me. Bandits in Central Asia, opal thieves of the Outback." He was clipping the gun back together now with practised precision. "It helps combat the unexpected."

"You're deranged."

"You won't say that when some woolly-haired Somalian pirate pokes his head over the gunwale and gives you the eye."

"Well, leaving aside the racism of that remark, for now, my response would be, I should be so lucky. Anyway, if we're attacked by pirates they'll be armed with AK-47s and rocket-propelled grenade launchers. What will you do with that little thing?"

"Defend us for as long as I can. Sell my life dearly. It's what any man would do. We serve. We sacrifice ourselves to protect our loved ones."

"What is this macho bullshit? Women serve in the military too."

"Ah, but men are genetically programmed, adapted if you like, to fight. Sure women do it now, in some cultures, but it's an abomination."

"You mean we're not capable of it."

"Of course you're capable of it. In some instances more capable, as long as it's not a straight comparison of physical strength. No, it's an abomination because if women fight then men have nothing left to defend."

"But women can fight alongside men. Think of revolutionary Russia or the Spanish civil war. What about the Kurds, where women helped defeat ISIS? There's no distinction."

"Other than the distinction of Nature, which remains intact, no matter how much social mores are trying to erode it."

"Jesus, I can't believe the views you come out with, Horace. I know you're old, but that's not a licence to be a complete arse."

"I'm just saying that men are warriors. Some are foot soldiers, some are officers, but all are warriors."

"You're not, you're a bloody dinosaur."

"A dinosaur who still has a roar. Here feel it." He had finished reassembling the pistol and, holding it by the barrel, offered it to me with a smile. "It's not loaded. See." He depressed a small lever on the gun to break it open and show the empty chambers."

"I don't want it. Why would I want to touch it?"

"Thank you, Lizzy, you have just neatly proved my point about gender distinctions."

Even as he was retracting his hand, I reached out and seized the gun. I had never held one before and was immediately struck by how heavy it was, how much effort was involved in just holding it level. It was also desperately utilitarian: its oiled metal surface, scuffed and scratched, still bore the mark of the maker's lathe, and its black Bakelite grip was chipped. On the left side it had a worn stamp saying "WAR FINISH."

I tried to hold it casually, aspiring to an air of limp-wristed insouciance, but its weight pulled my hand earthwards. His mocking smile annoyed me and made me more determined to regard it inconsequentially. I would not aim it. Instead I tilted it upright and traced my fingers over the bulge of the cylinder, stroking the indentations, feeling the curve of the trigger guard. I inverted it, looking down into the dark ellipse of the barrel. It was horrible, like staring at death. Glad to rid myself of it, I handed it back to him and he began wrapping it in an oiled cloth. My hands were discoloured with a residue of oil. I wanted to wash them.

"Do you have bullets for that thing?" I asked casually.

"Would you like to fire it?"

"No. But I want to know if you have bullets for it, here, on the ship."

"A gun is not a gun without bullets, although they are called cartridges, or rounds; the bullet is just the hard bit that flies out and kills people."

"Right, let's have them. Come on, hand them over. Right now." I extended my palm.

"You would disarm me? Have me surrender my weapon? Force me to give up my sidearm without having been vanquished in combat?"

"Horace, either you give me the *cartridges,* or I'm going to report the gun. Right now." I took a step towards the door.

He sighed heavily, and walked into the closet. When he returned, instead of the gun he offered up six brass cartridges, each topped with a lead tip. As they lay in my open hand I was shocked by how small they were, only two or three centimetres in length.

"Be careful with them, Lizzy. I will want them back if need arises."

"Do you have any more, Uncle?"

"If I had more, I wouldn't need them back." He smiled. "Come on now, let's take a turn around the deck. Cocktail hour is fast approaching."

We walked several times around the promenade deck with Horace chatting cheerfully about aspects of African and Aboriginal languages and the subtleties of pronunciation. He apologised for his earlier absence but explained that he had invited Selene to lunch. "You mean she actually accepted?" I asked, a little too incredulously. It seemed that the bottle of champagne he had sent to her dressing room had lubricated matters. Horace told me several times what a fascinating and thoughtful young woman she was, with an interest in the science of phonetics. Over lunch, apparently, she had instructed him in the history of African click languages where clicks formed a part, sometimes the most significant part, of their consonants. He helpfully demonstrated the difference between a popping click, with the tongue on the roof of the mouth, and the kiss click, which involved a sucking sound from the lips. I thanked him for the insight and said that one never knew when it might come in useful.

"There are a couple of others too, but I'm still working to perfect them," he said. "And do you know, Lizzy, when she said that there was only one language outside Africa that used click, I was able to shoot straight back with *Damiin*, the ceremonial vocabulary of the Lardil, an aboriginal people from Mornington Island, off the north coast of Queensland. She was bowled over. Couldn't believe I knew that, or that I'd been to the island. I even managed to remember a few words. And do you also know that *Damiin* was spoken only by a select few. All the young men of the Lardil underwent *luruku*, a form of ritual circumcision, as soon as they sprouted facial hair, and they undertook a year-long oath of silence during which time they learned a complex sign language. But *Damiin* was learned only by those men who went on to the second initiation, *warama*, which was voluntary. It involved subincision—the longitudinal slitting open of the underside of the penis and urethra—in a ceremony that honours the myth of the lizard god who found the first Aboriginals. But when he found them they were fused together and so he had to separate them with his knife, carving their features and openings. The split penis is seen to resemble a vulva and the bleeding is akin to menstruation. They traditionally reopen the wound for ritual bloodletting. In some parts of Australia it's called *mika*, which means 'terrible rite.'"

"Enough with the genital mutilation, please Uncle."

"I thought you'd be interested. Selene was." He sounded genuinely hurt. "Besides, because the urethra is open, those who have been through the ceremony usually have to sit or squat to pee. After what you said to me last night I thought you'd approve."

"I wasn't approving anything. It was just a suggestion. I was trying to assist. But you know what, Horace, what you do with your penis is entirely your affair." It came out louder than I had meant it to. Some fellow passengers standing at the rail looked over at us.

"Then why are you so concerned about my having lunch with Selene?"

"I was just concerned for you."

"Just like the government was concerned for the Lardil. Mornington Island is not what it was, you know. Now they've got wife-beating and child abuse, a lot of alcoholism. The government clamped down on booze and so the islanders had to brew their own, and it's much stronger. *Warama* has pretty much died out too, and that means *Damiin* is all but lost. The last fluent speaker of the purest form died a few years ago, but there are still some old men who can speak some of the simpler variations. And I'll tell you another interesting thing about the Lardil people, Lizzy."

"I'm not sure how much more I can take."

"It is absolutely taboo to speak the name of a dead person. The dead are generally unmentioned, and absolutely never referred to by name. The Lardil have many euphemisms and forms of linguistic circumlocution to avoid it. When the dead are dead they are gone, and they stay gone."

The ship was squeezing into the Mediterranean, Europe to its left and Africa to the right. We stood in silence, looking out at Gibraltar sliding by in the distance. It appeared as a dark mass, a mountain rising menacingly out of the sea. Horace practised quiet clicking sounds. I was thinking about the gun. It was hard to shake the memory of its heavy blackness, and how its hard, sculpted shape simultaneously embodied studied elegance and such banality of purpose. It was designed to fit so perfectly within the hand. It knew instinctively where to go, making itself instantly at home even in a hand unfamiliar with its form.

We went below for cocktails and then dinner. It was a little subdued, the conversation stiff at first, mediated by a mutual desire to find safe space in the form of subjects unlikely to cause argument. The alcohol helped loosen things up a little, but Horace looked tired. The questions I fed him were dealt with in a manner that was courteously sufficient but perfunctory. At least it was benign, without skirmishing, without provocation.

In the silences, I realised how incurious he was about me, how few questions he had asked about my life since our re-acquaintance. But I knew also that there was nothing personal that I wanted to share with him. Too much was painful or shameful and here, on the boat, there was an opportunity to be someone else, someone freshly formed, a person constructed at that moment who was free of all of the crud and the scars, accreted debris of the past. Afloat on the ocean in the company of strangers was perfect, the perfect opportunity to be anyone you wanted to be, and yet I remained shackled. It was hard to get beyond the gun, the weight and shape of that oiled shank of brutality. As we shared a sofa in the quiet of the Magellan Lounge, I braved the question that I had wanted to ask all evening.

"That gun, Uncle...."

"Speak up, girl. I think someone at that far table didn't quite hear you."

I lowered my voice. "Is that the gun my grandfather shot himself with?"

"Yes," he replied, with an exaggerated stage whisper.

"You've kept it all these years?"

"Evidently."

"But why?"

"It's an heirloom. It belonged to my father. He used it in the war. Shot Italians and Germans with it. At least one of each that I know of."

"But it killed your brother."

"It didn't kill Virgil. Virgil killed Virgil. Besides, it's a good pistol. It's a Webley Mark IV. Still shoots well, though it fires a little low. You have to compensate by raising it a few degrees when you aim."

"Well I'll try to remember that in the event of my ever having to use it."

"I'll tell you something, Lizzy, only last month I shot an Eastern Brown with it."

"Please say that's a reference to some sort of vermin."

"Snake."

"So what happened to your 'live and let live' environmentalist credentials?"

"Sometimes in life it's kill or be killed. Bastard was on the track, about a stone's throw from the house. I didn't see him until late. He was as mad as hell and went into that S-shape attack pose, chest high, mouth wide, about to strike. I had no choice. Shot him through the head. Killed him outright. You can't always reason with things, Lizzy, things or people. Sometimes all you can do is react instinctively. Sometimes it's you or them. Self-preservation. I don't feel bad about shooting him, not one damned bit. And of the two of us, I don't regret being the one who's still alive."

"Are we still talking about the snake, Uncle?"

"World is full of snakes, Lizzy. You know in Australia we have 170 separate species of them, and more than 100 of those are venomous. Browns are the second most poisonous land snake on the planet. A bite from one of those bastards will drop you in seconds. The venom paralyses you, like creeping death, and stops your blood from clotting. You'll die of a heart attack or a brain haemorrhage while bleeding from every orifice in your body, even your eyes."

"Please, Horace, please tell me what you know."

"About snakes or guns?"

"About Virgil. Tell me what you remember about my grandfather's death. Please, Uncle."

He sighed and his pale blue eyes looked at me hard. "Oh Lizzy, there's no great secret, nothing much to tell. He was on the ottoman that used to be in the library, near the windows that opened into the garden. There was a low table in front of him with a brandy bottle, almost empty, and an empty glass. There was an ashtray full of butts, an empty cigarette box and his silver-plated lighter. Also the oiled cloth that Father kept his old wartime revolver wrapped in, the Webley. We'd seen it many times. Sometime he let us help clean and oil it. But it was never loaded. But when Virgil died there was a box of cartridges on the table, too."

"And so the gun was fully loaded with bullets?"

"No, he only put one round in. He only needed one."

"And he died instantly?"

"A bullet through the brain tends to produce that effect. The wound was to the right side of his head. He was sitting upright but slumped, his head thrown back. His eyes were open and the look on his face... it's hard to describe. Terrible to behold. Unforgettable."

"You tell it as though you were there."

"The police inquiry concluded he was alone. Patricia, our housekeeper, she found him the next morning. Father was in London. I was in Cambridge when I heard the news. But later I saw some police photographs taken at the scene. I wish I could forget them."

"Is that why you fled to the other side of the world after it happened?"

"I didn't flee. After the tragedy, some considerable time afterwards, I left England to travel. There was nothing to keep me. Fresh start and all that."

"Were you there, when it happened, Uncle?" I tried to keep my voice slow and steady. "Did someone shoot Virgil?"

He took another drink and then looked straight at me. "The police inquiry concluded that he was alone when he died."

"That doesn't answer either question."

"You mean me, don't you? Don't be so bloody ridiculous. Of course I didn't bloody well shoot him. He was my brother. His death was one of the three great tragedies of my life."

"I'm sorry, Uncle."

"But maybe I'm fortunate in only having three. For some people they come not as single spies but in huge herds."

He rubbed the deep crease at the top of his nose. He looked suddenly frail as well as old, and I felt ashamed for having posed the question, for pressing him too hard, for giving him a tough time over Selene. I put my hand on his, touching his worn old skin, scarred, snake warm and paper thin.

"Yeah," I said, "Huge herds. And who needs herds when just one tends to be more than enough."

I walked him back to his suite. We swayed in synchronicity with the ship, our arms interlinked, woven like lovers. We didn't speak but there was a closeness and harmony in our tread. We walked via the promenade, which was almost deserted. The stars were hard and bright, glinting like the points of nails that had been hammered through the blackness. Around them the heavens were smeared deep with the millions of constellations of the Milky Way, all shiny cold, impassive. We paused momentarily, he leaning heavily on his cane, and stared up towards the heavens.

"I miss seeing the Southern Cross," he said. A cough rattled harshly in his chest.

At the door of his suite Monique greeted us with silence. I left him in her care, bidding him goodnight with a kiss on his cheek. I tasted the salt of a tear, or maybe it was just the tang of the night breeze from the sea.

ELEVEN

The next morning was overcast and we were pounding circuits on the Promenade deck, pausing occasionally to look out across a surprisingly grey Mediterranean. Horace seemed sprightly, having apparently benefitted from his early night. I was making an indirect approach, steering the conversation round to Horace's father. He was unexpectedly forthright in his assessment of my great-grandfather.

"You know, Lizzy, ultimately his was a negation of life. Where was the passion? If the woman I loved had been interned I would have moved heaven and earth to get her out. I would have caused the most almighty stink, broken her out if necessary."

"By storming the Isle of Man singlehandedly? Armed with what? The trusty Webley?"

"If need be, yes. I might have failed, shot down like a dog on the highway, but by God I would have tried. He did nothing. He put his country first, he even got a medal for shooting Italians, but he did nothing for her, nothing other than to betray her trust, ignore her pleas, and deny her the consolation of contact with Virgil and me, the children she loved. And you know why? He didn't want the scandal. He just wanted it to go away, at any price.

"After the war he returned to Oxford; went back to his books as though she had never existed. He got rid of most of her things and he cleared out every mirror from the house.

I'd like to say that it was shame over how he had treated Mother, or a manifestation of grief. I'd like to say that but it wouldn't be true. Even after Virgil died he didn't show any real emotion. It hit him like a train but he just absorbed it, bottled up the impact. He buried his son, paid off the debts, and went on as usual. Father preferred books to the real world; life was just too messy for him. You know, when he died they found the old bugger sitting in his pyjamas with an open copy of Ovid in his lap. He'd had a massive stroke.

"I had to come back and sort everything out. I sold most of it, the house included. Just setting foot in that place made me shudder. I was glad to see the back of it. Most of the contents too. Stuff. It slows you down, Lizzy. People covet it, exchange their lives for it, lie, steal, swindle and kill for it, but it's not worth the candle. Makes you fat and sluggish; furs up the arteries of life. I only kept a few things. Some crates of books, some papers and photographs. And my mother's dressing table. It was a family heirloom, given to her as a wedding present. It was made from walnut and had the most exquisite Italian marquetry and an ornate, gilded mirror. As a child I used to watch her sitting at it, putting on makeup and brushing her luxuriant hair. After Father's death I found it in the cellar, and because of his mirror phobia he had wrapped it in brown paper.

"Maybe he was protecting it. Keeping it safe for you."

"God only knows. He was very odd towards the end. Anyway, the money was useful. I invested some of it in an annuity, for Amelia and the baby, your mother. It paid a tidy monthly sum, inflation indexed. After the sale I left England as soon as I could, and never went back."

"Did you attend the inquest?"

"There wasn't one."

"No, I meant the inquest into Virgil's death?"

"There was no formal inquest. The police were satisfied. It was an open and shut case as far as they were concerned. He had gambling debts; he was drunk and depressed. Besides, the coroner was a friend of my father. They belonged to the same club. There was more of that in those days. Father wasn't well and I think there was an effort to spare him further suffering through any unnecessary unpleasantness. So the findings were a formality. The police even returned the gun."

"The trusty old Webley."

"Old Mr Webley."

"And you kept the gun and the dressing table but not the house?"

"It was an ugly old pile. Too many memories."

"Like a memory of Virgil's suicide? Tell me, Uncle, how long does the smell of cordite and blood linger in a house?"

"Hours maybe? I don't know, Lizzy, I wasn't there." He paused and frowned. "At least, I don't think I was."

"Uncle!"

"It's hard to be certain. It's more than half a century ago."

"You must know."

"My memory's not what it was. I've seen photographs, of course. You know how it is with childhood memories, where it's hard to distinguish between an actual memory of something you saw or did, and a memory of something you've seen yourself doing in a photo, or heard in an anecdote about your having done."

"Yeah, when I was three years old, maybe, but not twenty."

"That's because you're still young. When you reach my age all memory becomes a bit like that. There's so much of it, and it fuses with other things. I've thought a lot about Virgil's death, of course I have. I've dreamt about it, nightmares they are really. I dream about it often. I wasn't there though. I'm sure I wasn't there, but I have been there in dreams, that I admit, in my imagination. I feel I've walked there in other worlds, other lives."

We proceeded in silence for a few minutes. Then Horace said cheerfully, "What would you do if you won the lottery, Lizzy?"

It was classic Horace distraction strategy. He probably had a military-sounding name for it, maybe even an acronym, but it all amounted to the same deflection strategy: when faced with an issue that you want to evade, pose a direct but unrelated question on an unrelated subject.

"I don't do the lottery, Horace. I don't approve of it." It sounded more prim than I had intended.

"Of course not, neither do I. Old Adam Smith nailed it when he called lotteries a tax on stupidity. But supposing you were to do it, hypothetically, and supposing you won, hypothetically. What would you do?"

"Won what? Real or hypothetical cash?"

"Real cash, but in a hypothetical scenario."

"It would depend on the amount."

"Squillions. More than you could ever reasonably spend in a lifetime."

"I'd give up teaching."

"Yes, that's what most people say, give up work."

"I'd travel, I'd write. I would live a more reflective life. It could be more considered if you didn't have to sell yourself each day. I'd give money to charity. Not big, bureaucratic, bloated charities, but local ones, and to worthwhile individuals. On my travels I would look for people who were deserving of assistance, and I'd help them out."

"Ah, so you would move amongst the people and dispense good works, and they would tug at your sleeve, and kneel before you, showing their scars, and you would heal them with the power of money."

"Not heal, but help. I know it sounds idealistic, but I would offer the practical assistance that money can buy. And I would do it anonymously, through an agent, so nobody would ever connect the help they received to the unassuming traveller who had passed by that way some time before.

Imagine going through a village that had no water and then, a month later, a team of people arrive and install a pump. Imagine the same scenario with a village school or a clinic. Think of the difference that would make to individual lives."

"Gifts from the gods. But what if the money you gave was siphoned off and stolen, or wasted by the recipients who proved themselves to be less worthy than you had supposed."

"I would build in safeguards, of course, accountability. But you can't control a gift after it has been given. That's the nature of gifts."

"No more than you can control a bullet that has been fired. But you can control money. In fact, you must. Otherwise it will control you, it'll ruin you."

"I'll have to take your word on that. I've never run that risk."

We were standing at the rail, Horace collecting his breath. Near us was a man writing in a small black notebook. Horace approached him with extended hand. "Good day sir, Horatio Bosanquet. And you are?"

"Stephen," said the stranger, extracting his hand from Horace's grip.

"Delighted to meet you, Mr Stephens. How are you enjoying the voyage?"

"It's interesting. Some funny moments."

"Quite so. What brings you aboard."

"My wife is giving some talks. She's a university lecturer, an authority on the Romanovs."

"Ah yes, my wife attended one of her lectures yesterday. You said it was excellent, didn't you dear? I might drop in on one myself if I have a mo. I saw her photograph in the programme. The blonde, right?"

"She has blond hair, yes. She has a name too, and a PhD from Cambridge."

"Good show. I almost had one of those myself, you know, many years ago. But I changed my mind midway through. What are you scribbling?"

"Notes."

"What sort of notes?"

"The private sort."

"Very good. Carry on then."

Horace strode off in the direction of the bow. The guy with the notebook gave me a glance of quizzical sympathy as I scurried past, trying to catch him up.

"What the fuck was that about?" I asked as I overhauled him. "We've already discussed this. I told you not to pass me off as your bloody girlfriend. Remember? I assumed you'd understand that it also included not being passed off as your fucking wife. It's demeaning."

"I thought that wife would be a promotion."

"What the fuck is wrong with you? What's your issue with women?"

"What issue? I don't have an issue."

"We're not an alternative species, you know. Not some mutation from the norm."

"Of course not. You're just unknowable."

"Unknowable? Has it ever occurred to you that you just don't try hard enough? Maybe you don't use the right words. Think about that next time you're swinging gently on the breeze, alone in your chimp bed."

"Men try, Lizzy, we really do. We have to. You've got the *Thing*."

"And which thing, precisely, are we talking about?"

"*The Thing*. That which we do not have but must possess. And you have a monopoly upon it. So we have to be chivalrous and kind. We have to love, honour and protect. Go through courtship rituals and marriage. It's all a tax. Christ, we've turned it into the foundation of an entire civilisation. Layer upon layer of supplication and obscurantism that surround the *Thing*."

"Will you stop saying that. I don't like the terminology, 'the *Thing*'. It sounds like a fucking alien."

"How about l'origine du monde? Or the burden of dreams and promises, the centre of all desire, the garden of earthly delights, that unknowable object of attainment?"

"Christ. I think I prefer 'the *Thing*'. Jesus, Uncle, have you been mixing brandy with your meds again?"

"Not guilty."

"Then I genuinely think you might be mentally ill. Actually deranged, mentally unhinged."

"I fear I am. I'm a sad and terminal case. It was the *Thing* what got me." He looked at me, his wrinkled eyes twinkling with mischief. "Oh come on, Lizzy, crack a smile. Come up to my rooms and have a drink, there's something I want to show you."

"It's not your etchings is it?"

"No, something else."

"Yeah? Well you'd better bloody well behave yourself, or I'll set Mr Webley on you."

Horace told me to fix drinks whilst he retrieved something from the safe. He went into the closet and I saw him punch in a combination and swing open the hefty steel door in the wall. I had thought that his safe would be the same size as the one in my room, biscuit tin sized, large enough for phone, wallet and keys. But this was a monster. I should have known. I mean, if you can afford a suite, then it stands to reason that you have more stuff to stash away than the lowly mariners of the lower decks. I wondered about the crew's quarters—those poor devils in their hutches down in the bilges. They must have safes the size of tobacco tins.

Horace had his head and shoulders inside the safe, rifling its contents, when Monique ghosted in. She looked at me without acknowledgement and then, seeing Horace's body protruding from the wall, asked if there was anything she could do for him. He replied in the negative, his voice simultaneously muffled and echoing. After she left he called me over to assist. "It needs a bit of sorting," he explained, passing me a heavy cardboard box. I took it to the table; he followed, carrying a second with a file of documents balanced on top of it. I went back and looked into the cavernous interior of the safe. The gun was there, wrapped in its oiled cloth, together with its cleaning materials. There was also a large steel strong box.

"You can leave the rest," he called. "It's just some cash and a few stones, as well as the unmentionable."

I joined him at the table. He was rootling through one of the boxes.

"Christ, Uncle, what is all this?"

"Well they give you a big safe. Seemed only right to use it."

"So you brought an archive?"

"Just bits and pieces. Things I wanted to read again, at leisure. Also my Will." He tapped the file of documents. "I want you to know where it is, just in case I get knocked off by pirates or fall overboard when drunk."

"You should lodge it in the ship's strong room. It would be safer."

"Nah, it's not completed yet. I haven't signed it."

"You should do that, Uncle. I'll witness it if you want."

"No, that could complicate things. But this is what I wanted to show you."

He handed me a creased black and white photograph of two boys in school uniform. One was blond, his square face smiling at the camera. The other was more slight, his hair much darker, the face thinner and more delicate.

"You and Virgil."

"Yeah, about to go to school. He's the blond. Don't look much like brothers do we?"

I looked at Horace's scored old face, trying to blot out the lines and wrinkles, trying to imagine a skin unworn and unweathered, a skin at the start of its life, full of elasticity and optimism. If you stare hard enough, sometimes you can peel things back, peel back the years and see the ghost of the past hovering, its flickering presence momentarily superimposed upon the present. And so it was that I saw fleeting flashes of the child, the young man, in that battered face with its tattered skin. I looked again at the photograph. It was undeniable. I could see more of me in Horace than in Virgil.

"Here's another of us." They were teenagers in fencing gear, arms around each other in a sweaty embrace. Horace's head was turned slightly from the camera, smiling shyly, his eyes looking down. It wasn't just his hair and eyes that were dark, but his skin too. Dark like mine. Virgil was still straw-blond, his face pale, as pale as his eyes. The camera shutter had frozen his laugh and in his free hand he held aloft a small trophy.

"We got first and second place. First time two brothers had competed against each other in the final. You can guess who won." He passed me two more photographs. "Here's a couple of your grandmother. This is Amelia."

The first picture was of a seated blonde girl, with an open, golden face and dark eyes. She was sitting formally in a high backed chair against a wall of books. She was holding a glass of wine and had a curious half-smile, the left side of her top lip suggesting the tremor of someone trying to keep a straight face. Behind her were Horace and Virgil, white flannels and dark blazers, Horace glancing down and Virgil once again looking directly at the camera. The same girl was in the second picture, more casual this time and more troubled. She was sitting on a garden bench beneath a cherry tree. Virgil's blond head was resting on her shoulder, his face pressed towards the hollow between her chin and neck. His eyes were closed but hers were looking out over his burrowed head, looking out towards the middle distance without the hint of a smile. Her jaw was fixed and resolute in the sunlight, her eyes hard.

I could feel Horace looking at me intently. "My colouring is more like yours than Virgil's," I said with as casual a tone as I could muster. "My face is more like yours was too, finer features than his." I could feel my voice catching in the top of my throat. "Are you my grandfather, Uncle? Is that what this is all about? Is that why I'm here? Just tell me. Tell me it's true. I would be happy, so happy to have found you."

"Oh, Lizzy, my dear girl. I would be happy too. I would be honoured were it so. But it's not. I'm not. And he is... he was."

"But you have the same birthmark as me. On your right hip. I saw it in the pool. The little dark patch of skin shaped like a leaf." I could hear the desperation in my voice and feel the sting of approaching tears.

"Yes, I have it, Lizzy. But so did he, and so did Father. It runs in the family."

TWELVE

I woke in the night, back at my house in Cambridge, except I wasn't awake and it wasn't my house. There was a dark silhouette at the open window, someone wanting to get in and do me harm. I tried to close it but couldn't, so I ran to get Wat from his bed. I wanted to lock us in a room where we'd be safe. But the stairs to the upper floor went on and on and the carpet was stained and loose and wrapped itself around my ankles. I tried to kick it off, but when I looked down I saw that it was a roiling mass of snakes and by kicking at them I had made them angry and sure to bite. And I could hear Wat screaming but when I reached his room, which wasn't his room, his little bed was empty. And I heard the door close behind me and in the blackness I could feel the presence of the person who had been at the window.

I woke trembling, wet with sweat, the duvet rucked around my legs. I put on the light, swigged some water and then hugged Benny until the terror subsided. I got up and ate some fruit and drank a glass of water and then one of white wine. Outside, beyond the balcony, was unbroken blackness; inside there was only the dull throb of the ship's engines. Time behaves strangely when there is nothing against which to measure its passing.

I remembered a quote from St Augustine that I had stuck on my wall when I was a teenager. "How can the past and future be, when the past no longer is, and the future is not yet? As for the present, if it were always present and never moved on to become the past, it would not be time, but eternity." This felt like being trapped in some shabby, low-budget eternity, but I knew that it wasn't real. There was a past and a future. I could remember boarding the ship in Southampton, and I could project to the end of the voyage (for me at least) in Cape Town. And the past is never no longer with us, I mean reach out your hand and feel its shackle. And what if the future is already formed, what if it's there and always has been? And so the past and future are running alongside the present, each jostling and grinding the other, bumping along and determining how it all unfolds. So Time is not an orderly progression, it is more akin to a traffic snarl, a demolition derby where all you can do is grip the wheel and sustain damage, keep going until the end of the journey, the end of the chaos. And when it ends for the individual, when your car ceases to move or your leaking boat sinks, what then? Nothingness? An absence of existence? And does the jostle of past, present and future continue, unfolding without you, unfolding forever?

I thought about Horace, the way he had looked at me when showing me the photographs, that detached stare of curiosity, the half smile and the twinkle of his eyes. He enjoyed the power of knowing, just as he enjoyed the power of money. He got to decide those to whom he would give; who would receive and how much their portion. And I felt fury that he had co-opted me as a wife, deliberately demeaning me after I had told him that it was unacceptable. It was like he got off on it, some twisted sexual thing like the power and the money. And then I thought of the vulnerability I had seen when he spoke of Amelia, and the genuine sadness in his face when he told me that he was not my grandfather.

But maybe that's the thing about the past. Maybe it's only a coherent narrative when you arrange it as such. Maybe until then the past is just a random pile of stuff, shit that happens. But the pile keeps shifting, changing size and form and content. And we all have different privileges, differing levels of access to the pile. And though you know that the truest narrative can only be realised by having access to the whole heap, you also know that that's impossible. Only God has that, and I don't believe in God any more. God watches us suffer; God watches over the senseless killing of infants and otters and pregnant fur seals and He does nothing.

And then I thought of something else that St Augustine had said in *Confessions*: "The punishment of every disordered mind is its own disorder." I had come to Horace seeking clarity but the information that he had provided only confused the picture. The image remained clear in my mind, my grandfather's body, slumped and bloody, but the sequence of events that had preceded it was more incomprehensible than ever. For years I had scoured the same circular path. Why would a young man, whose whole adult life lay before him, have put a bullet through his brain? A young man from a prosperous family; a man who had enjoyed, and who could reasonably have expected to further enjoy, the privileges of rank, wealth and education; and, of course, the supreme privilege of gender. Virgil had had a beautiful fiancée, and the prospect of a child. His golden cup was immeasurably full and yet he dashed it to the ground so that its contents puddled away, mingled to nothing in the dust and the dirt. It made no sense. The family legend as to his motive—gambling debts and depression—seemed less credible after speaking to Horace. Their father would surely have covered the debts. As for the depression, Horace portrayed his brother as too unreflective, too superficial in outlook, to be inclined to melancholy. Virgil was the golden boy of privilege, a shiny youth not prone to guilt, despair or gloomy introspection.

The fact that Horace had evidently loved him, despite his flaws, gave that assessment greater credence. And the more that I heard of an idle, vain and irresolute young man, the less credible his suicide became. I once read an article about San Francisco's Golden Gate bridge being the most popular suicide destination in America and the second-most popular in the world. More than 1,600 people have jumped since the bridge was opened in 1937. Apparently it takes four seconds to fall the 250 feet to the bay below. Then you hit the water at 75 miles an hour. Amongst the 5 percent who survive the impact, most then drown or succumb to hypothermia in the cold water. I read two survivor accounts. One was from Ken Baldwin, 28, who on 20 August 1985 tried to end his long struggle with depression. He found an epiphany in his descent, recalling that the instant he let go of the railing he "realised that everything in my life that I'd thought was unfixable was totally fixable—except for having just jumped." He saw the faces of those he was leaving behind—his wife and baby daughter, his parents and three brothers—and he felt their pain as a profound sadness. He regained consciousness in the water imbued with a fierce will to live, and despite his injuries he kept himself afloat for seven minutes before the Coast Guard pulled him out.

Fifteen years later, nineteen-year-old Kevin Hines, a sufferer of bipolarism, succumbed to the voices in his head that told him he needed to die. He cried on the bus journey to the bridge, cried as he spent 40 minutes looking down at the distant water, making a bargain with himself that if one person were to approach him and ask if he was okay, then he would tell them everything and beg for help. Eventually a woman walked up to him but only to ask him to take a photograph of her with her camera. Afterwards, he recalled, "I was like, 'Fuck this, nobody cares.' So I jumped." Like Baldwin before him, he felt instant regret and the certainty that he did not want to die. During the descent he managed to pull out of his headlong dive, but the impact was still hard enough to break his back. He descended 80 feet into the frigid water, disorientated by the blackness, feeling pain greater than he had ever experienced. He clawed his way to the surface but could not stay afloat because of his injuries and his waterlogged clothes. He was drowning when a large marine creature saved his life, supporting him on its back until he was rescued by the Coast Guard. Observers, who saw the animal, afterwards described it as a dolphin or seal, or maybe a sea lion, manatee or shark. I like to think that it was the ghost of one of Steller's sea cows, offering its forgiveness.

I thought again about Virgil. I tried to imagine the act of putting a gun barrel to your temple; the cold, heavy pressure of the hard metal, the resistance of the trigger. I tried to imagine the courage that it would require. Only once in my life had I considered self-destruction, really, seriously, considered it. It was after Wat's death. There was no gun, of course, but I laid out an array of pills, enough I think to have managed the task. I tipped them on the kitchen table, emptying every bottle and packet in the house and then arranging the jumbled mass into orderly lines of neat segregation. Even as I was doing it, I knew that I wasn't going to swallow them. I should like to say that my hand was stayed by a sense of responsibility to William, to Mum, to my friends, but, in truth, it was just a failure of will, an absence of sufficient courage.

I was in pain, certainly. I wanted it to stop, undeniably. I wanted to end the heartache and the thousand natural shocks. But not at the cost of non-existence. The knowledge that the ordinary room in which I sat would be the last room; that chair, the last ever chair; the familiar table upon which my hands moved in arranging the coloured ranks of capsules, the last table, the last surface that I would see or touch. Ever. It was so momentous a feeling, so overwhelming in its magnitude, that I instinctively rose and stumbled from the room, as though retreating from the precipice. No, not retreating, that sounds too controlled. I reeled away from the cliff edge. I recoiled into the garden. Gulping for air I leaned against the wall of the house, pressing my body into the solidity of the bricks, inhaling the scents of Autumn. The sun was shining and a blackbird was singing in the old apple tree, its song so full of joy, its feathers gleaming like oil and flame. A grey squirrel was dashing up and down the hazelnut tree and looping across the lawn in fractured loping starts as she paused to bury nuts, storing sustenance for days as yet unlived. As long as life continues there is always a future.

And as I stood in the low sunshine, pressed against the warm brick, I knew that I lacked the courage to end my life. I lacked it because my pain, though immense, was not so vast as to overcome the fear. The fear of that frozen foreign land from whose bourn no traveller returns. The land of non-existence. And while I watched the squirrel going about her work, careless of my presence, I was struck by the mathematical improbability of that single egg—one amongst hundreds of thousands—and that individual sperm—one of a spawn of billions—meeting, fusing, lodging in my mother's womb. And then I thought of the same impossible odds multiplied across the thousands of generations of my ancestors, and I was awestruck by the sheer mathematical miracle of having been given this opportunity to live. And with that opportunity comes self-awareness, the knowledge that an individual human life is infinitesimally small and brief, a tiny spasm of consciousness within the infinity of non-existence. And I knew then that I would never end it prematurely. To do so would be a dereliction, and would require a level of desperation, of black courage, that was unimaginable. And thus conscience really does make cowards of us all.

And yet the consistent description of Virgil's character, by Horace, the twin brother who knew him better than anyone, was that he lacked courage, lacked the necessary insight for true desperation. Why then would the golden boy have killed himself? How had it happened? And if it was not he who fired the gun, who then? He was alone at the time of his death. There was no sign of a forced entry, no intruder, no crime. *"I wasn't there... I wasn't there... I don't think I was..."* But what if Horace was there that night? What if he knew it all? What if Horace really had fired the gun? *"You mean me, don't you?... Lizzy, I wasn't there. At least, I don't think I was... I'm sure I wasn't there."*

Previously, I think I had seen the past, the unknown past, as an unmapped blank upon the chart. And I was an explorer, equipped with machete and pith helmet, hacking through the jungle in a bid not to observe the contours of the land but rather to arrive at a specific destination, the source of some mighty river system or mountain range. The jungle was nominally the domain of Horace, but his title was unenforced and lacking legitimacy, for here was a province large and neglected, overgrown and left to Nature. But now I saw the limits of this metaphor. Now it seemed less a jungle and more an estate, Horace's private estate, whose shape and character were the subject of vague report and rumour but whose detailed geography lay unseen behind tall and forbidding walls. And what if it was not unexplored at all? What if it comprised formal gardens and sculpted landmarks. A landscape of the mind, artfully constructed by a human hand and brain. And if I could but scale the perimeter wall then its topography would be plain to behold; exotic blooms or poisonous fruit, all laid bare beneath the sunlight of the morning.

I threw on some clothes and washed my face. I left my cabin and wandered the silent empty corridors. There were a few crew, ghosting about in silent industry, standing aside when I passed, asking politely if I needed assistance. Their daytime smiles were absent now, replaced by uneasy frowns, concern that I was in need of something that had not been anticipated and provided. I passed through the main atrium where an army of cleaners was hard at work, vacuuming and polishing. I headed for the Magellan Lounge, the one place that I thought would be open. But it was closed, inhabited only by the night gang with their vacuums and their polish. As a last resort I went up to the reading room. It was deserted, apart from a man sitting on one of the plush sofas drinking coffee. He was in his thirties, with curly dark hair and a Mediterranean appearance. He did not raise his eyes from his newspaper when I entered. I took an unused cup from the stack by the door and tried the coffee urn but it was empty. "Shit," I said.

"I have a pot of coffee here if you want some. Please," the stranger indicated to the chair opposite. "You can join me." He was wearing a light suit with an open-necked white shirt and expensive looking trainers. His English was accented and overlaid with American pronunciation. I thanked him and filled my cup from the white ceramic pot. He apologised for the absence of milk or sugar and I assured him that they were not required. We read in silence.

I returned to Steller, determined not to allow my twenty-first century sensibilities to prevent me finishing my great-grandfather's book. I had moved on to the section on Sea Lions. "These beasts are indeed most terrible to look upon when alive." That qualification should have been a warning sign, I guess, "...and they far surpass the sea bear in strength and stature as well as in endurance. They give to the eyes and mind the impression of a lion." Oh most majestical creature! Next came his familiar and strangely anthropomorphic description of mating practices. "They copulate like the sea bears. The males hold the females in great respect and do not treat them so harshly as the sea bears do their wives. They delight exceedingly in the caresses of the females and count their affection worthy of much more demonstrative return." I liked the sound of these sea lions. They were good mothers too, for Steller observed with some tenderness how, "At eventide the mothers with the young go forth into the sea and swim quietly near the shore. When the pups get tired of swimming they are wont to perch upon the backs of their mothers and rest." I liked them even more.

And though they could be as fierce as lions, Steller noted that "they fear so much the very sight of man that if they see one even at a distance they hurry in headlong flight from land to sea. But if, when they are sound asleep, a man comes near and wakes them with a blow from his stick or by a loud noise, they take to flight at once, panting like a furnace, their limbs shaking so with fear that they cannot control them." My heart sank. There he was, at it again, striking out with his wretched stick like some psychotic Noah. I mean, who wakes a peacefully sleeping creature with a blow or a loud noise? He also noted, however, that "they are hard to overcome and fight most viciously when cornered." Under such circumstances, with "all possibility of flight removed, he turns upon his enemy with a great roar, shakes his head in wrath, rages, cries out, and puts even the bravest man to flight. The first time that I tried this experiment was almost the last of me." Once again I found myself rooting for the creature rather than the scientist.

But Steller also captured their gentleness, describing how "they low like cows and the young bleat like lambs, and while I was among them it seemed as if I were playing the part of a herdsman mingling with cattle." And "although these animals are exceedingly fearful of man, yet I have seen them grow used to him and become tame by meeting him frequently without injury... I lived a season in the midst of a herd of them, and for six whole days... they watched my fire and observed all that I did, and so no longer ran away even when I walked among them and took their pups and killed them and examined them." And thus is the pastoral idyll broken by the cold and savage hand of science.

There was also, inevitably, the passage on hunting, for "the blubber, as well as the sweet flesh, is well flavoured and highly prized, and the gelatinous flippers are considered a prime delicacy... The fat of the young is sweeter than mutton tallow and resembles the marrow of leg bones." The ferocity of sea lions meant that the Kamchatkan tribes never hunted them at sea, but sneaked up on the animals sleeping on the shore and harpooned them with iron or bone spears. Thus tethered, the animal was then shot with arrows or stabbed until, "when its strength is gone," it could be finished off with clubs. Alternatively, the poor creature would be shot with poisoned arrows and though it might retreat to the ocean, it was "compelled by the poison to return to shore, for the salt sea water increases the pain of the wounds; and then, if the place is a convenient one, he is stabbed, or otherwise, if left to himself, he will die of the poison in twenty-four hours." Ah, the importance that a place of slaughter be convenient. As for the killers, Steller recorded that "all who have the skill and daring to hunt this beast, and who have killed many, are held in great honour by their fellows, and are regarded as heroes. Thus the love of glory, as well as the excellence of the flesh, turns many to the hunt and makes them ready for so hazardous an enterprise."

I tore myself away from the tales of such heroic deeds. Glancing up, I saw the coffee-drinker staring at me. His smile morphed into a yawn which he half-stifled with his hand.

"You know your lips move a little when you read? Is it a good book?"

"It's interesting."

"You could not sleep?"

"No."

"Then you did the right thing. It's better to get up than stay in bed and stress about it."

"Are you speaking from experience?"

"Sure. I spend many nights awake. I'm nocturnal, I'm used to it. I work a lot at night."

"You must miss a lot, all that happens by day."

"You miss some, but you also see a lot. There's a whole bunch of stuff goes on only in the dark. My name is Raphael," he said, extending his soft, olive-coloured hand.

"Elizabeth. Nice to meet you."

It turned out that Raphael was Israeli. He spoke of having business interests in Europe and America, and houses in Tel Aviv and Maryland. He cruised a lot. His grandparents were Holocaust survivors from Odessa and Riga, and his father had fought in the Sinai during the Yom Kippur war. He had studied international relations at UCLA and had done his military service in the West Bank. When I asked how it felt to live in a pariah state he just laughed and said that it felt good to live in a regional superpower. He told me he supported a two-state solution to the Palestinian issue but that there was nobody on the other side willing to negotiate in good faith. "The Palestinians must let go of the past and accept the reality of the present. For sure, defeat is bad, but to keep hold of victimhood is worse. If you cling to that, you keep losing forever and cannot move forward."

"Have the Jews let go of Holocaust victimhood yet?"

He laughed. "Not yet, but maybe we should. Maybe we will when the last of the survivors is gone. But it's not the same. The Shoa was a loss on an individual level, of course."

"Six million individual levels."

"Precisely. And all the family connections multiply that number many times. But you know, beyond the millions of individuals, as a group it defined our place in the modern world. Transformed it, actually. Whisper it softly, but it's hard to give up a blank cheque when your name is on it. Hard to give it up even if you no longer need the money."

"So the Arabs should just accept the loss of land that's been theirs for thousands of years? Accept it and move on?"

"Land changes hands all the time, Lizbet. Bought, sold, conquered, bequeathed."

"Stolen?"

"In the space of a couple of generations we've made the desert bloom. That can't be reversed, it shouldn't be. It would be a denial of progress. But there are solutions, deals that could be done if they would just sort their shit out and negotiate instead of trying to kill us all the time."

"You make it sound easy."

"I didn't say it's easy. But it starts by accepting reality. They don't have to like the reality, but they have to accept what's happened. They have to make that choice: stop clinging to victimhood and start moving on. And you know what, it's a smart choice, even if you have to give shit up, because you're choosing life instead of death."

I went back and slept for a while, calm and easy as the dawn rose silent all around me. I woke refreshed and breakfasted on my fruit basket. I ate even though I was worried that I was putting on weight. There were no scales in the bathroom—for the same reason that there are no clocks in a Vegas casino—but I could feel the freshly piling pounds. I checked the ship's TV channel as I demolished the last of the pineapple. We were crossing the Tyrrhenian Sea at 20 knots, with calm water and a light south-easterly wind.

I was going to swim but by the time I got up there it was too crowded. So, I donned my sneakers and hit the teak, pounding circuits of the Promenade Deck, travelling at a brisk walking speed, 3.3 laps to the mile. I was on my fifth, breathing hard, when I ran into Horace, who was descending from the Eye of Zeus, binoculars hanging around his bony neck. We went for coffee in the Magellan Lounge, where Horace enthused about a pair of ospreys that he had been watching. "Marvellous birds... so easy in their action, such grace and elegance, economy of movement... It's as though they hang in the air utterly without effort, like clouds. They have a natural authority, a majesty. Remember what Shakespeare wrote in *Coriolanus*, '...he'll be to Rome/As is the osprey to the fish, who takes it/By sovereignty of nature." But I though not of *Coriolanus*, but of Yeats's Pre-Raphaelite masterpiece *The Wanderings of Oisin*, where he wrote of "the grey wandering osprey, Sorrow."

Horace was remarkably chipper, and when I commented on his cheery mood he said, "The sun is shining, I'm sitting with my favourite niece, and we are approaching the Holy City." When I pointed out that I was his only niece, he called it a mere statistic that did not affect the sentiment. "Athens," he said, "is the cradle of Western civilisation, and Judaism its spiritual root, but the two were fused in the furnace of Rome, which then exported its achievement via its roads, its armies and its trade routes, throughout the world. Rome...," he paused, his eyes raised slightly, "Rome is the great teat from which we are all still suckling."

I felt that I was nibbling rather than suckling, but I almost choked on my almond croissant when he mentioned, so casually as to be premeditated, that he had promised Selene he would show her the sights. "Just imagine," he said with genuine astonishment, "she's never seen the Pantheon, or the Forum, or the Sistine Chapel!" He invited me to "tag along" if I wished. I told him maybe, but that I was thinking of staying on board. I had seen what Rome had to offer. What I didn't say was that I felt slighted, demoted to second-class status by a second-rate nightclub singer. Even to myself, I didn't admit that. I processed my resentment as concern, concern for Horace. After all, he was old, wealthy, unworldly, and she was what? Young (comparatively), ambitious (probably), avaricious (almost certainly). There was a part of me that thought, okay, let's see her put up with the outbursts and the outrages, the coughing fits, the bizarre behaviour, the unsteady aim, the semi-autistic disregard for normal social mores. Let her guide him over the city's streets, the uneven cobbles of the day. She was welcome to it, for the idea of being a chaperone to an unleashed Horace at large in Rome filled me with horror. And yet I felt deeply irritated at my demotion. I felt it even as I smiled and said how nice it would be for her to see sites of such significance in the company of so knowledgeable a guide. Horace purred.

I went to get another croissant to suckle on and when I returned he was already working on an itinerary for the visit, musing about how best to guide the aging ingénue through two millennia of culture and history in the space of eight hours. I picked at my pastry and wondered what to do with a day of unanticipated emptiness. I tried to feel excited, but as I watched the people come and go, sit, talk, consume, and leave, I felt only a draining of energy, a creeping sense of sadness moving over me like a plume of lengthening shadow.

Horace completed his list and read it to me. I endorsed it with feigned enthusiasm. I characterised it as comprehensive but exhausting, and promised that I would let him know if I wanted to join the shore party. He looked at me with concern and asked if I was feeling okay.

"Fine," I said, "I just don't really know what I'm doing here."

"Where?"

"On this cruise," I said with exasperation.

"It's a gift. I thought you deserved a holiday. Some luxury and indulgence. The brochures say that this company's mission is to pamper its guests to death."

"And then what? When it's all over I return to my ordinary life? Isn't that a bit like giving a terminally ill kid a trip to Disneyland?"

"Is it better that the poor child does not get the holiday?"

"I'm just not used to being pampered."

"Lizzy, it's not hard to adjust to. Adjusting up is never difficult, it's adjusting down that's the killer. And that brings me to the purpose of your presence here, the core of my gift. It's not just about being pampered, it's about becoming accustomed to being pampered. And therein lies an important lesson."

"Which is what?"

He laughed, and the laugh turned into a harsh coughing fit. He took some breaths, dabbing his lips with a napkin. "It wouldn't be a lesson if I told you." He took a sip of water. "The most profound lessons always come from experience. You have to discover it yourself."

"Is it a good lesson?"

"It's a necessary one."

"How will I know when I've learned it?"

"You'll know. One day you will think something, or say something and in that moment you will have a flash of insight and know you've learned it."

"You talk in riddles, Uncle. I think it makes you feel in control. You like that, don't you?"

"If it makes things easier, Lizzy, think of your presence here as an indulgence to an old man. An ill, old man whom they would not otherwise permit on board. And I did so want to see the Indian Ocean one last time."

"Ill?"

"Yes, I was required to have either a companion or a nurse. Those were the cruise company's terms for my passage. I have cancer you see. Adenocarcinoma of the lung, to be precise, though it's not just in my lungs now. I'm at the end of the journey with it. It's metastasised."

"What about treatment?"

"I had treatment, but that's over now. I have secondary tumours, lots of them. It's beyond treatment."

"My God. I'm so sorry, Uncle."

"There's no need, Lizzy, really. My life has been long and has encompassed much happiness. And I am happy now, being with you. And this voyage is a wonderful way to say goodbye." He smiled. "Think of it as my trip to Disneyland."

"What's the prognosis?"

"Six months max. Probably nearer three. This is my swansong, you see. After this voyage I shall go home to die."

I hugged him gently, aware of the shape of bones, sharp beneath his clothes. "I'm here for you, Uncle. Just tell me what you need."

"Dear girl." He smiled. "There's really no need for sadness. Listen, I have to take care of a few things, but let's meet for tea. Shall we say four?"

I watched him saunter off with that stiff, jaunty walk. It seemed impossible that he would be gone forever in a matter of weeks. I did a few more laps of the Promenade, but my heart was no longer in it. I went back to my room and showered and checked email.

Later, Horace and I took tea on his terrace. Monique served and then withdrew. We sat for a few minutes, the silence broken only by Horace's ragged cough. Eventually, he looked at me attentively and spoke in a steady and unemotional voice.

"There's something I should tell you, Lizzy. I've been thinking hard about the past in these last days, revisiting times and places that I don't much inhabit. I was thinking particularly about Virgil's death. I might have unintentionally misled you. You see, I think I was there, when it happened..."

"You *think*?"

"Well it's complicated. I was there, but not present. I mean I didn't see it, which is the same as not being there, really. I was in another room, upstairs in fact. I heard the shot. But I didn't know it was a shot. It wasn't a ringing sound, it was more a loud, flat slap, like if you slam a heavy book down on a table. I didn't think too much about it. I was upstairs in my room. I was getting my things together as I was going back to Cambridge that evening. I'd only come home on impulse. I mean it wasn't planned, I just needed to pick up some books. I didn't think anything about that noise until I was set to leave. That's when I came down downstairs and found him. He was in the library, just like I described to you. He'd been dead for a while. There was nothing I could do for him. I left everything as it was and caught my train back to college."

"You *left* him there? Dead. Your own brother?"

"I know it doesn't sound good. That's why I didn't mention it before. But you have to understand the context, Lizzy. There was nothing I could do for him, nothing to be done. And I didn't want to be involved. I mean I wasn't involved, but I would have been involved if I had been the one to call the police. I was in shock, I didn't really think about what I was doing. It was shocking because it was so utterly senseless."

"Did you argue with him? Before it happened."

"Look. It didn't just happen. He chose it. He did it. He picked up the gun and put it to his head and pulled the trigger."

"I thought you weren't in the room."

"I wasn't, but you can surmise. It's clear what happened. How else would he have done it?"

"Why did you conceal that you were there?"

"Because I wasn't there. Not really. I was just in the same house. Besides, I was respecting his privacy. And I didn't want to complicate matters. It was neater if he was in the house on his own. It made no material difference, really, it just made things easier, the narrative, the circumstances, it made them neater. I didn't want to be involved, because I wasn't involved. It was his decision. I was upstairs. I didn't see it. That's the same as not being there."

"Did you shoot him?"

"No, of course not. How can you even ask me that? Virgil shot himself."

"Why?"

"Don't keep searching for a reason. There was no reason. Yes, he had some debts but they had been covered by Father. And it wasn't to do with depression or shame (though he had plenty to be ashamed about). He shot himself because he didn't care. That's what you have to understand about Virgil. He didn't care about anyone, not even himself by the end. You know, it's like Mayakovsky said, after his fellow poet Sergei Yesenin cut his wrists, wrote a suicide note in his blood, and then hanged himself. Mayakovsky wrote 'In this life it is not difficult to die/ It is more difficult to live.' And then he went on to prove it by putting a bullet through his own head five years later. It's like Camus said, 'Suicide is prepared within the silence of the heart.' That's how Virgil's heart was, and always had been. Silent. In that sense it was a logical suicide. Read Dostoevsky. Man invented God to be able to live without killing himself, but if you don't believe in God, or anything in His place, then it's all utterly pointless. Why hang on, having to suffer the slings and arrows, the whips and scorns of time? You might as well put a bullet in your head and get it over and done with. Cash in your chips and get out. And that's what Virgil did. Simple as that."

THIRTEEN

I woke early and pondered the nature of inheritance. To inherit is to be the recipient of a legacy: something unearned that is beyond a gift, something traditionally bestowed by virtue of one's lineage, one's accidental place within a generational sequence that retains and recycles wealth. Therefore, you receive with that inheritance an obligation not to squander the legacy but to pass it on, ideally enhanced, to the next generation. But not everyone honours their obligations.

Aside from DNA, does inheritance exist in any living being other than humans? There are creatures that use tools, but none that pass them down to their offspring; life skills yes, but not property. There is hierarchy within a pack, but leadership is established and maintained by force. The principal reigns until overthrown by a challenger; authority is transferred by combat, it is not bequeathed.

Our closest ancestors, chimps and bonobos, don't bequeath property. Is the explanation simply that they have no possessions worth inheriting, or is that just the skewed perspective of a twenty-first century materialistic human? Certainly the notion of inheritance is embedded for humans. In Genesis, God promises Abraham and his descendants an inheritance—the Promised Land of milk and honey. And perhaps that's the point. It was when humans made the transition from hunter-gatherers to farmers that we began amassing stuff that was worth passing on, principally land. And as economies evolve, money replaces land as the symbol of wealth but the principle of inheritance remains unchanged. And though it is not specifically patriarchal, it underpins patriarchy by subjugating women, controlling their reproduction in order to guarantee bloodlines, because only thus can the paternity of those who inherit be guaranteed.

Prior to the voyage, the possibility of inheriting wealth from Horace had never been more than a passing daydream, too remote to be worth the effort of serious fantasy. But this had changed with the recent realisation of the extent of Horace's wealth and the possibility that he could be seriously ill. The change was sort of inevitable. I mean, I have never considered myself materialistic, but believe me, if you find yourself in a position where you are one of a limited number of candidates likely to inherit a fortune, you cannot help but speculate. It's impossible not to. Like it's a hot day and you walk by chance under a tree that's about to drop a giant fruit; it is impossible not to wonder how tasty it might be and how much it could alleviate your savage thirst. Except the tree has agency and can toss its fruit in the direction of any one of a number of passersby. And not all that is tossed reaches its intended recipient. But if Horace were truly dying, to whom would he leave his fortune? Maya, his mysterious Australian companion, or me, his only surviving close family member? Either of us must be in with a good shout. Who else was there? Selene? Did that explain her encouragement of an old man's folly? My mother? Unlikely, and anyway I had power of attorney so it would mean me, in effect. Of course, there was always the wild card, the possibility of Horace leaving his entire estate to a wombat reserve or an orphan-kangaroo adoption service.

As with so much that surrounded Horace, the position was infuriatingly opaque. Was he really about to die? Did he really have an unsigned Will in his safe? I knew, even before I fully acknowledged it, that I needed to steal a peek behind the door in the wall. When I did admit it, I framed it as a necessary means of obtaining an insight into the past. After all, he had documents and photographs in there, boxes of evidence relating to a past that was mine as well as his. I could wait patiently and hope that he might show me more, or I could take matters into my own hands. It might answer my questions surrounding Virgil's death and, possibly, provide certainty as to my line of descent. But though I framed the matter of the safe's contents in terms of understanding the past, I recognise now that there was also an issue that related to the present and the future. Maybe I knew it at the time, but thought that it was okay. I mean, how could it be unreasonable to want to be sure of Horace's state of health, or to seek reassurance that he was not being pressured into signing over his money—wealth accumulated by generations of my ancestors—to a nightclub singer?

My plan, if it could be worthy of so grand a title, was to cry off the Rome expedition and use the opportunity of Horace's absence to have a little snoop in his rooms. I did not know the combination of the safe, but it would be a chance to scope it out and it was just possible that he had been lax about locking it or had written the combination down somewhere. In the event, however, my chance came sooner than expected. I was having an early breakfast with Horace on the morning after we had docked in Civitavecchia. He broke the news to me that Selene had been forced to pull out of the excursion to Rome at the last minute. Naturally, I expressed my sorrow over the missed opportunity to meet her, and said that I would be pleased to accompany him in her place. Later, as Horace ate, he announced that he had forgotten the scarlet pocket square that he intended to wear that day. Having finished my toast, I offered to fetch it from his room and he handed me his key without a moment's hesitation. Even as I galloped towards his suite, I was amazed at how, sometimes, fate conspires to assist in so roundabout a manner.

I made straight for the closet. I say closet, but it was actually a small dressing room that connected the sitting room to the bathroom. It was impeccably tidy, with the crimson handkerchief laid out on the dressing table just as Horace had said. I opened the wardrobe and checked the safe, which was locked. The shelves and drawers offered nothing but clothes and a row of neatly arranged and highly polished shoes. I went through to the bathroom and then to the bedroom, where the huge bed was unmade, though Horace's pyjamas were carefully folded on the pillow. A cursory check of the surfaces revealed nothing of interest. I moved on to the sitting room, which was perfectly ordered apart from a few scattered books.

A battered, brown canvas bag lay on the sofa. One of the things that I have learnt in my life is that transgressive behaviour involves a sequence of small transgressions, each a little more significant than its predecessor. Thus, with every cataclysm, there is always a debris field of escalation that leads to the corpses. Entering Horace's suite had been legitimate; searching the dressing room had been inquisitive; casing the rooms had amounted to snooping; but to rifle someone's personal bag was of a different order of surveillance; that was a violation. I approached. The top flap was in place but provocatively insecure, wantonly unbuckled. Perhaps I touched it, perhaps I would have flipped it open, but at that moment there was the sound of a key card in the door and a cleaner entered with the singsong cry of "Housekeeping." I smiled at her, held up the red square of silk, and then left her to her duties, pushing past the trolley in the corridor outside.

I was still cursing the timing of the cleaner's intervention when I got back to Horace. He seemed agitated, keen to get going. He stuffed the square into the top pocket of his jacket and headed towards the debarkation point. I hurried after him and tried to return his room key. "It's okay, you keep it, it's a spare," he said. "Help yourself to booze. They stock my drinks cabinet faster than I can empty it."

Rome was crowded; hot, grubby, airless and—as always—utterly ravishing. We stood awestruck beneath the coffered concrete dome of the Pantheon with its central oculus, a staring eye more than 40 metres above our inclined faces, unsecured against the sky, open to God. Almost two thousand years old and it was still the world's largest unsupported concrete dome. And it doesn't matter how many times you stand beneath that vault of heaven, its power remains beyond the pull of words.

Afterwards, we shambled out through its giant portico and fumbled our way through the Forum, with our every step seeming to scuff across the tracks of long-dead paladins. Horace was distant and brooding.

Lunch was a subdued affair and after a couple of conversational false starts we lapsed into a silence that endured despite our finishing a bottle of white wine. In the afternoon we gawped through the Sistine Chapel before going on to the crushing grandeur of St Peter's. I spent a long time staring at the Pietà, the most beautiful sculpture in the world, the only piece of art that Michelangelo bothered to sign. A beautiful Mary, uncorrupted by time or age, cradling her dead son with a tenderness, an aching sadness, and a serenity of acceptance almost too heartbreaking to look upon. It was hard to look but impossible to leave, and even as the tour parties ebbed and flowed around me, I stood before her incorruptible purity, marvelling at her dignity, her strength.

Horace found me there, transfixed, and after a moment's silence he put his bony arm around me, light as a bird wing, my head resting against the jagged angle of his shoulder.

"She looks good for a woman who would have been fifty or older at the time of his death and who'd been around the block a few times. But it's an incredible thing. You know, Lizzy, there was a mad Hungarian geologist who emigrated to Oz about the same time as me, Laszlo Toth his name was. He walked in here in May 1972, and stood right here, where we're standing, normal as you like. And then suddenly he started shouting like a lunatic, yelling that he was Jesus, and jumped up onto the statue and began laying into it with a rock hammer. The bastard got in fifteen blows before they got him on the ground. By then he's knocked off her left arm, smashed off her nose, and damaged an eye. He spent a couple of years in a loony bin and then the Italians deported him back to Oz. I always kept an eye open for him. I tell you, Lizzy, if I'd ever met the bastard I'd have happily used a rock hammer on his head. And that's why the statue's behind glass now, restored but beyond reach. How can you give people beauty, when there's always going to be an asshole who wants to take a hammer to it? And I'll tell you another thing. In the confusion, most of the fragments of broken marble were picked up and stolen as souvenirs. Some were returned later but not her nose. They had to carve a new one by taking marble from her back where the cut wouldn't be seen. If they'd used new stone it wouldn't have matched. Imagine, someone, somewhere still has Mary's nose, a piece of marble shaped by the hands of the greatest sculptor in human history. And sometimes they must pick it up and think that it looks better in the palm of their thieving, bastard hand than it did when it was a part of her perfect, white face. In other words, their private possession is worth more to them than any amount of shared beauty. That calculation alone suggests to me that the human species is irredeemable."

"Maybe they don't have it anymore. It's almost half a century ago. The person who picked it up is probably dead by now. Maybe they left it in a drawer and it was thrown away when someone cleared out their apartment. Someone who didn't know what it was."

"Nah, I reckon they're either still alive and hoarding it, or else they passed it on. If you have something of value it's natural to want to choose what happens to it. You pass it on."

"Do you?"

"Yeah, it's human nature. But it doesn't change the equation. It just means that the thieving bastard who's now hoarding it, and no doubt gets it out from time to time for a secret slobber, is younger than the original bastard who looted it."

"But they're not directly involved in the original crime."

"Yeah they are, of course they are. The moment they inherited it they were involved in the original crime. That's how possession works. And inheritance."

I was still thinking about Mary as our car battled through the chaos of traffic, taking us back to the ship. We passed the Colosseum and Horace asked if I wanted to stop. I shook my head. "Nah, me neither," he said. "It's impressive, no doubt about that, but it gives me the creeps. I've never walked around that site without thinking of all those animals that were butchered there for public entertainment. We'll never know how many, but it's got to be tens of thousands. Maybe a lot more. They didn't matter, so nobody bothered counting. Imagine those poor, frightened creatures—lions, giraffes, rhinos—dragged all the way from Africa to be maimed and slaughtered in the sand of that hateful place for the pleasure of the sweating crowd."

Horace sat back in his seat and closed his eyes. I thought of Mary, with her amputated arm and broken face, sitting serenely, patient with her pain, blemished but unspoiled, her core still beautiful. And then she was restored, made once more intact, intact with her secret, unseen wound.

Back at the ship we found that we had been invited to a 6pm drinks reception hosted by Captain Philippe D'Azio in the small clubroom, next door to the library. I told Horace that I would see him there, and then we went our separate ways, returning to our rooms to rest, shower and change into evening wear.

The reception was the first outing for my ivory dress. When I arrived, there were about thirty people present, plus the captain and a couple of senior officers, standing in knots of conversation whilst trays of fizz and canapés did the rounds. The steward on the door presented me to Captain D'Azio, who exuded the sort of polished charm of a man who had come to accept the necessity of social duties. He looked surprisingly frail, his skin tanned but his posture a little stooped. He seemed to ask everyone the same 'How are you enjoying the voyage?' question, and then dealt patiently with inquiries that ranged from "How do you know where you are when there are no landmarks at sea?" (Sat Nav, apparently), through to "Have you ever seen any bizarre sea creatures?" (whales, sharks, dolphins, flying fish, and atmospheric mirages, but no sea monsters. I felt Steller would have been disappointed, but then Steller would probably have wanted to kill them). I asked him how difficult it was to manoeuvre such a huge vessel into port. He said it was a lot like parking a large car and was a skill that became better with practice. He wasn't exactly patronising, but I wondered if he would have given that answer to a man. Still, at least he didn't compare it to manoeuvring a large pram in a crowded shopping mall. He went on to say that in Civitavecchia it was compulsory to "park" the ship's port side (which he helpfully explained was the left) alongside the dock, as it made it faster for ships to cast off and leave the harbour in the event of an emergency evacuation, without having to turn around.

I could see Horace across the room. He was talking loudly and was looking somewhat florid. I waved and he nodded, without breaking stride. He was telling a story about nineteenth-century gold miners in the remote Australian outback. In their makeshift camps water was more valuable than gold. It was in such short supply that it was used for drinking rather than personal hygiene. And one miner, desperate to wash, took the opportunity of an approaching storm cloud to strip naked and lather himself up with soap, and then stood in the middle of the camp awaiting the rain. But the wind changed and the cloud dispersed without a single drop having fallen. The unfortunate miner was reduced to scraping off the dried soap with a razor. "It took the poor old bugger hours and cost him all of his body hair and a good few chunks of skin," said Horace, with his distinctive high-pitched laugh, half cackle, half wheeze. I had a momentary image of the miner, disfigured and bleeding beneath the public gaze, and I thought again about the silent, white figure of Mary.

I found myself chatting with a trans-couple who were celebrating their marriage. The bride, Joyce Neumann, was a tall MtF blonde, who was rather beautiful but a little standoffish, apparently regarding my cis-gender status as an unearned privilege. Her husband, Jimmy Daty, a small but gym-honed black guy (FtM), had a great sense of humour, perhaps necessary when you're a ball of muscle adorned with a wispy beard that looked suspiciously like transplanted pubic hair. But the more I laughed at his jokes, the more pissed off Joyce became.

Then Horace joined us and things quickly deteriorated. I had no sooner done introductions than Joyce announced to Horace that they were "both trans-gendered" but he heard it as "both band members" and caused immediate consternation by asking if it was just the two of them, or whether there were more. Then he inquired, with genuine interest, if they would be performing for us on the main stage or in the smaller Celestial Lounge, saying how much he'd like to see them in action. After I had spent an excruciating minute or two untangling the confusion, Horace engaged the subject with his usual fearlessness, bolstered by the enthusiasm of one who is making amends for earlier failings. It wasn't plain sailing, however, as he struggled to remember the direction of travel of each of them and made repeated pronoun blunders which Joyce pounced on and sharply corrected. Then, in what I honestly believe was a misguided spirit of scientific inquiry, he began to ask about "the surgical state of play down there," and responded to the ensuing awkwardness by trying to phrase his questions with greater anatomical precision.

Horace's "mis-gendering" wasn't helped by the tangled soup of pronouns, involving ze, hir or zir, hirs or zirs, hirself or zirself. I mean, I'm a liberal woman, naturally sympathetic to discriminated-against minorities, but there is something truly irritating about the spectacle of trans-women (many of whom still have penises for God's sake) demanding from the rest of us (many of whom have never been in possession of said organ) a list of concessions that in some instances are obviously not conducive to women's rights and interests. Yet the nature of the times decrees that they are unquestioningly pandered to, and the demands—as illustrated by the carnage of the pronoun battlefield—increase with every concession. Pronoun proliferation and the right to insist on others using whatever newly-invented nonsensical term you can come up with, looks much like a small group of noisy people, self-appointed spokespersons of their group, shouting "jump" in order to enjoy the power-thrill of everyone else replying "how high?" I'm not trans-phobic, I believe in diversity, and I believe in the right to determine your own gender, but I object to being lectured by entitled, freshly-minted and surgically incomplete "women", who are looking for offence and demanding that the entire world adapt to their every whim. And I particularly object to being lectured by them on the issue of being a woman. I mean, I've been female from before I was born. That gives you, in my view, a unique insight, a perspective and experience that should count for something. Being a woman isn't a theory or a set of feelings, it's not a state that is chosen or even surgically assigned. It's way more fundamental than that.

The thing is though, as always with Horace, it was not easy to tell if he was trying and failing, or simply taking the piss. In any case, whichever it was, it turned out that he was not trying hard enough for Joyce, and later he stopped trying altogether.

"You've got to accept that the world has changed," she told him. "It's evolution, adapt or die. So just accept it. Yolo."

"Yolo?"

"It's an abbreviation, Pops. Y-O-L-O."

"Oh, you mean an acronym. What's it stand for? Young otters lose organs? Yanks only like onanists? Your orangutan loves only your own little orifice. There," he said triumphantly. "That's a double yoyo."

"Yolo, Uncle. It stands for 'you only live once'."

"Amen to that," said Horace.

"Look, we live in a non-binary world now," went on Joyce. "It's gender-fluid. What don't you understand about that?"

"Gender fluid?" Horace frowned. "You mean like sperm or vaginal secretions?"

"What?"

"Well I'm familiar with those sort of gender fluids, obviously. You know, genital secretions." His voice seemed to have risen a notch and I could hear the hush sliding out across the room from our epicentre. "Like Cowper's fluid—pre-cum, you'd probably know it as—or vaginal lubrication."

"Uncle!" I hissed.

"Or do you mean gender fluid as in fluid that you actually rub on the genitals? Is that a post-operative thing? I'm not too familiar with it, though I did have a nasty experience with engine oil once. What does this fluid do and do you have to wear protective equipment—you know, gloves, goggles and whatnot—when applying it?"

"Fuhgeddaboutit Pops."

"Wait, I get it. You mean fluid as in something that's in a state of flux. The poor old genitals can't make up their minds. A sort of block and tackle conundrum. They've been whipped from pillar to post and now they're unstable, always changing from one to the other?"

"You're the fucking unstable one, you boof." She took Jimmy's arm, "Come on Hon, I'm not wasting time with this white, mad, rich, cis, geriatric asshole."

"Goodness, racist, mentalist, classist, sexist and ageist. And all in one sentence. Madam, I salute you, you've got some balls. Bit hard on the asshole though, but I guess you're used to that."

"Fuck you, granddad. I know your angle, but you're wasting your time hitting on me. I'm not into necrophilia."

"That's not really my thing either. Though I must confess, where I come from we do like to crack open a cold one from time to time."

"Horace!" I meant it to be an urgent aside but it came out as an anguished groan. It made no difference either way, there was no holding him.

"But I'd draw a line at you. I wouldn't hit on you if you were the last person on Earth. God alone knows what kind of muddled malformation you've got going on beneath that shapeless tent you're wearing, but you'd have to be deranged to think that anyone in their right mind would want to find out. The scar tissue alone would make a sane person vomit all over you."

Joyce lunged at him. I stepped between them, just in time to receive the contents of her wine glass full in my face. I spluttered, Horace laughed, and Joyce turned on her heel and stalked out, followed by a scampering Jimmy who looked back at us with bewildered anger. Horace dabbed my face and shoulders with his handkerchief but I pushed him away. A steward came to assist with a clean napkin.

"Just a minor mishap," chimed Horace, his voice sounding way too loud in the silent room. "Still, lucky it wasn't red."

FOURTEEN

After the wine-throwing debacle, I went to change. I put on the black evening dress, as Horace had insisted we eat in the dining room. He was already seated when I rejoined him. It was the second shift and we were alone at our table. I wondered if our isolation was purely a matter of chance.

"Have some of this," he said. "It's a 1964 Saint-Emilion, an excellent vintage. There are so many fakes out there but this is the real deal and it's terrific." He filled my glass generously. "Taste the fruit, savour its rich, ripe opulence, all those silky tannins from the sun-soaked soil of France. Do you know, Karl Marx loved a decent claret. Taste it, Lizzy, there's history and geography right there in your glass."

"Horace, I'm angry." I tried to speak calmly, as though explaining to a child.

"You're still cracking the shits over a little spat with that show pony? I'm telling you, Lizzy, that Tranny's got a kangaroo loose in his top paddock, her top paddock, whoever the fuck the top paddock belongs to."

"Are you trying to be offensive or are you just plastered?"

"Neither. I just don't like the word-police. They're destroying the complexity of a rich and beautiful language on nothing more than a selfish whim. And they're suppressing free speech. The way it's going, soon you won't be allowed to even think some things, never mind actually say them."

"That's got nothing to do with what you just said. It was fucking offensive. You'll have to apologise, to the Captain and to that couple."

"To the Trannies? No way."

"Will you stop calling them that."

"You ever head of the *Eudyptula minor*, Lizzy?"

"You know I haven't. And stop trying to change the subject."

"Just hear me out. It's the smallest species of penguin in the world."

"Jesus, Horace...."

"Nah, just listen. They're cute little fellows, about a foot tall, blue and white, with slate-grey beaks and ears, and little pink feet with black soles. They're hanging on despite loss of habitat and being killed by overfishing, oil spills, plastic pollution, dogs, cats, foxes and a dozen other predators including bastard humans who murder them just for fun, for sport, without going to the bother of building a Colosseum. In New Zealand they're called Blue Penguins, but in Australia we used to call them Fairy Penguins, a good name for them because they're so small and delicate, sort of magical. But recently it was decided by someone in an office somewhere that you can't call them Fairy Penguins any more because it could be construed as offensive. Not to fairies, of course, but to gays and trannies. And, although it's okay for those types to use the term fairy to describe themselves, to appropriate it, we can't use it for the penguins any more in case those new fairies are offended. So now the penguins are called Small Penguins. How prosaic is that? So tell me, Lizzy, which world would you like to live in, one where there are Fairy Penguins or one where there are just small penguins?"

I never got to answer that question, although I've pondered it since then. I've pondered it and I'd opt for a world where words don't have to be appropriated or reclaimed, and where sexual preferences are irrelevant, where they're neither despised nor trumpeted as a defining feature of a self. A world where flying fairies, and gay fairies and fairy penguins could all peacefully cohabit. I never got to answer it because at that moment the waiter arrived to take our order. He greeted us, starched and smiling, stiff as a buttress.

"Tonight's special is genuine Japanese Wagyu steak. It's beautifully marbled, exceptionally tender and perfectly prepared to your individual preference by our expert chefs. I would most definitely recommend it."

"Would you indeed," said Horace. "You do know that the level of cognitive dissonance required to sanction the taking of a sentient creature's life, merely because you like the taste of its flesh, is beyond comprehension?"

"I'm sorry sir?"

"I am too. Sorry for the animal, sorry for the genocide. I can't stop it, but we do not countenance it. We don't eat dead animals."

"What my uncle means is that he is a vegetarian. I am not. Please tell me about the steak."

"Is it dead?" demanded Horace.

"Yes sir."

"Slaughtered on board ship was it, the poor beast?"

"No sir. All supplies were taken on before we sailed."

"Must be rotting by now then. Full of maggots I shouldn't wonder."

"They have refrigerators, Uncle."

"It is Kobe beef, from *Tajima-Gyu* cattle that have been born and raised in Hyogo prefecture," said the waiter. "It is a premium product with a marbling ratio above level six. The cattle were fed on organic food and distilled water. They were also given beer and sake, and massaged every day."

"Good," I said. "I approve of animal welfare. Meat should be a seldom eaten luxury that is expensive. The price should reflect a high level of care for the animal." Ah, I can hear my voice still, clear and sure in those days of ethical confidence, the age of the conscientious carnivore.

Horace leapt straight in. "Don't be such a Dill. They feed it like that and massage it not because it's nice for the animal, but so that it's more tender when eaten."

"Does it matter what the motive is if the net result is a happier life for the cow?"

"Dear God, Lizzy, that's not the issue. It's not a question of motive. It's not even a question of whether the poor beast was treated well or not..."

"But it's better that it was well treated, surely?"

"So if the Jews had been transported to Auschwitz in luxury sleeping cars rather than cattle trucks, and been given deluxe accommodation in the camp with fine dining and daily massages before being gassed and incinerated, that would have been an improvement over the historical reality? Would it have mitigated to any degree whatsoever the absolute unacceptability of what was being done?"

"That's offensive. You know it is. There's no..."

"What's offensive is industrialised genocide, the construction and operation of slaughter factories. The conditions of the soon-to-be slaughtered are immaterial. You are focusing on the irrelevant and, in doing so, missing the real issue, the unforgivable offence against Nature, against Morality, against God."

"You don't believe in God."

"You don't know what I believe in."

"It's served with asparagus and beetroot salad," said the waiter quietly.

"Is it now. Well throw it overboard. Give the poor creature a decent burial at sea. She'll have the soufflé, like me. Two soufflés and a large salad to share."

"I'll have the steak," I said firmly to the waiter. "Medium rare, please."

"Have you forgotten who signs the cheques on this trip? She'll have the soufflé. Two soufflés."

"Fuck you," I said. "I'm out of here."

As I stormed away from the table I heard Horace say, "Make that just one soufflé. And another bottle of the claret."

I say stormed, but in reality I walked with a slow determination. For one thing, I really didn't want to trip over in my smoked glass heels. For another, I harboured the small hope that he might come after me. I was still harbouring it when I reached the Promenade deck, but the cool of the night and the darkness of the ocean served as a rapid corrective. That's the thing about being on a ship, you can storm out as often as you like, but you can't storm far. I stood looking out over the rail, trapped in a mirage of gaudy light and throbbing music, while beyond me was the untouchable freedom of sea and sky. I cried.

An hour later I was in the Magellan Lounge. I'd had a couple of glasses of wine and a club sandwich and was watching the broiling wake of our progress disappearing beyond the lights, a flurry of white bubbles and churn sinking into the past. My anger had faded and what remained was a curiously grey sadness, a sense of pointlessness. I wanted to go home. But I also wanted answers, not just to the past, but also, why was I here and what was Horace playing at? Was he really considering bequeathing money to me? Was he even really ill? I wanted to go home but I also wanted certainty.

On the little platform opposite the bar a beautiful girl, nineteen or twenty, was mid-way through an acoustic set. Her face, partially obscured by her long hair, had a strange intensity, as though oblivious to her surroundings, existing only in the focus of the moment. Her voice was pure and, as I watched her long fingers moving over the frets and strings of her guitar, I wondered how someone could have the courage to be so exposed. This wasn't like performing in a play, protected by costume, and surrounded by other actors and props. This was being utterly alone in the white glare of a searchlight. In between songs she smiled shyly, adjusting the tuning of her strings or moving the capo, sometimes wryly commenting on the circumstances of a song's creation. The realisation that the songs were her own compositions made what she was doing even more astounding—like standing naked in a beam of cold, white light, protected only by your talent. I wondered how it must feel to be that young and fearless, that talented; your whole life still ahead of you with nothing bad having happened yet.

One of her songs, 'Sink in Solitude', had a chorus: "How long are you going to remain content with this life? If you waste time, it'll waste you in the end." Shelley and Shakespeare forged into a single couplet. And when she had finished her set and slipped away, with her guitar slung casually over her shoulder, that refrain continued to echo. After squandering so much, what had I settled for? And why pretend that this marking of time, this waste, amounted to contentment? For here was waste indeed, an expanse of emptiness, amid which I had truly sunk in my solitude.

At that moment Raphael appeared. He asked if he could join me. I hesitated for a moment, unsure if I wanted company. But his smile was warm. The waiter came by and I ordered another glass of wine; Raphael asked for a black coffee.

"Are you okay? You look a little down," he said.

"Yeah, long day, shit evening." I tried to remember how long it had been since anyone had asked me how I was.

"You want to talk about it?"

"There's not much to say. You know, I'm babysitting an elderly relative. That's why I'm on this fucking cruise, and he's not being easy."

He asked if I had been on the shore excursion to Rome. I explained, without too much personal detail, that Horace and I had made a private expedition. We talked about the sites, about the city. He said that he had stayed on board ship all day, but he was evidently familiar with Rome. He said he had studied there after graduating and he made me laugh with tales of the gauche mistakes of an Israeli-American in

Italy. He was easy to talk to and I liked his confidence, his self-deprecating humour. I told him about the evening and he said not to worry. That he had seen far worse behaviour on cruise ships. Boredom, the disinhibiting effect of the sea, excess alcohol and prolonged confinement were all, in his view, contributory factors for displays of behaviour that people would not ordinarily countenance and which, at their worst, were outrageous. Besides, he said, old people could be difficult. He told me about his grandmother, a survivor of Auschwitz-Birkenau, who stockpiled food in her Tel Aviv apartment to such an extent that the family had to remove it surreptitiously from time to time to keep down the smell and make room for new imports.

"Does she eat meat?"

"Sure, if it's kosher. She loves corned beef knishes. Smoked salmon too. But she keeps the blinds closed and has piled mattresses up against the windows. In summer the place stinks and we have to take her out for a day so that the cleaners can go in. It is not possible to reason with her. You know, when she was a child she knew only hunger. Behaviour is fixed early and it becomes more marked with age. I love her, of course, we all do, she's great but she can be impossible. Those are not incompatible states."

"Yeah, I sympathise." I told him a little about my mother.

He listened with concern. "That's tough," he said, putting his hand on my arm. "You know, Lizbet, we don't always get to choose the cards we have to play. The old can be hard work, a burden even, but when they are family, what can you do but care for them? They've earned it."

"The old can certainly be hard work." I felt his touch, light and supportive, but his hand lingered and I wondered if he was hitting on me.

"Hard work for sure. But we have a saying that 'the man who works is blessed'."

"Does that apply to women too, or is it just taken for granted that we work?"

"To all, I think. It's from before the time when you must include every group by name. Work is good. I work a lot. Hence the coffee."

"Well I needed something stronger than coffee tonight." The waiter came by and I ordered another glass. I knew that I had had enough but I wasn't slurring and I felt it was earned. Besides, on a ship you're never far from your bed. Raphael ordered another coffee. "No wonder you don't sleep," I said.

"You lose a lot of time in sleep. Our days are scrolls, we write on them what we will. Life is short and there is so much to see and to do."

"And what do you do?"

"I'm a security consultant, a facilitator if you like. I help people to get things done."

"That sounds suspiciously vague. Like a spy," I said, laughing.

"If I was a spy I would not say it."

"True. Unless it was a double bluff."

"That happens only in movies, Lizbet."

"Okay then, as a security consultant, let me consult you about something secure. I have a small problem. I need access to my uncle's safe. I need to check some details about his health and his treatment plan. He's sick, you see, dying in fact, and he's forgetful. He can't tell me everything that I need to know, so for his sake, I need to see the paperwork."

"And he will not show you this?"

"He's proud and stubborn. Hates to admit any weakness."

"You know, Lizbet, I can't advise you on how to do something that is unlawful."

"Well just tell me hypothetically. I mean, I'm a writer. So if I were to consult you as a technical adviser for a script I was working on, what would you suggest?"

"Well, first you would have to gain access to his room. Getting a master room key would be the simplest way. They're not uncommon, housekeeping staff have them and so do many other crew members."

"Okay, then what?"

"Then you'd have to open the safe. That would be more difficult, but there will be an override code, there always is. Passengers lock their safes and forget the combination they've chosen. It happens a lot. Sometimes in hotels the override code is left as the manufacturer's default, four zeros usually, but that's bad practice. It should be set by each separate establishment and it should really be changed frequently. And of course, there are restrictions on who has access to it."

"Do you know what it is here, on the ship?"

"No, but I could find out, hypothetically, if I wanted to."

"Would you, for me?"

"No, it would not be legal." He put his hand on my arm, that same light but sympathetic gesture. "Lizbet, you can't do it this way. You would end up in jail. Go to the Purser and tell him the situation. Do it by the book."

"But I don't want my uncle to know. He's only got months to live, I don't want to upset him. He's old and sick and sometimes drives me insane, but he's the only family I have left, and I'm all he's got. I used to have a husband but we split up. I used to have a son but he died. He was four years old. Please will you help me, Raphael?"

"Not the way you want. I can't."

"Well can you get me another drink at least?"

"Sure, that I can do."

"What's the national drink of Israel?"

"We don't really have one. Jews are not great drinkers. We produce some fine wines though."

"Every culture needs something stronger than wine."

"Well I guess it's Arak, although technically that's from Lebanon."

"Well one day that will be Israel too, won't it? I mean after you've digested Palestine you can gobble up Lebanon and then move on to Jordan."

He laughed. "Maybe. We'd sure do more with the land in a couple of decades than the Arabs have managed in five thousand years. Anyway, Arak is grape alcohol with anise. We drink it with water or lemonade, or grapefruit juice. It's nice, but only if you like anise."

"I don't like anise."

"Then you need something different. You could try Tubi 60, it's a lemon-based spirit flavoured with spices and floral extracts. It was invented a few years ago by two brothers who paid a bunch of foodies and botanists to do the research. The recipe is top secret. It's become very popular, particularly with the young, because it produces a feeling of euphoria, a bit like Ecstasy, and it's rumoured never to leave you with a hangover."

"I like the bit about the hangover. I'm sold."

He signalled to the waiter and I headed to the loo, weaving in time with the motion of the ship. On my return Raphael was sipping another coffee. On the table was a shot glass of pale cloudy liquor. There was also a large glass of crushed ice that contained the same pale liquid.

"You can drink it either way," said Raphael. "As a shot or a slushie. I didn't know which you would prefer. Be careful though, it's an acquired taste."

I sipped the slushie. It tasted like diluted limoncello with a hint of ginger and flowers. I downed the shot with an affected nonchalance that was hard to maintain as the fiery bitterness coursed through my system. My first thought was what kind of culture produces a national drink that is so acerbic, so unforgiving? I used the slushie to quench the burn and we sipped in silence for a while. I didn't feel drunk exactly, though I knew that things were more blurred than usual. But I felt good. There was a warmth between us, and it felt so nice to be interacting with someone who wasn't Horace, and wasn't one of the shallow, boring crowd that herded around the decks. Raphael had remarkable skin, very fine for a man, and it glowed with a golden hue that was more than a mere suntan. He had an exotic quality and though I was aware that we were travelling in that liminal borderland between acquaintanceship and attraction, I was okay with it. He was attractive, he was new, and I liked him. That doesn't sound much, but I couldn't remember the last time I had met someone of whom that was true.

"Do you ever sleep with that much coffee?"

"Enough," he said.

"What do you do when you can't sleep?"

He laughed. "Read, walk, listen to music, watch TV. Depends if I'm alone."

"Are you alone?"

"Right now, yes."

"So there's no Mrs Raphael?"

He looked over both shoulder in an exaggerated gesture. "I don't see her."

"Are you an actual spy?"

"No, not actually."

"Let me check." I remember giggling as I reached out to feel for a gun. There wasn't one, though I did find, directly at the back of his belt, a pair of handcuffs. "Hmmmm, kinky." I put my hand on his chest to steady myself and felt the hard lump of a shoulder holster. "Is that really a gun? God, you actually are a spy aren't you, or a policeman."

"I'm not a cop. I'm part of the ship's security team."

"Can I see it, the gun?"

"No."

"Come on, get it out for me."

"No!" He was laughing as we grappled, our arms playfully entwined, wrestling in the borderland.

My recollection of the walk back to my cabin that night is not as sharp as it could be. I remember taking Raphael's arm and saying that I wanted a turn around the Promenade. Maybe I thought that the night air would clear my head, but in the event the walking, together with the cool air and the movement of the ship made me feel a little unsteady. We stopped at one point and looked out over the rail. There were twinkling lights in the distance, flickering like fireflies dancing on the dark ocean. He said they were the Straits of Messina, which sounded anciently romantic and, on his breath, unutterably exotic. I thought that he might try to kiss me, I was prepared for it, but he didn't.

He opened the door to my cabin with a card that I couldn't remember having given him. Neither of us moved to switch on any lights. We stood poised in the darkness. I could see the angles and hollows of his face, his golden skin smeared orange by the glow of the shivering distant lights of Messina. His eyes were locked upon me, wide and still, and there was the ghost of a smile around his silent mouth. Time seemed to bend and warp as we stood becalmed, fixed in our secret stillness, close enough to whisper but not to move. I could feel my heart beating out of time with the ship's engines, and the orange light was unstable and garish, making me feel dizzy and slightly nauseous. I longed to lie down.

I broke the unbearable silence by asking if he wanted anything, but then clumsily added "coffee" as a qualifier, a retrospective nod towards decorum. The word sounded slurred in the silence. He shook his head. I longed for something to happen, something to lance the throbbing tension. I missed the easy intimacy and laughter that we had enjoyed back at the bar.

"You know the ship's protocol absolutely forbids intimacy between crew members and passengers," he said, his voice barely more than a whisper. "In fact I shouldn't even be in your room." He said it as though he believed it, but he was making no attempt to leave.

"Do you always obey the rules?"

"Not always. Anyway, I'm not really crew, I am an independent contractor."

"You're a cop, the ship's cop."

"No, not a cop."

"You're a spy, an Israeli spy, or American, or both."

"I'm just here to keep people safe."

"But not to help them retrieve stuff from safes."

"From their safes maybe, but not other people's."

"Raphael, I need your gun. I need to borrow it, just for a minute."

"What for?"

"I have to shoot my uncle's safe open." He snorted with laughter. "Please, let me have it."

I reached for him, lurching across the translucent but impenetrable barrier, my hands squirreling inside his jacket, following the contours of his chest, as though reaching for the gun. He was protesting and laughing, and then his hands closed around my wrists, warm and forceful like manacles fresh from the forge. We grappled for a moment, wrestling cheek-to-cheek into an embrace, and then we were kissing, hot, fierce kisses, passionate and intense. It felt illicit and wrong but also overwhelming in its excitement. His body was unfamiliar and unexplored, his smell unrecognised and unnamed, the connection between us as yet uncelebrated. And the voices in my head were silenced by a descending cloud of soft crimson for it had been so long since I was kissed, so long since I was held folded in someone's arms.

I felt my back braced hard against the wall as he pressed against me, his hands moving on my body. My hands were round his neck and our lips were locked, my eyes closed against the orange light. I could feel his tongue, his hands, his groin pressed hard against me. It was hard to breathe. He was fumbling with the fastenings of my dress, and I heard him swear softly in Hebrew. One hand was beneath my dress, I could feel it moving over my thigh as it sought to find a way past my tights.

I felt an overwhelming surge of anxiety. I feared he might rip the dress, I was horrified when I thought about the laying bare of the magic pants which would look anything but magic. I opened my eyes and immediately felt sick with the movement of the ship and the spinning orange light.

"Wait, I have to use the bathroom."

He released me and sat back on the edge of the bed. I shed my shoes and weaved a path to the bathroom. After a moment to recover from being blinded when I turned on the light, I wrestled off my tights and pants. Ideally I would have liked to have replaced them with something suitable for the occasion, but that would have required going out to the wardrobe unit. I decided instead to go without, imagining myself sexily shimmying off the dress like a snake shedding its skin. I rooted through the clutter of my wash bag until I found the emergency condom, I used the loo, and then sat resting with my eyes closed, willing the room to stop spinning. I'm not sure how much time passed, but evidently not enough, as I got up too quickly, pitched forward and bashed the top of my head on the wash basin. After ascertaining that I wasn't bleeding, I remained for a while on all fours, waiting for the stabbing pain and nausea to recede. I wondered if it would be wiser to call the whole damned thing off, but I wasn't sure how. Besides, I'd waited long enough, too long, this was my moment and I was determined to enjoy it.

Using the basin for support, I hauled myself upright and ran a facecloth under cold water and pressed it against my skull. After repeating the procedure a couple of times, I felt able to return to the fray. I plumped up my hair; took a swig of mouthwash, gagging briefly after I swallowed some by mistake; and treated myself to a generous couple of air squirts, moving through the perfumed cloud for an all over ambient scent. This was probably a mistake as my eyes were smarting before I got out of the bathroom, and in my half-blinded state the lock on the door proved hard to overcome.

The room seemed much darker than I remembered, but certain of its topography I moved towards the bed where I could just about make out the prone shape of Raphael backlit in amber. I paused at the end of the bed to unfasten my dress. I teetered, stepped forward to rebalance but turned my ankle on one of my discarded shoes. I heard my own cry as I went down, my left shoulder hitting the bed base with considerable force. I knew immediately that I was going to be sick, but had the presence of mind to poke my head under the desk and throw up into the bin.

I'm not sure if Raphael was stirred by the fall or the retching, but I remember the awful flood of light as he turned on the bedside lamp and came to my aid. He held my hair back until I had finished vomiting, and then helped me onto the bed. I kept my eyes clenched, blocking out a world where pain and humiliation were spinning me in circles across an endless dance floor of unforgiving light. I could hear him telling me that everything would be fine. He gave me some sips of water and lay me back down with a cool cloth on my forehead. I think I thanked him but maybe it was just a groan. I think I flinched when he kissed the top of my head, his lips brushing the bruise. I told him I was seasick, I think, but I might have dreamt it.

Time flowed away from me like dark water being sucked through a sinkhole, sucked down to a place where there is no light, no feeling, just the movement of the water and the flicker of fractured dreams. I dreamed of a hand gently stroking my face and hair, and of my mother undressing me at bath time, the cool of air against my skin, only the child was not me, it was Wat, and I was tucking him up safe and warm in his little bed, beneath his kangaroo duvet. And I could feel the insistence of his hands upon me as I lay with him in the soft warmth, and he burrowed within me as I rocked him to sleep, rocking into blackness, gentle without memory, gentle as the sea.

FIFTEEN

Time is not an arrow, nor a winged chariot. It doesn't have such coherence. It's a splodge, an incoherent mess, an ocean of inconstant currents. And it's full of discarded trash that will haunt us forever; jumbles of junk circulating in clumps that gob the water, contaminating it in perpetuity with the tainted stain of the past. And we swim or drown in this heaving and inescapable mess, held fast by its binding weight, its pockets of blackness, tugged and pulled and buffeted by its unending spite.

And that is why we drink: not to forget but to lessen the weight, to loosen the ties and associations, and through disconnection find a form of freedom. Freedom from the burden of the past, of course, but also from the lumbering boredom of the present and the stifling fear of the future. And here's the thing: it works. There is a weightlessness within the laughter and the insight, the euphoria that grows from the glass. The problem with drinking is not the alcohol, it's the pain that returns when the alcohol departs.

For afterwards, always there is that awful pain. You wake and the first stirrings of consciousness are accompanied by a Viking symphony, the savage clanging of metal on metal and the jarring, beating blows of some mighty hammer, beating from the inside, beating as it tries to burst out of your brain. And your mouth is a dried up river bed of stones and dust, and your bed is the trench, a hole into which you fell in those ebbing moments of consciousness back on the other side of the dark. And your body aches, wracked by sweats and chills, and in the rank sweat, stewed with corruption, you can smell last night in the booze oozing from your every pore.

And you know what it is, this cycle, and you know that after Pain comes its trotting, ever faithful hound, Shame. Shards of the evening returning, the fractured pieces making you wince, and in every flinching grimace there is more pain. And you long to shrink away from it all, to forget, but you cannot sleep and you cannot even drift on the ocean's flow for the pain is too ragged and unpitying. And though your need is overwhelming—to pee, to find water to slake your intolerable thirst, to find medicine to dull the pounding throb—the pain is too jagged and you know that any movement of eye or limb will burst the web of delicate vessels in your brain and bring forth a deluge, a drowning ocean of blood. And so you lie absolutely still, paralysed as the memories come like predators, circling, jabbing forward from the dark to nip and tear and bite. And when they discern your helplessness they close in to feed. And it's then that you see the true horrors, the awful things that lurk in the deep dark, where the pressure is too great for anything but the aberrant. And the shame lingers long after the pain has become bored and floated away. The shame sticks and stinks and you are like those hunched seabirds that you see on TV, reeking and black, the blinding crude oil coating their feathers and leaving them adrift on the water, unable to feed or feel or fly. And when some stranger picks them up they do not struggle for they are beyond resistance. They are motionless, waiting to die with the patience of the dying.

So much then for the generalities; so much that one need not dwell on the specifics. That is how I was on the morning after I passed through the Straits of Messina, after I passed through my night of humiliation and shame. And in the days that followed I skulked in my cabin, scrubbing and picking away the tarlike stickiness of shame.

More detail is required? On the morning after Messina I awoke to the dry humping, agony of pain. And as I drifted on my shipwrecked spar it gradually became apparent that the noise was not confined to the inside of my skull. Someone was on the outside, knocking at the door. But by the time I groped my way to open it there was only a breakfast trolley standing fresh and abandoned in the deserted corridor, with scrambled egg, toast, marmalade, coffee, orange juice and a single stem rose. There was a handwritten note too, with a phone number and the injunction "Call me, R x."

The smell of the food in the enclosed space made me heave. I left it in the corridor, taking only the note, the coffee and the rose. I tried the coffee but threw it up almost immediately. I locked the door and engaged the "Do Not Disturb" sign and then returned to the semi-darkness of my bed, curled and foetal, alone with my pain. But, of course, Pain was not alone, for there is always a berth for Shame, who looks on as a grinning voyeur. Incomplete images of the evening came like a stuttering cast of phantoms, shambling figures reeling through the ruins, emerging from lost places. They were bad—they are always bad—but worse were the gaps, holes of lost time, empty but for speculation, the whiff of manufactured memory and desolate dreams.

I was aware of having woken naked, but had no recollection of when or how my clothes had wandered over to the chair where they had folded themselves neatly. I wondered if my drink had been spiked. I remembered Raphael's presence but not his leaving. I didn't think that we had made love, but could not be entirely sure. A superficial examination of my body revealed no conclusive evidence either way, but raised the awful question of how fucked do you have to be before you don't know if you've been fucked? And had it happened, would it count as rape? Technically, yes, I had not given consent, or at least I had no memory of having done so. But then if you stage a clumsy drunken seduction that goes horribly wrong when you pass out, what jury, which court, would convict your rapist? I mean it's not right, or fair, but it's the way it is and always has been.

I went to the bathroom and threw up the water I had drunk, leaving the residue unflushed in the bowl as the mere idea of the hurling force of that atom-shredding toilet was too much to bear. I washed my throbbing face and gazed at its sullied ruin in the forensic light of the mirror. And then I stumbled back to bed, curling corpse tight against the light.

And thus the day passed as a negation, leaving me less molested with each passing hour. By evening I was keeping down the painkillers and water and had moved on to some black coffee. The pain was in retreat, leaving more room for drifting banks of memory moving like breaks in fog, creating more room for shame. A couple of times there were knocks at the door, but they ceased when ignored. Once the phone rang but went through to voice mail; I did not check for a message.

By day two, I was sufficiently recovered to order room service but I remained mentally ravaged, shunning all human contact. When we reached the port of Split, I stayed wounded in my lair. I concentrated on cleaning up, tidying my room and bathing and washing my hair. Healing. I recalibrated my life, sipping water, looking out at the sea whilst thinking of home, contemplating a life of permanent sobriety. When I was a Christian I learned how pain is a gift from God; a route to reconciliation with God by sharing the suffering that God had endured at the crucifixion. A route to reconciliation and thence to a form of redemption. It's like Pope John Paul II said, "Don't waste your suffering." I wondered if I could rekindle the faith I had lost, that I had abandoned, to give meaning to my life and help shape its newfound abstinence.

I returned also to Steller, still fascinated to understand the psychology of the man who had written the original account as well as the one who had laboured to translate and rearrange it, the one whose DNA I shared. The final section dealt with the sea cow, a giant mammal now extinct. An introductory note by great-grandfather explained dryly that the creature had been discovered by Europeans in the waters off Bering Island in 1741 and was declared extinct in 1768, just 27 years later. It was, in fact, the most recent extinction of a giant mammal, one of the largest mammals ever to have lived. It sounded like one hell of a creature, a Sirenia, an order of aquatic herbivorous mammals named after the Sirens, the mermaids of Greek mythology. It was part of a family of aquatic animals closely related to the elephant, a family now largely extinct, apart from three species of manatee and the dugong. But Steller's sea cow was much bigger than these surviving remnants; it was the largest Sirenian ever to have lived. A sea cow would typically have grown to nine or ten metres in length and could weigh up to ten tons.

Great-grandfather's introductory notes also pointed out that the sea cow section had been first in the originally published version of Steller's work, but that the current edition had rearranged the order of the four animals discussed, "to accord with the aesthetic logic of ascending subject size." Thus, the sea cows came after the otters, sea bears and sea lions and constituted the book's climax. Apparently, the original had also begun with a list of measurements of the sea cow's body parts and organs, though my great-grandfather, in his extensive rearrangement of the content, had relegated this to an appendix, "for fear that its taxidermological approach might alienate the general reader." I flicked to the back of the volume to consult the list and was astonished by its detail. The mass of measurements included the length from the extremity of the upper lip to the extreme right *cornu* of the caudal fork (296 inches); the diameter of the trachea below the glottis (4.2 inches); the greatest circumference about the middle of the abdomen (244 inches); and the narial septum (*columna narium*) to the anterior angle of the eye (13.5 inches). The largest single measurement was the whole intestinal tract, from pharynx to anus (a whopping 5,968 inches) which, as Steller helpfully pointed out, "was 20½ times as long as the whole animal." This mania for measurements made me think of a passage I had read as a child in one of the Narnia books, where an opinionated character describes a star as a huge ball of flaming gas, only to be corrected by a wiser head who points out that this is not what a star is, but only what it is made from.

Whereas Steller's manuscript had then moved on to a detailed description of the organs, my great-grandfather's version opened with an account of the sea cow's habits. "These animals are very voracious and eat incessantly." My appetite returning, I felt an instant affinity. "When they raise their noses above the surface, as they do every four or five minutes, they expel the air and a little water with a snort such as a horse makes in blowing through his nose. As they feed they move first one foot and then the other, as cattle and sheep do when they graze, and thus with a gentle motion half swim and half walk." He made these giants sound as gentle as elephants. And then, of course, came the dark stuff. "And because they are so greedy they keep their heads always under water, without regard for life and safety. Hence a man in a boat, or swimming naked, can move among them without impediment and select at his leisure the member of the herd that he desires to strike—all accomplished while they are feeding.

"These animals are fond of shallow, sandy places along the seashore, but they like especially to live around the mouths of rivers and inlets, for they love fresh running water, and they always live in herds. They keep their young and half-grown close while they feed, and are careful to surround them, always keeping them in the midst of the herd. When the tide came in they came up so close to the shore that I often hunted them with my stick or lance, and sometimes even stroked their backs with my hand." Once again Steller's syntax entwined the lust to kill with an affection for the subject of his observation. "If they were badly hurt, they did nothing but withdraw to a distance offshore, and after a short time they would forget their injury and return. Usually, whole families live together in a single community, the male with one grown female and their tender little offspring. They appear to be monogamous. The young are born at any time of year, but most frequently in autumn, as I judged from the new-born little ones that I saw about that time."

There was such delicacy in the domesticity of the images, made more poignant by the knowledge that these gentle creatures were gone from our world forever. "In the spring, especially in still evenings when the sea is smooth, they come together in the human fashion, the male above and the female below. But before their union they partake in many amorous preludes. The female swims gently to and fro in the water, the male following her. The female eludes him with many twists and turns until she herself, impatient with further delay, as if tired and under compulsion, throws herself upon her back, whereupon the male, rushing upon her, pays the tribute of his passion, and thus they fall into each other's embrace."

The physical description of the animals was full but, as ever with Steller, laced with unabashed references to slaughter. "It is covered with a thick hide, more like unto the bark of an ancient oak than unto the skin of an animal; the manatee's hide is black, mangy, wrinkled, rough, hard, and tough; it is void of hair, and almost impervious to an axe or to the point of a hook... And I observed oftentimes in animals that had been captured and hauled to shore with a hook, that great pieces of cuticle had been pulled off in consequence of the violent thrashing of its body and tail and its resisting with its front feet... As to voice, the animal is quite dumb and utters no sound, but only breathes heavily and seems to sigh when wounded... The structure of the animal is totally unfitted for moving on land. Indeed, if the tide went out and the waves receded from under one of them whilst it slept, he was left high and dry upon the shore, helpless and unable to escape, a pitiable object, at the mercy of our cudgels and axes."

In his extensive notes on anatomy, Steller emphasised that "the strangest feature of all, in which this animal differs from all other animals both of land and sea and from amphibia, is its arms, or, if you prefer, its front feet; for its two arms, 26.5 inches long, consisting of two articulations, are joined immediately to the shoulders at the neck... at the ends of the arms are something not unlike like claws, or rather like a horse's hooves... He performs with these arms various offices: with these he swims, as with brachial fins; with these he walks on the shallows of the shore, as with feet; with these he braces and supports himself on the slippery rocks; with these he digs out and tears off the algae and seagrass from the rocks, as a horse would do with its front feet; with these he fights, and when taken with a hook and dragged from the water upon dry land he resists so vehemently that the cuticle surrounding these arms is often torn and pulled off in pieces; and finally with these the female when smitten with the sting of passion, swimming prone upon her back, embraces her covering lover and holds him and permits herself in turn to be embraced."

But for the most part, the poetry of these majestic creatures, and their nuzzling, breathy culture of touch and tenderness, was submerged in a butcher's shop of anatomical detail. "I opened the heads of four animals, an arduous and difficult undertaking... the substance of the vagina was so hard that I could scarcely cut through it with the knife... The gland when sliced open poured forth a great quantity of juice. But after that I was unable to examine any further stomachs because I lacked the necessary assistance for, with the few men I had, rarely could I turn a carcass over upon its back... When the peritoneum is cut the intestines gush out violently... If only a very slight aperture should be made with the point of a knife, the liquid excrement (a ridiculous thing to behold) would squirt out violently like blood from a ruptured vein; and not infrequently the face of a spectator would be drenched by this powerful fountain whenever someone opened a canal upon his neighbour opposite, for a joke." Ah, the humour to be had even on so barren an island.

Inevitably, Steller also dwelt on "the uses to which the parts of this animal are put." Its fat "when exposed to the sun becomes yellow, like May butter... Its odour and flavour are so agreeable... that we lost all desire for butter." It was also used in lamps for it burnt "clear without smoke or smell." Nor was "its use in medicine... to be despised, for it moves the bowels gently, producing no loss of appetite or nausea." The poor creature's breasts, described as "different from those of most other animals, but in place and form exactly as in woman" were also a delicacy. "The milk is very rich and sweet, in consistency very much like sheep's milk, and oftentimes it was my wont to take it in large quantities from dead ones in the same way as from cows... and when the glands are cut they give out milk and the breasts, when boiled, are a little harder than beef and give out the mild odour of game." In general its flesh, "somewhat tougher and coarser than beef," was easy to preserve, and though it needed to be cooked longer, "when ready was an excellent taste, not easy to distinguish from that of beef." With a dash of added salt "it becomes quite like corned beef and very excellent in flavour." By contrast, "the fat of the calves resembles fresh lard, so closely that you can hardly tell the difference; but their flesh is just like veal... The internal organs—heart, kidneys, and liver—are very tough, and we did not try to do much with them, because we had a great abundance of meat without." Who needs heart when you have so much flesh?

I looked again at my great-grandfather's introductory notes on the sea cow. Like elephants, they had had no natural predators. Their natural buoyancy made it hard for killer whales to drown them, which is how those predators hunt.

And the sea cow's predilection for grazing in shallow water, with rocks and ice, protected them from sharks. But an adult specimen could feed a 30-man ship's crew for a month with tasty meat that was nutritious and easy to preserve. And after Steller's visit there were plenty of crews in the region, sometimes staying on Bering Island for months as they hunted the fur of otters and foxes. And so within three decades sea cows were extinct. But it was not just the crime of Europeans, for that colony of sea cows on Bering Island was the last of a population that had once ranged all along the Aleutian island chain and had been preyed upon for millennia by native Aleut hunters. Bones dating from the late Pleistocene age showed that these gentle mammals had been around for thousands of years, perfectly adapted to their cold waters, but they could not coexist with man. By the time that they were discovered by the Europeans, they had already been driven to the brink of extinction with maybe only 1,500 left in their most remote and extreme location. Bering Island wasn't their home, it was their final redoubt.

And as I charted the sedate progress of our stately ship, watching the map on TV, gazing from the window as we passed through the Ionian Sea, I pondered on the sea cows, their lost lives and their sudden, senseless destruction. The ethnicity of their killers was irrelevant, the cruel, squalid, short-sighted, psychotic impulse to kill is not modulated by race. And the result, the loss to the world of these amazing, mystical, giant creatures, these sociable, gentle, friendly elephants of the sea, was just the same. And it was irreversible, lost forever; that's what extinction means.

Eventually I decided to vacate my cabin so that the cleaning fairies could do their work. The catalyst for ending my period of purdah was our arrival at the curious island of Santorini. I had not seen it in years, but it remained fresh in my memory: a thin, curved rim, high above the sea, flanked by several offshore islets. It's what remains of a huge volcano that erupted 3,500 years ago, triggering a series of tidal waves and earthquakes that destroyed the Minoan civilisation, thereby giving rise to the myth of the lost city of Atlantis.

Our ship anchored off Skala, the old port, and tenders took passengers over to the harbour that lay at the base of a 1,000 foot cliff. Above was the sprawling whitewashed capital, Fira, but to get there you had to negotiate 600 rough steps, which zig-zagged their way up the cliff. Passengers were put on donkeys and then led up the precipitous route. I chose to walk, despite being told by the donkey men that it was impossible. In part my decision was motivated by concern for the poor beasts condemned to convey their human cargo up and down those steps, although there was also an element of instinctive self-preservation. It was so bloody steep and the passengers, who were invariably heavier than the donkeys, swayed alarmingly as they made their jolting ascent. I walked steadily, rhythmically. My legs and lungs burned but I accepted the pain as a rightful penance. I stopped regularly for water breaks and sucked in air while looking out over the ocean. To the north west was the smaller island of Therasia, another part of the old volcanic rim, and in between were two small uninhabited volcanic territories. Elsewhere all was blue. Below me lounged the *Evening Star*, serene as a painted ship upon a painted ocean, an ocean daubed in a swirling trance of azure and ultramarine, with luminescent highlights of sparkling cobalt and submerged coils of phthalo.

At the top, beyond the flies and the tethered ranks of sweating donkeys, there was Fira, charming and white but thronged with tourists. I visited the archaeological museum and walked round to a whitewashed, angular, eighteenth-century church, Catholic no less, with a blue dome of such vibrancy that it made my eyes wince with its beauty. The views from its cliff-top perch were stunning, but it was crowded with tourists jostling to take photographs, invariably of themselves. Why must people photograph everything, as though the act of seeing is no longer sufficient unless it has been validated by a snap taken on their phone? When did that happen and where will it end? In the absurdity of photographs taken as an alternative to actually looking at an object, actually connecting with the real world?

It wasn't just the church that was crowded. The whole damned island was packed, for there were two other cruise ships anchored off shore which had also disgorged their human cargo. The island was beautiful and historically significant, but I hated it. Once, it had been real, a place where real people had lived real lives. Now it was a tourist attraction, a mere representation, a cliché of itself, a parody of what it had once been. Besides, touring alone in a crowded place accentuates one's loneliness. Amid the parties of friends and families one walks like a pariah, a vagabond widow who has no place at the chattering table of the attached.

I was tired and hungry but the tavernas were full. I longed to escape the crowd and so I retraced my route, picking my way down those switchback steps that were slippery with urine and donkey shit, heading back to the port. The return journey was less physically arduous but more perilous, as the loaded donkeys were coming head on, braying their distress and fatigue, driven on by the muleteers whose iron-tipped sticks and springy whips encouraged them. Every blow produced a fresh bellow of protest: the raw sound of uncomprehending suffering, like when an iron hook strikes an abscess. So here is a vision of Hell. Here is reincarnation to be feared: come back next time around as a Santorini donkey and labour up those 600 steps a dozen times a day carrying bloated, privileged, ignorant dullards slouching in an ill-fitting saddle that rubs and cuts deep sores in your flesh. And do it without water or shade or rest; do it every day of your miserable existence, running to the rhythm of the whip.

With several hours to spend before I could get a tender back to the ship, I bought a ticket for a boat trip to Nea Kameni, one of the uninhabited islets created in recent times by continuing subterranean volcanic activity. After a short hop in a crowded boat we moored at a concrete pier in a little bay amid a moonscape of jagged, black volcanic rock. I walked with the straggling herd, following the rough track inland across a lifeless landscape. We ascended more than 100 metres to the rim of an enormous crater. I saw smoke and could smell the choking stench of sulphur. Here the rock was stained white and brown and yellow. The volcano had not erupted since 1950, but it felt as though it was limbering up for a repeat performance. I felt light-headed and found a quiet spot where I sat watching the smoke and sulphur plumes, looking back over the blue water to Fira. I thought again about the donkeys being whipped up that vertical path, toiling until the end of their lives without ever knowing why. I wished that I had brought more water.

In surroundings of such unworldly desolation it seemed unreal to be gazing across the sunlit sea to a white city perched on top of the cliff, as though one was looking from Hell to Heaven. Yet, I also knew that Heaven was not all that it was cracked up to be: the casual cruelty that littered the path to its attainment was more than capable of poisoning the promised ecstasy.

I heard footsteps behind me and then that dry, racking cough.

"It's like crossing the Styx into the Underworld isn't it?" Horace sat down next to me and offered his water bottle. I wiped away a smear of rust-coloured dust from the rim and drank a long, deep draught. "Do you know, Lizzy, about 30,000 people used to live on Santorini before it blew up?" he said cheerfully. "It's actually a cluster of shield volcanoes, and this current caldera was formed during the big Minoan eruption, but there were others before that, before human history. Right here is the most volatile spot on the South Aegean volcanic arc. You see, the African tectonic plate is being sucked under the Aegean sea plate, which is part of the Eurasian plate. The subduction rate is about five centimetres a year. That's got to produce volatility. Most of the inhabitants probably escaped because it began rumbling and spewing quite some time before the main event. You can tell from the ash deposits. Anyone with any sense would have got out. Get out while you can. Never stay to the bitter end." He laughed. "The clue is in the name, it will be bitter."

"Could I have some more water?" I asked.

"Sure, of course. I have bread, olives and some feta too, if you fancy it." He passed me a bag and I ate gratefully. "I say, Lizzy, you look completely bushed. I've got a water taxi waiting in the harbour: comfy seats, shade, snacks, even a bar. We can take a loop around the island and be back on board the mother ship in time for cocktails. No pressure, your choice. But it'll be nicer than going back to the main island with that lot and then having to wait for a tender."

I accepted. Of course I accepted. But before you judge me, ask yourself what you would have done in my position. Anyway, it gave us time to straighten things out. We both apologised in our respective ways, and I will say this of my uncle, he never held a grudge. Whatever happened, it seemed, he was willing and able to just begin over again, putting the past behind him and moving on.

As with so many of Horace's offers the return leg was not entirely without incident. We did whizz around the little black island but he also insisted on a diversion back to the main island to show me some sites of "family significance". He explained how he had wanted to take me on a tour but had been unable to contact me for the last few days and so had been forced to make the expedition alone. He pointed out the cove where, in April 1944, a squadron of British commandoes had secretly come ashore to attack the German garrison.

"My father was among them, your great-grandfather," he said, shouting above the engine noise of the boat. "Mostly he was involved in training and intelligence work, but on this occasion he actually participated. The raid was a conspicuous success and Father was among those who were decorated. Got the Military Medal. He fought bravely by all accounts. Shot several of the blighters. Just think, Lizzy, old Mr Webley was firing in anger, just up there in that scrum of tourists." He nodded towards the white town that was receding from us as we headed back to the ship.

"Why?" I asked. "What was the point of attacking such a little island?"

"In part, to destroy the radio installation at Imerovigli," he pointed to a tiny white village on the cliff top. "Long-range radio: essential part of communications between Athens and Crete. Also to wear down the enemy by wiping out the garrison and taking the commander back for interrogation."

"That sounds ambitious. How many were there?"

"Not many. They landed at night and marched to Vourvoulos, which is over there," he gesticulated through the spray. "They were guided by local Greeks and hid in a cave. After a few days of reconnaissance, they split into three groups: one blew up the radio installation, while the other two went to Fira, one to the house of the commander and the other to attack the barracks in the town centre. Your great-grandfather was in that last lot. They were helped by the locals and achieved total surprise. The commander managed to evade capture, but the radio was destroyed and the barracks taken. The fighting was intense. Two Brits were killed and about forty Germans. Afterwards they hopped back into their boats and escaped into the night."

"You make it sound very heroic."

"It was," he said, "in the British version, at least. And that's the official version because history is written by the victors." The driver swung the bow of the boat away from the coast and accelerated into open water. "From the German perspective it probably looked different. Different again for the Italians. The past is a slippery business, Lizzy."

"Did it really help shorten the war?" I shouted. "It was almost over by 1944."

"After the raid the Germans had to increase all their Mediterranean garrisons. Thousands of troops were deployed to the islands, which meant thousands fewer in France or on the Eastern Front. You don't always win by attacking head on."

While Horace reminisced with a misty eyed—and hitherto entirely unrevealed—sense of patriotism, I just wanted to rest on my bed with the oblivion of my sleep mask. But getting back on board the ship was a fucking nightmare. They were deeply suspicious of us trying to come aboard from an unidentified local craft and kept us bobbing alongside the towering white hull until thorough checks had been completed. Even then we were greeted by a rather irate officer and a posse of security officials. Amongst them, smiling wryly, was Raphael, though he did not speak and gave no indication that we had met. Horace blustered but I submitted to the pat down and accepted the bollocking about contravening security regulations. I just wanted to sit somewhere quiet and rest. After the ritual humiliation had run its course we were allowed to return to our quarters.

I showered and wrapped myself in the fresh white bath robe. Then I sat on my terrace eating fruit and drinking sparkling water, watching as the tenders brought weary passengers back from Santorini. I thought over what Horace had said about his father's wartime experience on the island as I finished the last of my mango. I had a few pangs of desire for a glass of wine but the impulses, once resisted, melted into a health haze of oblivion. *Refrain tonight,/ And that shall lend a kind of easiness/ To the next abstinence, the next more easy:/ For use almost can change the stamp of nature.*

When the doorbell sounded I assumed that it was Horace. It turned out to be Raphael, who asked if he could come in. It was confusing to see him. I mean, there is standard advice about how to deal with the aftermath of embarrassment, but there are no guidelines for how to relate to someone with whom you might or might not have had sex during a night of humiliation and shame.

He was polite and not intrusive, although his smile and the way that he looked at me made me uncomfortable. I pulled the dressing gown more tightly around me. I told him that I was due to meet Horace shortly and was getting ready to go out. He said that he had just wanted to check I was okay and to apologise for the officious way that Horace and I had been treated when we made our unorthodox return to the ship. "Security is going to get tighter," he explained. "We've reached the wild end of the Med now and the terrorist threat goes up. When we get to the Indian Ocean we'll be on high alert for pirates. A ship like this is a rich target and it's most vulnerable in port or close to land. Until now the voyage has been easy, but from here, that's where people like me earn our shekels."

He said how much he had enjoyed our evening. I apologised for having fallen asleep. He smiled and I looked away. We both knew that 'passed out' would have been a more accurate description. He said that he had checked I was okay and then left, after making me comfortable. I thanked him, resisting the urge to ask if making me comfortable had included fucking me whilst I was unconscious. He asked if I had felt okay in the morning. I said that I had been a bit thick-headed. I blamed the Tubi. "I feel bad for that," he said, "I want to make amends." From his bag he produced a bottle which, once he had stripped off its ice sleeve, turned out to be a 2010 Bollinger. He informed me that it should be drunk immediately and asked if I had time for a glass.

I did have time. I mean, when does one not have time for a bottle of Bollinger? And, despite my new-found sobriety, a decent bottle of cold champagne on a warm evening is a prize that's worth a few bent rules. He placed the bottle on the table and I could see the mist of condensation on the thick green glass. I could feel the explosive charge of the cork restrained only by its cage, that delicate latticework of wire beneath a thin, golden skin of fragile foil. I lusted after it; I could already taste its smoky flavours of white cherry and oak. After all, I had had the sort of day that made one susceptible to the solace in its embrace. A moment of consensual pleasure.

"One glass," I said.

"Of course. I'm on duty later, until midnight."

I got the glasses and he poured. I tried to interpret his last statement. Did it mean, 'Relax, I'm not going to try anything, I have to go to work?' Or was he really saying, 'I'm not free now, but I'm available after midnight?' Because the thing is, Raphael was quite attractive, and I was interested, sort of, particularly as the Bollinger had infused the evening with a spume of iced rapture. We chatted about Santorini, about the preparations of the ship as it made ready to get underway. Of course we finished the bottle. Its crisp golden bubbles just slipped down unobstructed. It's possible that I drank more than my share. As we sipped our final measures he said, "You know, Lizbet, you are very beautiful." He put his hand on mine.

"And I shall be very late if I don't go soon," I said, withdrawing my hand.

"I almost forgot. I found out the override code for the cabin safes. They change it for every voyage. I know what it is for this one."

"Oh really?" My insouciance sounded a little too forced. "I took your advice and decided to sort it out officially, after the voyage. Besides, my uncle has calmed down a bit."

"Good. It's for the best like this."

"But tell me the code, if you like. He sometimes forgets which numbers he chooses and then he has to call down to have it opened. It would be more convenient if I could do it for him."

"Will you be around when I get off work? I'd love to see you."

"Maybe, it depends. Sometimes my uncle gets tired early, sometimes not."

"I can't tell you the override code directly, but I could give you a hint."

"I don't have time for games right now, Raphael. I'm going to be late." I stood up and went to the door.

He followed. Before I could open it he put his hands on my waist and looked hard into my eyes. "Maybe I will see you later?"

"Maybe."

He kissed me lightly on the lips, and then once again, for a little longer. I did not resist but nor did I encourage. His body pressed against me but I felt only a detached sense of curiosity and a nagging worry that I was already late for Horace.

He pulled away and said, "Memory needs every method of nurturing its capacity, but only in disguise."

"What?"

"Think about it," he said. And then he was gone.

SIXTEEN

Having stowed away half a bottle of Bollinger, and achieved reconciliation with Horace and Raphael, as well as obtained a clue, albeit in cryptic form, as to how to open the safe, I was feeling pretty cheerful as I descended to dine. The idea was to have a light supper and then go and listen to Selene crooning to the old folk. Or at least that was Horace's plan, but I was already working on an alternative. If he was at the show, then his room would be empty. I had a key; all I needed was the code. So I sauntered down to the buffet turning over Raphael's enigmatic parting remark, *Memory needs every method of nurturing its capacity, but only in disguise*. It meant nothing to me as a quotation, but a quick online search by phone revealed it to be a common mnemonic for spelling out 'mnemonic'. How very droll. There was, however, no clue as to the meaning of the final four-word qualifier. Searching for the precise phrase brought up nothing useful. I paused near the entrance to the buffet and noted the four words down on a paper napkin: 'but only in disguise'. There seemed no obvious connection between them.

I heard Horace before I saw him. "It is not only evident, it is undeniable. It would be obvious to a blind man on a galloping horse." His voice was high pitched with excitement and his declaration was followed by that dry, hacking cough. I glanced over to the edge of the main drag and saw him holding court at a table with a number of other diners. I moved closer, standing in the lee of a large pedestal upon which sat a mature aspidistra in an ornate, reproduction Grecian urn. I recognised the dreadful Miriam, dressed in what appeared to be a safari suit. She confirmed her presence with that unmistakeable and combative bray of privilege.

"I hardly think that you are a reliable authority on the subject. You are a man who advocates sleeping in filthy monkey nests."

"Ape nests are not filthy. They are extraordinarily clean. Much cleaner than human beds."

"That, I doubt."

"Then your doubt is misplaced, for you are mistaken. It's been proven by peer-reviewed scientific research. They are almost entirely devoid of bacteria or parasites, unlike human beds which are full of that stuff and are a significant cause of ill health. Do you know, a third of the bacteria in a human bed comes from the owner and is oral, faecal or skin-related in origin? And it's everywhere, the mattress, the sheets, the pillows..."

"Please!"

"And consider this," said Horace, with obvious relish. "If the bed's occupier accounts for a third of the filth, where does the rest come from? And how do you get faecal matter on your pillow, or saliva on your sheets. I understand pillow-biting, when occasion demands, but who licks their sheets in the night?"

"Really! This is not a conversation fit for the table."

"Calm down, mother," said Brian the Bore. "We should all relax about our beds."

"About them, on them, in them or under them," said Horace.

"It's true," said Brian. "A few mites never killed anyone. Even bed bugs won't kill you, though they can give you a nasty bite."

"Actually, bed bugs are the principal source of Chagas disease," said a female voice, its owner out of my eye line. "It kills tens of thousands every year."

"Shagger's disease?" said Brian. "What on Earth is that?"

"A nasty condition spread by beds," said Horace.

He was having fun and it was hard not to smile, but I was also nervous. I knew I ought to go over and supervise. But I was not keen to get entangled with Brian. Besides, there was a part of me that screamed, 'I'm tired, too tired for this shit. I'm not his keeper. Let him have his fun, he's paying his way after all. He's an adult and so are they. If they don't like it, they can choose not to share a table with him.'

"Actually, they're not the principal source. Chagas is spread by kissing bugs (*Triatominae*) rather than bed bugs (*Cimex lectularis*) or dust mites (*Dermatophagoides*)." This was another woman, smartly dressed with closely controlled hair and minimal makeup. She spoke with firm authority.

Her companion, a slight young man with fluffy blond hair, patted her knee as a gesture of solidarity. "Valerie's quite right," he said. "She knows about this. She's a vet."

It occurred to me that watching people was invariably more interesting than having to talk to them. I knew that I should go over, but I delayed, choosing instead to lurk on the sidelines. I looked down at the napkin once more and pondered Raphael's four word mystery.

"Kissing bugs? Why in heaven would anyone wish to kiss one?" I knew it was Miriam, even without glancing up.

"You kiss them as a means of immunising yourself against Shagger's disease, of course," said Horace with glee.

The little blond guy laughed with a high-pitched nasal cackle. "That's very witty."

"I agree with this fellow," said Horace. "What's your name again?"

"Benjamin, but people call me Benjo."

"Well I agree with the Banjo, here. You should always listen to a vet, but you shouldn't get overly hysterical about bed cleanliness. Life is microbial. We are all covered in bacteria from head to toe, inside and out. More than half of our cells aren't actually ours. We're covered in mites too. Do you know, you even have eyelash mites. *Demodex* they're called. They've evolved into an elegant tubular shape so that they fit perfectly inside the pores of our eyelashes. They live there happily, eating dead skin and eye gloop, and drinking our tears. Technically they're parasites, of course, but the little buggers are perfectly benign and cause no bother. Unlike some things I could mention, like the bastard botfly larva that I picked up in Costa Rica. When that little sod burrowed into my scrotum the pain was like being stabbed with a white-hot knitting needle. And then it kept wriggling about trying to get comfortable. Luckily there was a local fella, Juan, who showed me what to do. You have to cover the entry hole with a big gloop of engine oil and then wait for the little sod to stick its head out for air. Then you grab it with a pair of tweezers and pull it out in one deft movement with a turn of the wrist. If you miss the bugger it'll dive down again and you'll have to wait, sometimes for hours, with oil all over your knackers until it comes up for another breather. Fortunately Juan had a steady hand and got it first go. Never been so grateful to a bloke in my whole life for standing guard over my nuts."

There was a momentary pause as people—me included—floundered with the image that Horace had just conjured.

Then Miriam spoke. "It's not just beds," she said, evidently keen to steer the conversation away from Horace's genitalia. "Books can be awfully filthy as well. I hate even the thought of a second-hand book. I can't help but imagine all of the people who have touched it, all those filthy fingers passing over the pages. I see the finger marks in my mind's eye and it makes me shudder. It's why I never frequent second-hand bookshops or libraries."

"Yes, you strike me as someone who has lived a life protected from the perils posed by books," said Horace.

"One has to. One cannot be sure where they've been. And they attract dust, too, especially when stored on open shelves."

"And some people make the problem worse by reading in bed. Mucky books in a dirty bed leads to grubby thoughts and filthy habits," said Horace.

"Mind you," said the invisible woman. "Looking on the bright side, if all that skin and faecal matter rubs off in your bed, imagine how clean you'd be when you wake up in the morning. Imagine, Cheryl," she said to her more elderly companion, "No need to shower. Think of the time you could save." She giggled.

"Actually," said Valerie the vet, "I recently read an article by a dermatologist who swore that soap strips skin of its protective oils. Sometimes she rubs herself with a drop of cold water but she hasn't showered or bathed in fifteen years."

"Christ, I bet she honks," said Horace. "Does she use toilet paper or just allow her undies to rub off the leftovers."

"Please don't return us to the lavatory." Miriam was becoming exasperated.

"Actually, she insisted that she had no discernible body odour. She claimed she'd never felt better or been healthier. She also said she had a wide circle of friends."

Horace laughed. "Yeah, I bet they form a very wide circle. I'm telling you, Val, I worked with some soap-dodgers when I was in the Outback. Those buggers had one thing in common: you always had to stand upwind of them. Everyone gave the cruddies a wide berth."

"That's one of the difficulties, isn't it? People can't usually smell themselves," said the invisible woman.

"Not unless they're double jointed," replied Horace.

"No, I mean they're not sensitive to it." She leaned forwards and I saw her dyed red hair.

"That's true," said Cheryl. "A friend of mine's brother gave up washing. He said the body cleanses itself naturally if you let friendly microbes live on your skin. Apparently they eat the ammonia from sweat so you get no body odour. Mind you, he smelled dreadful. Her children used to call him Uncle Stinky and would run away whenever he came near them."

"Yes, and we were in China last year, weren't we Cheryl?" said the red-haired woman. "And we were amazed by how there was no deodorant in the local shops, only in the hotels. But I will say this about them, even in the summer, in crowded places, you never smelled any body odour. There was a lot of smoking, and far too much spitting, but no body odour, not so much as a whiff."

"Certainly nothing offensive," agreed Cheryl. "Sometimes there was a distinctive oriental smell. Sort of sweet."

"But not sour," said Horace. "And you know why? East Asians have fewer apocrine sweat glands than whites or blacks, and so they have less body odour. It's because of a genetic mutation. Almost all East Asians have a non-functioning version of gene ABCC11. It affects their ear wax too, which is dry and flaky, and largely colourless, unlike the gooey orange-brown stuff we have in the West. But they do still sweat. They have eccrine sweat glands like other races. We all have those, all over our bodies. They're a thousand times more numerous than apocrine glands, but they don't produce odour."

"Why have they developed like that?" asked the redhead.

"No idea, but the racial differences are clear. Blacks have more apocrine glands than whites."

"Isn't this a bit racist?" said Benjo.

"Why? They're just biological differences."

"I don't know, it just sounds racist."

"It's natural. If it's racist you should take it up with Nature or God. Anyway, it's not just race. There are gender differences too. Men have larger apocrine glands than women. Mind you, there's no consensus on which sex has the greater number."

"That is not a contest of which one would wish to be declared the winner," said Miriam.

"When we reach puberty everyone starts to produce scents that are a sexual attractant," said Benjo.

"Are you looking forward to it?" asked Horace.

"I just meant, in a sense we are designed to smell. It's how we get together to reproduce. It's just that we're not familiar with our smell anymore because we've become conditioned to disguising it with artificial scent. So much so that we now confuse smelling like perfume with smelling good," said Benjo.

"Well the thought of even conversing with an unclean mouth is an anathema to me," insisted Miriam. "As for anything more, well in my view those parts of the body prone to odour are the parts that need most attention. I couldn't imagine being intimate with a person who did not cleanse those areas."

"I couldn't imagine you being intimate either. I think your best hope is to be attentive to your own parts without worrying about the smell," said Horace.

"I shall take my coffee elsewhere." Miriam rose to leave, and Brian followed.

"Check the cup's clean and the coast's clear," Horace called after her. "I think I saw a botfly circling earlier, and he was looking hungry."

Cheryl and her companion trotted after them, leaving only Valerie the Vet and Benjo the Boyfriend for Horace to torment.

"I think men are much worse than women when it comes to hygiene," said Benjo. "When I was still able to work I used to be a physio. Believe you me, I had some stomach-churning experiences. Some just don't know how to keep their things... their bits... clean. It's gross."

"You don't strike me as an expert on cleanliness, Bongo," said Horace.

"Actually I am. I wash often but very carefully. I have total body neuropathy and it's aggravated by hot water, friction and chemicals. They burn me and leave my skin covered in itchy lumps. I just use a little distilled water, at room temperature, to wash. And even then I'm careful not to overdo it."

"Christ," said Horace, "So you're another of those bloody crusties?"

Valerie intervened. "He's just saying that he allows self-regulation by permitting benign bacteria to flourish at the expense of malign varieties. As you yourself said, most of our bodies are bacteria. Medicine is beginning to realise how closely our gut microflora is connected with overall health. So it makes sense to stop trying to wipe out all bacteria and instead aim for a balanced relationship by encouraging the good ones."

"Yes," agreed Benjo. "Kill the bad but encourage the good, the ones that are our friends."

"Sounds a bit racist to me. Tell me, Bingo, are the bad bacteria born bad or can they be rehabilitated?"

"You may mock, but I do have a significant disability. It forces me to avoid crowded places because of the odour. I can smell the residue of red meat in the sweat of crowds, and artificial scents make me nauseous and trigger migraines. As for non-distilled water, the merest possibility that I will accidently come into contact with it terrifies me."

"So, crowds and water are your great fears, are they? Well tell me then, why in God's name did you come on a bloody cruise? And though I'm with you when it comes to the stink of meat in the sweat of carnivores, there are other smells that are equally revolting. And the putrid smell of an unwashed body is one of them. Water is your friend not your enemy. It's a miraculous substance, Boso. Just think, water can wash away almost anything; it can dilute deadly poison; it has carved and shaped our world; it lubricates and cools, and it evaporates in air like magic before returning to us as gentle rain. Imagine a world without water. Why is outer space so hostile? What do we look for first when exploring other planets? What substance is even more precious than air? We think of ourselves as terrestrial animals, but that's just a memory lapse. We came from the sea, Blowjo, and we carry its legacy within us. You too, despite your migraines and feebleness, your bloody virtue-signalling. Two-thirds of our bodies are water; probably more in your case. Over 70 percent of your heart is water, same for your brain, if you've got one. It makes up more than 80 percent of those watery lungs of yours. Even those weak and wobbly bits that you call bones are 30 percent water. So I strongly suggest that you re-familiarise yourself with water's many miraculous properties with immediate effect. Because let me tell you, you piss-filled drongo, I could smell you from another room. So stop moaning and do something to help yourself. Do us all a favour, Banjo. Tighten up your strings and sluice down your nether regions rather than just waiting for the crusty bits to clump up and drop off. And if you can't bear water, try rubbing with a rough stick."

Of course, at this point I intervened. I walked swiftly across the hushed room and got to the table just as they were leaving. I couldn't bear to look either of them in the eye. I sat down next to Horace, who was tucking into a bowl of peach melba with childlike relish.

"Dining alone, Uncle?"

He looked up with a innocent smile. "Ah, Lizzy. Good to see you. I was wondering where you'd got to. Here, have a drink." He poured me a glass of wine.

"You really are amazing, Horace. You look normal and you can act normal, but only for a while, right? Then it all gets too much and the madness returns and you just have to offend people."

"What? That pair of pot screamers? Nah, I was just kidding around with them."

"No, Uncle, that wasn't kidding around. That was a different thing. It's called being grossly offensive. There's something wrong with you, Horace. You just can't be trusted to interact with ordinary people."

"Well I do try, Lizzy." Incredibly, he actually sounded a little hurt.

"You know, I'm not sure that's even remotely true. And supposing it is, the fact that you try but fail so spectacularly, so miserably, just proves what I'm saying. I think you may be insane. I'm no expert on these things, but I mean actually mad, clinically insane."

He thought for a moment and then shook his head with conviction. "Nah, just a bit high spirited. But I can't be doing with pious, mealy-mouthed, hypocritical bastards."

"You can't be doing with people, Horace. Look, you've cleared the table. All the ordinary people, the sane people, they've all gone. They've been forced to leave. See that? They didn't even finish their meals. The table looks like something from the Marie fucking Celeste. Now what do you think it was that caused them all to leave?"

"Maybe they weren't hungry."

"Oh you think so? Well I think they probably were hungry, at least they were before you unleashed your latest rampage and drove them all away. Let me tell you something. Though I love you, Uncle, I have noticed that you have a tendency to offend and bully people. And you do it for pleasure. And I have to tell you, that is not an attractive trait."

"You're still gonna come to the show with me tonight though?"

"No. I've had enough for today. I'm going to bed."

"But Selene is on in twenty minutes. She's doing a whole set from *Phantom of the Opera*."

"Well enjoy, Uncle. I'll see you tomorrow."

I walked purposefully to my room without a backward glance. I poured myself a glass of wine and tested my theory as to the override code for the ship's safes. The mnemonic of the last four words had to translate into numbers on the safe's keypad. As the keypad contained only the numerals 1-9, the active part of the mnemonic must be the first nine letters of the alphabet. So, taking the first letter of each of the four words, and treating o as a zero, I came up with 2-0-9-4. I tried it on my own safe and it slid open, the buzz of its yielding lock offering an entry to the past.

I took an empty bag and made my way to Horace's suite. I let myself in with the spare key. There was a light on in the lounge area but otherwise the place was in darkness. I went into the dressing room, turned on the small desk lamp, and keyed the code. The door to the safe opened. I stood for a moment, aware that I was poised on some threshold. The room felt oppressively silent, hushed but for the dull throb of the ship's turbines and the sound of my breathing. As I opened the heavy steel door fully, the interior light of the safe came on, illuminating its contents. The gun was there, wrapped in its oiled cloth. The strongbox was locked. I took out the two cardboard boxes and the file of documents. I heard someone walk quietly along the corridor outside. I quickly put the file and boxes into the bag and carefully closed the safe. It would not lock unless I keyed in a code and so I tapped in 1-0-0-1 and heard the bolts slide into place.

I turned off the desk lamp and then went to the fridge and helped myself to one of the bottles of white wine. It seemed sensible to have a legitimate reason for having visited the room. At the front door I paused and listened until satisfied with the silence. Then I left, trying to walk casually, trying to walk without guilt or shame as I retraced my steps, back to the sanctuary of my room. Once there, devoid of their context, the contents of the bag looked paltry, lying stranded on my bed like beached sea creatures. The boxes looked smaller and more scruffy than they had when stacked within their steel cave. I felt shabby, sticky with the tackiness of guilt. But I knew that the boxes were the only route into a land whose borders were patrolled by a bloody maniac. I also knew that I could live with guilt, for there are emotions, many emotions, way more corrosive than an occasional shiver of necessary guilt.

My intention had been to rifle through the boxes and then return them to the safe before Horace emerged from the evening show. I quickly revised this when the scale of the task became apparent. The heavier of the two housed a random collection of artefacts whilst the other contained half a dozen tightly packed albums. The file was stuffed with what seemed to be an unordered confusion of invoices and bank statements, though tucked inside its front cover was a brown envelope marked 'Last Will and Testament of Horace Cunningham'.

I poured a drink and flicked through the document file. It suggested that Horace's financial affairs were hopelessly disordered and spread across a series of bank accounts in Australia, Lichtenstein and the Bahamas. There were accounts in different denominations, but though significant sums of money ebbed and flowed, the lack of any chronological order amongst the records meant that it was impossible to determine whether he was even solvent. Accounts opened, accounts closed, money moved and routed through different jurisdictions, from business to personal accounts and back again. The invoices and bills of sale were equally opaque. It would have taken a team of accountants days to tame the jungle of paper and figures.

By contrast, the Will was crisp and had been drawn up and dated by a lawyer in Sydney less than a month ago. The structure was complicated but seemed to involve the establishment of a trust for Horace's property, administered by the lawyer and Maya, with conditions about providing a habitat for wildlife and a home for local aboriginals. There were also extensive bequests, some small and some seemingly huge to individuals and charities. Specific opals were also singled out as gifts, to be distributed either individually or in groups. His mother's dressing table and all items relating to family history were bequeathed to me. Finally, the remainder of his estate was to be liquidated and the cash divided equally between Maya and me.

This was intriguing. It would be ridiculous if I were to suggest otherwise. I mean who is not interested by the possibility that they will receive unexpected and unearned cash? But it was also frustrating on two levels. First, it was impossible to know how much money was involved; Horace's affairs seemed in such a ramshackle state that it could be millions or nothing or anything in between. Second, and more to the point, it was entirely hypothetical as the Will had not been signed and was, therefore, utterly worthless. I carefully returned it to its envelope and replaced it in the file.

The box of artefacts was even more oblique. Its contents included: a small hand-painted wooden Spitfire; two locks of hair; a woman's antique vanity mirror and hairbrush; an empty miniature brandy bottle; several stones, of varying size and colour; a tooth; a small bronze statue of a dog; a threadbare soft toy that appeared to be a cross between a teddy bear and a monkey; a signet ring; four brightly coloured feathers; a tortoiseshell comb; a pair of sunglasses with one lens missing; two harmonicas; a small box of white sand; several pre-decimal British coins; a medal; a number of expired passports that showed photographs of Horace at different stages of his life; and an old rag with what looked like rust stains.

As I examined them I was struck by the thought that you can touch such things but what can you do with them? They are part of someone else's life, objects kept back and venerated either because they were special in some way or were made special by the longevity conferred through hoarding them. So maybe they were special or maybe they had just been randomly preserved. The point is, it was impossible to tell. When something lacks intrinsic value it is impossible to guess at its individual worth to the hand that saved it. And maybe it had been saved further up the generational track, thus adding an additional layer of ambiguity. Did the vanity mirror belong to Horace's mother or to some former lover? You can guess but you cannot know. An object divorced from its context is just an object. Its emotional charge is known to the person who saved it but, without their cooperation, their willingness to share that past, the object reverts to its most base character; it becomes merely an object rather than a relic. That box of Horace's artefacts highlighted the nature of the past as a personal preserve, a private world within which I was an intruder, travelling without map or guide.

I poured another glass and moved to the second box, taking out the albums and leafing through them. From the battered covers there was no indication of the content or date of each volume. All were filled with an ephemera of paper glued to the thick dark pages: photographs, drawings, letters, cards, menus, banknotes, recipes, newspaper clippings, receipts, school reports, and dried flowers. Of course, there was no order to the pages, and the overall chaos was enhanced by the numerous items, particularly letters and handwritten notes, that were stashed loose between the leaves. But though confusing and disordered, here was a past that could be deciphered through language, a past that could be read. And thus, as we sailed through the night towards Alexandria, I drank and I read.

SEVENTEEN

Alexandria: ferocious sunlight and pools of dark shadow; a city where the air reeks with the slop of the throng and throbs with their noise. The streets shrill around you, a shrieking mosaic of hundreds of millions of individual sounds and smells that swirl and babble together to create a link with the past—the immediate past of the moment, or a deeper past that survives the tramp of centuries. I sat on the terrace, in a puddle of shade cast by the canopy, looking out over the writhing city with its twisted streets and skewed skyline. And it occurred to me that the past is alive with echoes, as noisy and chaotic as a metropolis, whereas the future is silent in its unpredictability. Still and patient, the future waits for echoes to arrive, sounds of the past travelling like radio waves through space and time, to confer form and animation. And then we arrive, bustling in, footsore and burdened, and we dump our luggage and take in the view, sniffing the freighted air and squinting through the tangled haze of echoes. And this we call the present.

It was mid-afternoon, but time was acting strangely. We had spent too much of it exploring the old city as Horace searched in vain for a particular cafe that he had frequented half a century earlier. We trudged through a latticework of narrow, crowded streets, made wrong turns into dead ends, retraced our steps and blundered anew, fumbling within a landscape richly textured but unmapped and unstructured.

In the end we had given up and retreated to the shade of this nondescript restaurant where we ate baklava and ice-cream and drank several pitchers of cool, locally-brewed Stella. It had been recuperative and, with the morale of the shore party beer-bolstered and restored, I mused on the noise of passing time while I waited for Horace to return from his seventh visit to the toilets.

I took off my sunglasses and rubbed my eyes. They felt prickly and inflamed from the dust of the day. The city heat and cool beer made the afternoon slow and slumberous. My drowsiness was in part derived from having spent two nights enmeshed in the tangle of Horace's scrapbooks. On the first, I had fallen asleep with them strewn open on my bed. I was trying to work quickly but there was so much material. It was like scrabbling through an archive in the shadow of the sweeping arms of a giant clock. I had bought myself some time on that first evening by returning the two boxes and the file of documents to Horace's safe. But I left the scrapbooks in my room and filled their box with a pad of paper, several brochures, and the copy of the *Guardian* that I had bought in Southampton on the day of our departure. The weight was about right, and once returned to Horace's safe all appeared undisturbed. But I was conscious that, at any time, Horace could try to open his safe and find that his combination no longer worked. He'd complain, some steward would come and unlock it for him, and then, if he opened the scrapbook box, the unforgiveable scale of my subterfuge would be exposed. It was only a matter of time.

The next day I had spent a lot of time keeping Horace occupied so that he would not try to retrieve anything from his safe. We had swum and spent a while in the steam room, sweating out our sins and opening our pores and airways to the cleansing vapour of menthol. We lunched, and inevitably had a few drinks, which was probably a mistake. But it was going pretty well until we took in a basket-weaving class, where Horace became embroiled in a fierce altercation after an elderly lady complained that the phallic penis gourd he was weaving was offensive. If he had just made the damn thing quietly he might have got away with it, but quiet was not in Horace's nature. As he wound the willow into an elaborate sheath—called, apparently, a *koteka* in the Eastern Highlands of Papua New Guinea—he kept holding it against his trousers and asking for my opinion. He also insisted on loudly supplying a surfeit of ancillary anthropological information, whilst he attached beads and feathers, describing how the sheath was the only garment worn by men of the region and so had to be sufficiently capacious to also accommodate keepsakes, valuables and money, "including their loose change." Apparently the Indonesian government in the 1970s had launched a massive operation to eradicate the *koteka* from Irian Jaya, encouraging the men there to dress in shorts and shirts instead. But the unfamiliar and unwashed clothes caused skin diseases and so they went back to their gourds, whilst deploying the shirts as bags and the shorts as hats, and so the government gave up.

It was after he had decorated the wretched thing and was busy fixing loops of string to its tip and base—helpfully describing how the former was for attaching to the chest and the latter looped and cinched around the testicles, which were "always left naked" in tribal society—that the instructor was called over to intervene and was dismayed to discover the true purpose of what she had hitherto assumed was a basket for dried flowers. There followed a brief but fierce argument over the limits of decency. I say argument, but it was more a Horace rampage, delivered without quarter whilst masquerading under the guise of an anthropological lecture. It included the shameful legacy of white cultural imperialism on indigenous societies; how the shapes and angles of phallocrypts varied by tribal region but that size and erectness were not, interestingly, a signifier of wealth or status; how the tightness of the scrotal ligature could affect the tonal quality of the voice, which he demonstrated with some guttural cries; and how Australian aborigines eschewed the gourd in favour of the *Lonka Lonka,* a form of genital ornamentation apparently carved from pearl shell and suspended from a thong of twisted human hair. I think it was when Horace declared his intention to move on to making a *Lonka Lonka,* just as soon as he had completed his gourd, that our fate was sealed.

After being ejected by the basket-weavers, we paused to take stock. I needed a drink. Even then he insisted on displaying the damned gourd in the centre of our table at the Paper Moon. I affected insouciance, for I was trying a new approach with Horace. Having come to the conclusion that he fed on conflict, I had resolved to avoid any further arguments. I would endure the inevitable embarrassment of being his companion, and find solace in the looks of appalled sympathy that came my way from observers and victims of the Horace pageant. I told myself that I was a carer. I could enjoy the glossy sheen of altruism and embrace the martyrdom inherent in the role. After a few drinks we hit the cinema, which I was keen to do as the darkness concealed the hideous gourd (though it also contained the awful possibility that he might take off his trousers and try it on). It was a crap movie, but it provided some respite. Horace dozed off and I took the opportunity to gently remove the gourd from his lap and slide it under the seat in front. When the film finished I bustled him out and we were mercifully rid of it.

After a couple of quick toilet and drinks stops we joined a lecture by the Russian historian. We were a little late but could have slipped in unobtrusively had Horace not changed his mind several times about where to sit. When he insisted on moving a second time, the lecturer stopped mid-sentence and glared as we shambled our way along a crowded row to get closer to the front. She was backlit at the lectern, perfectly still, with the soft yellow glow of her reading light catching her blond hair and cultured cheekbones. She stared at us, head cocked slightly in a parody of patient inquiry. There was silence for a moment and then she asked with acidic courtesy whether we would be moving again soon. Horace had given a reassuring and cheerful answer in the negative, with a tad too much accompanying detail concerning his hearing difficulties and need to find the room's acoustic sweet spot. The lecturer gave an almost imperceptible nod of resignation and flashed me a look of sympathy before resuming her talk, picking up from the interruption with effortless poise. I slunk lower in my seat. The subject was Rasputin: projected on the screen was a photograph of the deranged holy man, his eyes staring out at us, as mad as a fruit cake. There was something a little Horace-like in that stare. I looked across at my companion who was listening with enraptured attention; one fucking maniac from the present hearing all about another, a kindred spirit from the past.

In fact, the lecture was pretty interesting. The speaker knew her stuff and could explain it to an audience of mixed ability without having to dumb it down or sex it up. And as Horace later said, she was "very easy on the eye" and had a voice that was low enough to be easy on the ear without being "huskily vampish." I think we would have stayed for the whole session had not Horace's concentration been broken by the sudden and shattering realisation that he had left his creation behind in the cinema. He let out a half-stifled wail of anguish. "I forgot the gourd," he said in a strangled whisper and then began squeezing back along the row, heading determinedly for the aisle. The lecturer paused, staring at him.

"Just remembered something," Horace called out. "Got to get it immediately."

"Medication?" she inquired caustically, one eyebrow impressively raised.

"Valuable art work, actually. Cultural artefact from the South Seas. Back in a jiffy. Do carry on."

I followed him, clambering the obstacle course of shame, glancing neither left nor right, heading for the exit. I knew how she would be looking at me. They were all looking. The room was silent. We reached the door, where we were momentarily delayed by Horace trying to open it in the wrong direction and declaring it to be locked, before loudly lamenting that we were trapped. After I freed us we made our way back to the cinema where, after more explanation and embarrassment than I can bring myself to recall, we retrieved the penis gourd from the third of the rubbish sacks that we were permitted to root through. Horace, whilst complaining that it had been squashed out of shape, smelt of stale food, and had lost some of its beads and feathers, was ecstatic over the gourd's deliverance, for, as he reiterated several times during the course of the evening, "Anything could have happened, Lizzy. It could have been lost overboard."

There was no possibility of rejoining the lecture and so we went to the bar where we had drinks and I cadged a large paper bag "to keep your gourd safe, Uncle," and to ensure that, though it remained on the table, its hideous aspect was concealed. We ate, drank more, and then, after a bad coughing attack, Horace declared that he was tired. I escorted him back to his room and helped him put the gourd on the table, turning it until he was satisfied that its most attractive angle was foremost to anyone having the misfortune to enter the room unawares.

"You know, Lizzy, I have a photograph that I took years ago in the Papuan Highlands. I trekked there for months. Do you know, they have hundreds of different languages up there, not dialects mind, but actual languages. Country is so rugged that there are tribes separated by only a few miles who have never clapped eyes on each other. Never. But they're friendly people, for the most part. I have a picture that I took with a self-timer, me posing with a group of them wearing these amazingly long and curly penis gourds. I'll get it and show you. It's in one of my albums."

"No need, Uncle. Don't go to any trouble."

"It's no trouble, it's in the safe." He got up unsteadily.

"Not now," I said. "We're both tired and we should make an early start tomorrow if we're going to do Alexandria."

"Won't take a mo," he insisted. I looked out towards the sea as I heard him make several attempts to open the safe. "That's funny," he said. "It's not working."

"Are you sure you're using the right combination, Uncle?"

"It's 3141, he said. "It's Pi, Archimedes' constant, without the decimal point of course and with no rounding up. A non-rounded Pi, that's how I remember it. It's what I always use for passwords. That way you don't have to remember numbers, you just have to visualise an odd-shaped pie. You can calculate the figures if you need to, and so it will provide as many as you need. Infinite decimal places. I'll have to call the Purser and get someone to come and look at it."

"Sure. But not now," I said, getting up and taking his arm. "Come on, I'll help you to bed. Busy day tomorrow."

I waited while he used the bathroom and then, after he emerged in his pyjamas, I tucked him into bed and returned to my quarters. There were two phone messages from Raphael. I lay down and resumed mining the albums, taking notes when I found a record of anything interesting. There was a soft knock on the door. I peered through the peephole and saw Raphael, spruced up in a jacket and holding a bottle of wine. I retreated quietly back into the room and after a second knock went unanswered I heard his footsteps recede into silence.

I read until late. I read until I fell asleep and then woke dry-mouthed in the dark. The ship was delicately tip-toeing into harbour. I watched the shore lights sliding by before I went to bed.

And now, red-eyed and exhausted from searching the streets of Alexandria's old quarter, I was sitting on a sleepy terrace having listened to Horace extolling the many virtues of a grandmother I had never met, but some of whose letters—always written in blue ink and with a neat and regular script—I had read only a few hours earlier. I looked at two passages that I had copied into my notebook, transcriptions from two separate letters, neither dated, which had been stuck on facing pages of one of the albums.

> "My darling boy, it is hard to wait until Wednesday. I break the intervening days into hours and minutes in the hope that the barrier of time that lies between us will seem reduced, but the numbers rise so rapidly that I am not sure it helps. I'm trying to read but my mind wanders back to you and to last night. Darling H, your memory possesses me, for you touched me in a way that was beyond my imagining. I meant what I said last night, about two bodies being fused by the seal of love, and now, alone once more, it is impossible to be focused or content, for your absence is like some missing piece of me that is fundamental to my life, to my wellbeing, to my very soul. Travel speedily, my dearest one, and return safely to me. I will live in shadows until Wednesday. A xxx"

> "..and so I repeat what I said to you yesterday. It was not a conscious or deliberate betrayal but rather a fall from grace. What happened happened, and we cannot remake it. I want only an end to all deception. I have never lied to you but I confess that I have withheld information from you both, information that I knew in my heart you would wish to possess. It's impossible

> to tell what the future will bring but it is my most fervent hope that we can remain friends. I know that we can no longer rejoice in the exultation of physical passion, for that is in the past, but I trust that we can return to the friendship—that deep and abiding friendship—from whence our journey began, and that this can serve forever in its stead and bring you solace and comfort. Your true friend, Amelia."

Horace returned, and insisted on describing, in way too much detail, the state of the Gents. "I'm telling you, Lizzy. It was as though someone hadn't even attempted to get to the bowl. They'd barely got into the cubicle before letting fly. It was absolutely disgusting in there, a total shit shower. I have never before in my entire life seen such... what are you reading?"

"Some notes. Things I wanted to ask you about my grandmother."

"Oh?" He sounded immediately guarded.

"I'm interested in what you leave out when you talk about her. You fell in love with her, right?"

"I make no secret of having loved her."

"And you became lovers."

"Yes, I loved her. She was the first woman I ever loved, the first I ever made love with."

"So you had an affair with her? And that's why you fell out with Virgil. He found out, maybe she told him, and you fought with him?"

He laughed, a snorting maniacal laugh that was loud enough to turn heads at the neighbouring tables. "An affair? She was mine before she was his. She was my girlfriend, you idiot. I took her to meet my family. That's where she met Virgil. And he seduced her, ruined her. He never loved her, he seduced her just for sport, just for the fun in possessing what I had, what I cherished. He got her pregnant and couldn't face the consequences, so he shot himself."

"Is that really true?"

"Lizzy, we had been together for six months. She came to stay after Christmas. By then I knew it was serious, in fact I knew that from the start. I wanted her to meet Father and Virgil. The visit went well, they liked her, everybody liked Amelia. She had the most delightful manners, you see. Not in an artificial way, but naturally. She was fundamentally a kind and considerate person. It was her nature. She stayed for a week or so. Strictly separate rooms, of course. Father's rules. I fell ill for a few days with a gastric virus or some such. They looked after her when I was laid up. She said Father talked to her a lot about a paper he was working on and about Italy. Virgil took her riding and was kind, even though she wasn't that good at it. He showed her around town too. He behaved himself. He was charming, actually. She got a full-on performance of the Virgil extravaganza.

"We broke up in the summer term, a few weeks shy of our first anniversary. I say broke up, but actually I mean she broke it off, out of the blue. She said we were too young, that it had become too serious too quickly, that she needed time and space to sort out her feelings. Time and space—I know now that when someone tells you that, what it actually means is that they want to spend time with someone who is not you, in a space where you are not present. But back then, I was young and it made no sense. It was just an incomprehensible blow, a wound so deep that it could never heal. Years of loss and yearning. I miss her still. Impossible to get over.

"Later, I found out that they'd been seeing each other, she and Virgil, in secret. It made the pain that much greater. You know, even by Virgil's standards of duplicity, it was a spectacular betrayal. Cut me to the core." Horace produced a voluminous white handkerchief and mopped his brow, discreetly dabbing his eyes as he did so. He blew his nose with alarming force and then coughed, wiping his pale lips with the handkerchief before carefully folding it back on itself and returning it to the pocket.

"So was there no chance of a reconciliation between you and Amelia? I mean after Virgil's death."

"Too much had happened, Lizzy. Too much hurt. Too much pride as well, maybe. You have to understand, we were all so very young. If I could go back and redo certain things I would, in a heartbeat, and I'd do them differently. But you can't. The past is not like that. Besides, Amelia was heartbroken over his loss, as well as being swollen with his bastard."

"My mother."

"Yes. Sorry. The circumstances were not of Amelia's own making, obviously. But it was an impediment, a constant reminder of what had happened. It takes a rare man to adopt another man's child, you know. Especially when that child is the symbol, the very product, of such betrayal."

"So that was your revenge, to cut her out of your life forever?"

"I'm not sure that financially supporting someone and their offspring for life can be justifiably described as an act of revenge or as cutting them out forever."

"You know what I mean. You denied her your presence, as an act of anger, vengeance for what she had done."

"That wasn't it at all. You know, Lizzy, even the most beautiful and robust thing can be destroyed at a single stroke by a single lie, a solitary act of betrayal. And there is not necessarily any balance in that equation. It's like an armoured knight shot down by an anonymous arrow; a queen taken by a pawn; a Jove-like, sleeping king, destroyed with a draught of leperous distilment dripped into his ear. And it doesn't just destroy the present and obliterate the future. It also negates the past. It invalidates even the memory of happiness because it hollows out the foundations upon which that memory stood. It poisons and denies, so all that once existed as real and true and fine becomes a worthless fiction. And then the infection is complete. All is destroyed. The pain is intolerable, unendurable. All you can do is cauterise the wound and limp forward with your scars and stumps.

"So, you see, I could never see Amelia again. It wasn't about anger, and certainly not vengeance. It was about self-preservation. And I know the mantra, people said it to me a hundred times over the years that followed. You know it, that moronic cliché, 'There's plenty more fish in the sea.' My response was always, 'Fuck you, I loved that one particular fish.' And now she's dead; she's been dead a long time."

I poured the last of the beer. "You know, Uncle, if that's the way it was, I wouldn't blame you if you had shot him. What he did was unforgiveable."

"I'm not sure that anything is unforgivable, Lizzy. If you can't forgive, it cripples you. It's a negation of life. But I take your point, it was hard to forgive. I hated him for a long time, even after his death."

"Enough to kill him?"

"Probably, yes, but I didn't. I didn't kill him. But I did see it, the moment of his death. The thing is, I was downstairs when it happened, not up in my room. But I wasn't involved. I didn't know he'd be at the house. I'd avoided him like death ever since I found out about what he had done with Amelia. I couldn't bear to look at him. I had gone back to pick up some books. He was there, wallowing in self-pity. He didn't want to marry her, he didn't want to be a father. The thing about Virgil was that he was never capable of bearing responsibility. He had been drinking, of course, and he wanted help, of course; sympathy, advice, a way out of the bloody mess that he had created for himself, for all of us. He wanted forgiveness but I was not in a forgiving vein. I was harsh, I admit that. I told him the truth, what I thought of him. I told him that the gun was just another of his poses. I knew, you see, that he didn't have the guts to shoot himself, he wasn't that brave. I laid into him and he took it, took it all, and he was weeping and snivelling, whimpering like a whipped dog.

"When I was done I told him I was leaving. I told him I never wanted to see him again for as long as I lived. And then he stopped crying and sat up straight and looked at me, straight and clear. He was sitting on the ottoman with the low table in front of him, exactly like the photographs the police took. We stared at each other. He looked so vulnerable with his tear-stained face, like we were kids again, but I felt nothing, just utter contempt. And then he smiled, and raised his glass, and said, 'Morituri te salutamus,' you know that apocryphal old gladiators' salute, 'We who are about to die salute you.' Then he did it. Just raised the barrel of the Webley to his temple and fired. And it was all in one complete movement, without any pause or hesitation. It was all one completed action, just like any everyday thing, like suddenly snapping closed a book and putting it on a shelf. I never thought he had the balls for it. I was shocked. The look on his face was one of shock too. I've often wondered if he miscalculated and thought that the gun wasn't loaded. I stood there for a moment watching the blood flow. He was obviously dead, I mean there was nothing I could have done for him. I didn't touch anything. I closed the door, grabbed my stuff and left. On the train back to Cambridge I found blood on the sleeve of my jacket." Horace mopped his face with his handkerchief. "I suppose I ran away. There was nothing else to be done. I didn't want to be involved. Yes, I ran away, and I just kept running."

On the drive back to the port Horace had a bad coughing attack. Afterwards he sat quietly in the back of the car, his head resting on my shoulder, as light as a bird. He looked shrunken and wasted within his baggy clothes. I rested my hand on his thigh but then pulled it away. It was as though there was no flesh inside the linen trouser-leg, only bone.

They brought him back on board in a wheelchair. I escorted him to his room where Monique insisted on helping him to bed. I kissed him goodnight, my lips cool on his creased forehead, but he did not stir. I think he was already asleep.

EIGHTEEN

The next few days are somewhat hazy. They began well enough but then sort of tailed off, spinning out of control a little. Though I did not know it at the time, in retrospect I think Horace had been, paradoxically, a stabilising force, as I felt a duty of care towards him. It felt like a burden but it also provided a definition and purpose for my time on the ship, and its removal, whilst it should have been liberating, was actually somewhat hard to adjust to. Burdens can be like that. Certainly the world without Horace was less colourful and I wonder if, subconsciously, I engaged in some compensatory patterns of behaviour.

That night, when we left Alexandria and sailed towards the Suez Canal, Horace was taken ill. The evening had begun normally enough. I had settled down to continue working my way through his albums. I ordered room service but it was disappointing. The salad was overly chilled and the balance of crab to lettuce was wrong. I picked at it disconsolately while I read the letters that Horace and Virgil had written to their mother during the war, the ones that were never posted and which she died without ever having read. There was a desperate poignancy to them. Not in the words so much as the childish script, with rounded, Sunday Best letters formed with such care; drawings in bright crayon, portraits of a family forever lost, stick figure children holding hands on either side of a smiling mother with profuse hair who was, by then, already dead. I had to take regular breaks, sipping white wine and looking out towards the darkening sea, despairing at the cruelty of the world. I ordered dessert but it took an age to arrive. By the time it did I was no longer hungry and so left it untouched.

Towards the end of one of the albums I came upon a letter from my great-grandfather, typed on Oxford notepaper and dated 7 April 1948.

> Dear Sir,
>
> I write in response to your letter of 25 March regarding my publication of an English translation of "De Bestiis Marinis" ("The Beasts of the Sea").
>
> I reject categorically your suggestion that I have in any respect infringed your copyright in relation to the English translation of Herr Steller's work that appeared as an appendix to "The Fur Seals and Fur-Seal Islands of the North Pacific Ocean" (Washington, 1899), or that I incorporated any of this material when making my own translation.
>
> Whilst I am familiar with the aforementioned work, I am of the opinion that its somewhat utilitarian rendering of the original Latin text fails to replicate the soaring spirit evident in Herr Steller's masterpiece. It was for this reason that I undertook the labour of a new translation, working from the original text, and, moreover, restructured some of the material to better capture the grandeur of this neglected opus and thereby make it more readily accessible to the non-specialist reader.
>
> I have nothing further to add with regard to this matter and wish to receive no further

communications from your firm. Should you have need to contact me, please do so via my representative at the enclosed address.

Yours faithfully,
Professor Alexander Cunningham

Attached was the business card of a local Oxford solicitor. On the opposite page, held in place by an aging cross of sticky tape that came away in my fingers, was a medal. It looked like an old coin, the colour of dull pewter, and had the remnants of a faded blue ribbon with red and white stripes that had been cut off near the ornate clasp. On one side was a royal crest and the words 'For Bravery in the Field' surrounded by an open laurel wreath. On the other was a profile of George VI with a crown that looked to be sitting too low on his head and an ear that seemed overly large. Below it was a certificate, inscribed in the name of Alexander Cunningham, stating that the Military Medal had been awarded for 'acts of gallantry and devotion to duty under fire'. I felt an unanticipated stab of pride, knowing how it had been earned and having visited the island where the battle had taken place. It seemed a shame that it was not displayed more prominently than inside the pages of an album of neglected miscellany.

Overleaf was a captioned photograph of my great-grandfather, evidently taken in a studio. He gazed sternly out from a painted backdrop of distant pyramids, mid-ground camel-train and artfully curated foreground palm trees and ruins. A second photograph, heavily creased in black and white, showed some men in a small wooden fishing boat. It was cluttered with packs and rifles which cast dark shadows. The men were scruffy, almost all with beards, and dressed in torn and greasy clothes, mostly a sort of hooded jacket. They had large knives hanging from their belts and pistols, and looked for all the world like bandits. Next to it was a small piece of ripped newsprint, maybe from *The Times*, with a fragment of Parliamentary transcript, undated apart from '1944', written next to it in neat blue ink. A Tory MP, Simon Wingfield-Digby, had posed a question to Churchill: "Is it true, Mr Prime Minister, that there is a body of men out in the Aegean islands, fighting under the Union flag, that are nothing short of being a band of murderous, renegade cut-throats?" The last three words had been underlined in blue. Churchill had replied: "If you do not take your seat and keep quiet I will send you out to join them!"

The facing page was blank, but bore the traces of having once had something affixed to it. Overleaf was a pair of 1955 typed letters, signed by great-grandfather.

> Dear Mr Rowley,
>
> Thank you for your letter of the 27th.
> Regretfully, I must decline your request for a meeting to discuss the matters that you raise regarding your research. It is true that I had some wartime involvement, in a training and administrative capacity, with the SOE and SBS, but I am not at liberty to speak about such. Even if I were, I believe that no constructive purpose would be served by airing the operational details of wartime missions.
> On a more general level, I can confirm that operations were conducted against enemy targets in the Mediterranean, and that these were successful in both demoralizing and tying down significant numbers of Axis troops. The men involved in such missions came from a variety of backgrounds and were highly trained and capable of great endurance. They were skilled in close combat and the use of explosives for demolition; able to move swiftly and

undetected over both land and sea; and to subsist without supply or support within enemy-occupied territory.

The casualty ratios that you cite should not be interpreted as evidence of "one-sided" engagements, at least not in numerical terms. Invariably our men fought from a position of significant numerical inferiority, but this was negated by superior training, equipment and morale, as well as the advantage of surprise.

Prisoners were taken when circumstance permitted, but rarely in large numbers as engagements were fought on a relatively small scale. The strictures under which our forces operated also militated against being able to bring back large numbers of POWs. Prisoners need to be transported, fed and guarded, a task hard enough when operating from a base, but almost impossible when moving fast through enemy territory laden with ammunition and supplies.

I cannot comment on the issue of surrender amongst our forces, other than to say that such instances were rare. There were no official instructions as to how to proceed if men found themselves in a hopeless position. It was widely known, however, that the nature of the operations meant that, if captured, our men faced interrogation, torture and execution. In that sense, death was preferable to capture, not because of what you term "a culture of fostered heroism" but as a means of avoiding the torture that would inevitably precede execution.

I cannot comment on the use of Benzedrine other than to say that wartime missions sometimes require huge reserves of stamina and long periods without sleep, and there were instances within the military of all nations where stimulants were used, most notably caffeine, to assist with this.

Yours faithfully,
Professor Alexander Cunningham

Dear Mr Rowley,

Thank you for your recent letter.
I am afraid that I cannot add further to the general remarks that I made in my earlier reply.
Having taken advice on the matter, however, I can confirm the facts that you put to me regarding the April 1944 operation against Santorini, as these are a matter of public record. I can also offer some contextual explanation as to why the oft-used appellation "Lassen's Bloodbath," which you cite in your letter, does not accurately reflect the true nature of this mission.
A force of around 20 men landed on the island on the night of 22-23 April. They were led by Captain Anders Lassen, whose heroism during the war was widely acknowledged and who died in action a year later in Italy. (As you may know, Lassen was awarded a posthumous Victoria Cross, the only non-Commonwealth serviceman throughout the entire war to have received this highest gallantry award.) The expedition had sailed from a base in Turkey, travelling for three nights and concealing itself by day to avoid detection by enemy aircraft.

In the early hours of 24 April our men simultaneously attacked three designated targets. One was the wireless telegraph station at Imerovigli, which was utterly destroyed. Another was the house of the German commander, Lieutenant Hesse, which was taken. The main target was the barracks in Fira, which housed the German-Italian garrison. This was the scene of fierce fighting. The assault was successful but two of the raiding party died in the attack; a significant portion of the enemy garrison was also destroyed.

With regard to the point you make about casualties, I should stress that the fighting was intense, and took place in pitched darkness inside an unfamiliar and smoke-filled building. Our men were not equipped with torches and there was, inevitably, a considerable degree of confusion. The building, originally a bank, was strongly fortified and entry proved more difficult than anticipated. The initial attack was repulsed by heavy enemy fire, but after regrouping, a second assault, this time from the rear, succeeded. Even then, our men had to fight their way to the upper floor where the garrison was housed. There were many rooms, and in each case the door had to be forced and then grenades and machine gun fire used to subdue the enemy.

This explains why such a high proportion of the garrison was killed. Some also died as they tried to flee by jumping from upper floor windows, a drop of 30 to 40 feet. After the barracks had been secured, our men provided medical assistance to enemy wounded, though they had limited supplies of such and little time before having to withdraw from the town.

There was further fighting as the assaulting force clashed with scattered enemy units along the way. Despite a delay because of bad weather, our men were evacuated by boat and all returned safely to their base.

After German reinforcements arrived on the island they executed five civilians from Vourvoulos, including the mayor, as a reprisal for the raid. More would have been shot had not Lassen sent a message to Lieutenant Hesse, emphasising that the German commander would be answerable after the war for any atrocities committed by those under his command.

In conclusion I can say without hesitation that the Santorini operation was a conspicuous success. Though there was a comparatively high casualty rate on both sides, the raid was merely one of many conducted against that particular island and against other strategic targets in the Aegean. It that sense, it was a routine operation, without any exceptional features.

I wish you every success in obtaining your PhD but regret that I cannot assist you further. Please do not contact me again.

Yours faithfully,
Professor Alexander Cunningham

There seemed to be no further correspondence on the matter. The following pages of the album consisted of two menus from formal college dinners, the minutes of several departmental meetings and some book reviews, all unrelated and entirely inconsequential. Then, on the last page of the volume, was a glued down sheet whose ragged edge suggested that it had been torn from a notebook. It was a handwritten diary entry, but there was no indication as to its year.

25 April.

Difficult night. It is that time of year again, when spirits stir abroad by light of day and, in the darkness, sleep is all but impossible.

It is unseasonably cold. Took an early walk on the Meadow and found pleasure in simple things – the sunrise, the tracery of frost on grass, a glorious cloudscape, the cacophony of bird song.

The anniversary of the landing was on Tuesday, but the assault was the night of the 23rd or, technically, the early hours of yesterday. These markers in time inhabit the mind oddly. I dreamed of it again last night, but the rooms were different and the faces changed. The only constant is those eyes.

Standing in the Meadow with the cold sunlight it was easier to go through it all methodically, confront it coolly, without unnecessary emotion. When there is a monster in the house you must turn on the light, rather than cower in the dark.

It is important to retain a hold on necessity. That operation was not decisive, but it was instrumental. It was a small piece of a campaign that helped shorten the war by drawing enemy forces away from the beaches of France. And though war is brutal by necessity, we were on the side of right. There is no ambiguity about that; History has been the judge. Further, the operation was successful in its own terms. We lost two and they lost 40, as well as suffering the deprivation of supplies and the disruption of radio communication in the entire region. Within those margins lies the calculus of victory. What was done was 'cruel necessity'. Cromwell knew how the first of those words was counteracted by the second; poison and antidote. It was war and those chaps had been trained for that specific type of work: to kill at close quarters, in cold blood. They were terrorists. Their job was to terrorise the enemy. But Lassen enjoyed it too much. He enjoyed the cold savagery. He was tough and courageous, no question, but he was also a reckless, bloodthirsty madman. No sane mind finds joy in hurling grenades into the dormitories of sleeping enemy men, or responding to surrender pleas by emptying Bren gun magazines into the darkness.

There was no need. The garrison would have surrendered but he wanted a bloodbath. We had total surprise but he botched the initial attack. That's when Lieutenant Casulli was shot. Stefan the handsome Greek, quiet and dependable, the nearest that Lassen ever had to a friend. He was killed outright, and after that there could be no prisoners. Lassen was like Achilles after the death of Patroclus: no amount of blood could slake his fury.

Later I heard that the Germans had shot ten men from the village, though the official number was half that. Another 13 islanders died when the radio was blown up. The explosives had been left on a timer and when they blew there were

> locals in the building searching for food and loot.
>
> So, the final count was two of ours, 40 or so of theirs and more than 20 civilians. I'm not sure where that stands in the calculus of victory, but I know that the medal was a joke. I think it was to remind me to keep my mouth closed about what happened that night. I think, too, that I have been forever marked by it. "Tempus erit quo vos speculum vidisse pigebit."
>
> This is no longer a diary entry, it is becoming a confession. Enough.

I looked up a translation of the Latin online. It meant, 'The time will come when it will disgust you to look in a mirror.'

I checked the reverse of the paper, prising it gently from the album. The old glue cracked but came away easily. There was no writing but there was a folded sheet of paper taped behind it. I carefully pulled it free. It was another page, though the top half had been torn away, and was written in the same hand.

> I did not ask for the role. I was there to observe. But perhaps there was also the need to see action before the war's end – the base instinct of a staff officer stabbing an enemy corpse in order to blood his sword. But by being there I was a participant; there was never any room for observers.
>
> After the firing had ceased, a small group of prisoners was taken to the back terrace and dispatched. I did not see it but I heard the shots. Elsewhere, whilst our wounded were treated in preparation for the withdrawal, several of us were charged with checking the bodies. We moved amongst them dispensing the mercy of

oblivion to those still alive. It was routine and had to be done quickly and efficiently.

The first was a German. He was haemorrhaging blood from grenade shrapnel in the abdomen and was in great pain. He would have died, I am sure of that. I followed procedure: from the side, find the spot, get the pistol barrel close but not touching, cock, steady, look away to avoid the spray, fire. It's simple really. The other was an Italian. He was young and had taken several shots to his right shoulder and arm and was bleeding but calm. He asked for water and I gave him some from my canteen. That was my mistake. I shouldn't have hesitated and given him that drink. He didn't need water where he was going. He said "Grazie compagno" and I answered "Prego." My use of Italian was instinctive, but that was another mistake. His face was very pale under the starlight. He looked at me with wide black eyes and said, "Per favore, non uccidermi." He told me he had a wife and two daughters. I was kneeling next to him with the revolver hot in my trembling hand. He felt it touch his temple and he stared at me with those wide eyes and said "Aspetta." I whispered "Perdonami," for indeed I wanted his forgiveness. I cocked the hammer and he said "Tempus erit quo vos speculum vidisse pigebit." It was only after I fired that I recognised the quote. His last words were from Ovid.

And because my hand was shaking the shot was not clean. He was still alive and so I fired again, too fast, from the front without proper aim. The bullet entered through his right eye socket and killed him instantly, spraying my face with blood and matter. And through the jagged hole

> in his skull, the hole where his eye had been, I saw the seepage of brain. Smelt it above the cordite, the pink and red disorder that until a moment ago had, like me, held Ovid's poetry within its scope. Held and treasured it.
> I was throwing up when Lassen came by. He kicked that shattered head and told me that one bullet would have been enough.

I went out onto the balcony. The night was warm and I sensed the scale of the black sea all around me, the Greek islands scattered within it, littered with their silent dead. I could feel the looming presence of Africa where my great-grandfather had served, and beyond that, the perfumed winds of Arabia and the great canal that would take us through to the Red Sea and thence to the Indian Ocean. I felt a yearning pull of homesickness, a desire to be amongst my own people. I sat and drank and listened to the noise of the ship, the clatter of passengers and the throb of music.

I went back inside to the bed and flicked through more pages of the past. There were notes between Horace and Virgil, birthday cards, letters, casually dashed off lines on scraps of paper that charted the passing of the years. There were nicknames, references to unknown anecdotes, manufactured words and abbreviations; an island language and culture in which no outsider could ever be fluent and which, like some dying dialect, was passing with the lifespan of its last speaker. I felt shabby as I sifted through the detritus of their lives, but envious too, hankering after their closeness. I wondered what it would have been like to have a sister or a brother, a confidante upon whom you could rely.

There were random notes between Virgil and Amelia, including some flowery love letters and a poem or two. On the last page of one of the albums, was a small note in Virgil's handwriting dated three days before his death. There was no indication as to whether it had ever been sent and, if so, to whom. It said simply, "Agreed. Wednesday evening. I'll be waiting. V." It was written on the usual letterhead which bore the address of the family home, but the bottom of the paper had been torn off. It shared the page with a typewritten copy of the last stanza of that well-known Alan Seeger poem, the only well-known Seeger poem: *I Have a Rendezvous with Death*.

God knows 'twere better to be deep
Pillowed in silk and scented down,
Where Love throbs out in blissful sleep,
Pulse nigh to pulse, and breath to breath,
Where hushed awakenings are dear...
But I've a rendezvous with Death
At midnight in some flaming town,
When Spring trips north again this year,
And I to my pledged word am true,
I shall not fail that rendezvous.

The paper was yellowing and dog-eared and had a small flower doodled in one corner. It had been smoothed out and stuck down but bore the marks of having once been crumpled. It was stained with red wine. Below the text was a handwritten doggerel.

A shot to the head
is a terrible thing,
makes the eyes smart
makes the ears ring,
but the eyes of the dead
don't say anything
blackened with shock
bloodshot and ringed
they shriek in their silence
of a soul that's now binned.

A shot to the head
doesn't cure anything,
it just left you dead
and made my ears ring.

It was undated and unsigned, but the pronouns in the last two lines were interesting.

I got the call at about 10pm. Monique had raised the alarm after she found Horace collapsed on the bathroom floor. He had been taken to the sanatorium where they diagnosed dehydration resulting from diarrhoea. They suspected a stomach bug or mild food poisoning. They told me he would be okay, but were keeping him in for observation because of his age and underlying health issues. I went to see him but he was sleeping peacefully under crisp white sheets in the little medical bay.

On the way back I made a detour via his suite. I let myself in and opened the safe with the override code. The contents were exactly as I had last seen them, although when I examined the strongbox I found that it was unlocked. Inside were numerous small plastic pouches containing bags of opals. There were hundreds of stones in an array of sizes and colours. I also checked on the Will, still in its brown envelope and still, disappointingly, unsigned. I left all undisturbed and locked the safe using Horace's 3141 combination, the non-rounded pie.

I went into the sitting room and scanned the surfaces, looking for anything of interest. I saw his briefcase tucked under the table but I had only taken a step towards it when the main door opened. I turned, guiltily, and there was Monique. We stared for a moment, each equally surprised to see the other. She closed the door and advanced towards me.

"Can I help you with something, Madam?"

"I was just checking to see if there was anything that my uncle might need."

"But I already took for him all he needs."

"Good. That's good. Well there's nothing more I need to get him. I've just seen him. He wanted me to check on his cabin."

"I have just come from him. He is sleeping."

"Yes, yes of course, he's asleep now. I meant before he went to sleep. That's when he asked me to do it... to check."

"It is not necessary, Madam." She made the honorific sound like an insult. "Would Madam like anything from the drinks cabinet?"

"No." I felt myself flush. "What are you doing here when he is not in residence?" It was an attempt to wrestle back control of the conversation.

"I'm his butler, Madam. What happens in his suite is my responsibility. It is my role."

"Good. Okay, well carry on. I shall drop by and visit him when he wakes." I left with what I hope was a quiet dignity, but it's hard to be sure. I could feel her doll-like stare burning between my shoulder blades as I let myself out.

On my way back I stopped for a drink. There was some sort of party going on at the Magellan and I bumped into Raphael who had just finished his shift. After the unsettling encounter with Monique the Mad Butler, I was rather pleased to run across someone who seemed genuinely happy to see me. We had a few drinks. I was adamant that I would not drink any more Tubi 60, ever, but we did have a couple of glasses of wine. We danced too. I wasn't really dressed for it, but there comes a time in life when such invitations are in sufficiently short supply that it does not do to pass them up. He was a pretty good dancer actually, rhythmical and silky without being too flash.

It was hot and loud and so later we went out on deck. The night was warm and still, clear but almost moonless. There were a number of people taking the air and gazing at the stars. After a couple of turns around the deck he said there was something he wanted to show me. Checking that we were not being observed, he furtively unlocked a small steel door and ushered me through, quietly locking it behind us. "Follow me," he whispered, "But hold on tight." He began ascending a steel ladder and I followed. We climbed four or five lengths, each demarcated by a small platform. I could feel the layers of accrued salt on the steel. Eventually, after cautiously popping his head up to check, he pulled himself through a steel hatch. His face then reappeared from above. "Come on up, it's okay, totally secure." I clambered through, his hands reaching down to guide me. I stood up and found that we were on some sort of lookout platform high on the ship, higher even than the Eye of Zeus observation deck. There were no lights but the platform was surrounded by a wire screen with cut out sections on all sides. The views were breathtaking. Passengers moved far below, oblivious to our existence, and beyond the ship's pool of light lay the silent sea, wine dark around us. To the rear was the white churning water of our wake. Above was a flint canopy of stars backlit by the wraithlike glow of the Milky Way, so clear and close that it seemed almost possible to reach up and touch it.

"This is amazing," I whispered. "What is this place?"

"Very secret," he said. "Off limits even to crew. It's a reconnaissance platform. A redoubt, too. The floor is double plate steel and the mesh is armoured. Even RPGs will just bounce right off. It's got awesome fields of fire and the angles mean it's hard to return fire from below. And see that cabinet there?" he nodded to a locked steel bunker door set into the one solid side of the platform. "That's a fully equipped arsenal with emergency water and rations. It also gives access to the ventilation system so you could, if you needed to, crawl through and get back into the main body of the ship."

"Who are you planning on going to war with?"

"There's plenty of bad guys out there, Lizbet, pirates, hijackers, terrorists. But this," he gestured proudly, "this is impregnable. It's beautiful. We call it the Sky Fort. From here we could hold out indefinitely, interdict activity below, and even counter-attack through the ventilation shafts. Those motherfuckers wouldn't know what hit them. From here we could take back the ship no matter how many of them there were. You see, it's not numbers that count, it's training and firepower."

"You're really saying that we might be attacked?"

"Where we are headed, absolutely. Why do you think the company employs guys like me? Believe me, we don't come cheap. This is a valuable asset, full of rich people. The onboard security detail is here to keep you safe from those fuckheads. Until now, all I've had to worry about was the possibility of a drunken brawl or some asshole pushing his wife overboard so he can marry his mistress. But soon we'll be in bandit country. After the canal, it's the Red Sea and the Gulf, with plenty of towel heads who are full of al-Qaida poison and who would love to blow up the ship and take you all hostage, cut a few throats. After that it's Somali pirates, the Indian Ocean is crawling with them, like fleas on a dog's ass. They operate from the shore or from mother ships out at sea. Either way they use speedboats to get close enough to board. They take the ship and then ransom it back, along with the crew and cargo, though some like to rape and loot also. They used to be fishermen but now they're making millions of bucks and don't need to fish. Companies pay because it's cheaper to buy them off than to lose the ship and cargo. It's mostly tankers and container vessels, but they're interested in cruise ships too, they just haven't managed to get one yet. They've tried, but guys like me have kicked their sorry asses."

"Are you for real about this?"

"Totally for real. But there's no call to be scared. They're opportunistic, drugged-up vermin, looking for easy targets. They've got RPGs and Kalashnikovs but they're still assholes wearing shorts and flip flops. We're armed and trained. As long as we spot them we can drop them, and we can do it before they get within pissing distance. But the risk to passengers is real. Cruise ships have been hit by automatic fire and a few grenades. You'll know if an attack is imminent. They'll sound an alarm and muster everyone to a safe space. If you hear it, drop what you're doing and follow instructions. Me and the guys have predetermined posts, maybe I'll be up here. There's no cause to worry, those fuckheads won't get past us. You'll be safe."

Actually, I was not worried in the least about the fuckheads. I was gazing up at the brave o'erhanging firmament, the majestically arching canopy of sky and thinking about how its scale and grandeur dwarfed everything: the fuckhead pirates, our miniscule hidden platform, our tiny painted boat, with its trail of spittle, trudging across a small inland sea on an insignificant planet that was circling a middle-aged and distinctly average star. And though the scarred space above us was pockmarked with diamonds, billions of furnaces whose ferocious blue heat leached tracks across the void, even they would one day burn out. I read somewhere that that was how the universe would end, not with a bang or some massive contraction, but with the last star burning the last of its fuel and sputtering into darkness. And then there would be nothing, no light or time, just the faint presence of background radiation. So even after all was gone, the Earth long gone, the Milky Way consumed by a giant black hole with all matter shredded to a sub-atomic level, even after all this, some dark approximation of sky would remain, its congregation of vapours and blackness stretching forever. In that sense it was vaster than Time itself; as immortal and limitless as the God in whom I had once believed but whom I lost through carelessness or neglect. And at that moment there was a part of me that wanted to step off that tiny platform, climb over those screens of armoured mesh that let you see but not touch, and leave this prison ship forever, falling upwards into the darkness and starlight, stumbling into Heaven, and finding there, finding once again, those whom I had failed to hold close enough.

Raphael moved next to me. "You know Lizbet, what I've told you is absolutely confidential. And this place, you've never seen it, okay? I'd be fired immediately, no severance pay. This place is way off limits. We're not even allowed into guests' rooms."

I laughed. "Well you've already contravened that rule."

"Yeah, and I hope I do again. Maybe stay longer next time."

It was getting schmaltzy and I guess I knew what was coming next. My knees weren't exactly knocking in anticipation, but nor was I about to dive back through the hatch. I was sort of mildly curious. The first kiss was quite nice, gentle, almost hesitant. More like a poet than a warrior. Those that followed grew quickly more passionate as he pressed against me, pushing me against the salt-caked steel. I could taste him, feel his tongue, his hands inside my shirt. I could hear the sound of our breath above the throbbing pulse of the ship's turbines and the distant clatter of voices far below us.

He struggled with the waistband of my trousers but I stayed his hand. "Let's go to my room," I said.

NINETEEN

When I woke the next morning Raphael had gone. I had a dull headache. I called the sanatorium to check on Horace and was told that he was continuing to improve. Then I ordered room service. The coffee was good though it could have been hotter, but the croissants were cinnamon flavoured when I had distinctly requested almond. I ate them anyway. I breakfasted on the balcony, in my dressing gown, whilst the maid cleaned my room.

Raphael had left a note. "Gotta work. Thanks. Much appreciated. Catch you later – R." Thanks? Much appreciated? That sounded almost dismissively slight. When you open your bed, your heart, your body to another, it ought to feel consequential. But this was like, 'Thanks for running that errand, it was much appreciated;' 'Thanks for the use of your lawnmower;' 'Thanks for whatever minor service was performed, it was much appreciated.' I mean, I wasn't expecting to be kissed awake with champagne and roses wreathed in a freshly minted love poem, but maybe something more substantial than 'Thanks'.

Actually, it was a shame because the evening had gone pretty well. We had got back to my room without mishap or detection. The sex was not earth-moving but it was easy and pretty nice. He was in decent shape from all his macho man security work, clambering up ladders so he could spot and shoot the fuckheads who would otherwise run amok in the world, killing us all. His moral universe was fixed and certain. There were good guys and bad guys and his life was lived in the fault lines between these two warring tribes. And he was always absolutely certain that he could identify the good from the bad, it was one of the odd things about Raphael. That and his acne-scarred upper back and shoulders where the skin felt as rough as barnacles. He was undemanding but not without bedroom skills and after our in depth exploration of country matters we lay in the dark, my head on his chest, the scent of Africa wafting in through the open balcony door on the warm sea breeze.

Raphael was strangely incurious; he asked almost nothing about me or the course my life had followed before our paths overlapped and mingled. He talked about his dilemma over whether to live in Israel or America, and about how his father had defended the Suez Canal in 1973, and how the return of the Sinai to Egypt had been a strategic blunder by unworthy politicians. He talked with immediacy about a girlfriend in Jerusalem who, though he overemphasised the past tense, sounded very much an inhabitant of the present.

I thought of William, but not with guilt. We weren't together and for all I knew he was seeing other women. It was understood when we separated that there would be no ties, but it still felt odd to be with someone else. Not wrong but odd; one becomes habituated to the individuality of a particular body. Some people find that a problem, they get bored, particularly men I guess. But I have always found it comforting. It's like when you live in a particular area for a while, you learn the geography through familiarity. And while there is always more to explore, you know the basic layout and you know your secret places of preference, like where to walk, where to eat, where best to park or shop. With an unfamiliar body there is the excitement of the new, but new is not necessarily better. Besides, with the new you have to explore uncharted terrain, never quite sure what you will encounter. Internal wounds and external scars lie in wait like swathes of sharp barnacles.

The thing is, it takes years to truly know the body of another person with its idiosyncrasies of form and feeling, its curves and hollows and secrets, its weight, its scent, its sighs. I remember having read how hard it was for the Norman victors to identify the corpse of King Harold amongst all those mangled bodies on Senlac Hill in the aftermath of the Battle of Hastings. Eventually they had relied on his lover, Edith Swanneck—how I have coveted the elegance of Edith's name—and she identified the corpse by what the chroniclers described as 'secret marks, known only to her'. Bodies are like that, each with its secret marks, secret sites, that only lovers know. I knew I would be able to identify Will's body even now, even after so long, so much elapsed time, by following the route of familiar paths and the waypoints of secret marks. And thinking of Will, and bodies, made me think of Wat, and then I felt the rise of that familiar nausea of unquenchable pain, suffocating grief. And I pushed it away as I didn't want it to come crashing into a night made soft with the small tenderness of shared skin. And it worked, for there, in that insignificant but genuine moment of intimacy, I drifted into sleep.

Breakfast on the balcony turned into a protracted affair, not least because the maid took an age to clean the room. There was some debris from the night before but nothing Carthaginian, and I had asked her to take a little more care in scrubbing the chrome of the shower fittings, which seemed to have been skipped in recent days. For whatever reason, she moved at glacial pace. I ended up ordering a second breakfast from room service just to while away the time. Besides, I was feeling lazy and it was interesting to watch the Suez Canal slip by. It was wider than I had imagined, and I had not realised that there were no locks, as the sea level difference between its northern and southern points is inconsequential. We were in a convoy of vessels that left Port Said, moving slowly south with the Sinai on our left and Egypt to the right. The land that we cut through was largely baked brown desert, low and arid but for a smear of green that grew next to the freshwater irrigation channel running beside us. This had been dug in the nineteenth century to provide water for the poor bastards who had excavated the main canal, toiling in the desert heat. Recently, the Egyptians had completed a vast canal expansion project that enabled ships to pass up and down simultaneously by using two separate lanes.

Over the sandbank that divided the two lanes you could see the tops of ships making their way north, as I discovered when I had finally been able to shower—in a bathroom where the chrome could have been cleaner given the ocean of time taken—and go up on deck to observe the canal from both sides of the ship. The scale of the project was impossibly impressive and there was ample evidence of ongoing construction, with tunnels and bridges, settlements being built or expanded, vehicles scurrying between the military checkpoints that littered the road running like a ribbon along the bank beside us, parallel to the railway tracks. And all around was the swarm of other craft: speed boats and tugs, pilot boats, ferries carrying people and cars, and tiny fishing skiffs unchanged since the time of the pharaohs where sun-dark men with headdresses and oars cast their nets. I imagined Raphael perched somewhere, perhaps in our secret love nest, watching, scanning his allocated stretch of waterway, checking for possible pirates, looking for lurking bands of fuckheads.

By afternoon we had passed Ismailia and entered the Great Bitter Lake, which opened out around us, as vast as an inland sea. I got talking to a guy who told me that the lake had, prior to the canal's construction, been a dry salt valley since ancient times. It was flooded when the canal was cut, but had retained a level of salinity several times greater than that of the sea. I was still mulling this over when I went to check on Horace in the sanatorium. I was told by the nurse that he was much improved and would soon be returning to his suite. He certainly looked lively, sitting in a chair in his dressing gown and pyjamas, peering out at the landscape and purring about the canal.

"Isn't she a beauty," he said. "What a marvel of engineering, what confidence. It's a monument to a civilisation that believed in its own future. And to think that all this, like the pyramids themselves, was built by illiterate labourers with picks and shovels, hacking their way from one sea to another without thought of failure."

He told me how much it had changed since he had sailed through it in the 1950s, when ships would have to wait in designated passing places so that another could come by from the opposite direction. He related how from 1967 the Great Bitter Lake had been the anchorage of fifteen international merchant ships, trapped in the canal for years after it had been blocked during the Six-Day War.

"Do you know, Lizzy, they were called the 'Yellow Fleet' because of the sand which covered their decks, but they stayed afloat, manned by skeleton crews who whiled away the years. One was an American vessel that was trapped further north in Lake Timsah. But the others were close to each other and they established a little community called the Great Bitter Lake Association. And their relations were far from bitter for they socialised freely. There were movies shown on the Bulgarian freighter; swimming parties in the pool of the Swedish merchantman; church services on one of the German vessels (Lutheran, I would imagine); and football matches on one of the British ships, the one with the largest deck space. They competed in lifeboat racing, deck games, and even held a 1968 Bitter Lake Olympic Games to mirror the real Olympics that were going on in Mexico City. And do you know, when the canal was finally reopened in 1975, two of those ships—both German, naturally—were actually able to depart under their own steam. Think of it, after all those years they just weighed anchor and resumed their voyage, continuing their route back to their original destination, Hamburg, where they were greeted by a cheering crowd of tens of thousands. In the end, their voyage from Australia took eight years, three months and five days." He emphasised the five days with the snap of precision that derives from an accuracy of days when Time is measured in units of years. "What do you think of that?"

"It sounds like a prison sentence."

"Nonsense. It's as much a tribute to the indomitability of the human spirit as the canal itself."

"But to be trapped there, with those other people, having to find ways to pass your time, ways of fighting the boredom while you watch life draining slowly away around you, draining into the sand."

"Just like being on a cruise, really. Most people adapt. That ability to adapt is one of the greatest strengths and, simultaneously, curses of humanity."

I tried to ask him about his health but he insisted he was fine and returned the conversation to the canal. As dusk began to fall the canal talk slackened. He yawned and the nurse suggested that he return to bed. He bade me a warm goodnight and arranged to meet tomorrow. "I'll be up and about by then. In the meantime," he said with sleepy tenderness, "Go and have some fun. Get a nice dinner. Do some shopping. I hear they have some swanky stores on the ship. Just charge it to the room. It's all taken care of."

I kissed him on the forehead and then went out again into the desert, or rather, into the gaudy streets of the vulgar city created in the desert. Over the next few hours I hit the shops in a manner that was, when viewed in retrospect, a little excessive. In my defence I can say only that it was not a regular occurrence. I had not bought anything—well, not much—since the last time and on this occasion, unlike the last, it was an officially sanctioned expedition. The first time it had been motivated by anger and was a sort of revenge shopping; this time it was the response to an invitation that—had I refused—would have appeared unnecessarily rude to an old man who was being generous, and could afford his generosity. To have spurned it would have been not just rude, but also churlish in denying him what was, clearly, a source of vicarious pleasure.

Furthermore, the weather was getting distinctly warmer and was set to become warmer still. So I did need some additional sun wear. I admit though, I got a little carried away. I think I became a bit desensitised with regard to prices. At the outset I bought a lovely Claudie Pierlot floral print frock with a plunging neckline that looked like an oriental painting in blue and gold. It seemed expensive (£250), but after I had been snagged by an exquisite Zimmerman, eight-ribbon-tie number in crisp linen (that was £599) with a flattering mini length—that had, I was told, leg-lengthening results, which, let's face it, is always good—together with elasticated bow embellishments and this season's Poppy Print blossoming across the sleeveless body, the first one seemed pretty cheap. And that meant by the time I got to the divine Dolce & Gabbana stuff I was very much in the groove. I gobbled up a cashmere leopard print sweater (for 925) and an Italian-crafted sequin collar shirt in soft cotton with crystal buttons for only a few pounds more. After that, the silk polka-dot dress—with flattering silhouette, delicate butterfly sleeves and a cinched feminine figure-accentuating waist, falling to a modest midi length with a subtle peplum hem—seemed reasonable (1,650), as did the lace eyelet dress, part of Dolce & Gabbana's recent Runway collection, with bustier-inspired bodice embellished with eyelets and laces to give a shapely and defined silhouette with infused sensuality, which was actually 100 cheaper. I realised then that I had to get away from Dolce & Gabbana but in doing so I fell a chance victim to Valentino, where the loose fit but strikingly elegant, chromatic giraffe print dress was an interesting take on the original 1960s version and an alternative to the ubiquity of leopard print. The price (2,350) did make me wince a little but when there is no cash involved, and the money is not yours, the wincing is just a reflex twitch of conscience rather than a spasm of meaningful pain. Besides, it passes in a moment.

And it's not like I did not buy straightforward sun wear too. I got two pairs of shorts: Ralph Lauren, cotton chinos in navy blue (55), and Armani, high-waisted, distressed denim (95). I got into a bit of a dither about sandals and ended up gorging on a logo-print pair from Balenciaga—red-pink with black silhouette sole and a steel stiletto heel—which were half price (500); a pair of Yeezy thong heels, in beige (450), that were muted and classy; some Tory Burch flats; a pair of Studio Amelia sandals in white leather with a thong that coiled up the leg almost to mid-calf—very Greco-Roman; some Gianvito Rossi leather flats that were amazingly versatile as they perfectly captured that tricky 'formal-to-beach vibe'; and a pair of low-cut, pink sneakers from Nike that were irresistibly cute. There were a couple of bags, too: a faux leather tote that would obviously be immensely practical rather than frivolous and a Chanel mixed fibre, lambskin and silver tone metal, with matching coin purse, which was, I admit, more of an indulgence. I also got some new sunglasses, because they're something that always get misplaced or broken. I tried for ages to decide between Dior and Gucci, which were similar though with subtle but important differences, and ended up resolving matters by getting both. There were also a few sundries: bits of impulse jewellery, mostly just earrings; various skin and hair products, necessitated by the corrosive exposure to heat and salt; and a few odds and ends, the most adorable of which was a leopard print, water resistant trench coat. It was, I admit, not strictly sun wear, but I loved it and besides, it was versatile enough to protect from sun and also spray.

I arranged to have everything sent to my room, but even though I was not laden with baggage it was still an exhausting session. Oddly, it was less satisfying than I thought it would be. You know the fantasy—free shopping, buy whatever you like with no cost or cash involved. But there was something less enjoyable than the first time, something almost dispiriting about it.

I was about ready to call it a day when I ran into Raphael. He had just got off shift and was solicitous, apologising for having had to leave so early, wanting to make it up to me. So we went for a few drinks and then ate at the buffet. He was pretty twitchy and was drinking his customary lake of black coffee because he was on call. I was not on call and so relaxed a little more. He said we were entering the Red Sea and so were now officially in "towel-head territory." I told him that was racist but even in the saying it felt like the echo of a position once held, rather than a real flesh and blood opinion with a beating heart of outrage. I told him that Arab headdresses looked amazing, in fact Arab robes in general have always struck me as the most glamorous garment a man could wear. He snorted and said I had a Lawrence of Arabia complex typical of the English, but when I drilled down into that it turned out he was woefully ignorant about Lawrence and his achievements. I mean, I'm no expert but at least I've seen the movie. And when it became obvious that there was a disparity chasm between our respective levels of knowledge on the issue he quickly changed the subject.

We had more drinks and then, inevitably, we ended up back at my place. I was actually a little ambivalent, worn out from the shopping, but he was keen and I went along with it. Back in the room I had to clear the mass of purchases from where they had been laid out neatly on the bed. He gave me a hand and whistled slightly through his teeth at the quantity of stuff which did, admittedly, look a little extravagant in the cell-like confines of my little cabin. He asked if I was very rich but I ignored the question and went to make some coffee to stop myself yawning. He offered me a line of coke instead. It had been some years since I had indulged, but once tried, when coke blows into town who do you know who ever refuses? He rubbed the glass top of the bureau but it was still smeared and so I did it properly and then he cut four lines. I rolled a 20 pound note—and was struck by the realisation that it was the first actual money I had touched on the entire voyage. We did the lines and that immediately sorted out the tiredness and the ambivalence of desire. We got down to business with the usual agreeable results. It was only days later that I realised he had kept my twenty.

The sex was okay; better than okay, actually. I mean it was coke-sex, which is always better than okay. It took a while and afterwards we lay sprawled and naked on the ruined bed, silent in the darkness, slipping on towards the Indian Ocean. The smear of light coming in from outside picked out the shadows of the discarded bags and strewn clothes. I felt low and was waiting for him to leave. I remembered what Horace had said about those poor stranded bastards in the Yellow Fleet, trapped for years on the Great Bitter Lake. Like theirs, this was a prison-ship, a floating palace-prison where you eat and drink, and shop and fuck, because there's nothing else to do. And the sun comes up on a new day but it's not really new because you know that you're going to do the same stuff that you did the day before, and the day before that. And you will keep doing it until the voyage ends because there's no alternative; the great array of choice on offer is a sham, just inconsequential variations, elaborations on the same tawdry theme. But even though you know this, you go along with it all and do it anyway, just like everyone else. And every day is the same as its predecessor and always will be. And you realise how bored you are. And you want so much to go home, though you've been drifting so long that you're no longer sure where home is exactly. And so you have another drink and you wait for it all to end.

"You want to sleep, Lizbet?"

"I don't think I can."

"You want something to drink?"

"No. I'm tired but not sleepy. Tell me something interesting. Tell me something that you've learnt from all your time on these ships."

He laughed. "The dirty secret of cruising is that although they sell these trips as being all about fresh sea air and a shiny clean environment, they're actually filthy."

"In terms of hygiene?"

"No, though that can be pretty bad also. No, I meant in terms of their environmental damage. They fuck up the places they visit, distort their economies, but that's tourism. The locals get some benefit from it. The real damage is to the wider environment. They're filthy. A ship like this can burn through 4,000 tonnes of fuel in a single voyage. Tonnes, not gallons. They can burn a gallon just by travelling ten metres. Some produce as much sulphur dioxide as 13 million automobiles. And they do that every day."

"Christ, I didn't know it was that bad."

"And what's worse is they use heavy fuel oil, the dirtiest gasoline in the world, and there's no requirement that they're fitted with abatement systems or particulate filters like cars and trucks. And because they're floating hotels, they have to keep their engines running 24/7 even when they're in port so they can power up all those spas and showers, and restaurants and bars. They can use the same energy as a mid-size town. They can burn 150 tonnes of fuel a day, which emits as many particulates as a million cars. I always laugh when I see those assholes standing on deck, breathing in the fresh ocean breeze, because the air they're sucking in has twenty times the emissions you get on a busy highway.

"And think of the numbers on board. A cruise ship carrying 6,000 passengers generates a quarter of a million gallons of raw sewage each week, give or take, and most of it is dumped directly in the ocean."

"Is that permitted?"

"They're allowed to do it as long as they're more than three miles from shore. But even if they're inside that three mile limit they do it anyway They're at sea for fuck's sake, who's watching? And that doesn't even include the oil-polluted bilge water they regularly dump, or the millions of litres of grey water from all those showers and basins."

"If you're so outraged about it why are you on board?"

"Because I get well paid, well fed, meet nice girls like you, and can outgun the fuckheads that I might have to fight. What's your excuse? Why are you here?"

"Funnily enough I've been asking myself that very same question."

"And I'll tell you something else that's not widely known. Every year hundreds die on cruise ships. Passengers and crew."

"How?"

"Some in accidents. With crew it's more likely to be fire, getting crushed during docking manoeuvres, electrocution, asphyxiation. With passengers it's stuff like drowning in pools, falling down stairs in rough seas, allergic reactions. Alcohol and drugs also, of course. I once saw a drunk try to climb the mast; he fell before we could reach him."

"Into the sea?"

"No, onto the Prom deck. Nearly hit some guy and his wife who were taking a stroll. Doesn't really matter where you land. Sea or deck, you'll likely die either way. Look at the height of these boats. Hitting the water from that altitude isn't like jumping into a pool, it's like hitting fucking concrete. I once saw some fuckwit jump overboard from his balcony after going crazy on ketamine. He was hallucinating and he thought the Devil was in his stateroom, so he climbed onto the table and jumped over the rail. That was a rare one because we recovered the body. But actually, most passenger deaths are age-related. Remember, you're quite young but most of these guys are in their sixties or older. You know that Brit, David Frost, the guy who interviewed Nixon? He dropped dead with a massive heart attack on the *Queen Elizabeth* a few years ago. He was a guest speaker. He was on board to do a gig talking about his life and career."

"Did he die before or after his speech?"

"Who knows. Does it matter?"

"Maybe to him. Almost certainly to his audience."

"The point is, Lizbet, passenger deaths are routine. You want to know a secret? 'Operation Bright Star' is what they announce when there's a medical emergency, and 'Operation Rising Star' means a passenger's croaked."

"That doesn't make sense. Surely it should be 'Fading Star' or 'Setting Sun' or something. Why rising?"

"Fuck knows. They're just code names. They don't have to be logical, they just have to be understood."

"So when someone dies what do they do with the body?"

"Same as on land, they zip it up and take it to the morgue. Every ship has body bags and all ocean-going ships have to have a morgue. They site them away from food areas."

"You surprise me."

"Away from passenger areas I mean. They usually have room for four corpses, maybe more. Depends on the size of the ship. If it gets full they have to find somewhere else to put them, you know, alternative accommodation."

"I'm not going to ask."

"After that it depends. Some ports insist on immediate transfer. The body gets removed discreetly, and then it's repatriated to its home country."

"Do the dead have a home country?"

"You know what I mean. But if the port is okay with it, then the bodies stay in the morgue. That way it's less disruptive and the dead person's partner can continue their holiday." He laughed at my grimace. "Yeah, I know, but it's not uncommon. Ships used to have chaplains but not so much now. Unnecessary expenditure. But they still try to be supportive. You know, bereavement counselling and that sort of shit. And they usually move the survivor to a new cabin, a space without associations."

"Sounds like a hell of a way to wangle an upgrade."

"It depends a lot on the cruise line and the ship. Those morgues can't keep bodies indefinitely, not much longer than a week really. But people usually want to stay on board. I know of cases where the survivor has had the dead person cremated and then brings their ashes back on board so they can both complete the cruise. I even heard of a guy who tried to conceal his wife's death by keeping her covered up in bed so that they could finish the voyage."

"That suggests either true love or a determination to get your money's worth."

"You wouldn't believe some of the things I've seen people do. And then, of course, there are the suicides."

"Ah yes, the suicides. They used to say that there's a special place in Hell for those."

"That's a Christian 'They'. Not my bag. But suicide's a common cause of death for crew and passengers. Top three methods, in reverse order?" He gave a little drum roll with his fingers on the pillow. "In third place, the ever dependable Hanging," he paused. "The runner up is Overdose," there was a longer pause, "but the runaway winner is Jumping Overboard. It makes sense. It's like, the sea is all around you. One leap and you're in it, home free. Chalomot paz. No more worries."

"Christ, I was hoping to hear something interesting, not unrelentingly depressing. Can we talk about something else?"

"Okay, here's something interesting. There's another category, one that's between the living and the dead."

"Don't tell me, we've moved on to fucking zombies."

"Those who disappear."

"Disappearing zombies? You're taking the piss."

"Disappearing passengers. Sometimes crew. Nobody knows how many because the cruise companies don't want it to be known. But people disappear from cruise ships every single year."

"Disappear?"

"Yep. Some must be suicides. People jumping without anyone seeing them. A quiet night, a blind spot from the cameras. Some are probably murders: a wife pushes her husband overboard when he's drunk; a husband strangles his wife and drops her over the side. It's so big out there you can lose most anything once it's gone over. A weighted body for sure. But that still leaves others, those who just vanish. Sometimes happy people with everything to live for, who are on holiday with people they love. One minute they're there, enjoying themselves, and the next... Puff! They're gone."

"Maybe they just get off the ship and start a new life. Lots of people have stuff they want to run away from."

"Passengers are logged on and logged off. There's always a record. I'm talking about people who *don't leave* the ship, but who, when you look for them, just *aren't there* anymore."

"So what's the explanation? Random de-materialisation? Alien abduction?"

"I'm serious, Lizbet. You ever hear of Amy Lee Bradley? Rebecca Coriam?"

At that moment Raphael's phone pinged with a message. I was a little relieved, as the conversation I was having—alone in the dark, with a guy I hardly knew and who had never officially set foot in my room—was beginning to creep me out.

He checked the message and then said, "Sorry, Lizbet, I've got to go."

He put on the light. I wrapped myself in the sheet and watched him dress. "Pirates?" I asked innocently.

"It's probably nothing but I have to check it out." He tidied his hair in the mirror before bending to kiss the top of my head. "Catch you later."

And then, like all those legions of vanished passengers, he was gone.

TWENTY

It was late afternoon when Horace called and told me he had been released. He invited me up to his suite. It was a welcome distraction in what, until then, had been a pretty shitty day.

I had woken up depressed. My head ached from a dull but manageable hangover. The coke had left me with a blocked nose and with that familiar jumpy anxiety that needed—or, rather, demanded—another line. I tried to walk it off but the sea air didn't help. I just kept thinking of what Raphael had told me about the pollution. As I breathed and looked out at the Red Sea I could feel the billions of micro-particles irritating my red eyes, sticking to the walls of my congested nose and settling at the base of my tired lungs. I went inside and had breakfast but it was hard to work up any enthusiasm for the food.

I returned to my room and felt a wave of self-disgust at the tangled bed and strewn clothes. I thought of last night and how little pleasure there had been. No love, certainly, nor any connection beyond that most basic bridge between two people. It had, at heart, been just another empty moment of consumption, just like the eating and drinking, the shopping, that had preceded it. I hated all that I had bought and gathered up most of the bags and spent the next few hours returning their contents. I thought that this would be an act of expiation that would improve my mood; that it would feel cleansing. It should have felt cleansing. But in the event, it made me feel no better. The ever-helpful, buffed and burnished retail operatives tried so hard to accommodate, to preserve the thrill of consumption for me. They offered different sizes, shades, models, they offered advice and encouragement, without being able to comprehend that I did not want alternatives, more variations on the same theme. I wanted nothing that they had to sell. I wanted to go home.

After I had got rid of the stuff I felt sad and empty. I found a spot to sit and look out over the sea. Later I came back to my room and ate some chilled and unripe mango that was as tasteless as ice. Then Horace called, and I was glad to go and see him, anything to escape the prison even for a moment. I have to say, he seemed remarkably well. He had a freshly laundered look about him, his hair still damp from the bath, his face freshly shaved and fragrant, his eyes smiling and alive.

"Never felt better," he declared. "Fit as a flea and twice as lively."

"It's great to see you looking so well."

"Oh, you little flatterer. Still, keep it coming. Thing is, Lizzy, I was just tired, tired and dehydrated from the shits. I'm sorry to have missed so much of the canal, but I feel fine now. Never better, truly."

"I'm delighted to hear it, Uncle." And I was, truly.

"Mark you, Lizzy, I felt the breath of the Reaper on my cheek, his shadow at my shoulder. Reminded me of how much sand has trickled through the hourglass."

"All that lives must die."

"Quite so. Perhaps I should get my Will signed. Maybe I should take it to the Purser so it can be stamped and witnessed."

"Maybe you should." I tried to sound as uninterested as a disinterested party should sound. "They say that everyone should have a current Will. I mean, life is unpredictable. I hope you live for decades, obviously, but one never knows."

"Indeed, *they* do say that, but I have never been entirely clear who *they* are. Still, one never knows and it pays to be prepared." He laughed but it descended into coughing. "Might be a few bob in it for you, Lizzy, you never know."

"That would be kind, but I hope I won't inherit it for many years."

"Maybe I will sign it. Right now." He got up and walked over to the safe. I heard him jabbing the keyboard several times in a futile attempt to open it. "Damn thing won't work."

"Let me help, Uncle." He watched as I keyed in the combination, 3141. The door slid open and I took a discreet step back in order to be seen not to pry.

"Well I'll be damned," he said.

"You told me the combination, Uncle, remember? You said it was Pi, a non-rounded pie. Remember?"

"I do, Lizzy. But it wouldn't open the last time, remember? So I had it opened by a fellow from the Purser's office the morning that we went to Alexandria. Before we went ashore I had it opened and then I reset it to a different combination." He paused and peered into the interior of the safe. "It must have somehow reverted back to the original combo. How very odd. This safe seems to have a will of its own." He took out the documents file and extracted the Will. Then without checking anything else he closed the door and keyed in a combination to lock it.

"The non-rounded pie?" I inquired innocently.

He put the Will down on the desk. "I think we should take a wander. Celebrate my restoration to good health."

"Did they say you could go out?"

"Ah, there's that *they* again. I never pay much heed to what *they* say. Besides, everyone knows that sea air is restorative. *They* know that. Come on, it'll be fun."

"And the Will? You're going to just leave it there?"

"Sure. Who's going to steal it? I'll sign it later."

We took turns around the deck, making our circuits with industrious regularity like hamsters in a wheel. It was hot and I suggested several times that he should ease off. He wouldn't hear of it. If anything, each of my suggestions that we take a break was met with an increase in pace. Eventually I sat down on an unoccupied bench near the stern and said that I needed to rest for a moment.

"Shame on you, Lizzy. You're a fraction of my age. What's wrong with you?"

"Nothing. I just feel a little dizzy. Tired."

"Rubbish." He put his hand on my arm. "Tell me truthfully. What's wrong. You've hardly said a word all afternoon."

"I don't know. Sometimes I just feel tired. I just feel a bit weepy and sad. Today I do. A bit depressed, I guess."

"I feel weepy and sad and depressed sometimes. Everybody does. It's the human condition. Life is hard and involves suffering. And it's unfair, so there's more suffering for some than others. And because it's unfair bad things happen to good people for no good reason. No reason other than they were in the wrong place at the wrong time. And you know, Lizzy, the natural desire, the political impulse, of any decent and enlightened person is to try to mitigate that unfairness where possible. And it can be mitigated but it can't be eliminated. It's part of life. It's not possible to eliminate it, and even if it were, it's not desirable. Suffering is how we learn."

"Well I..."

"So the choice is how you respond to this stuff. It's a test of character. Most people want to be victims because it's easier that way, the fault then lies elsewhere. They want the special status and privileges of victimhood. It gives them resources, attention, and a free pass to behave as obnoxiously as they wish, without consequences. And if they're not victims they pretend to be, looking everywhere for victimhood and screaming in rage, anguish and pain when they find it.

Victimland is a responsibility-free zone of milk and honey. Victimhood is its hard currency, a cultural fucking disease symptomatic of an entire civilisation that has lost its bearings, lost its marbles, had its foundations eaten away and is sinking back into the swamp."

"I just meant..."

"But within that context, as an individual who is alive within this culture of decline, you still have choices to make. Everyone does, some more than others. You can choose to try, choose to exercise agency, to acknowledge that you are the architect of much of the stuff that happens to you. And once you accept that, it empowers because then you can choose different options. Sure, it might be hard to do. But like I said, Life is hard. Hard but doable. It's either that, or you choose to opt out. Blow your brains out. Finished. No more choices. No more feelings of sadness. No more feelings at all. Come on, let's do ten more laps and then we'll have some drinks. Take my arm. I won't go too fast for you, I promise."

And so we did ten more circuits, toiling in the windless heat, pressed close like a pair of lobsters in a pan, our claws entwined in some small act of tenderness or solidarity. Afterwards, we had a couple of drinks, looking out over the empty water. Behind us was the Sea Garden. The shy octopus had left her barnacle-encrusted anchor and was close to the plate glass, her arms delicately tracing the smooth surface in restless exploration. In the backlit water, her eyes were dark and fixed upon us, her beak raised as though in supplication, but her skin was dull brown.

"Feeling better?" Horace asked.

"A little, maybe. Exercise helps. I just feel... I don't know, a loss of faith. I think I've been struggling with that."

"Faith? In God?"

"No, I mean faith in humanity, in progress. I've always believed that people aren't born bad, they're just born. But then they get made bad by bad circumstances. They get bent out of shape by society's pliers, by poverty and alienation and misery. That core belief is the starting point for any progressive view of society, of politics. If you believe that then you can see a route for improvement, see how people can be made better by material changes. But I'm struggling to hold onto that belief. Wherever you look the world seems to be getting worse, people more selfish and short-sighted. Don't you feel that, too?"

"I've never had any time for politics, Lizzy. Politicians tend to be venal or idiotic, or, more commonly, they're venal idiots. Never trust leaders, they'll always shit on you. But I'm okay with it. I never had your faith to begin with. I'm curious why an intelligent girl like you would have it when all evidence is to the contrary."

"Is it? History is littered with acts of self-sacrifice and altruism."

"Yeah, littered is right. History is also littered with martyrs, but it would be a mistake to use them as a yardstick for measuring people at large. Let me tell you something, Lizzy. In 1974 a Yugoslavian performance artist called Marina Abramovic gave a six-hour performance at Studio Morra in Naples. She had done stuff before involving the limits of her own physicality, but this piece, called *Rhythm 0,* was the culmination. There was a table, covered by a white cloth, rather like an altar. On it were seventy-two objects. I don't remember them all, but they included a bell, candle, lipstick, fork, rose, mirror, feather, chains, paint, spoon, nails, needle, knife, brush, bandage, flowers, pen, water, book, comb, hammer, hat, axe, newspaper, scissors, saw, soap, coat, pipe, spear, shoes, wire, bread, scalpel, sugar, whip, apple, scarf, salt, honey, medal, perfume, flute, dish, grapes, oil, a sprig of rosemary, bone of lamb, box of razor blades, and a handgun with single cartridge. There was a sign on the table which said that any of the objects could be used on her as desired. Note that conditional and the transitive verb. Members of the public were invited to respond according to their desires and were given carte blanche because the notice also stated 'I am the object. I take full responsibility.'

"And so she stood there for six hours, from eight in the evening until two in the morning, enduring all that was done to her. It began quite gently, people coming forward shyly with smirking acts of exploration, self-consciously posing her body, moving her limbs like those of a mannequin, copping a stealthy feel. Remember, this was being filmed and was happening in a public space. As the time passed they warmed to the task, for an absence of resistance always triggers further exploitation. That's an iron law of life. So, they used the blades to cut her clothes off, they examined her body, daubing it with paint, lipstick and slogans, draped it in chains, tearing skin with the thorns of the rose, tasting the blood. They even loaded the gun and put it in her hand, the barrel pressed to her head, her finger on the trigger, a tremble away from extinction."

"Was the audience male?"

"Nah, you can't get away that easily. It was mixed. There were enthusiastic women participants. I also saw some of them egging on the men. It was crowded in there like a dark carnival, Naples heat, audience and perpetrators crowded into the same space, indistinguishable, and there was excitement, you could smell it, like at a lynching."

"You were actually there?"

"She was compliant throughout, utterly silent, but afterwards she described feeling violated. And imagine what would have happened if this had been done off camera, in private space. What had begun as an experiment to see how far ordinary people will go, when there are no consequences of their actions, showed that there are no limits. Why? Because they find joy in cruelty. That wild, dark atavistic joy has always been there. What holds it in check is not personal morality but simply the fear of punishment and the shame and social stigma of being seen to transgress. Take away those constraints and give them power, they will kill you. And what's more they'll take pleasure in doing it. So, my advice to you, darling girl, is to let go of the notion that people are perfectible and then you won't be so disappointed. Never mind perfectible, the truth is most of them aren't even improvable. And you know why? Because they don't want to be improved. It's too much effort. Offer them your hand and they'll use it to drag you down into the hole that they're in, and then they'll use your murdered carcass as a stool to climb out just far enough to grab the ankle of the next poor sod they're going to feed on. They're worse than bot flies."

"God, Uncle, that's so irredeemably bleak."

"Not totally bleak. We can still party a little as we tiptoe on the edge of the abyss. In fact, now that I'm restored to health and have worked up an appetite with exercise and aperitifs, I feel the hungry call of a good dinner wafting to me on the breeze. Shall we dine?"

I accepted the invitation, but I really wasn't in the mood for dining table conflict. So I extracted a promise that there would be no arguments with diners, crew, or any other humans. I thought that should cover it and was encouraged when he gave me his word. I went to shower and change and agreed to meet at our table in time for the first sitting.

By the time I got there Horace was already ensconced, drinking a martini and chatting to Fat Pamela and her husband, Even Fatter Stanley. They were the only diners at our table and it was impossible to ignore the suspicion that other regulars were making a conscious effort to avoid us or, to be more precise, to avoid Horace. Still, I was encouraged to see that my uncle had washed and changed and was listening politely to their opinion of the Red Sea, even though this seemed to involve a degree of surprised disappointment at its absence of pigment. They greeted me warmly when I arrived, and Horace rose graciously, kissing my cheek. I was filled with optimism that tonight, with such limited company, we could negotiate a normal evening. Benign and ordinary, it would be a foundation stone upon which to rebuild wider relations with the ever-growing list of those who had been injured in recent Horace attacks.

I checked my phone, as Raphael had tried twice to call. There was a long text, the gist of which was that he wanted to meet later. I replied briefly, putting him off. To my right I could hear the conversation meandering along, with Fat Pam extolling the virtues of Burnley and Horace saying—with implausible but passably credible sincerity—that he had never been there but would definitely make a point of visiting on his next trip over to England.

We ordered food and I stiffened slightly as Horace's choices led, despite my best efforts at deflection, to a discussion of vegetarianism. I deployed my pre-planned strategy of keeping Horace sweet through solidarity—I, too, ordered vegetarian fare—while also seeking to ensure that I stayed fully engaged in conversation with him so that he could not isolate and prey upon a less robust victim. When the Fats jumped in on vegetarianism I gave a courteous explanation, without blame, guilt or aggression, and then sought to move the conversation briskly on. Horace watched from the sidelines, prowling like a tag wrestler impatient for his moment in the ring. When he did come in, I was encouraged that he declaimed with sorrow rather than launching an all out assault.

"When you see a dead creature on a serving platter, it is impossible to look the other way or to avoid the overwhelming realisation that this being was once alive. It was born and grew, it was sentient and miraculous, and now it has been reduced to such pitiable ruin, to this," he gestured to an imaginary platter on a table that as yet contained nothing but drinks and bread rolls. "Killed for no reason but that its flesh is to be gorged on for lunch."

Fat Pam, her mouth half-full of buttered roll said, "But animals, and I include humans in that, have always killed and eaten other animals. Ever since we first evolved they've been at it. It's natural. It's all part of the great circle of life."

"And what a harrowing and sorrow-filled orbit that has been. But it is not one that we are forced to maintain."

"Well my canine teeth say otherwise," said Fat Stan. "So does all the meat-eating that our relatives, the apes, get up to. It's like Pam says, it's the way of the world. Always has been."

"You know physiologically we are not carnivores, not even true omnivores actually. We're herbivores or possibly frugivores. No self-respecting omnivore gets atherosclerosis from eating animal products, but we do. And so do herbivores. Of course we've eaten meat during our evolution, as have chimps, and like them we have also eaten our own species. We can survive on meat, as we can through cannibalism, but it's not good for us, not good on so many levels."

"If you think that chicken nuggets or a bacon sarnie makes us cannibals you've got some very funny ideas," said Stanley.

I jumped in quickly to head off any further chimpanzee or cannibal talk, as it was only going to end one way. I tried to dial down the emotion by concentrating on the Environment rather than the issue of animal cruelty or ethics. I mean, almost everyone these days cares about the Environment. "You know, vegetarian diets need much less land than meat-based food production. We could feed a lot more people if we grew crops for human consumption rather than using them to feed animals that we then eat."

Horace took the bait. "That is absolutely right, Lizzy. Do you know how long it takes to generate three centimetres of top soil? A thousand years! If we keep going as we are, the planet's top soil could all be gone in the next sixty. We've already degraded about a third of it. And we've done that by intensive, chemical-heavy farming, global warming and deforestation. We're losing thirty football pitches of soil every minute and it's a vicious circle because the more we lose, the less carbon the Earth can absorb, so the world gets hotter, and then even more land is lost. So if the plight of animals does not move you to pity, think of our poor planet."

I barely had a moment to celebrate my own diplomacy before Fat Pam said, incredibly, "To be honest, we don't much worry about the Earth. I don't see the point. It's obviously getting used up but that's what happens when you use something. Eventually it gets used up. Maybe it will get uninhabitable one day, but not in our lifetime, and certainly not yours," she nodded towards Horace. "But even if it does, humans will find new planets to live on. There must be loads of them up there that we can colonise. Millions I should imagine."

"My dear woman," said Horace. "The answer is most definitely not to find another planet. If we are incapable of looking after our original planet what makes you think we can do a better job of looking after a replacement?"

"We don't have to. Once we get better spaceships we can keep finding new ones to expand onto."

"This is not like just buying a new car when you've trashed the old one, or dipping into the box to get another biscuit because you've licked the chocolate off the one in your hand. These are worlds, and the solution is not to fuck up a new world because we've fucked up the old one. The answer is to recognise what we are. Look in the mirror. What do you see in the hideous glass? Death, that's what. Ours is a culture of death. Humans are a plague of locusts upon the Earth. It's essential that we die out, and quickly. Ideally before we've killed off all the big animals. But even in the worst case scenario, just as long as we disappear before we've extinguished all other life, the Earth can recover. As long as some life still exists. It will just take time. And without us the world would have that time. Time to heal herself."

"What if we change our ways?" I asked.

"We won't. We can't. Too stupid, too selfish, too short-term. We'll never stop, not of our own volition. We're like a bunch of pissheads locked in a bar. The only effort we're putting in is deciding which dancing juice to chug down next."

"God, Uncle, that's so harsh. What about the children. Do they deserve to die? The innocent?"

He stared at me with pity. "The innocent die, just like the guilty."

"So children and babies, those who have done nothing to anyone, they deserve to die?"

"On a micro level, no, of course not. Not as individuals. But then nor do the billions of creatures we treat like garbage." The scarred fingertips of his left hand rubbed his brow wearily. "But on a macro level, yes, but it's not about what's deserved, it's about what is essential. Those infants may not have done anything yet, but that's because they haven't had the chance. They'll do plenty when they grow up. Humans are a plague, a virus. Stopping it from spreading before it destroys all life is essential, even if that requires the death of innocents. Think of it like fire fighting: the Earth is on fire; we are the flames."

"I'd prefer to find another planet," said Pam. "We should start with Mars."

"Dear God," said Horace. "Living on Mars would be like living at the top of Everest. It's got one percent of our atmosphere and it's very, very cold. It would be like living in Antarctica, except it would be orange, much colder, and there'd be no penguins."

"I thought it would be hot," said Pam. "In the pictures it always looks like a desert."

"There are experiments going on with people living in Antarctica as a trial run for a space colony on Mars," said Stan. "It was on TV. And, looking on the bright side, unlike Antarctica there's not much wind on Mars. Makes it easier to build cities."

"I think we're doing enough damage to the Antarctic as it is," I said, trying to steer a course back towards Earth.

"Don't encourage them, Lizzy. Don't treat this as a sane conversation. It's pure lunacy. Listen, the low gravity of Mars would mean our bones and circulatory systems would struggle. Bones like jelly, blood that doesn't flow, how's that sound? And Mars has no magnetic field so it's being bombarded constantly with cosmic radiation."

"You'd be alright living underground," said Stan. "You'd be warmer that way too."

"God in heaven, why would you want to live underground in an inhospitable wilderness where you couldn't set foot outside without a protective suit?"

"They must have some warm days up there," reasoned Stan.

"Who are the 'They'? There's no one up there. And it's uninhabited for a good reason."

"Antarctica has nice days. It has a summer. Not like our summer in England but not too bad from what I hear. Not bad for Antarctica."

"It's probably better than some of our summers," said Pam. "Some of the ones we've had recently at any rate."

"Are you taking the piss or are you really this stupid?"

"Horace..."

"Listen. It's not at all like Antarctica."

"You said it was a minute ago," said Stan.

"And you couldn't get there even if you were foolhardy enough to want to go. Not until we develop a method of space travel that does not rely on chemical rockets." Horace's voice was rising. "Our current rockets are barely able to get to the Moon and back. More than 90 percent of the weight of an Apollo rocket was the fuel."

"So you build bigger rockets," said Stanley.

"You can't. Very quickly you reach the point where the mass of the extra fuel exceeds the thrust that it provides. There's a general principle at work. It's called the diminishing rate of marginal return."

"The programme I watched said we should send a manned rocket to Mars with just enough fuel for the outward journey. Just one way."

"Oh well, that makes perfect sense," said Horace. "And what happens when they want to come home? Fill up at a local Martian gas station?"

"No. Once they get there, while some of the crew are exploring for a few months, setting up camp and whatnot, the rest will be distilling the fuel they need to get back."

"Well that's all sorted then. What could possibly go wrong?"

"Whether we can get there now isn't the point," insisted Pam. "We will be able to, at some time in the future, when we invent better spaceships. It's what humans do. Think of when we discovered America. The New World, it was called. It was a long way away and there were no radios or phones to stay in touch with England. But we colonised it. It'll be like that with Mars, only it will be easier to stay in touch because we'll have radios and such like. It'll be the new New World."

"It won't be remotely like that with Mars. The Americas was a natural paradise. At least it was before we got there."

"We brought civilisation," said Stan.

Horace snorted. "We brought our civilisation, if it can be called that. Let me tell you something. One of the first Europeans to be hanged in the New World was in Plymouth Colony, New England, in 1642. His name was Thomas Granger, he was sixteen years old. He was hanged by John Holmes after he had been convicted of buggery with a mare, a cow, two goats, numerous sheep, two calves, an ostrich and a turkey. The animals weren't spared, of course, every one of them that he was accused of buggering was killed before his eyes before they hanged him. That was a portent of what we brought to the Americas."

"What, buggery? I don't think so."

"Senseless cruelty. They killed all of those innocent creatures. Every one."

"Maybe he was only trying to stuff the turkey for a roast and just got carried away when he was basting it."

Pam shrieked with laughter, spraying bits of half-chewed chicken back onto her plate. "Yes, and how come he cheated on all those sheep?" she squealed. "What was he doing, looking for a pretty one?"

"Well they'd all be better looking than you and a damned sight more intelligent, you sad pair of fat fucks."

The exact sequence of the events that followed was disputed. The contents of a water glass were thrown at Horace (though it might have been wine) and he responded with a glass full of wine (or water); several pieces of crockery were knocked over, and at least one (or many more) was broken in the initial lunge (or later); Horace and Fat Stan grappled with silent determination (or sound and fury), trying to strangle, restrain or subdue each other until separated by the intervention of other diners (or staff); Pam screeched, wailed or called for help, claiming that Horace was trying to murder, maim or stab her husband, before slipping, fainting, overbalancing or throwing herself to the ground with what appeared to be a coronary but later turned out to be a panic attack (or black out); in doing so, she deliberately (or inadvertently) pulled off the tablecloth and was bombarded with food, wine, plates and glasses, some of which were already broken (or not). Blood was drawn but no wounds detected, other than a scratch on Horace's cheek where it was snagged by the thorns of the rose which had been knocked (or thrown) from the vase on the table. What is beyond dispute was that I watched it all unfold in slow-motion horror wishing that I was somewhere—anywhere—else. Even Mars.

We were all told to leave the dining area and return to our quarters pending an investigation. Pam was wheeled to the sick bay to be checked over. I went with Horace to his stateroom for a couple of brandies. He was shaken but dismayed only because, in retrospect, he wished he had thrown the glass rather than just its contents. An hour later the ship's doctor and a passenger liaison officer came to take a statement. They wanted to interview Horace alone and so I returned to my cabin. Later they came to see me and I gave them an account of the evening which, they said, pretty much accorded with that given by Horace but was at odds with what the other principals, and some witnesses, recalled.

The liaison officer said that pending a decision by the Captain, Horace had been confined to his quarters and could only venture out if he was under my direct supervision. She accepted that there may have been provocation, but Horace was deemed to have engaged in physical aggression. Besides, he had form. His past had come back to haunt him in the form of a log of prior complaints from other passengers about his conduct. So, it would be up to the Captain to make a decision as to whether he would be permitted to continue on the voyage or would be put ashore at the next convenient port. It would then be his responsibility to get himself and his luggage home. Whatever the decision, I was told that Horace's misbehaviour could not continue as it was unfair to the other passengers and detrimental to their safety. The comfort and safety of all the cruise line's guests was paramount. Violence could not be tolerated under any circumstances.

I pleaded mitigation on grounds of his age and terminal illness. The doctor was sympathetic. He said that Horace's alcohol consumption was likely to be reacting adversely with his medication, and counselled me to stop him drinking. He recommended an immediate and absolute cessation and said that Horace had agreed to this. He also said that it was possible that Horace was suffering from frequent mini-strokes which, whilst not incapacitating, were interfering with his behaviour and cognition. He said that he had neither the expertise nor necessary facilities to test for this, but that I should get it checked out as soon as possible. The liaison woman emphasised that whatever the cause, pending the Captain's decision, the only way that Horace could remain on board was either secured in the sick bay or under my direct control. He had agreed to the latter but I had to consent in writing to play my part.

I signed, of course, and after they had left I went to see him. He was in his robe, about to have a bath. He seemed subdued but not exactly penitent. He promised to behave. I told him he better had or else he would be looking for a flight home rather than going by sea. He laughed and said that he could always try to swim.

I returned to my room and had a glass of wine. I doodled notes in my pad. Its empty pages reminded me of how I had ceased to write since coming on board this ship of fools. I tried to write a poem.

Fragments

Memories in a broken cup,
you sup, you sup,
you drink it up,
you soak your soul
but then discover
for with each shiver
gulp and shudder
you hear the gasp
as you ingest
another tiny sliver
from all that broken glass.

I gave up trying to write a poem and had another drink. In my misery I returned to Steller, flicking through the pages. Here was further misery. On sea lions he wrote, "The males, like the females, have a very indifferent love for their pups... and they were not the least bit disturbed when, as often, I slit the throats of the young, even before the eyes of their parents and threw the entrails to them." This was beyond dispassionate science. This was abominable cruelty.

As was his description of their treatment of sea bears. "Often I went with my Cossack and attacked one deliberately and knocked out his eyes; and when I had done that I pelted four or five others with stones. When these pursued me I took refuge near the one I had blinded. He could not see but could hear his brothers on the move. However, he did not know whether they were fleeing from or pursuing us, and invariably he would end up attacking his fellows. Meanwhile, quite at my ease, I would sit down in some high place and watch them fighting for some hours. The blind one would attack all that came near and was attacked by all as a common enemy. If he fled to the sea he was pulled again to land and torn by constant blows until he lost all strength. Falling down helpless, he breathed away his angry soul in forlorn groans, and thus became prey for the droves of hungry blue foxes which tore at him with their teeth as he lay powerless but still breathing.

"Often we entered a harem and stole the pups. In such cases, if the mother abandoned her pups through fear, the male would ignore us and instead snatch up the female in his teeth, lifting her high, and throwing her in fury two or three times against the rocks with such violence that she lay still as though dead. When her strength returned she would crawl like a worm as a suppliant to his feet, and kiss him, and shed tears in such profusion that they ran down on her breast. For a time he would walk back and forth roaring and rolling his eyes most terribly, and would shake his head from side to side like a bear; but at length when he saw that we were going to take the pups away, he would weep in the same way as the female, and just as copiously, so as to flood his whole breast, even to his feet, with tears."

And regarding the beautiful sea otter, "When it receives a vigorous blow upon the head it falls upon the ground, covers its eyes with its paws, and keeps them there, no matter how many times it is struck upon the back. But if one hits it on the tail, which is extended as the animal runs, it turns about to face the striker in the most absurd fashion. But more frequently they fall down at the first blow and pretend that they are dead, and then when they see us turn our attention to others they suddenly take to flight. From this it would appear that the animal is very cunning. Oftentimes we would drive them into narrow places on purpose, without any thought of doing them harm; we would hold our clubs ready, and they would fall down fawning and looking around in every direction. Then they would slowly slink past us like dogs, and as soon as they saw that they were out of danger they would hurry to the shore and seek, with a mighty leap, the safety of the sea.

"Whether they give birth twice within one season I would not venture to decide; but I have seen, and I have sometimes killed, mothers with two cubs, one of which was a year old and the other three or four months only... I have sometimes deliberately deprived females of their young, sparing the mothers themselves, and thence they would weep over their affliction just like women do. I once carried off two little ones alive, and the mothers followed me at a distance like dogs, calling to their young with a voice like the wailing of an infant; and when the young ones heard their mothers' voice they wailed, too. I sat down in the snow and the mothers came close up and stood imploring, ready to take the young ones from my hand if I had set them down. But I did not. After eight days I returned to the same place and found one of the females at that spot where I had seized the baby, and she was bowed down with the deepest sorrow. Thus she lay, as I approached, without any sign of flight on her part. Her skin hung loose, and she had grown so thin in that one week that there was nothing left of her but skin and bones."

Skin and bones; loss and memory. I put my head in my hands and wept.

It was midnight when I got the call from Monique informing me that Horace had escaped. She sounded breathless. "I cannot find him anywhere." Apparently he had said that he was going to bed, but when she checked in on him later, he had gone.

It was hard to feel involved, but at her urging we agreed on separate areas of search. I checked out several bars and she went to the auditorium. I found him eventually in the quiet gloom of the casino. He was in one of the corners feeding coins into a slot machine. He wore a hat pulled down absurdly low over his face and a pair of sunglasses. He looked somewhere between an aging incognito rock star and a pantomime villain on the run. I approached him calmly. It was easy as I no longer felt anger, only a tired sense of despair and resignation.

He looked up as I approached and gave me a wide, warm smile. "Hello, Lizzy," he said with childlike affection.

"What are you doing here, Uncle?"

"I'm hiding, hiding in the dark and having a little gamble. Combining the two."

"You know you're not supposed to go out without me. You agreed to it, remember? I agreed to it as well."

"I didn't think this counted. I'm not really out. I just nipped down to the casino. Haven't even played the tables, haven't spoken to anyone, honestly. I've been a soul of discretion, Lizzy, keeping myself to myself. Want a drink?"

I shook my head. He finished his brandy and waved at a passing waitress.

"I was told that you promised to stop drinking. It's another of the conditions you agreed to, promised to abide by, so that you could stay on board."

"It's only a brandy. It's strictly medicinal. I'm still technically in a state of shock at having been exposed to such utter and crass stupidity by those idiots at dinner. Don't berate me for one small brandy It's not worth being angry over, it'll be gone soon, down the hatch in a jiffy."

"Look at me, Uncle. I'm not angry. See? Your behaviour doesn't shock me anymore. You're just trying to get a rise out of me."

"Actually I was just trying to get another brandy. A splash of the Devil's mouthwash. The measures here are very small."

"It doesn't work anymore. I'm onto you, Horace. I know the game and I don't like it. I don't like it and I'm not playing any more. Not by your rules at least. I'm going to bed."

I walked away without looking back. Over my shoulder I heard him order the brandy.

TWENTY ONE

I lay in bed the next morning looking at shafts of bright sunlight dancing through the curtains. My limbs were as detached and useless as driftwood, my body an inert stone condemned to lie forever on the grey bed of that grey room, able to writhe but not rise, dragged by invisible currents across an infinite grey ocean. I was trying to remember home, not the home I had left two weeks before but the home that had once existed, the life that had once seemed possible, had been begun, but then shattered.

I was reading Steller's description of how they hunted the sea cows. "Their capture was effected with a large iron hook whose point resembled an anchor's fluke. The other end was secured by a long, thick rope to an iron ring. A strong man took this hook and was rowed by four or five others in a boat that was steered gently toward the herd. The spearman stood in the prow holding the hook aloft and struck as soon as he was within range. Immediately, thirty men on the shore with the other end of the rope in their hands held the animal, and in spite of its desperate efforts at resistance they dragged him laboriously toward the land. The boat was held steady by another rope, and the boatmen exhausted the animal by raining down constant blows, until, tired and rendered passive by the spears, it was subdued by their knives and other weapons and drawn to the beach. Great pieces were cut from the creature whilst still alive, but his only response was to work his tail vigorously and to brace himself with his fore feet, so stubborn that great pieces of skin were often torn off. Besides, he breathed heavily, as with a groan, and the blood from his wounded back spurted forth like a fountain. As long as he kept his head submerged the blood did not flow, but as soon as he raised his face to breathe the blood leapt forth anew. I believe this occurred because the lungs, being located at the back, were wounded first, and when they were filled with air they increased the pressure of the spurting blood. From this I have concluded that the circulation of the blood in this animal, as in the seal, is in a double manner—in the open air, through the lungs, but under water, through the *foramen ovale* and *ductus arteriosus,* although I did not find both. But I believe it happens that they breathe differently from fishes, so that they can better swallow solid food." Oh, the cold compassionless eye that sees science in such suffering.

"If one animal is caught with the hook and begins to plunge about violently, those near him in the herd are thrown into similar commotion and endeavour to assist him. Thus do some of them try to upset the boat with their backs, while others bear down upon the rope and try to break it, or to extract the hook from the back of their wounded companion with a blow from their tails, and several times in this they proved successful. It is a very curious evidence of their nature and of their conjugal affection that when a female was caught the male, after trying with all his strength, but ultimately in vain, to free his captured mate, would follow her even to the shore, even though we struck him many blows, and though she was dead he would often come up to her side, as surely as an arrow. When we came the next day, early in the morning, to cut up the flesh and take it home, we found the male still waiting near his mate; and I saw his vigil once again, even on the third day, when I came alone to that spot for the purpose of examining the entrails."

Grief lingers. We know this. But as a species we seem incapable of sufficient empathy to extend that feeling of aching loss to other creatures with whom we share this world. And from their perspective how do we appear? We cannot speak their language but we can infer. The evidence is clear, it was there for Steller. He saw it but failed to draw the obvious conclusions. "It is undoubtedly true in places where they are caught in great numbers they have learned by long experience that men are dangerous to them. It was the same way with the otter, seal, and blue fox, which lived on this desert island and never saw a man before and never were disturbed while lying at their ease. They were slain with no trouble at all when we first came to Bering Island, but now they have become just as wild as those living in Kamchatka, and take flight at once as they discover, not only with their eyes, but even with their sense of smell, the approach of an enemy."

I put aside the book and resolved never again to open its pages, for I felt only an absolute revulsion at the utter brutality of Steller's butchery, his cruelty in the name of science. Even though he could see the beauty of these creatures, anthropomorphising them in response to real and identifiable emotions—parental selflessness, courage, altruism, pain, loyalty, love, unquenchable grief—still he treated them with abominable cruelty, without a moment of doubt or shame. And this, not in some barbarous era but in the Enlightenment, the midwife of modernity, where humankind was liberated from medieval superstition. This is the poisoned gift of the Enlightenment, a loss of connection with the living world and in its place the elevated brutalism of science and reason, where all is reduced to a sequence of moving parts that can be mapped and understood: comprehension via vivisection.

Those shipwrecked wretches who survived on Bering Island were as much a microcosm as those who died on the *Medusa*'s raft or in the blood-soaked beauty of Pitcairn. For here was a society where most laboured and suffered; cold, hungry and exhausted, they dreamed of eventual freedom from their island prison, and their alienation from the land and its native creatures was palpable. Periodically these brutes were bribed and cajoled by the mad scientist, the deranged brain who required their help in hauling and butchering his victims. This was Steller's island, a prototype for the modern world where creatures knew not the fear of man until they met him and experienced his violence and cruelty. It was a harbinger of our world, a world where we have become the enemy of all living things.

It made me pine for a retreat from modernity, a return to Romanticism with its reverence for the Sublime, the natural world. For though Romanticism might have gestated the wars and hatreds of nationalism, it took modern science to produce effective extermination camps and the railways and infrastructure to service them with victims. Perhaps Horace was right, we are the contagion. The world is on fire and we are the flames.

I let the phone ring unanswered. It went to the machine and I heard Horace's voice, child-bright and cheerful. "I've been following orders, Lizzy, playing doggo like a good Horace. Got back over the wire last night undetected, so no harm done. And I haven't set foot outside my quarters yet this morning. Not even one whisker. Still waiting for my escort. Monique's sulking and I know you might be a tad cross, but let's make up. Thing is, I need to talk to you. Besides, I've ordered a breakfast banquet and I can't eat it all myself. So do come and help. Pop up and tuck in. It'll be fun." If I had not felt so low I might have laughed. The irritating thing about Horace, however hard one tried, was that he was impossible to hate, truly hate. Not in a sustained way, at least.

When I arrived at his rooms he was dressed in a white linen suit with a scarlet cravat. I was calculatedly cold with a dash of weary formality, but he was bouncy and exuberant. "Look!" He gestured towards the table which was garlanded with platters of breakfast goods: fruit, cereal, cheese, smoked fish, bread, pastries and hot steel trays of scrambled eggs, mushrooms, tomatoes, beans and hash browns.

"Very impressive," I said, with a studied absence of enthusiasm.

"No, not the food you dolt. Outside. See that?" He pointed beyond the sun-filled terrace. "That, my girl, is the Indian Ocean. It's the sea of distant dreams. I crossed it as a young man when I first sailed for Australia. Since then I've only ever flown over it. And now I'm back, scudding over its enchanted waters. It's like I've come home, returned to the root, and you're with me. We are a family reunited."

"Horace, we're the stumps of a stunted family whose tree has been overly-pruned by a mad gardener, shorn of limbs by a maniac."

He looked at me with tenderness and thought for a moment. "Nah, I'm a bit gnarled these days, I grant you. But though you're stumpy, you're a bud that's full of life and potential. Come on, load up a plate and let's do some scoffing on the terrace whilst we enjoy the ocean. I can't tell you how happy I am to see it again. Ocean of dreams. Later, if I'm allowed, let's go up on deck and view its full majesty."

And so we sat and ate as the sea of dreams slid by below us. Horace chatted amiably, telling me that the Indian Ocean was the world's youngest and warmest, and covered 14 percent of the planet's surface. Beneath it, apparently, was a 5,000-kilometre long ridge of mountains and a submerged micro-continent three times the size of Japan. "Vasco da Gama sailed across here to reach India in 1497. That voyage kicked off the age of exploration, but what most people don't know is that Eudoxus of Cyzicus, a Greek, crossed it sixteen hundred years before that. Did it twice in fact and then he disappeared somewhere around here while trying to circumnavigate Africa. This mighty sea was once a paradise of coral and marine life, its sky alive with birds, before it contracted 'humanicitis'. Now it has been raped, its delicate inhabitants murdered on an industrial scale. Now there's a 5 million square kilometre garbage patch in this ocean." Periodically he broke off his monologue to point out storm petrels and cormorants, and even a pair of frigatebirds, angular and black with forked tails. "Beauties," he exclaimed, passing me the binoculars. "You won't see those in Cambridge." I thought they looked sinister, but I was also aware that drinking in that sparkling morning with my freshly squeezed orange juice had lightened my mood. I was trying to remain taciturn but it was hard to maintain silence in the face of Horace's childlike enthusiasm and wonder. There was one sour note when he threw the platter of smoked fish overboard, saying, "You order a vegetarian breakfast and the morons include fish. I mean, when has a fish ever been a fucking vegetable?" I watched the plate flash down towards the waves like a falling discus and I said nothing. But otherwise, relations were amicable, and when not purring with pleasure over the birds and natural majesty of the ocean, Horace rattled on about his first voyage to Australia and his dreams of making a new life, away from the "mess that Virgil had left."

He looked at me hard. "The thing is, Lizzy, I know you're angry with me for not saying more about his death, but what you have to understand is that there isn't much more to say. You think of suicide as this massive thing, this huge transgressive act, but that's a recent mindset. The Ancient Greeks were pretty cool about killing yourself, as long as it was a rational response to immoderate circumstances such as disease or infirmity. For them it made sense. The Romans went further; they elevated it into an art. Dying well was as important as living well, it was a sign of virtue and character, a creditable response not just to adverse external circumstances but also to inner demons. Remember what Seneca said, 'Wherever you look there is an end to evils... Your neck, your throat, your heart are all so many ways of escape... You enquire the road to freedom? You shall find it in every vein of your body.' When you read John Donne's list of famous suicides in the Classical age it's like a Who's Who of antiquity, it goes on for three pages. As long as you weren't owned by someone else—so not a soldier or a slave—you were free to kill yourself without penalty. It was Christianity that demonised suicide. And it did so because Christianity was an ideology of hysterical martyrs for whom, logically, it made perfect sense to escape this vale of tears as quickly as possible and get yourself checked into the certain bliss of Paradise. But although it made sense on an individual level, it wasn't good for perpetuating the ideology. So, in order to stop Christians from killing themselves, Augustine—of course it was Augustine—decreed that life was God's gift and suffering was God's will and you could not wriggle out of either by opting for self-destruction. And suddenly, by the sixth century, suicide had become a mortal sin, a capital crime, an act of moral repugnance."

"The Everlasting who fixed his canon 'gainst self-slaughter."

"Indeed. And the Enlightenment, by removing God the Everlasting from our daily life, gave the act of self-annihilation more significance than it's worth. In a world stripped of gods, this brief spasm of life is all we have, and so to toss it away becomes a momentous act, the snuffing out of a universe."

Horace coughed raggedly into his handkerchief. I poured him a glass of water and I looked out over the shimmering blue sea as he drank, each gulp more laboured than the last. I thought about that micro-continent somewhere below us, half-hidden in dark green light and waving weeds, a place intact with hills and plains, where life had once walked and grazed, now glided over by fish and who knows what other creatures lurking down there in the darkness.

"What I'm trying to say, Lizzy, is that if you search too hard for a reason for what Virgil did you'll be disappointed. History is littered with examples of frivolous suicide. Zeno of Citium, the founder of Stoicism, killed himself as an old man from irritation at having tripped and broken his toe. There was a case of an English gentlemen in the eighteenth century who hanged himself because he was bored of having to put his clothes on and off each day. I once read of a woman who was hale and healthy, though her husband was dead and her children gone, who came home one day with the shopping, opened a bag of frozen sprouts—carefully emptying them on the table—and then put the bag over her head and suffocated herself. No note, nothing, just a corpse with a tranquil face flecked green with fragments of sprout leaves."

"But there would have been underlying reasons in all of those cases. You just said, the lady was old and lonely. Zeno was old. Maybe the English gentleman was depressed."

"Sure, there are underlying causes. But they are not necessarily rational or even knowable. Psychiatrists have been grappling with underlying causes for decades, and there are many theories of suicide, including, as it happens, the loss of a parent at an early age and the feelings of guilt that flow from that. But Virgil didn't feel guilt. I think he killed himself because he just couldn't be arsed to carry on living. People do that. It's a form of depression, of course, that permanent winter of the soul. But my point is, we'll never know. Remember what Auden said, 'The desires of the heart are as crooked as corkscrews.' And he knew a thing or two about desires and corkscrews. Let it go, Lizzy. Spend your time and energies on Life not Death."

"It would be easier if I was sure you had told me all you know."

"I get that. I've been thinking hard in the last few days, trying to recall everything about the circumstances of Virgil's death, every last scrap, so that I can give you a total picture with nothing omitted. It was a long time ago, but I'll try. But first I want something from you. You're in such pain, Lizzy, it hurts me to see it. I'm family. Unburden yourself to me. Shall we exchange tragedies as a step towards healing?"

I squinted out to sea and could hear my voice as though across some great distance, dry and disconnected. "The facts of my little tragedy are in the public domain. There was a public inquest, unlike your brother's case, and police reports, a trial, coverage in the local paper. There are no secrets."

"So tell me about it."

"I'm not sure what to say, Uncle. I wish that you had met him, Robert Charles. He was named after Will's father and grandfather but we called him Wat, that was his nickname. He was an independent spirit, a rebel like Wat Tyler. And he was loved, so very loved. We tried very hard to conceive him. It wasn't easy, Will had a low sperm count, but we tried and were so happy when I got pregnant. We used to talk to him when he was growing inside me, lying for hours on the bed talking to him, playing music to him and speculating on who he might look like and what amazing things he would do with his life. And he was a sunny baby from the moment he was born. I gave birth to him at home, in the same bed where he had been conceived. And because he was my first child they wanted me to be delivered—that term always strikes me as ludicrous, makes me think of a parcel—in hospital but we insisted on a home birth. And it went so well. I was in good shape, I used to do yoga in those days, did it throughout my pregnancy. And the midwife was local and I had built up a bond of trust with her. It was so calm, and Will was there holding my hand and encouraging me. It was all so natural, the most natural thing in the world, and calm, so very calm. The day began with the three of us and by the afternoon there were four, with the addition of this tiny perfect creature with a massive fuzz of hair, who didn't cry much, just looked around with these big dark eyes, taking it all in. And then the midwife went and there we were, a little family, with Wat sleeping in a Moses basket like a little hedgehog.

"And the days that followed were tiring and we didn't get everything right but I tell you, Uncle, I have never felt more content, more fulfilled, in my entire life. It's like he was a little magic counterweight and suddenly Life was balanced, wonderfully full but perfectly balanced. And he grew, like kids are supposed to, and he became this cute little boy with copper blond hair and dark blue eyes, who was curious, and clever and so much fun. I can still hear his laughter, it was like water burbling over rocks. And I went back to teaching and Will's job was going well and Wat was happy at the nursery and looking forward to starting school.

"And then he died. He was four years old. The boy who killed him was seventeen, driving his parents' car; passed his Test a month before; driving too fast to impress his girlfriend. She was sixteen. It was early summer and I had a parents' evening, so Will was collecting him from nursery. Wat was riding his trike on the pavement and Will was walking on the outside, carrying the bag. It's a stretch of pavement I had walked a thousand times. The kid was driving too fast and lost control on the bend. The car swiped Will but he wasn't badly hurt. It dragged Wat's little red trike for 20 metres. It was unrecognisable. Just shards of twisted metal.

"And the thing I learned about tragedy is that it has no end. There was an inquest and a trial, which was mercifully short. The kid pleaded guilty. When I saw him in court I almost felt sorry for him. He looked so small and frightened in his oversized suit, and I felt sorry for his parents. And then he was talking with his solicitor and I saw him smile and then I hated him, wanted to tear his flesh with claws. He got a three-year driving ban, a fine, and 100 hours of community service. Judge took account of his good character and said that he didn't want to destroy his life. Said he would have to live with his mistake forever. But I also have to live with his mistake forever, and his parents got to leave the court with their child, got to drive him home, offer comfort, rebuild a life for him. I never even got to say goodbye to Wat, not even hold him one last time. They picked up my beautiful little boy, picked him up from the road in pieces. I can't get that image out of my head. Pieces."

I felt Horace's gnarled hand warm upon my own. My eyes were itchy and blurred and I kept my gaze fixed on the ocean. "It never ends. Not ever. Waves pulsing out from that senseless epicentre. Grief is a physical pain. A moment of shock and then a tidal wave of pain that seems literally unbearable. It's like being overwhelmed with love, only it's not love. And when you run, it hunts you down, and when you stand, it annihilates you. And in time it ebbs and flows, but even when it ebbs it's like a huge muted sadness where the world is muffled in grey cotton wool. And you function because you have to function, roboting through the senseless days. And in time people think you're getting over it because sometimes you go out in the evening, or you laugh, or do something other than grieving. They think you're better but they can't see the pain or the guilt that says, 'How can you do anything normal, how can you do anything but grieve?' And the truth is that none of it makes any sense because the shape of the world has changed, and the shape of you has changed, and you no longer know how anything fits together because there is just this twisted, swirling mix of sadness and madness, the grief and guilt and pain and horror, slopping over the rim and pouring through the cracks of your fractured fucking life."

I dabbed my eyes and paused, twisting the paper napkin into a hard ball. "At the beginning, it brought Will and me closer together. Us against the world. You know, keepers of the sacred flame. We sat in the court together holding hands. We helped each other with the madness of the days. We looked for signs; we looked for him. We tried for another child—not to replace Wat, but just as the sister or brother that he would never know but who we'd always planned for him to have. We tried but we didn't manage it. Grief is exhausting. And I'm tired of being tired. So fucking tired of being so fucking tired. I feel that death has made me selfish and hard, so it's hard to care about a lot of stuff. You can't escape the pain and you can't avoid the memories. You don't want to lose the memories because that's all you have left. And you can't avoid the places and associations, the places where the memories call to you, the birthdays and anniversaries, thinking about what might... should have been. You can't avoid dreams where the dead inhabit, or imagined rites of passage for a life that will never be lived. And then there are the Whys. Why him? Why us? And the million What Ifs.

"Over time, grief corrodes. Even if you try to pack it away, make time to live, it rusts in the dark. Will and I didn't make it through. Deep down I could never entirely absolve him of the blame and he could never get free of the guilt. It's awful. I mean, he didn't do anything wrong. They were on the pavement. Wat was on the inside, farthest from the road. He was wearing his little blue helmet and there was even a safety harness on his trike. Will was just doing what he had done a dozen of other times, what I had done hundreds of times before. It could just as easily have been me, I know that. But I also know that it wasn't me; it was him. And there was some part of me, even when I first saw him, at the hospital with his cuts and bruises, there was some part of me that thought, 'Why are you still alive when our child is dead? How dare you be alive, when he is not.'

"And the thing is, on the evening it happened, Will had gone back to the nursery because he forgot to pick up Benny, Wat's little blue bear. He'd forgotten to check that Benny was in the bag and so they went back for him. They had to, because Wat won't sleep without Benny. But although it was the right thing to do, I still can't get past the knowledge that if they hadn't gone back, if Will hadn't forgotten Benny in the first place, then they wouldn't have been on that stretch of pavement, on that bend, when that car span out of control. And then Wat would still be alive. Even if some other child was dead. An unknown, unnamed child. I could live with that if only my darling boy would still be here."

"You can't think like that, Lizzy." Horace spoke softly. "Random things happen, even terrible things. Don't look for logic where there is none. That way lies madness."

"Madness? Well, I'll bow to your authority in that particular field of expertise, Uncle." I stood up and walked to the rail. The sea was vast and calm around me, a shivering ocean of tears not dreams. In the distance was the white wake of tiny boats, their hulls invisible but for the tracks they left; just like shed tears. I felt Horace's wiry old arms around me as he folded me into the crumpled white linen of his suit.

"I'm so sorry, Lizzy. So sorry for your loss. It's unspeakable."

Then he suddenly moved away, seized the binoculars and trained them on the distant white trails of wake. At that moment the ship's alarm sounded, a harsh and repetitive whoop broken only by a relentless looped demand that all passengers report immediately to the main dining room. Even without the binoculars, now I could see three open boats with powerful outboard motors carving over the waves, their bows out of the water at an impossibly high angle, closing on us fast.

"Bastard pirates," shouted Horace. "We need the Webley."

He passed me the binoculars and dashed inside. I stared at the approaching boats. Under magnification, the nearest seemed alarmingly close. I could see its half-dozen occupants, their dark skin and hair, behind a veil of spray and speed. There was a young guy, handsome with a close cut beard and moustache. He was smiling with what seemed like perfect white teeth, gesturing with hand signals towards the ship. Several of the men had rifles and one was aiming some kind of rocket launcher. They opened fire. I could see the tiny flashes but it was impossible to hear the shots above the noise of the ship's siren. Then there was the dull thud of an explosion somewhere towards the stern. It felt surreal that people were actually shooting at us, like in a movie or a dream. It was impossible to take seriously.

Horace appeared in the doorway. "Jesus, they're using RPGs. Stay down, Lizzy, and get inside!"

I crawled in and he locked the glass door and closed the curtains. Both the glass and the heavy drapes seemed ridiculously insubstantial. It all seemed too absurd, almost laughable, to be crouching in the lee of a table that was laden with sufficient food for an entire village. Horace had retrieved his gun and was waving it at me but it was hard to hear what he was saying above the whoop of the alarm.

"The cartridges, Lizzy. Where did you put the damned cartridges?"

"In the safe. In my room."

"Come on," he shouted. "Let's go!"

He stuffed the gun into the waistband of his trousers, like a bit-part bandit in a two-bit movie, and pulled his shirt down over it. The corridors were chaos, harassed stewards ushering us downstairs and panicking passengers demanding to know what was happening. Some people had already donned lifejackets and several were pulling large suitcases which added to the tangle of confusion.

In the dining room people were sitting at crowded tables. Many were drinking and there were throngs around the windows as the crowd jostled to enjoy the drama despite official pleas to stay in the middle of the room. There was a palpable and distasteful thrill, as though this was a sporting contest or some public blood sport. *"There was excitement, you could smell it, like at a lynching."* We veered away, pushing through the mayhem. We made our way to my room and Horace had me open the safe. He seized the cartridges and loaded the revolver, his hands shaking, though I was unsure if it was from fear or anticipation.

"We should head up to the dining room with the others," I suggested.

"No way, Lizzy. Death loves a crowd. This is where we'll make our stand. Barricade the door. Let's get the mattress and pillows up against the window. Cushions too. And arm yourself with something, Lizzy. This will be our Thermopylae. The wave will break here, and here we must prevail or else be swept away."

The *Evening Star* was travelling faster than I had thought possible, the turbines high-pitched and straining as she zig zagged back and forth, rocking across her own turbulence. I felt disconnected from the events, though mildly curious as to how it would turn out. I poured a glass of wine. From the corner of the window I watched the small boats weaving like dancers, making darting runs towards us and then curving away. I was reminded of those nature programmes where you see hyenas circling an isolated water buffalo, looking for the chance to get in close and clamp their jaws on some undefended area of flesh. There was the dull crump of shots, some louder and more regular that seemed to be coming from on board. Horace crouched in his homemade sniper's nest, peering out from the corner of the mattress, drawing beads on the moving boats and their crews of T-shirted boys with tousled hair and white smiles.

Eventually the firing stopped. The small boats dropped back and then were suddenly gone, swallowed in the infinite blue as effortlessly as a cloud melting in the silent summer heaven. The ship slowed and sounded the all clear, with passengers being informed that they could return to their staterooms. There was cheering and some victory chants repurposed from the football terraces.

"Right has prevailed this day," declared Horace without any apparent trace of irony. He flicked the safety catch on the Webley and then stuffed it back into his waistband. "I think this calls for a drink, Lizzy. I'm going to check on my suite while you put your room back together. Meet you in the bar in thirty minutes for a celebratory snifter."

Horace had barely gone before Raphael was at the door. He was wet with sweat and spray, breathless and pumped with adrenaline. I could smell cordite and exultation on his skin when he embraced me.

"I can't stay," he said. "I just needed to be sure you were okay."

"I take it you won," I said coolly.

"Never in doubt, Lizbet. We took out two of their boats. I dropped at least one of the fuckheads for sure." He paused, staring at the chaos. "What the fuck happened to your room?"

"It's a long story, " I said. "But before you dash off, can you help me get the bed back together?"

He helped with the heavy stuff. And inevitably, with the heightened post-combat emotion of survivors, we ended up sharing a kiss. And then another. There was something strangely compelling about letting go, putting down the burdens of the past few days. Borne along on a tide of victory, what followed was fast and urgent, its heat and sweat like an adjunct to combat. And, naturally, the bed got messed up again.

TWENTY TWO

Under the circumstances I was, inevitably, a little late in keeping my appointment with Horace. I found him sitting quietly, alone at the table of an outside bar, sipping Scotch and water and staring out to sea. He seemed strangely still, disconnected from the excitement around him as the ship shivered in celebration of the great triumph, our blessed deliverance from the peril of pirates. A fancy dress party was already scheduled for the evening, though its theme had been hurriedly changed, inevitably, to 'Pirates'. When I sat down he stared hard at my eyes and I looked away; I think I blushed. He asked what had kept me, saying that he had almost given me up for dead. I initiated a discussion of what costumes we should wear to the evening's event and he suggested that we black up our faces and wear T-shirts, ragged shorts and flip flops. I told him that would be extreme bad taste. I said we should aim for specific rather than generic pirates, characters from the eighteenth century's Golden Age of piracy, for pirates of that era were the best known and the costumes were the most glamorous.

"There are plenty of well known Australian pirates," he said petulantly. "Well, outlaws, anyway, which amounts to the same thing."

"Well, you can dress up as Ned Kelley if you like, Uncle, but I think you'll find he never sailed the high seas. All that heavy armour would have been distinctly disadvantageous in the event of falling overboard."

"Falling overboard is invariably disadvantageous, unless it's planned. And how come you're so cheerful suddenly?"

"I feel relief. We've been through an intense experience. Look around you, everybody feels it. That's why they want to party tonight. I'm actually looking forward to it. I've already decided who I'm going as."

"I don't suppose if I say 'Don't tell me' it will make any difference?"

"None whatsoever. Ann Bonny, the most famous and feared female pirate of the Spanish Main. See, I've already made some notes. She was born 1697, the illegitimate daughter of an Irish lawyer from Cork, William Cormac, who got his housemaid pregnant. They eloped with young Ann to Charleston, South Carolina, where Cormac made a fortune. When her mother died, Ann took over running the household. She was pretty wild, reputedly stabbing a serving girl in the stomach with a carving knife when she was only thirteen. She eloped with James Bonny, a feckless sailor, and was disinherited by her father. While they were in the Bahamas, where the husband was a government informer, she fell in love with a dashing pirate, Calico Jack Rackham, and they stole a ship, the *Revenge,* and raised a crew, attacking and taking several merchant ships. On board one of their prizes was a young sailor who turned out to be a woman, Mary Read, an illegitimate child from London who had been raised as a boy. And so it was that the two most famous women from the Golden Age served together on the same ship, fighting as equals of the men. In fact, when the British navy captured the *Revenge* off the coast of Jamaica in October 1720, most of the crew were incapably drunk after celebrating their latest catch. But Ann and Mary rallied resistance, fighting like wildcats with pistols, cutlasses, and boarding axes..."

"What's a boarding axe?"

"I'm not sure, but they sound ferocious and the women used them... until overpowered by sheer numbers. As women, they were tried separately but it didn't make any difference because, like the men, they were condemned to death. Ann's last words to Rackham before he went to the gallows were, 'Had you fought like a man, you need not have been hang'd like a dog.'"

"Christ, that's a bit harsh. Not what you want to hear on the eve of your execution."

"But whereas the men were hanged, Ann and Mary—both of whom were pregnant—received a stay of execution until their babies were born. The governor considered it bad form to execute unborn children. Mary died of fever in prison in early 1721, during or shortly after giving birth. But Ann, like all great outlaws, just disappeared. There's no record of her death, by execution or natural causes, nor of her release. Some say she escaped or was quietly freed; that she became the lover of her jailer or that he was bribed with the loot that she had amassed from piracy. It was said that her father bought her release and that she went back to live on his estate, giving birth not just to Rackham's child but ten more besides after she married for a third time. They say she lived to be over eighty before dying in 1782." I put down my sheet of notes. "I guess we'll never know. She just vanished into legend. From real life warrior-mother-lover. Puff! She disappeared into romantic fiction. So, that's who I'm going as. Ann Bonny. You should come as William Cormac, Ann's father."

"Don't be bloody ridiculous. Nobody's heard of him. I shall go as Blackbeard. Teach his name was, he used to go into battle with lighted matches in his hair and beard. He crippled Israel Hands when he discharged a couple of pistols under the table during a card game. It was his idea of a jest."

"Oh yeah, he sounds like a real joker. Why don't you come as my father, then we'd be related?"

"Don't be absurd. The father wasn't even a bloody pirate, he was a lawyer. You said so yourself. And I can't abide lawyers - bloody parasites. Give me an honest pirate any day. I shall come as Blackbeard. He was the archetypal pirate. He was successful and then made the transition into respectable society in the Carolinas after a royal pardon, married a respectable young lady, but he could never quite give up his piratical ways."

"It's different for men, they have so many options to choose from."

"Yeah, but they die earlier."

"Some earlier than others." I winced even as I said it. "So what happened to him, old Blackbeard?"

"They cornered him and he went down fighting like a maniac. Shot, slashed and bashed from every side, he died in a welter of blood and gore. They cut his head off and hung it from the bowsprit and chucked his body overboard to sleep with the fish. His bones must still be down there somewhere, drifting with the currents."

The party was in Poseidon deck's bar complex but also spilled out around the swimming pools. Beyond the bar and buffet a dance floor had been laid and there were tables dotted around its periphery. Above us, rockets were being launched from the Eye of Zeus, which was also the site of a laser show where pulses of lancing light mutated through an array of colours as they skipped over the dark ocean or speared up into the night sky. White-jacketed serving staff moved among the guests with trays of glasses and canapés, offering grog and victuals to the pirate throng. Most people had made an effort with their costumes; some sporting lavish attire that must have been designed and packed before setting sail.

Horace was late but I felt calm and unstressed. I had rested in my cabin and then Raphael had dropped in and we spent some time together talking. He was reflective and vulnerable, feeling bad about the pirate boy he thought he had killed. He spoke about his mother and Israel and about how much he wanted to lead a normal life back on land. I thought at one point that he was going to ask me to come out to Israel. There was a moment of closeness when the issue seemed to hover just beyond the eye line, but then he had to go. He promised to see me at the party.

I spent time perfecting my clothes and makeup. I opted for the classic Ann Bonny, the one in all the contemporary pictures: wild hair protruding from a floppy brimmed hat; loose linen shirt (borrowed from Horace), as unbuttoned as decency permitted; an open scruffy jacket and baggy trousers with a heavy leather belt and boots. I made a cardboard cutlass which I covered in silver foil and cut out a cardboard pistol. I painted a scar on my right cheek, blackened my skin a little for a weather-beaten look, and used blood red lipstick to enhance the contrasting femininity of lips. I entered the fray with a confident swagger. There were a few others who, I think, had chosen the same character, but none that seemed as convincing. There were a lot of Blackbeards though, a choice second only to Captain Jack Sparrow, who was well represented, interestingly, amongst both men and women. It seemed that History had been trumped by Hollywood.

I saw Horace arrive, weaving through the crowd with his cane. He was wearing a long dark coat and a wide brimmed black hat beneath which a lank, dark wig poked out at odd angles. He had a ridiculous beard, raggedly uneven, somewhere between Osama bin Laden and Ali Baba. As his slight, stooped frame moved towards me in that voluminous coat he looked for all the world like a pantomime Fagin. I tried not to laugh, as I could tell from his sullen face and slumped posture that he was feeling cranky.

"Ahoy ship mate," I called out in best pirate dialect.

"I'm pissed off with this bloody beard," he said. "Every time I drink it falls off. And it was supposed to be bushy. Look how threadbare it is, and straggly. It's a bloody joke, more like Bleakbeard than Blackbeard. Or Lackbeard, maybe. I might as well have glued some bits of black string to my chops. It's pathetic."

"You look very dashing," I lied.

"It's the only one I could get and it's utter crap. Now I see why. Look how many Blackbeards are here, dozens of them. They obviously bought up the entire ship's stock of beards. And this is what I was left with. And I'm not even allowed to put lighted matches in it. Health and Safety."

"You surprise me."

"It's acrylic for God's sake. It's fire retardant. You couldn't burn it with a blowtorch." His mood was not improved when he flopped into a chair beside me and sat on his cardboard cutlass, bending it neatly in two. "Well that's buggered as well now," he said, waving the piece of flapping cardboard. "What am I supposed to do in the event of a duel, fan my opponent to death?"

Things did get a little better after he had downed a few rum cocktails. When his beard kept falling to one side he even laughed, albeit in a pissed off growly sort of way, which was actually quite piratical. We ate and drank but did not interact with any other guests. I couldn't tell if I was being paranoid or whether they genuinely were keeping their distance, having formed a cordon sanitaire around us. And Horace refused point-blank to dance with me, insisting that he was too old to make an exhibition of himself.

"Okay," I said. "So let's talk instead. Tell me the truth about Virgil."

"Oh, Lizzy, not that again. Do you never stop?"

"You promised. Remember the bargain? 'Shall we exchange tragedies?' That's what you said."

"I just wanted this evening to go well, you know, and everything to look good."

"It is going well, Uncle. We're having a nice time. Just relax about the costume. It looks fine and it's all pretend anyway. It's not real or permanent or important. Just tell me the truth about Virgil. You said you would."

"And what if I'm not in a giving vein this evening? You know, Lizzy, you should watch your step. I don't have to leave you anything at all in my Will."

"Horace, I expected more of you than that. Do you really think I care about the money? I'm not expecting any; I don't need any. One of the things that this cruise has confirmed for me is that consumption is crap. It doesn't satiate, it just makes hungry where most it satisfies." He laughed. "I don't want your money. I want the truth, even if it's painful. Tell me and then I promise that I won't ever ask you about it ever again. It'll be over."

"The past is never over, Lizzy."

"Okay, so let's call it closure."

"It's never even past."

"Then you should be able to remember it easily."

"Do you want to dance?"

"No. I want you to tell me."

"Be careful what you wish for, Lizzy. Fear not the haunted house but rather the house that ghosts are scared to enter."

"Tell me."

He plucked another cocktail from the tray of a passing waitress and took several gulps. He smoothed his beard back into place and frowned. He looked old and tired, the reflected coloured lights picking out the bones of his worn face.

"Okay, Lizzy, if this is really what you want." He coughed into his handkerchief. "I've been trying to remember everything. I was definitely there when it happened. Like I said, we'd arranged to meet, to sort things out between us. But what happened wasn't exactly how I described. The thing is, I had seen Amelia a couple of days before that meeting. I ran into her by chance in Cambridge, in the town. She looked terrible. She had bruises on her arm and swelling around one of her eyes. She said she had fallen but I could see that she had been hit in the face, and the marks on her arm were from being grabbed. So, when I went to the house to meet Virgil, I was already pretty furious, even before I had to listen to his self-pitying whining. We argued. I told him he was a bastard. I mean what sort of man hits a woman? I told him he was despicable. I guess we both said some home truths and it did get pretty heated. He had the gun but he wasn't going to use it. He didn't have the guts. It was just for show. I told him that. I told him he was a coward. And then things got a bit physical. I had assumed that the gun was not loaded but even so, when he pointed it at me I guess I lost my temper."

There followed an episode of ragged coughing, and he gulped some more of his drink. "Go on," I said.

"I tried to grab it, the Webley, and we ended up sort of grappling. We both had hands on it, struggling to control it as we wrestled on the floor. He got on top, using his body weight to pin me, but I managed to dislodge him with my legs. He was trying to reassert control, his face was right above mine, really close and flushed, and his teeth were clenched. He was grunting with the effort. We both were. The gun was between us, our hands were wrapped around it, but we were locked so close that I couldn't see it. And then he did something really odd. His face was above mine, just inches away, and he kissed me on the mouth. In the middle of this ferocious struggle that was consuming all of our strength, he kissed me tenderly, gently, on the lips. And at that instant the gun went off. I got powder burns on my neck; Virgil got a bullet in his temple. He just collapsed on top of me, stone dead. There was a lot of blood, a fountain of warm, viscous blood, smelling of iron, thick and sticky.

"I didn't know what to do. I was in shock. I remember holding him for a while, supporting the weight of his head. Blood from his nose was dripping on me. Eventually I got out from under him and I dragged the body to the ottoman and got it slumped into a sitting position. The bullet was lodged in his skull and so it wasn't like I had to line him up with an impact mark in the wall. I did put some blood and some... matter on the wall behind him. It was part of the cleaning up I had to do. I mopped up the traces. It took some time but I worked methodically. There was no real pressure as we had the place to ourselves, and you know, it's not like I had to remove evidence of my entire presence from the house. It was as much my home as his. I just had to make it look like he had shot himself whilst alone. I wiped my fingerprints off the gun and put it in his right hand, lifted it to his wound and then let it fall. When everything was in place, I slipped away and got the train back to Cambridge. I think if the police investigation had been really thorough they might have turned up flaws, but it wasn't. They weren't looking for inconsistencies. They were looking at a suicide."

"My God, Uncle, so you really did shoot dead your own brother?"

"No. I never said that. I was wrestling with him when the gun went off. So, in a way, it was a suicide. I mean it was he who had brought out the gun and pointed it at me. He'd loaded it. I was fighting him in self-defence. And who knows whose finger actually pulled the trigger. It's impossible to say, there was so much pressure on the gun. It was being pulled in different directions. I didn't knowingly discharge it. My finger was not actually on the trigger. At least I don't think it was. I didn't kill him, Lizzy, I was simply there when he died."

"Christ, Uncle, it was more than just being there. And you know what, despite all of those bullshit rationalisations, I think you killed him. I've suspected it for a long time. He'd taken your girlfriend just like he had taken other things from you throughout your life. You were jealous of him, and always had been. You told me how he was better than you at everything."

"Some things. I said better at some things."

"You were rivals. Deadly, jealous, sibling rivals. And jealousy became hatred. You hated being second-best. You fought him because you hated him. You shot him because you hated him."

He laughed. He put back his head and laughed until his laughter was consumed by coughing. "Oh Lizzy, you make it sound like something from a soap opera. It wasn't like that at all. I didn't hate my brother. Sure there was rivalry, there always is between siblings, but love too, much love. Too much love in fact. You could say that we had a history of love. Virgil's capacity for exploring physical love was without limit, as was the shallowness of his understanding of the nature of real love, true love."

"What are you telling me Horace?"

"Remember when I said that Amelia was the first woman I ever slept with? I said woman, not person. The distinction of my first sexual partner, though it hardly merits the term 'distinction' or 'partner', was Virgil. It began when we were thirteen. Well, actually it began a lot earlier than that but it was only by about thirteen that it became more technically feasible. It wasn't terribly penetrative, but it was exploratory in a fumbling sort of way and was invariably taken to a satisfying conclusion. I broke it off eventually, when we became older. I think sometimes that's why he seduced Amelia—from spite. But then you could never be quite sure with Virgil, it might not have been so grandiose and elevated an impulse as spite. The thing is, I don't think Virgil ever liked women very much. Maybe it stemmed from maternal abandonment or some such stuff. I've never been too keen on all that Freudian nonsense. But I know he didn't like them. He was very much a man's man, if you know what I mean."

"He was gay?"

"I guess. We didn't have that term in those days. Life was a lot simpler. Gay meant being happy."

"Still does for some people, Uncle, still does."

"Yeah, but not the same people. In those days homosexuality was illegal. It ruined lives. Men went to prison for it."

"So his relationship with my grandmother was all a lie?"

"No, not for her. She fell for him alright. People usually did. At his best Virgil could be irresistible, at least until you got to know him. So for her it was genuine, she was that sort of girl. For him, I think it was an act of vindictive acquisition, but one that his proclivities were perfectly able to encompass, to shape according to his nature and preferences. He was an omnivore, really, an omnivore operating in a moral vacuum."

"Did he hate you as much as you hated him?"

"No, quite the reverse. He was always desperate for my approval. Narcissists are like that—bottomless pits, black holes that suck in love without ever being sated. Actually, he even tried to leverage his relationship with Amelia as a means of connecting with me. He suggested that the three of us could be an item."

"You're kidding me."

"These days it would probably be seen as a legitimate relationship choice."

"I'm not so sure about that."

"Back then it was beyond the pale on several levels. Though my love for Amelia was sufficiently strong, and the pain of her loss so acute, that I did agree to it. It only happened once... no, twice. And it was a fucking disaster. I did it for her and she did it for him. He did it because he could, because it gave him pleasure to have us perform like sea lions in the Virgil circus. And like all performing animals, beneath our docility we were silently howling. I put a stop to it and severed all connection with both of them. I had to cauterise the wound before I bled to death. And so he ended up with her, even though he didn't love her, or even want her, and she was no longer of any use to him. I'm sure he would have left her but she got pregnant and he was expected to do the honourable thing and marry her. That was the price of the financial settlement that Father was prepared to give him, the wiping clean of his gambling and drinking debts. I think that his physical abuse towards her was symptomatic of his frustration, but maybe it was also an attempt to make her leave him. That would have got him off the hook. But Amelia was not that kind of girl, she was too loyal, too decent for that. So you see, it was an act of vindictive acquisition that ended up trapping him and he died squirming in the trap. That's what caused his death, regardless of who pulled the trigger."

"And the child, my mother, was she yours or his?" The question was whispered, barely audible above the music.

"His, I think. I'm sure. I wish I could tell you it was otherwise, Lizzy. I would be even more proud of you than I already am."

I reached over and took his hands in mine. His beard was falling off again and his eyes looked tired and watery, full of the sadness of years. I wanted to look after him, see him safely through this final voyage and let him return home, for however long he had left, without the burden that he had carried for so many years.

"Thank you for telling me, Uncle. It's shocking, but it's better to know. You shouldn't blame yourself. I believe you. It was an accident. My grandfather sounds like an utter bastard. And I'm glad that the police didn't find out the truth. I'm glad that you have unburdened yourself of the secret. You can trust me with it, Uncle."

He smiled weakly. "Any chance of another drink?" he asked. "I'm as dry as a dingo's bumhole."

I went to the loo and then hunted down a couple more cocktails. The party was in full swing, the dance floor a heaving pirate carnival. I felt a sense of satisfaction, of genuine closure and a feeling of gratitude towards Horace for having provided it. I imagined an impossibly young Horace sitting on a train back to Cambridge that night in a state of shock, trying to blot out the sound of the pistol shot still ringing in his ears. And the incessant travelling that had followed as he fled the demons, always trying to stay a step ahead of the sound of that shot, the flood of his brother's blood. And now here, with me, afloat on this ocean of dreams, he had put down the burden that he had carried for so long and which had bent and twisted him, made him misanthropic. We would both be lighter now. At Cape Town we would go our separate ways. I could fly home with that old ache now resolved, and he could go back to Maya and live out the rest of his days in the paradise refuge he had created, relieved at last from the burden of the past. I did not just feel affection for the old rascal, I think for the first time I also felt admiration. He had survived, albeit misshapen. He had survived and I was determined to make the final days of our time together happy and fulfilling. After all, we had both been freed from the past by my persistence in cracking open its carapace and letting the cleansing light stream in.

When I returned with the drinks he was looking out at the dance floor, sitting perfectly still. "You look happy," he said.

"I am. For both of us. You dodged a bullet, Horace. Literally, but also with the police investigation. What did you do with the clothes?"

"What?"

"Your blood-soaked clothes. How did you destroy them?"

"I don't think I did. They weren't too bad. I probably just sponged them off a bit."

"Surely you changed before getting the train back to college?"

"I remember using my handkerchief. I've still got it somewhere. A memento. Just a rag now, of course, with brown stains. Time erodes everything."

"But you must have been covered in blood. You said he bled over you. You were holding his head above you when the shot was fired."

"Well maybe he wasn't actually above me. It's a long time ago, Lizzy."

"And there must have been blood to clean up from the floor or it wouldn't have looked right to the police. You must have used towels or sheets to mop it up. How did you dispose of them?"

"It's hard to remember the details."

"But you fought with him. You wrestled with him for the gun, grappling on the floor."

"I think we did."

"You think?" I could feel the rigidity of the ship flex, its angles moving in uncontrolled opposition.

"Either we did or I imagined we did. We often used to argue. It was a long time ago, Lizzy. I wonder sometimes if I dreamed it all."

"You can't say that, Horace. You must know."

"Sometimes I dream he's still alive."

"Things either happen or they don't."

"Well, not always. Are you familiar with Schrödinger's cat?"

"I'm not interested in Schrödinger's fucking cat. I want to know what happened between you and Virgil. Have you just told me a pack of lies?"

"Not lies exactly. The Copenhagen school of quantum mechanics suggests that something can simultaneously exist in all possible configurations, but observing it forces it into just one of those possible states. Now although Schrödinger disagreed with this interpretation and..."

"You've done it again, haven't you? Unbelievable. I don't believe this is happening even though we're both sitting here and it's going on right now."

"Ah well, that's exactly the point I'm making with Schrödinger's cat. But I don't understand why you're getting so upset. You were happy a moment ago."

"Unbelievable. You can't be this obtuse. I was happy because you had finally told me... Correction, I thought you had finally told me, the truth. That means a real and factual account of something that really happened, in the real world. Now you're saying it might not be what happened, which means it might not be the truth, which is another way of saying it definitely isn't the truth, which is another way of saying it's a pack of fucking lies."

"Not a pack, exactly. That's almost like saying it's a herd. I grant you that some of the details might be a little imprecise. But it's a satisfying narrative. That's why it worked for you and made you happy."

I rose with dignity, or as much dignity as it is possible to muster when one is dressed as a bloody pirate. I was determined to stay icy cool. "Uncle," I said, with what I hoped was magisterial calm, "I'm leaving. You're on your own. I've had enough of this fucking voyage, of you, of the lies and equivocations. I'm done. Understand? I'm getting off at the next port we come to and I'm going home. Goodbye. Have a good life, or what remains of it."

I turned on my heel and I heard him call after me, "Leave your cutlass will you? Mine's all bent to buggery."

I headed for the exit. Crossing the floor I saw Raphael over at the far side. He was dancing and I started towards him but then saw he was with a young woman. He looked over towards me and I waved. He turned away without acknowledgement.

TWENTY THREE

Back in my cabin I cast off my pirate garb and slouched on the bed with a glass of wine. I ordered a snack but it took an age to arrive so I had a few more drinks to fill the time. I thought about having some fruit but the contents of the bowl did not look appetising. I would have eaten the chocolate mint that was always left on the pillow by the maid who came to do evening turndown, but on this occasion what had been left for me was a thin biscuity affair with a sludge of chocolate on its upper side. I threw it in the bin in disgust and then flicked through the pointless TV channels while I had another glass of wine.

And then, when the tray finally arrived it was disappointing: the crudities were irregular, cut without care and way too chilled, and the proportion of carrot to peppers was totally unbalanced. And a speck of sauce from the dip had splashed the white linen covering of the tray, making it look sad and spoiled and unclean. And, having been kept waiting for twenty minutes for it to arrive, I felt overwhelming anger at its glaring imperfections and I was torn with indecision over whether I should bawl down the phone to get it replaced immediately or call back the steward who had delivered it and make him acknowledge and explain its inadequacies before taking it away, out of my space, out of my sight.

And that was the moment, as I stood with the phone in my hand, looking with disgust at the tray of food with its frigid red rose, that was the moment I realised I had learned Horace's mystery lesson. Here's the thing. You eat, you drink, you indulge in entertainments of your choosing. You socialise, within the parameters of your companions; you consume, within the confines of available choice. And at the end of the day, tired, and full, you sleep. And then you get up and do it all again. And though tomorrow is another day and the activities that you choose may be different, they will still be selected from the same menu, as will the food, and those with whom you converse will still be from the same small pool. Maybe there will be some new novelty, but by tomorrow's tomorrow it will be less novel, and no longer new.

And as with every line of cocaine that follows the first, you try harder to chase that initial feeling of euphoria. How? By consuming more. But though you consume, it's just more of the same. And so you increase the quantities and make the experiences more hardcore, even though this brings no joy or fulfilment. And that which once seemed the epitome of luxury becomes ordinary and routine. You look at your stateroom and see that it has become a cabin, and though you lust for a suite or dream of a penthouse, in time those too would shrink to cabins. You long to swap your balcony for a veranda, your veranda for a terrace, but wait a while and watch as that terrace retracts into a balcony. And as the days pass, that luxurious basket of fresh fruit that appears each morning on your cabin table diminishes and you feel disappointment, which becomes irritation, that its contents are not plumper, shinier, riper and more exotic. And the sandwiches you have had brought to your room by white gloved hands should be fuller, more precisely filled and cut more geometrically; the chocolate mint that appears each evening on your pillow should be larger and more minty; and the hospital corners on your freshly made bed, with its crisp white sheets, should be sharper and their angles more regular. And the throb of the ship's engines, which once felt like the familiar pulse of a maternal heartbeat, is transformed now to discordant noise, a braying irritant that keeps you from sleep. And even the ocean, that azure womb of the world that once shimmered with unbounded beauty and possibility, becomes an empty and imprisoning desert whose malign otherness presses in upon you from every side as a foul and pestilent congregation of vapours that delights you not.

I remembered Horace's words, *It's not just about being pampered, it's about becoming accustomed to being pampered.* For indulgence is indeed a futile highway that leads to a single destination: perdition. Everyone feels the frustrating futility of the road, but most are spared its awful terminus. Most get to travel only a little way along its seductive length because they can't afford to pay the tolls. They think that more money would unlock greater happiness by providing them with more stuff, more experiences, more indulgence, more distance down that highway. But in reality, the limit of their means is the brake that saves them from ruin. For those whose purses are deep enough, you can just keep on rolling, picking up speed as you go, and with every passing unit of time and distance your dissatisfaction is more assured. Hell, when it arrives, is not a place of fire and brimstone, nor of darkness and desolate ice. It's a paradise carved from luxurious plenty, where excess feeds appetites that cannot be sated, only amplified. And there, in this garden of plenty, lost souls in designer labels feed in perpetuity without satisfaction, for their food seems dull and tasteless. And the overwhelming beauty of their environment appears as a dreary, grey monotony, a sterile promontory, a quintessence of dust.

At that moment there was a soft rap at the door. I opened it expecting either an apologetic Raphael or a penitent steward, but it was Horace. He had ditched the beard and wig, but was otherwise still in his pirate costume. He stepped inside without waiting to be asked.

"Sorry to disturb, Lizzy. I know I'm in the doghouse, but there was something I meant to say. Well two things, actually. What you said earlier, about consumption being crap, that's an important thing to have learned. It took me ages to work that out but you're a bright girl, a chip off the old block."

"Except I'm not sure which block."

"Did you read through my old scrapbooks?"

"Some of them. How did you know it was me who took them?"

He laughed. "A thief who takes old letters and whatnot but leaves behind cash, jewels and a gun? Not hard to identify."

"Sorry. I was desperate. I have them here."

"Nah, keep them. I'm tired of lugging that stuff around with me. And I want you to have this too, now that I know it won't screw up your life." He passed me the envelope containing his Will. "It's all signed and official. Ready to go when the time comes. I'm sorry for saying I might disinherit you. I was just pissed off about the costume. The thing is, Lizzy, I always wanted you to have this."

"I would have preferred the truth about my grandfather, if that's who he was."

"Yes, I believe you would. Well, I've been thinking about that and I have remembered a bit more." He took off his coat and sat down heavily on the bed. "Do you have any brandy?"

"Only wine."

"That'll do."

"It's late, Uncle, and I've been here too many times before. I'm tired." I handed him a glass.

"It's come back to me."

"Has it now? And what happens in this version? Virgil gets eaten by the croc who pouched Jimbo? Or murdered by pirates? I know, the gun gets dropped and goes off and the bullet ricochets off the ceiling and walls, passes right through your shirt and vest, leaving you miraculously untouched, kills old Jimbo and then lodges itself in your brother's head."

"Nah, nothing as colourful as that. Life's rarely as rich as the imagination. But this is the definitive account. I didn't shoot Virgil, but I guess I did participate in his death, in a manner of speaking. I went to meet him. It was like I said, we were alone in the house. We argued. I was furious about Amelia and the fact he'd hit her. I told him it was a rotten thing to have done, to have seduced her. He didn't even love her, it was just spite. It was a rotten thing and showed how rotten he was. Rotten to the core. I told him so, to his face.

"His eyes were red and swollen. He hadn't slept in God knows how long. I thought he'd been crying, but now I'm not so sure. It was probably just the booze. He was wasted. That's what they say these days isn't it, 'wasted'? Curiously appropriate for such a waster like Virgil. And he was certainly feeling sorry for himself. Although he had ruined her, he didn't want to face the consequences and marry her, as Father was insisting. He wanted my help. He wanted me to intercede on his behalf and get him out of the mess he had created by his own selfishness.

"I was unflinching. Aloof. I let him wallow in his self-inflicted misery. When he produced the Webley I didn't bat an eyelid. He threatened to shoot himself and I just went to make my supper. I told him he was a coward. I said I had a train to catch and I just carried on making my sandwich. That was the one they found uneaten when they discovered his body. The police took it as symptomatic of his state of mind, his mental disturbance, that he had made the sandwich and then killed himself without eating it. He threatened to shoot me, but I didn't believe him. I told him he didn't have the guts. Actually, I didn't think the gun was loaded. He said I was the coward and always had been. He said he could prove it.

"And then he proposed the contest: Russian roulette. He decided the rules, of course, he always decided the rules. I went along with it. I'm not even sure why. I guess because I was furious and didn't want to back down. In any case I still thought it was just drunken bravado; I didn't think we would actually do it. I just didn't want to back down. I had done that all my life and now I was determined that it would stop, right there, in that kitchen on that evening.

"One cartridge in the Webley, alternate shots, each man to spin the chamber before pulling the trigger. So the odds would remain a constant one in six. And there were to be an equal number of shots by each of us. Even if one was already dead, the other had to reload and take the remaining shot. We both swore to abide by that, swore by everything that was good and holy. Swore on our father's life and our mother's memory.

"We went into the library and each had a brandy. He emptied the Webley of all but one cartridge and then span the chamber. It suddenly seemed real at that point and I remember feeling very afraid. We sat on either side of the table. He was on the ottoman. He put the gun on the table and span it. It stopped with the barrel pointing more towards him than me. He looked at me and smiled. I wanted to tell him to stop, to call it off, but when I thought of Amelia I felt such loathing towards him that the idea of being the one to blink first was too much. He shrugged and then suddenly swooped on the gun, cocked it and raised it to his temple in one movement, and fired. There was just the dull heavy click of the hammer. He laughed and it sounded shrill and too loud and then he put the old Webley down gently in front of me, staring at me, his eyes burning with triumph.

"I heard him pour another glass and swig it down. I could hear his breathing. But my eyes were locked on the gun. It looked so ordinary. I'd seen it and held it many times before. It seemed utterly impossible that it could end everything, snuff out an entire universe. It was too pedestrian an object, too ordinary. I could feel his eyes on me. I picked it up in my right hand and it was much heavier than I remembered. I was thinking of ducking out but I was so damned angry. I felt trapped but I didn't see why I should be the one to back down. I mean, I was the wronged party in all of this.

"I thought about the one in six odds. You know, when you think about it, they're not that bad. Chances are it will be an empty chamber. Decent odds but if you get unlucky... I just couldn't imagine Death, you know, I was too young. I was at an age where Death is just a hypothetical possibility. He said that if I apologised he would consider honour to be satisfied. He said it but his voice had that tone, the one I knew so well, that mocking superior tone that had trumpeted a lifetime of his victories and my defeats. And I knew I was going to take my turn and suddenly my greatest fear was not Death but the moments left to me before death, the fear that my hand might shake.

"I was focusing on controlling my breathing. I span the chamber and slowly and deliberately I raised the gun to my right temple. The posture felt weird, you know, it's not a position that you ever normally adopt. The barrel was flush to my skin, nestling in my hair, the metal impossibly hard against the thin bone. I cocked the hammer and it sounded louder than I had ever heard. I closed my eyes so I didn't have to see his smiling face. I closed them too because I wanted to choose the last image that my mind might ever conjure. And you know what, Lizzy, I couldn't think of one. Not Mother, not Amelia, nothing, just emptiness. Crouched there, poised on the edge of death, there was nothing, just black.

"I felt so wretched at that moment, so utterly alone, that I just wanted it to be over, to be resolved one way or another. So I pulled the trigger.

"There was a flood of intensity, a sort of excitement that passes through your body like an electric current, like an overwhelming spasm. The physical sensation was extraordinary. There was the resistance of the trigger and then I felt the heavy slide of the gun's parts moving, but slowly, very slowly. Then the metallic thump of the hammer that seemed to pass up the length of the barrel and into my temple. This might sound crazy but it actually hurt. I don't know if it was the vibration or if it was my brain imagining the torn path of the bullet that never came, but it actually hurt. I could feel it for weeks afterwards as a sort of bruise. Some days I can still feel it. I put the gun down. I was too shocked to speak. I just kept thinking, 'I'm still alive but what happens now?' Virgil picked up the Webley, span the chamber, emptied his glass and said 'morituri te salutant.' He was smiling and looking right at me. Then came the explosion. He was killed outright.

"The shot was incredibly loud and the blood came instantly. And so much blood. A bright red torrent gushing from his nose and mouth. And there was darker blood, brown and thick with lumps of matter and clots sprayed in a plume on the wall behind him. His head was rocked right back, his eyes wide open and staring up at the ceiling. They were wide, like he was in shock. The hole in his temple was quite small, about the size of a ha'penny piece, old money. It was dark scarlet and oozing. On the other side, a portion of his head had been blown away. You could see the brain matter and shards of bone fragments. The gun had dropped from his right hand and lay on the floor near his right foot.

"I knew immediately that I was not going to honour the oath. There was no way that I was going to pick that thing up and put a fresh cartridge in it, spin the chamber, put the hot barrel to my temple and pull that hateful trigger. No way. It would have been insane. I didn't touch anything. I backed away slowly. It was hard to take my eyes off his face. It was like dull wax . The initial rush of blood had slowed. Now it dripped lazily off his chin and onto his sodden chest.

"I backed away until I got to the door. I went out of the room. I collected some stuff and I left the house, locking the door, unobserved. There are some old blood spots on the book I gave you, the Steller. They came from my sleeve. I was reading it on the train. When I got back to college that evening I showered. When I washed my hair there were some traces of blood and minute fragments of bone. It went down the drain. I laundered my clothes. After that it was just like I said. I've never spoken about it until now. Told no one. Not even Maya. You're the first."

"Why me?"

"You're my closest living relative, Lizzy. My family. Besides, nobody has ever badgered me about it as much as you have. Most of the time the past just slips away. The important stuff, or the stuff we preserve at least, we call History; the rest just atrophies into nothingness as memories fail and the participants die off. It's probably better that way."

"I don't believe that. I think the past carries on resonating, like ripples spreading out on a pond. It shapes who we are, shapes future generations. That's why the past is so important. And that's why it has to be true and accurate. Is this version true, Uncle?"

"As true as I can make it, Lizzy. Cross my heart."

"But is it really what happened?"

"It is. I believe it is. To the best of my recollection."

I laughed. "That's the best I'm going to get, isn't it?"

"It's all there is, Lizzy. The world is full of endings, but most aren't definitive, most don't even end anything, not really."

"Thank you, Horace. Thank you for telling me." I embraced him with quiet affection for that frail frame, that leathery vessel stretched across crumbling bone that had stared down the barrel of death more than half a century earlier. Or maybe not. But either way, he had lived to tell the tale.

"It's hot in here," he said. "Let's go back out on deck. I can hear music. If we're lucky we can still catch the end of the party."

I took his arm and he walked stiffly beside me, leaning on me swinging his silver topped cane. "You know," he said. "I wish I'd told you earlier. I feel much lighter now. Speaking the unspeakable is not nearly as hard as you think it will be. I wish I'd done it years ago."

"We didn't know each other years ago, Uncle."

"Yes, and I regret that too. It's so easy to get distracted, to lose sight of what's important."

The party was winding down. There were knots of people still drinking and some couples smooching on the dance floor. Stewards were clearing tables around them, carrying towers of used plates and glasses. We got fresh drinks and staked out a table on the edge of the light. The music was slow and easy and Horace stood up and said, "You know, Lizzy, even an old man could manage to dance to this. Would you do me the honour?" He held out his arm and we walked a little unsteadily to the dance floor. And there, as the stewards moved around us, we danced among the dregs.

It was some form of waltz, and we were a single creature; fused lobsters sharing a single outstretched arm. My other hand rested on the carapace of his bony shoulder while his claw lightly held my waist, guiding us through the wreckage. The soft lights played on his face, colouring his skin. There were times when he looked too ancient to belong in the world but other moments when I thought I could see a youthful Horace, even a child, flickering uncertainly within his features.

"Tell me, Lizzy. What are you going to do after the voyage has ended?"

"I'm going to patch things up with Will. I'd like us to try again. Maybe even try for another baby; try to look after it better this time."

"It wasn't neglect, you know, just rotten luck."

"Well then I'll try to be luckier."

"Good on you, my girl. Trying again is a great idea. If you don't keep trying you die. That's the thing about those poor old sea cows. They weren't wiped out by Steller getting shipwrecked on that island. They were already doomed by that time. That island was their last redoubt. They were wiped out by their placidity. They were too nice."

"We should talk about that in more detail. Steller, I mean. There's a couple of passages I'd like to re-read. I admire the work that your father put in but I have some issues about the changes he made to the original text."

"He just moved some stuff around a bit to make it flow better. The underlying message wasn't changed. Life is a struggle and if you don't fight you die. The men fought and survived but the poor old sea cows grazed placidly in the shallows and were butchered. It's wrong but that's just how it is. The world is without morality, Lizzy. And we're alone in it except for the people we love. So cherish them. I think you guys will make a go of it. You'll be fine. And you have to come out and visit Australia, see my old place and meet Maya and all the other creatures."

"I'd like that. Just as long as you're still in residence."

"I love that place, Lizzy. I'll always be there."

We went to the bar to get a final brandy and then walked down to the stern. We stood looking over the rail where the black water was being churned to luminescent white by the ship's propellers. Above us the moonless sky was full of silver stars. If you looked at any patch of black, every second or so there was a shooting star darting down towards the Earth.

"I've never seen so many shooting stars," I said.

"See, didn't I say it was the Ocean of Dreams? We should both make a wish."

"There are so many."

"Then make lots of wishes." We stood in silence for while and I made a wish for Wat, and then for me, and finally for Horace: mercy, happiness and peace.

"I wished for serenity," he said. What about you?"

"You can't say what you wish for, Uncle. Everyone knows that about wishes."

"Damn. I've buggered it up. Oh well, you never know, might still work. And there's another thing," he said, fumbling in his pocket. He opened my hand and I felt a smooth, cool stone fill my palm. "I want you to have this. As recompense. I know the trip hasn't always been easy."

I looked down at a perfect oval of black polished stone flecked with dots of blue and green. It looked almost artificial in its beauty, manufactured and manicured. But very beautiful. It felt like looking into the night sky through a portal. "I couldn't, Uncle. You've already been so generous. Besides, you already gave me a beautiful opal, remember?"

"This one is special, Lizzy. It's that big pinfire black I told you about. I've never seen one like it, not that size and tone. And the marking is exceptional. But what makes it unique is the rolling flame deep inside. You won't see it in this light but it's a profound red. It's in the heart of the stone, but the black is translucent enough for it to flash red when you hold it at certain angles. It's really rare, very special, Lizzy, but what makes it extraordinary is hidden. You don't always see it and when you do, like with a shooting star, you have to be looking. It's valuable, very valuable in fact, but I never sold it. I wanted to give it to the right person. Please accept it. It would make me happy. Think of it as a going away present."

"Are you leaving?"

"Well, our time together is coming to an end. The ship will be in Cape Town in a couple of days. Time to go our separate ways, wherever that might take us. I think it was Tennessee

Williams who said 'There is a time for departure, even when there is no certain place to go.' I just want you to know that it's been a blast. Thank you for making an old man happy. I wanted so much to see this ocean once again."

We hugged and I tried not to cry. "There'll be other opportunities for you to see it, Uncle. And we'll see each other again. I'll come over and visit soon. I've heard so much about it, you won't be able to stop me. I'll stay until you're sick of me. We could cruise the South Pacific. I've always wanted to. So I refuse, I absolutely refuse to say goodbye or to be sad. This conversation is ongoing and will remain so."

He laughed. "Well said girl, good on you. I say, Lizzy. There's a breeze blowing up. Would you mind awfully getting my coat? I left it down in your room."

"Sure. Anything else you need?"

"Nah, you've given me all that I needed. But put that stone in your safe." I turned to go and heard him call, "Maybe pick up a brandy on your way back. Purely medicinal."

I went to my room and retrieved the coat. Under the lamp light I examined the opal. It shone deep black with an astonishing luminosity. It felt as though I was holding a piece of the sky that we had just been gazing at. I went to put it in the safe and it suddenly flashed so red that it looked like an orb of molten fire. It seemed impossible that it was not too hot to hold, and yet it remained stone-smooth in my fingers, cool to the touch.

I left with the coat and picked up a brandy. I almost ordered one for myself, too, but decided against it. Time to clean up and get healthy, I thought, if this old body is going to be a vessel for new life.

I walked back towards Horace. He was standing in the distance at the edge of a cast shadow, his white shirt and skin pale beneath the starlight. As I drew near I saw that he had climbed over to the seaward side of the rail. He was looking back at the ship, holding on with both hands, his face angled to the sky. I shouted and I ran towards him. He waved cheerily and smiled a happy, wide, mischievous smile. Then he turned to the sea and raised his arms, his head tilted up towards the stars. The ship pitched and he stumbled back hard against the rail. Then, as it rolled forward, he stepped out, arms wide, treading lightly into air.

~~~~~~~~~~~~~~~
~~~~~~~~~~~~~~~

Printed in Great Britain
by Amazon

32054080R00189